Thirteen captivating tales from the best  *accompanied by three more from mon...... authors you've read before.*

In a world where monster killing and trapping is big business, one girl from a Hunter family decides she won't kill monsters. As a matter of fact, her best friend is one....

—"Agatha's Monster" by Azure Arther

A "book wizard" wants to help a pair of young orphaned brothers repair their relationship. But a powerful new magic book with problematic spellwork stands in the way.

—"The Magic Book of Accidental City Destruction: A Book Wizard's Guide" by Z. T. Bright

The daughter of Neptune Station's greatest hero is about to face her most daunting mission yet: elementary school on Earth.

—"The Squid Is My Brother" by Mike Jack Stoumbos

A bartender with a vendetta against the future must determine if his customer is a time-traveling tourist.

—"Gallows" by Desmond Astaire

Grant's Tomb—missing! Pennsylvania Station—missing! The Empire State Building—missing! New York City is disappearing piece by piece....

—"The Professor Was a Thief" by L. Ron Hubbard

A disgraced Lark is forced to take the job nobody wants. His songs can sway minds, but there's no margin for mistakes in the frozen north.

—"Lilt of a Lark" by Michael Panter

When a lieutenant with a mysterious past discovers an exotic creature held captive by a traveling farrago, they must decide how far they will go to save what matters most....

—"The Mystical Farrago" by N. V. Haskell

Alone but for her grandchild and a fox spirit, Emily braves Russia's winter and Napoleon's army to keep her family alive and together.
—"Tsuu, Tsuu, Kasva Suuremasse" by Rebecca E. Treasure

An abused boy finds an alien artifact that gives him the strength to reshape his life and stand up to his violent step-father.
—"The Daddy Box" by Frank Herbert

A son must decide whether to follow his father's footsteps and accept a responsibility he doesn't understand.
—"The Island on the Lake" by John Coming

When a desperate bid to recover stolen memories goes wrong, Alice must decide how far she's willing to go to protect her best friend.   —"The Phantom Carnival" by M. Elizabeth Ticknor

A botanist must cure a dying planet before an evacuation when she will be forced to leave her young daughter behind.
—"The Last Dying Season" by Brittany Rainsdon

When Fava, a Neanderthal shaman, discovers the men of metal driving away her mammoths, she must find magic powerful enough to save the herd.
—"A Word of Power" by David Farland

Technology suppresses crime on the generation ship *Eudoxus* until a body is discovered, threatening the years of peace.
—"The Greater Good" by Em Dupre

A genetically engineered assassin, concubine, and bodyguard has to unravel the entirety of her being to save her son....
—"For the Federation" by J. A. Becker

Tyson doesn't need to be psychic to know the invitation is a trap, but he can't refuse a poker tournament with the highest stakes imaginable.   —"Psychic Poker" by Lazarus Black

L. RON HUBBARD

Presents

Writers of the Future

Anthologies

"It really does help the best rise to the top."

—Brandon Sanderson
Writers of the Future Contest judge

"Writers of the Future is the gold standard of emerging talent into the field of science fiction fantasy that has contributed more to the genre than any other source."

—Midwest Book Review

"Writers of the Future, as a contest and as a book, remains the flagship of short fiction."

—Orson Scott Card
Writers of the Future Contest judge

"Writers of the Future is always one of the best original anthologies of the year." —*Tangent*

"It's a five-course meal that is a nice flow of different types of stories going all the way through."

—Kevin J. Anderson
Writers of the Future Contest judge

"Where can an aspiring sci-fi artist go to get discovered?... Fortunately, there's one opportunity—the Illustrators of the Future Contest—that offers up-and-coming artists an honest-to-goodness shot at science fiction stardom."

—*Sci-Fi* magazine

"The Contests are amazing competitions. I wish I had something like this when I was getting started—very positive and cool."
—Bob Eggleton
Illustrators of the Future Contest judge

"I really can't say enough good things about Writers of the Future.... It's fair to say that without Writers of the Future, I wouldn't be where I am today."
—Patrick Rothfuss
Writers of the Future Contest winner 2002

"This is an opportunity of a lifetime."   —Larry Elmore
Illustrators of the Future Contest judge

"The Illustrators of the Future is an amazing compass for what the art industry holds in store for all of us."
—Dan dos Santos
Illustrators of the Future Contest judge

"A terrific book and a terrific launch to the careers of the latest batch of the very best new writers in the field."
—Robert J. Sawyer
Writers of the Future Contest judge

"The Illustrators of the Future Contest is one of the best opportunities a young artist will ever get. You have nothing to lose and a lot to win."
—Frank Frazetta
Illustrators of the Future Contest judge

"I consider this to be the best short fiction contest anywhere. L. Ron Hubbard's vision of promoting and nurturing young writers has given thousands of talented people a forum in which their work can be seen and appreciated."
—Jody Lynn Nye
Writers of the Future Contest judge

L. Ron Hubbard PRESENTS

Writers of the Future

VOLUME 38

DEDICATION

To David Farland (1957– 2022)

Thank you for all the years
of great books and stories
and all your help to new writers.

You will never be forgotten.

L. Ron Hubbard PRESENTS
Writers of the Future
VOLUME 38

The year's thirteen best tales from the
Writers of the Future international writers' program

Illustrated by winners in the Illustrators of the Future
international illustrators' program

Three short stories by David Farland /
Frank Herbert / L. Ron Hubbard

With essays on writing and illustration by
Diane Dillon / Brian Herbert & Kevin J. Anderson /
Frank Herbert / L. Ron Hubbard

Edited by David Farland

Illustrations art directed by Echo Chernik

GALAXY PRESS, INC.

For information, contact Galaxy Press, Inc. at 7051 Hollywood Boulevard, Suite 200, Los Angeles, California 90028.

CONTENTS

Introduction

BY DAVID FARLAND (1957– 2022)

David Farland was a New York Times *bestselling author with more than fifty novels and anthologies to his credit. He won numerous awards across several genres, including the L. Ron Hubbard Gold Award in 1987, the Philip K. Dick Memorial Special Award, the Whitney Award for Best Novel of the Year, and the International Book Award for Best Young Adult Novel of the year.*

In 1991, Dave broke the Guinness Record for the world's largest book signing.

In addition to writing novels and short stories, Dave worked in video games as a designer and scripter, and worked as a green-lighting analyst for movies in Hollywood.

*He helped mentor hundreds of new writers, including such #1 bestselling authors as Brandon Sanderson (*The Way of Kings), *Stephenie Meyer (*Twilight), *Brandon Mull (*Fablehaven), *James Dashner (*The Maze Runner), *and others. While writing Star Wars novels in 1998, he was asked to help choose a book to push big for Scholastic. He selected Harry Potter, then developed a strategy to promote it to become the bestselling book of all time in English.*

Dave ran a huge international writing workshop where twice each week he interviewed successful writers, editors, agents, and movie producers, and offered access to his writing courses.

Dave also helped mentor writers through the Writers of the Future program, where for more than fifteen years he acted as Coordinating Judge, editor of the anthology, and taught workshops to winning authors.

Dave passed away just after he finished the final details on this volume. To say that he will be missed by all is a massive understatement.

Introduction

Welcome to *L. Ron Hubbard Presents Writers of the Future Volume 38*. Over thirty-eight years ago, L. Ron Hubbard founded this Contest to promote the writing of speculative fiction short stories—in science fiction, fantasy, and horror. The idea was to inspire, train, and promote young writers who very often have a hard time getting noticed by professional publishers.

Shortly after its inception, the Contest was expanded to provide the same services for illustrators.

The stories you read in this anthology come from budding writers. Some stories are the authors' first publication.

All new authors are invited to send stories from anywhere in the world. There is no charge for entering this Contest, and we show no favoritism. When we receive a story, as judges, we have no way of knowing the author's age, gender, nationality, race, or political affiliation.

In past years I've talked about how stories are selected and what I'm searching for. If you want to read about that, look at the introductions to the volumes I've edited over the last many years.

Today I'd like to talk about something else that is important to both me and this Contest: nurturing talent.

When L. Ron Hubbard founded the Contest, he created it to run every three months to help motivate new writers to compose on a regular basis. As a young writer some thirty-seven years ago, I did just that—until I got serious and wrote a story that won the grand prize. So inspiring authors was important to him.

More than just giving authors a goal to reach for, giving validation was just as important. In fact, teaching writers to believe in themselves may be the greatest motivator. So, we grant awards and certificates to those who win Honorable Mention, Silver Honorable Mention, Semifinalist, and Finalist places, as well as to our First-, Second-, and Third-place winners.

Authors who are struggling to break into the field need both *encouragement* and *training*. You'll find a free online writing course taught by me, Hugo and Nebula Award–winner Orson Scott Card, and World Fantasy Award–winner Tim Powers at our website www.WritersoftheFuture.com.

Training and inspiring writers aren't things I do only with the Contest. For the past fifteen years I've offered free writing tips (and free writing books).

I wish I could convey just how deeply I really want to help, but with thousands of writers who enter this Contest every quarter, I don't have time to do everything I'd like. I feel like Bilbo Baggins, who told Gandalf, "I feel thin, sort of stretched, like butter scraped over too much bread."

The bulk of my time for this Contest is spent studying anonymous entries and trying to gauge just how well each story succeeds and how much potential each author has.

Over the past three decades, I've discovered and mentored some great ones.

Part of my time with the Contest is spent training new authors in the week before the annual awards ceremony, or critiquing our semifinalists, or speaking at writing conventions.

Some of my time is spent editing this anthology so that we can present the fine new writers we've discovered. That's both an honor and a privilege. As an editor, I get to put together a collection of stories I truly love. I hope you love them, too.

In this anthology, you'll find tales by new authors and illustrations by artists from all over the world—stories that will make you wonder, make you laugh, make you cry, and hopefully will leave you inspired to create your own best future.

—David Farland
December 2021

The Illustrators of the Future Contest and the Importance of Art Direction

BY ECHO CHERNIK

Echo Chernik has been illustrating for thirty years and has been the recipient of many prestigious awards and accolades.

Her clients have included Disney, BBC, Mattel, Hasbro, Miller-Coors, Jose Cuervo, Celestial Seasonings, McDonald's, Procter & Gamble, Trek Bicycle Corporation, USPS, Bellagio Hotel & Casino, Kmart, Sears, Publix Super Markets, Regal Cinemas, the city of New Orleans, the state of Illinois, the Sheikh of Dubai, Dave Matthews Band, Arlo Guthrie, and more. She is a master of many styles including decorative, vector, and art nouveau.

She has been interviewed on CBS, PBS Radio, and countless publications in her career. Echo owns an art gallery in Washington State featuring exclusively her art, and she tours the world meeting fans and lecturing on illustration.

As the art director and Coordinating Judge of the Illustrators of the Future Contest, Echo prepares the winners for the business of illustration and a successful career in art.

The Illustrators of the Future Contest and the Importance of Art Direction

The illustrations within this volume were created by winners of the Illustrators of the Future Contest. I have the honor of being the Coordinating Judge for the Contest, and I also serve as this volume's art director.

An art director to a book is akin to the role of a conductor to an orchestra. It is the art director's responsibility to make the art flow together to create a cohesive and beautiful performance. As the Contest Coordinating Judge and art director for the Writers of the Future volumes, my objective is to ensure every illustration is the highest level of quality and does justice to the story it represents.

Illustrators of the Future is an international contest. It is free to enter. The anonymous judging means that anyone of any age, race, gender, from any country can and does win this Contest. The competition is based on the quality of the art alone. There are absolutely no biases. Every three months, illustrator winners receive a cash award and an illustration published in the Writers of the Future anthology. Additionally, all the winners are flown to Los Angeles for a weeklong workshop with the Contest judges, art directors, and the other winning illustrators to join the professional community in person. Finally, one grand prize winner will be selected and revealed at a red-carpet award ceremony in Hollywood, California.

Once an illustrator receives their fateful call from the Contest Director informing them that they are a winner, they are introduced to the anthology's editor and myself. The editor

5

assigns the illustrator one of the stories from the Writers of the Future Contest winners for that year. I then take over as art director and guide them to completion of the piece that will be published in the upcoming volume and will be judged for the grand prize award.

As art director, my goal is to do so much more than make the book look good. Winners go through the paces of a real illustration job, from being assigned the story, to submitting thumbnails for my review, creating a finished piece worthy of both the story and their vision, and managing a real-world deadline. Their piece should conform to the story but not give away the ending. It should be in the style that the illustrator wants to make a career with, and it should be a shining example of their artistic ability. In the end, the pieces will be published in the anthology, become a valuable portfolio piece for the artists to get more illustration work, and for one lucky illustrator, will be a grand-prize winning piece of art. Working with an art director is something that takes practice, and that can only be learned from experience.

With thirty years of experience as a professional illustrator, I've worked with absolutely phenomenal art directors. They provide the right direction for a piece without stomping on the artist's vision. When you work with a good art director, you are a team, with the goal to create an amazing finished product.

The talent that is brought to me through the Contest is astounding, and it is an honor to work with these artists at this early stage in their career, and to help them launch into greatness and success. If you are an aspiring artist or know someone who is, take the opportunity to enter the Contest. There is nothing to lose and everything to win. We look forward to seeing your entries.

ZAINE LODHI
Agatha's Monster

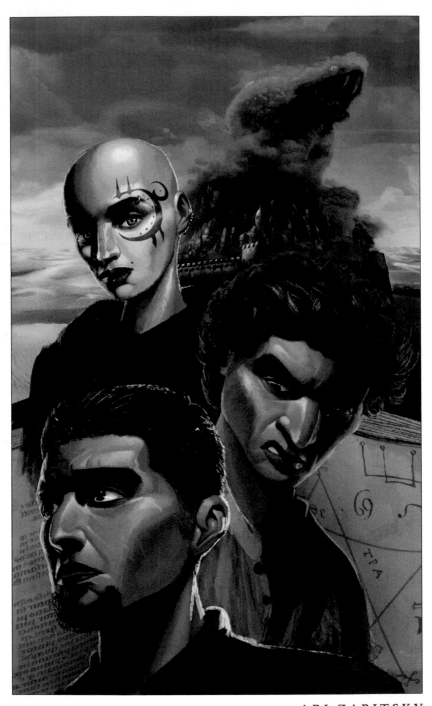

ARI ZARITSKY
The Magic Book of Accidental City Destruction

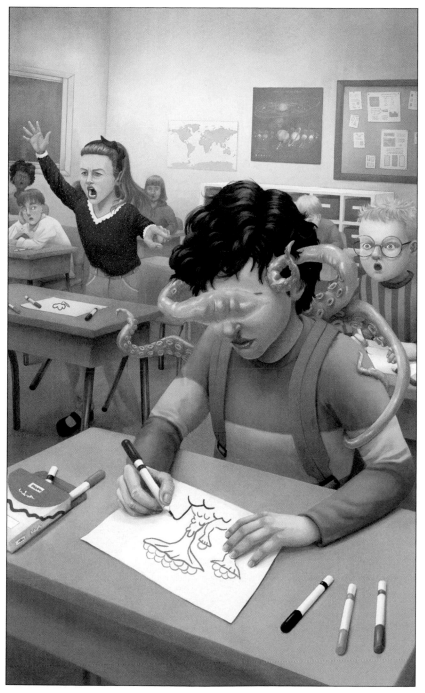

NATALIA SALVADOR
The Squid Is My Brother 9

NICK JIZBA
Gallows

MICHAEL TALBOT
The Professor Was a Thief

BRETT STUMP
Lilt of a Lark

ANNALEE WU
The Mystical Farrago

NATALIA SALVADOR
Tsuu, Tsuu, Kasva Suuremasse

ANDRÉ MATA
The Daddy Box

MAJID SABERINEJAD
The Island on the Lake

XIAOMENG ZHANG
The Phantom Carnival

17

JEROME TIEH
The Last Dying Season

BOB EGGLETON
The Mammoth Leaders

JIM ZACCARIA
The Greater Good

ARTHUR M. DOWEYKO
For the Federation

TENZIN RANGDOL
Psychic Poker

Agatha's Monster

written by
Azure Arther

illustrated by
ZAINE LODHI

ABOUT THE AUTHOR

Azure Arther is a native of Flint, Michigan, who resides in Dallas, Texas, with her husband, son, and Blazion the Betta fish. Azure began writing at a young age, and while her inspiration began with Grimm fairy tale stories and the Sleepover Friends, much of her current style has been heavily influenced by Octavia Butler and Henry James.

She is obsessed with literature and has found that her passions are evenly distributed between writing, teaching, parenting, and reading books with her son. Azure's stories and poems have appeared or are forthcoming in more than a dozen publications, but Writers of the Future is her first professional sale.

About "Agatha's Monster," Azure says, "Agatha began with some random questions. One day, I found myself wondering: what if monsters were born out of trauma? What would the world look like? How would humanity stay safe? Thus, Agatha came to life as a Hunter, a mage, a regular person with basic needs and worries. The ride Agatha and her monsters go on surprised me at times, and every rewrite shifted the narrative just enough to keep me, and hopefully future readers, guessing about what would happen next. The ending actually surprised me, too, and I feel it is one of my best-written endings thus far."

ABOUT THE ILLUSTRATOR

Zaine Lodhi was born in 1999 in the seaside tourist town of Sarasota, Florida. He feels as if his path as an illustrator was predestined— he has known the trajectory of his life since childhood. Zaine was surrounded by incredible fantasy art from a young age, collecting

Magic: The Gathering cards and whatever comics he could get his hands on. The art of Frank Frazetta, Alex Ross, and Gerald Brom were pivotal in his stylistic development.

Zaine is currently studying illustration with a visual development (concept art) focus at Ringling College of Art and Design. He placed the most importance on programs that value an unwavering work ethic and emphasize preparation for the workforce.

He has a strong classical painting background fostered by professors who specialize in figure and landscape painting. He combines traditional painting and drawing skill sets with his visual library to produce concept art for games and film. Currently, he is a student freelance illustrator looking to join a studio and make a mark in the video game industry upon graduation.

Agatha's Monster

"Hung-greee." Martin growled the word in my ear, drawing out the last syllable. I rolled over and batted at him. He scuttled out of reach and squatted on the other pillow, his tail lashing. "Hung-gree."

"Mouse?" I asked, not bothering to open my eyes.

"No mouse," Martin rasped. He whined. "No mouse left. Hung-greee."

"You can't be this alert when Mom comes." I sat up and yawned. The sun was rising, its beginning rays embellishing the shaded spots outside.

Martin crept across the patchwork quilt, hesitant, because I am not a morning person, but determined. He reached out a clawed hand to tap my arm, his four digits splayed, haunches ready to bolt back. When I didn't snap at him, he wrapped his small fingers around two of mine. I smiled slightly and asked, "What about a cat?"

"Permission?" Martin perked up, the short, fuzzy tufts of black feathers around his ears dancing. His breath, always slightly foul, wafted between us, but I was used to it.

"Sure. Get the one that keeps taking a dump in the front yard." I grabbed his scaly, clawed hand, and looked him straight in his round, yellow eyes. "Do. Not. Get. Caught."

"No get caught." Martin nodded, his large mouth already beginning to drool. He smiled, multiple rows of pointed teeth glinting in the faint light and widened his gaze, an attempt to look serious. "Return to Agatha. No get caught."

"Hurry." I opened my window and let him scuttle out into the backyard, his black skin blending into the last of the shadows as he slipped down the side of the house. I stretched, partially yawned again, and blearily watched the light slowly creep across the sky; faint purples and vibrant oranges mixed with the slow reveal of the neighborhood. In the hall, the floor creaked slightly, but other than that, there was just the soft whisper of movement on the hardwood planks when Mom crossed to my room.

"You awake?" Her voice was hushed when she poked her head in. I could barely see her face in the dim light.

"Yes, Mom."

"Good. Let's get this day started." She began to shut my door but reopened it. "Make sure to keep your voice down. Dad and Devon were out late last night."

"'Kay." I pretended to get out of bed, but as soon as the latch clicked, I was back at the window, whispering urgently. "Martin? Martin. Come."

And he did, bounding across the last patches of shadow, his body making liquid leaps from one scrap of darkness to another until finally, he was balanced on the edge of the window, bringing the scent of blood and outside with him. A white and brown cat leg was in his mouth. I felt bad for a moment, but Martin had to eat, and I didn't have enough magic to only feed him power. I threw an arm out, effectively blocking his path back over the windowsill. "Is that the one?"

"Maybe." Martin shrugged and grunted; his gravelly voice was hardly recognizable around his full mouth. His belly, which was dark gray against the blackness of the rest of him, was bulging. He was full, thank the gods, and a cat would usually hold him for a few days, sometimes a week. I ran my hand over the flat part of the top of his head, burying my fingers in the short fur for a second before giving him a brief caress down the soft, flexible spikes along his back. He purred, a deep rumble like the creature he was eating.

"Finish it," I said, motioning to the cat leg.

"Save." Martin clutched the leg to him, his spindly fingers forming a fist around the paw. He liked to wake in the middle of the day and have a snack. The claws on the limb flexed from the strength of his grip, and I gagged.

"Ugh." I looked around the room, grabbed a T-shirt off the floor, and handed it to him. "Wrap it up, and don't get any on my things."

He awkwardly stuffed the cat leg in the shirt and smiled at me, tiny bits of cat fur and grime stuck between the pointed triangles of his teeth. I rolled my eyes, scooped him and his package up, and tucked him into a drawer, right by his lodestone, a patch of white fabric with smeared, dried blood on it. He curled up in the back, beneath some old clothes, and immediately went to sleep, his long tail coiled around his body, the cat leg pillowing his triangular head. I stroked his scaly skin and closed the drawer. It was time to start the day.

I slipped out of my door, flipped the lock on my room—a simple spell that my little sister could probably break, but she'd be in so much trouble if she did—and headed down the hall.

"And now for the Hunter Report." In the kitchen, Gary Hedge, the digital announcer, chuckled. "My favorite part of the day." The anchor began to give a play-by-play of the top-rated monster killers. The Hunters. My dad was somewhere on the list, and I absently listened for his name as I went into the bathroom. I left the door cracked as I stripped and activated the shower. I scrubbed quickly, more to wake up than to wash, and was out before Hedge finished.

"As usual, I saved the top Hunter families for last. Devon Arbriger, who, before his little sister, Ardwin, joined the ranks, was considered the youngest Hunter ever...." He droned on, expounding on my brother's exploits and history. I rolled my eyes at the mention of Ardwin.

"Probably doesn't even know I exist," I muttered and slipped on the clothes I'd picked out last night; a yellow and black tunic that complemented my brown skin, fitted black pants, and black and yellow boots. I was a bumblebee today. I brushed my teeth and almost missed when Gary started in on Dad.

"His father, Jamaal Arbriger, reigning champion Hunter—I mean, no one has captured more monsters than this guy...." Gary rambled about Dad's stats. He sounded like a fan, but his coanchor brought him back to the point. "Ahem. It appears that the largest kill of the night came from both Jamaal and Devon's efforts. Great job, guys!"

I exited the bathroom and clicked up the hall to the kitchen. The space was wide, with muted gray stone floors and white and gray marbled countertops. It should have been a cold room, but the large, scratched table and chairs, and the decorations Mom had added over the years, gave it a homey feel. Mom, her sleep-mussed, honey curls wild and in every direction, was folded into a chair, one of her long legs tossed over the arm, her bare toes flexing repeatedly as she watched the digital that rested in the corner near the sink. The curved, transparent glass was full of images from a Recording. The news had switched to a video submission of a Hunt.

"Maybe you'll be a Recorder," Mom said without looking back. Of course, she'd felt me come in.

"Do you ever get tired of being an Auror?" I asked in response. She could feel the auras of almost anything, including monsters and humans. The smaller the creature, the harder it was for her to detect, which was why she hadn't found Martin. That and she wasn't expecting a monster to be in her house. This was where her guard was down.

"Of course not. If anything, I get tired of being an Adept. No mage should have this much power," she replied without missing a beat. "So, what do you think about Recording?"

"Maybe." I shrugged. "I don't know if I want to run around chasing after mages on Hunts, Mom. It's dangerous and boring. Besides, there's no guarantee that I'll be able to see after the procedure I don't need."

"Of course you will, and yes you do. You're an Arbriger. We just have to fix—" Mom flailed her hand into the air. All the magic in the world couldn't give my mother tact. She stood, turned, and kissed the top of my head. "Make coffee. It's Friday, and I want to watch the Hunt. They're chasing an Intermediate."

"Psh. Dad and Devon could do that alone."

"Your father and brother could take down two Intermediates and a High Novice alone."

"At the same time." I laughed.

"Make my coffee, little girl." Mom shoved at me and sat back down.

"I'll be sixteen in two weeks." I pulled the filter out and began prepping the machine. "Not so little."

"Shhh." The Hunt had started. I watched in snatches as I measured the grounds. The Recorder wasn't bad. He definitely wasn't the best, so they must not have had anything better for the Hunt of the Week. They had to play something, and new fodder was better than replays.

Recording was the only way regular people could see monsters, and since it was important that the nonmagical saw what the magical did, the news paid really well for Recordings. It was not a bad business, just...boring and dangerous. The Intermediate on the screen couldn't have been as big as the one Dad and Devon had caught, but we didn't have a Recorder that we worked with. Our last one, like all the others, had quit.

There were five mages in this Pack, six if you included the Recorder, not that anyone would: two Guards in purple, one Healer in green, and two battle mages—the Hunters—in red. I wouldn't know for sure where they classed at until they did something, but they were probably fire mages. Most battle mages were. The Pack chased an Intermediate, perhaps ten feet tall. The creature was brown with yellow fur. It wasn't that big, but it had to feed pretty well to hit that height. The Pack cornered the creature and slammed it with magic, the multihued spells pouring into the monster. Purple bands swooped around it. It was a containment spell from one of the Guards.

"Where's my coffee? This is getting good." Mom didn't look at me but held out her hand. I moved next to the digital and filled the pot with water.

"I can mix some grounds with water if you want?" I snickered. She blew a raspberry at me, and I poured the pot into the machine. "In a sec."

On the screen, the mages had contained the monster. I missed the battle mages' talents. The Healer surged forward, drawing out the negative emotions or trauma reaction that made it so big. There was a flashy show of colors when he released the power; no wonder Hedge had chosen this one. As soon as the creature had shrunk to at least half its size, the leader of the group blasted the Intermediate, and I watched as it thinned to a flat sheet that floated across the air to the lead mage. The Hunter held out his arm, and the sheet wrapped around his limb from wrist to elbow; other tattoos on his skin moved to make room for the new one.

"Not a bad haul. I wouldn't mind that monster to fight with," I said and turned to grin at Mom.

"Terrance," Mom muttered under her breath. "That trick gets old, and it's not like he can use more than one of those damn tattoos at once."

"You sound jealous."

She looked over at me and rolled her eyes. Monster tattooing was rare; we both knew it, but Mom had never been able to tame a monster to her will.

"Get the oats started." She got cream from the icebox and poured some into her cup before setting the carafe on the counter. The fragrance of freshly brewed coffee began to fill the room as we moved around each other, saying little; this was our daily routine. Mom broke the silence, her voice deliberately casual. "You know, as you said, your birthday is in two weeks. I thought we could go ahead and schedule your eye appointment."

"There's nothing wrong with my eyes," I replied.

"Agatha." Mom looked at me. I stopped and looked at her, holding the pot and the oats.

"I can see monsters."

"Prove it."

"I am not killing in a Hunt."

"Because you can't see." Mom smiled brightly and pointed at the digital. "You can be a Recorder."

"Just because I couldn't see that one time—"

"It has been multiple times, Agatha." She was right, but I knew I could see monsters. Otherwise, I wouldn't have been able to see Martin. I would have brought Martin out to show her, but she would have killed him in less than a heartbeat. Anyone in my family would have.

"I'll think about it." I said the words simply, but there was nothing simple about getting your corneas removed and having magical lenses put in, and two out of ten failed, so you had to do it over again.

"On the other hand, your monster could still be out there if you just listen for its Call." Mom was quiet. Waiting. She didn't believe that a monster hadn't manifested when my twin brother, Anthony, died. She was right, but she couldn't have Martin.

"You know I've never heard the Call." I wasn't lying. I had never heard the Call to kill a monster. Even though most Hunters could hear it, some couldn't. It didn't mean I couldn't see monsters. I just... couldn't see all of them.

"Mmm." She moved past me and turned the digital off with a short spark of angry magic from her hand. "This world, Agatha. This world only cares about money. There is a lot that goes into being a Hunter, but really, the world isn't much different than it was before the monsters appeared. Society deals with the manifestations just as they deal with everything else: by asking how much it is worth."

"I said I'll think about it." I added butter to the oats and stirred them. She moved closer and wrapped her arms around me, squeezing.

"You know, before the manifestations twenty years ago, your father and I were dirt poor."

"I do know, Mom." I glared at the oats. "You and Dad were some of the first Hunters."

"True, and that gave us an edge that we've managed to keep." She touched my chin lightly, and I turned to look into her hazel eyes. "You need to remember that while Hunters run the world right now, it can always change. The world changed out of nowhere. You must have a skill. Be useful, make connections, save money." She nudged me and smiled to lighten the blow. "Get your eyes fixed."

I nodded instead of answering. If you asked Mom, we were one bad Hunt from poverty, even though she was the most frugal, financially careful Hunter I had ever met.

I finished setting the table just as Ardwin came in. Her honey ringlets were a wild halo around her pixie face, and drool had dried on her caramel skin. She yawned, her light brown eyes still heavy with sleep. Even at twelve, everyone knew Ardie would grow to be a great beauty, but her looks would just lead people to underestimate her. That would be their downfall. Ardwin was vicious.

"Did I miss the announcements? What'd Daddy catch? Did Devon do good?" Ardwin scrubbed at the crusted drool on her face. She poured a glass of water and drank it down in one go, waiting for one of us to answer.

"Daddy and Devon took down an Intermediate," Mom answered her mildly. We looked at each other and smirked.

"Ooo." Ardwin smiled and sat in Mom's chair. She spun it to face the table and poured a second glass of water. "I wonder what happened for it to manifest." This was the part Ardwin liked. She got serious pleasure from finding out what happened to make a monster appear. The higher the monster, the happier she was.

I set a bowl in front of Ardie, and she scowled.

"I don't want oatmeal." My sister pushed the bowl away and hopped up. Opening the cold box, Ardwin pulled a grapefruit and a lemon from inside and kicked the door shut. She tossed the fruit in the air; a knife slid off the counter and flew up to cut both fruits in half. The surprising part for me was not that she cut them but that she managed to catch all four halves and the knife without cutting herself. Ardwin was a Kinetic. She could draw power out of anything, even the air, and use it to move other things or beings.

"Good morning, sweetie," Mom said, neatly plucking the knife from Ardwin's hand and kissing the top of her head. In profile, they were twins, except Mom's skin was dark brown, and her curls hung to the middle of her back, whereas Ardie was light brown and chose to keep her hair cut at her jawline. Unlike either of them, I didn't want hair at all, so mine was a buzz cut, perfectly highlighting the crescent scar that trailed from my temple to my jaw.

"Morning, Mommy." Ardwin dumped her fruit in the bowl on the table and proceeded to scoop the grapefruit out of its rind with a lazy twirl of her finger, her magic precisely setting the skin to the side. The lemon halves rose over the pink chunks and Ardwin hunched her head forward, her eyes wide as she concentrated. The lemons squeezed out juice and pulp, and my sister sat back, satisfied. I watched as she manually doused everything with sugar. She closed her eyes on her first bite and opened them to see me looking at her. "What?"

"Nothing." I shook my head and returned to stirring the oatmeal. Ardwin was in a class all her own, but that made sense; Ardwin was a Hunter-born, one of those rare children that had the talent to not only see but kill monsters damn near since birth. Supposedly, Anthony and I were like that. I didn't remember us that way, but Devon said we were.

I took the oatmeal off the stove and poured it into a ceramic pot. This I carried to the table and carefully placed in the center. I went back to the counter for the top, the carafe of cream, and utensils. I balanced them in my arms, all the while feeling Ardwin's eyes on me. It was my turn to glare. "What?"

"It must suck to not have any real magic," Ardwin observed, a smirk on her face.

"Whatever, Barfwin." I sang out the name that caused her first monster to manifest and zapped her spoon, a minor magic, just like everything else I could do. She dropped the utensil, and I grinned when she glared at me.

"Watch it, Agatha," Mom snapped.

"Yeah, Agony," Ardwin snickered, and Mom slammed her coffee cup down. Both Ardwin and I startled.

"You don't know what agony is," Mom said quietly. She looked at me, and for just a moment, I saw the anguish in her eyes. Anthony. Agony was so close in sound to Anthony. "Eat your breakfast."

Mom returned to her coffee. Ardwin raised an eyebrow at me, and I looked at her before mouthing my dead twin's name. I saw the moment when Ardwin made the connection and her face fell. "I'm sorry, Mommy."

Ardwin barely remembered Anthony, but we were all used to the bouts of melancholy that would spring up out of nowhere when Mom was reminded of him. Not that she ever forgot. She didn't respond to Ardwin's apology but got up and poured another cup of coffee. Behind her, while she was pouring sugar, the cover lifted from the oatmeal, adding the aroma of cinnamon to the air, and scooped into one bowl, while another spoon lifted half of Ardwin's grapefruit into a second one.

"Hey!" Ardwin laughed, snatching at the bowl. Mom smiled slightly and stirred her coffee. She turned and held out her hand, waiting for the bowl of Ardwin's fruit to float to her. My little sister squinted her eyes and concentrated. They played tug of war in the air, both smiling.

I rolled my eyes, dropped my spoon in the oatmeal, and stood.

"We're going to be late," I reminded Ardwin. "You haven't even gotten dressed."

"Mom will take me." Ardwin shrugged. Since I had broken my sister's concentration, the bowl flew toward Mom fast, and with her Hunter reflexes, she just as quickly caught it. Mom looked up from the dish, her expression just a tiny bit guilty, but not much.

"I'm sure," I said to Ardwin and headed to walk out of the kitchen.

"Wait, and I'll take you too." Mom's voice was quiet.

"I kind of want to walk." When I looked up and met her eyes, I saw that she understood, even if she didn't agree. Anthony was never too far from my mind, either. He was my twin, after all.

I walked slowly, feeling the heaviness that weighed me down. I may not have remembered how Anthony died, but there were times when I felt like I was missing something. There was this haziness in my mind whenever I tried to recall my twin and a sadness that came from the lack of memory. Sometimes, the weight of it all could drop me where I stood if it caught me unaware. Whether it was magical memory loss or a trauma block, neither seemed fixable.

It was the lack of closure that hurt Mom the most. She wanted to know. She wanted to enter my mind and experience it. She wanted to make sure that Anthony had died instantly or live with the fact that he died in pain. She wanted to torture herself some more. Sometimes, I was glad I didn't have my memories, just to save her from herself.

A horn honked behind me. I flinched and turned. Devon.

"Hey, little girl. Get in." My brother pulled over next to me and opened the door. I slid across his leather seat and bumped him.

"I bet your breath still stinks."

"Maybe."

"What are you doing out during the daytime, vampire?" I teased, but Devon's dark-brown eyes were inscrutable when he peered over at me. I sighed. "She woke you?"

"She worries." Devon shrugged one large, muscular shoulder, and I buckled up. "Why would you walk? You knew it was going to set her off."

"I needed some space." I told him about breakfast, and he nodded. He pulled back onto the street, and we drove. I stared out of the window, breathing in the fresh air, and watched the mix of magical houses, some that floated in the air, others that constantly changed, and normal houses that regular people lived in. I loved our neighborhood. It was the definition of diversity.

"I miss him too, you know," Devon said into our silence.

"Everyone misses him."

"I miss you, too."

"What does that even mean?" I laughed and looked over at my brother. I imagined Anthony would have looked just like Devon, muscular with Mom's brown skin and Dad's dark-brown eyes. Anthony would have had locs, though, and I, well, I wasn't sure. I had hated hair on my head since I woke up. Devon and I had the same haircut.

"It means I miss you. You don't remember. You were one crazy kid." Devon smiled. "Both of you were."

"You were fourteen. You were just a kid, too."

"I was." Devon grew quiet. He'd joined the Hunters on his fourteenth birthday. Even though the mandated profession choice is the sixteenth year, most Hunter children join at fourteen. Devon hated monsters. Honestly, I thought he hated them more than Mom did. He was merciless in battle, unnecessarily violent. He was the reason the last few Recorders quit. They couldn't sell any of the Hunt videos that Devon was in. He literally tore monsters to shreds.

That was the only reason he didn't know about Martin. Devon knew everything about me, except that.

Everyone had waited for Martin to manifest. Everyone knew that Martin would manifest. Whole families of Hunters combed the woods, trying to find my first manifestation. I didn't know how Martin hid from them, but he was so tiny when I woke, able to fit in the palm of my nine-year-old hand. He was this small little being who fed on air and was warm, so warm, and comforting, in a way my family hadn't been. Everyone was grieving a brother I barely remembered, and no one understood how I could forget him.

"All right," Devon said, pulling into the parking lot. His car growled and purred as we drove up, and I saw a couple students admire the sleek automobile as they headed inside. It was a regular brick-and-mortar building, nothing like the fancy mage school Ardwin went to across town. I was one of the few mage family kids here. I hated it, but I had hated the magic schools even more.

"School." I stared at the doors, not moving.

"Wanna skip?" Devon asked, and he wasn't joking. He would totally take off and drive me wherever I wanted to go.

"Nah. Tests."

He nodded at my response and reached into the backseat. "Forgot your lunch."

"I didn't pack one," I said and caught myself.

He smirked and held the bag out. "Mom."

I took it and leaned across the seat to hug Devon. For a moment, I felt safe in the warmth of my brother's arms before he shoved me. "Out, you bald-headed bumblebee. To school with you, peon."

"Like I said: your breath stinks." I leapt out of the car and bumped the door shut. He rolled down the window and fake roared at me, his voice loud. I couldn't help but laugh, even though we were both kind of sad.

I walked into the building with my head held high. In a school full of normies, even though I was basically nonmagical, even though I tried not to be, I was noticed, so I stopped hiding. I saw heads turning to look at me. I stood out in my yellow and black. They whispered, but they didn't come near me. It had taken one visit from Devon for my bullies to leave me alone. No one forgot that day. I went to class, listened, daydreamed, and thought about surgery and how I could avoid it.

"Are we going to catch her today?" Janice asked, startling me as she jogged up on the way to the cafeteria. We walked beside each other. Janice was in the grade above me, but we talked about our monsters during study hall and at lunch, whispering about what we learned from them. I shrugged.

"I hope so. I'm going to feed her to Martin."

Janice scrunched her nose up, her owl eyes behind her glasses even larger than usual. "Is that a good idea? Martin is already powerful."

"No, he's not, and he won't be."

"You don't know that."

"Yes, I do. Martin is good."

"No monster is good, especially not one that looks like a mini-Titan." Janice hunched into herself. "You know...when monsters decimate towns and kill whole cities, it's not Novices or Intermediates that do that. It's the Gods and the Titans."

"Everyone knows that." I stopped in the middle of the hall to stare at Janice. She blinked at me.

"Well, I was thinking...with Martin being from the trauma—"

"You don't know that." I snapped at her.

"But you said you woke up—"

"I say a lot of things." I started walking, and she hurried to catch up, huffing at my pace.

"I'm just saying. It's probably better to keep Martin in a cage like I do with mine."

"You hate your monsters. Martin is my friend. I would never trap and torture him like you do yours."

"Whatever." Janice glared at me. "No monster is ever your friend. You should just tell your family and let them take care of him."

"You should just tell the mage board rep that you can see monsters and get a new family," I said, taking a dig at her.

"No." Janice was firm. "I won't go live with some mage family that's gonna treat me like normie trash."

"It's gotta suck to live with the monster blind, though."

"Nah. It's kind of cool to know something they don't."

"I guess." My voice was doubtful, and Janice rolled her eyes. "Magekind shouldn't stay with the mageless."

"Mageless shouldn't stay with Magekind. Kill Martin and join your family," Janice said simply, her round cheeks curving into a malicious smile. "Put up or shut up."

"Shut up, Janice. I'm not mageless."

"You may as well be." We went through the double doors into the cafeteria, both of us making a beeline for the corner table by the window that we always sat at. We didn't say anything as we unwrapped our lunches. Mine was leftovers from last night.

38

I made a point of looking up at Janice as I zapped my food, the tiny spark of kinetic energy sizzling the sauce on my pasta.

"I am not mageless." We stared at each other until we both burst out laughing.

"Do mine," Janice said, holding out her sandwich. I snickered and almost burned the bread. It was small magic, but it worked. Janice gazed at me and shook her head, stopping the question I was about to ask. She didn't want to try. I shrugged and began eating.

If Janice wanted, my family could have helped her become a full mage, maybe even Hunterkind, but she didn't want that, and in a few months, it would be too late. Her core, the inner part that held her magic, would harden when she reached the age of maturity, usually at some point between sixteen and eighteen. She had to get proper training to fully access her power or kill her first monster by then to reach her full potential.

"You're running out of time."

"And I don't care," Janice said.

"Right now, but what about when you're older, and you're stuck as like…some…"

"Normie?" Janice asked. "A minor hedge witch or untrained parlor mage?"

"Yeah." I looked down at the table, uncomfortable.

"Like you?"

"You hate your monsters, though." I answered, avoiding the question.

"And you don't hate Martin. It doesn't make sense to me, just like I don't make sense to you. Leave it alone, Ag."

"Fine."

"I caught a new one last night," Janice mumbled around her sandwich, switching topics. She was hiding her bites behind her glossy brown hair. It did nothing to obscure the roundness of her face as she shoveled food into her mouth, but it made her feel more secure. Janice always ate ravenously but stayed generally fit. I barely ate, and we wore the same size. "I might kill this one."

"This makes four—all in one fish tank. Is this one even yours?"

"Nah. Probably a neighbor's. Nothing's been going on for a while at home." Janice shrugged.

"What are you going to name it?"

"I don't know. Something that fits with Ralph and John."

"And No Name," I quipped. Janice tilted her head to look me in the eyes and shook her head.

"He has a name."

"Well, you haven't shared it," I finished lamely. "You've got enough untrained power to keep three fed, but do you have enough to feed four?"

"Who cares if they eat?" she snapped. We argued about what she fed them a lot. Janice had enough magic to keep her monsters slightly satisfied, but I worried about them. They were tiny things that she barely fed, but even tiny monsters could become a problem with the right stimulus.

"I do. Unfed monsters find something to feed on. You know that." I tapped her tray. "You gotta feed them something."

"Crickets it is," Janice said seriously, but we both laughed. Crickets would do, but monsters fed on magic more than real food. My house was full of errant magic, while Janice's house had none except whatever well of power Janice naturally had. Martin stayed in a room, so he was cat sized. Janice's stayed in an aquarium, so they fit in her palm, but the ones that we saw on the screens just grew to the sky; they fed on more than magic. They thrived on fear and pain, the trauma and chaos that they had manifested from, and they grew fast, sometimes within minutes, but only as big as their environment.

"What are you going to name it?" I asked.

"I don't know." Janice shrugged. She grinned at me, a wicked curve of her mouth with a feral baring of teeth. "I've been after it for weeks. I finally caught it with my camera last night."

I nodded. There were many ways to catch a monster, but Janice and I had found that tape recorders and cameras worked best for us. The tiny ones got trapped in the reel, then you just had to extract them and decide where to keep them. It was different with Martin. I hadn't trapped him. When I'd woken up, he was just there.

"I should just bring them to your house." She grinned at me.

"There's definitely enough errant magic for them to eat, but you'll be a Hunter and a ward by the end of the night. The fam would figure out you're Magekind for sure."

Janice nodded. "No way, then."

"It wouldn't be that bad," I said. "Maybe you'd become a famous Hunter, and I'd be your Recorder."

"Are you finished?" Janice laughed, grabbing my container of barely touched food. I didn't bother to answer, knowing she would throw it away, anyway. I was thinking about the monster we had been chasing at school, the one only she and I could see. If I caught it, I could take it home and prove that I could see monsters. It wouldn't open my core, but it would stop Mom from trying to cut off my corneas.

Janice returned from throwing our trash away. "Let's go."

I got up from the table and followed her to the restroom, where Janice had once slammed my head into a wall, right behind that other group of girls who bullied her and hated me because of who my family was. Except, with Janice, we made up; we became friends. Once there, we tossed our backpacks on the ground outside, by the door, and went in. I washed my hands, pulled out my camera, and we waited for the monster to show up. She came out of the largest stall, but this time, I was ready for her.

On the way in, I silenced the new monster with a punch to my book bag. She stopped squealing.

"Mom!" I sang as soon as I closed the door. "I have a surprise for you!"

No one answered, so I slipped down the hall to my bedroom. I liked to check on Martin as soon as I got in, especially today. I didn't want him to hear them kill this monster. That wouldn't be fair to him. The window in my room was open, the glass shattered from something going through it. Martin's drawer was open, and there were scorch marks on my wall. "Martin?"

41

"Looking for something?" Mom was standing in my doorway, holding Martin's lodestone, the patch of red smeared across white fabric.

"Where is he?" I snarled at her, my hands curling with violence. I tossed the bag with the other monster onto the bed. Mom's eyes flicked to the bag, her focus wavering for a split second, but her anger redirected to me.

"We haven't caught it yet. Come." She turned away, walking fast, as if she didn't want me to see her face.

I followed, angry. "What did you do to him?"

When we reached the kitchen, my father was there, sitting at the table, his face pensive, his eyes staring off into the distance. He was rotating a large Hunter knife in his hands, the magicked blade moving intricately over and between his fingers, dancing faster than the eye could follow.

Devon was leaned against the counter, dressed in his Hunter leathers, his face flushed red and angry, matching his clothes. Outside, in the backyard, I could see Ardie. She had been sent out, but she was standing at the doorway, wearing an angelic white dress, probably from school this morning, glaring at me as she clenched her hands. She hated being left out of conversations.

"Tell me why you would keep a monster in your room." My mother's voice was distant. At the table, Dad mirrored Ardwin, his fists clenching and unclenching for just a moment before they began moving again. I could feel his power, angry and oppressive, building up in the room.

"How long have you been able to see them?" Devon asked. "Is it…was it because of Anthony? Have you been able to see them since then?" They all hesitated, the air vibrating as they waited for my answer.

I didn't speak but nodded, the memory of the Titan that killed Anthony hazy, still elusive, even after all these years. I didn't remember, didn't want to remember, but the spray of blood across my face, across my clothes, leapt to the forefront of my thoughts. I smacked the memory down.

They asked more questions, but I kept blinking, remembering.

My mother slapped me hard, and the concussion from the power in her hand rocked me back. I hit the floor, but it was Dad's power that lifted me up, gentle, a buffer that I hadn't even noticed. I met his eyes, and he looked at me, disappointed, but still Dad.

Mom, on the other hand. "You won't do this again." I focused on the spit around her mouth, on flashes of her teeth, how pink her lips looked against her brown skin. "You will not shut down when it is time to answer questions."

My gaze rose to her eyes, where I met her glare, angry, wounded, wild; my stare slid away from her face, and I looked around the kitchen for Martin. If they hadn't caught him, then he would be in the house, somewhere. My eyes shot to the lodestone my mother was holding, a piece of fabric soaked with my brother's blood, the token of my trauma, then to the counter, the table, the ceiling, back to the lodestone, the only piece of Anthony that was left. They had gotten rid of everything else when we moved; everything that was him was boxed up, in storage, somewhere.

I didn't want to look at it.

"Why does it matter?" I asked Devon. I gazed at the refrigerator. "Yes, I've had him since then."

"Why didn't you tell anyone?" Mom asked. My gaze darted under the table.

"I don't know if he's the same monster that manifested," I murmured, maybe in my head, perhaps out loud. I glanced into the hall. "He's my friend."

I kept looking for Martin. I leaned over to see under each of our chairs.

"What are you doing?" Dad finally asked, his first words deadly quiet. His whole body was tense, the veins of his neck straining outward, the muscles of his huge arms flexing as he continued moving the knife. He flicked the blade, embedding it into the wall and snatching it back with his magic. I stared at his fingers, so long, so like Anthony's.

"Looking for Martin," I said it simply, openly.

"You named it," he said, even quieter. I nodded my head and looked up at him, meeting his tortured stare.

"He's all I have left."

"That monster is not your brother," Dad said. I heard Mom gasp, a sharp intake of breath, as if she was just now realizing why I had kept Martin. She looked nauseous. I thought about the monster in my room. Was Martin hiding there? Would he let the new monster out? Would he stay with me?

"I'll kill him for you. I understand why you didn't," Devon said, and I looked at him, the rage a mottled purple beneath his skin, and for a moment, we were all silent.

"Do you?" I asked him, searching his gaze for an answer.

"We loved him too, Agatha." The rage left his face, and he took a shuddering breath. Strong Devon about to cry. He took his kill kit off the wall by the door and strapped it onto his broad back. "I can't do this."

"Devon, wait." Mom stood up, shifting into his path as he headed to storm out of the kitchen. "You can't go to battle angry."

"This won't be battle." Devon laughed and looked back at me. "You know, if you didn't blame her, maybe she would have told us."

"I don't blame her," Mom snapped at him, placing her hands on his shoulders.

"Yes, you do," I said. I felt a stirring in my chest then; for the first time, that thread of connection Hunters supposedly felt toward the monsters they were fated to kill unfurled inside me. The Call. I felt it even though the minor mages and the mageless supposedly couldn't. It was a bubbling up of power that I shouldn't have had, and I recognized the feeling, even though I didn't know where from; the scrabbling chaos called to me.

"Agatha." My mother looked at me. She could feel it, too, then. My father stood just as Devon slowly turned, each of their expressions vacant as they listened to the seductive demand to Hunt. I whirled and ran toward my bedroom, fighting the overwhelming siren quality of the Call.

"Martin!" I screamed his name, feeling my family thundering down the hall at my back. I thrust open the door and saw Ardwin on my floor, curled into a fetal position, held down as the new monster and Martin both bit into her, drawing away her power, each one growing as they did. We'd never heard her come in.

For a second, I didn't see Ardwin. I saw Anthony and the terror in his eyes right before the Titan killed him. I didn't need my father or my mother to touch the core of magic inside of me. I felt it crack and power I didn't know I had burst out and exploded across both monsters simultaneously.

Martin reached out to me as his skin split, leaking the magic I had filled him with in a show of light, then he tore apart, and the power returned to me, holding the writhing purple energy that was my best friend inside of it. I fell to the ground, feeling the ripping pain that was my mage talent sizzling through my veins. It was agony, and no one could help me through it. It would be all they could do to contain it.

My mother fell across my sister, screaming and holding her, her power washing over Ardwin's wounds. She was going to have scars. Dad enveloped them both, his shields surrounding me and the room and Devon—I looked up, and my big brother was watching me, watching my pain.

"You can do this," he said, but I couldn't. I felt the surge of magic through my body, and I could see it reforming my bones and flesh, the baby fat that had clung to me all through high school turning into hard muscle. I passed out, then woke seconds later. I was blind now, the pain and power exploding through my vision, remaking my eyes into a Hunter's. I passed out again. This repeated until the power was finished with me, finished with the changes it had made to my skin, my bones, my blood.

"Come on," Anthony said, grabbing my hand, and I went running after him, giggling in my brand-new purple dress that matched the cuff links and tie to his new suit. Mommy said we were her adorable chocolate drops. Our locs had been styled;

Bantu knots for me and cornrows into a ponytail for him. We looked perfect, which was why we were about to destroy the look. Anthony and I didn't do perfect. We did chaos.

"These shoes suck," I said, kicking them off as soon as we made it to the tree, our tree, deep in the forest, away from anyone else. The scent of the woods surrounded us—tree sap, foliage, and earth. Anthony shed his jacket and his shoes, rolled up his sleeves, and tugged off the tie; then, he climbed, light and limber, barely touching his hands to the trunk before finding the next spot to reach for. I scampered up after him, both of us squirrels who could find knots and grooves where others would only see bark. We chose a comfortable branch and grinned at each other.

"Let's see it," Anthony said, his brown eyes bright and full of mischief. I pulled the backpack from my back and held it out. He dug past the lunch we stole from the kitchen and brought out the two presents, clumsily wrapped, perfect for us, from us.

"This is yours." He held out the package gingerly.

"Duh," I said and shoved him. We were part of the tree, though. He didn't move, but he laughed, a flash of white teeth, joy infusing his face and making the dimple in his right cheek pop out. I had a matching dimple in my left. I hooked the bag onto a branch.

"That one's yours." I motioned to the other gift in his lap.

"Duh," he snickered and, without ceremony, tore the package open. He gasped at the contents before pulling out a set of monster cards, a full set. Devon and I had worked for months to collect them all. He gave me part of his old collection to start with, but we went online and bugged Mom and Dad, and my older brother shook down some kids at his school, too. "This is all of them, Aggie!"

"Obvious." I rolled my eyes and carefully untied the intricate knot he had tied around my package. It was about the length of my arm, and I knew what it was before I even opened it. I finished with the knot and tore the brown paper back, revealing the spelled knife I had been coveting for months. I squealed and hugged the Hunting knife and sheath to me.

"That was girly." Anthony rubbed his ears in fake pain.

"Thank you!" I nearly screamed at him, and he laughed. I marveled over the knife, finally able to touch it. The sheath was covered with famous Hunters and some of the Titans they had killed, each one with their insignia above it. Our family was there, our father and mother, among the famed poses and kills. They were part of the first Hunters, the teenagers who discovered that killing the monsters that formed from their traumas gained them more power, made them faster, stronger, better battle mages than any that had come before.

"Thank you, too." Anthony waved his cards at me. "I am the only one in third grade with all the cards. I can't wait for school."

I pulled the knife from the sheath and tilted the spelled blade so that I could see the soft glow of amber, blue, pink, and other layers of magic across the metal. "How did you get this?"

"Devon." We said it at the same time and grinned. Devon got us whatever we wanted. At fourteen, Devon was the youngest Hunter ever. We were going to beat his record, and he wanted us to. Everyone expected us to. We already had strong magic and agility individually, but as a team, we were unstoppable on the training grounds. We were the youngest trainees and had been since we were seven.

"Do you hear that?" Anthony cocked his head.

"Hear wh——" Then I did hear it. The monster sirens were going off.

"Titan class," Anthony said. He handed the cards to me, and I stuffed them in the bag. "We gotta go. Mom's probably already mad."

I watched him as he began to make his way down. "If she's already mad, why go home?"

He looked up at me and grinned. "Because it's our birthday, and we have other presents to open, Aggie."

There was a ringing in my ears, a high-pitched whine, and out of the corner of my eyes, I could see Anthony turn his head at the same time, toward the forest edge, toward the houses. It was like an itch in the back of my mind, something ravenous and angry but also seductive. *Go*, it whispered. *That way. You must go that way*. And we did. I leapt from the branch, an impossible height, and landed on my feet, not even acknowledging the jarring snap of my ankle fracturing. Then we ran, a tiny pack of wolves, tearing through the forest, following the Call.

The Titan was huge. I could see its legs before we burst out of the trees. Sirens and chaos were everywhere. There was a path of carnage behind it that I couldn't see clearly. I ran faster than Anthony now, my legs churning as I flew across the meadow toward it. It was black with spikes down its back, curved claws, and a wide, wide mouth. I could see black feathers sprouting around its huge ears, ears that heard me coming. It looked at me. I looked up at it as I put another burst of speed beneath my feet. At the last second, I leapt into the air, pulling the knife out of its sheath to plunge the blade into its leg. One hand went up to grasp the fur on the sides of its calf, and I climbed, stabbing as I did, watching the magic take effect.

The monster roared, each wound I gave it causing its blood to gush, weakening it. I stabbed again and again, dancing away from its arms and hands that reached for me, calling out all the battle spells I knew, whether they worked or not. I screamed at it and stabbed repeatedly, but then I heard him.

"Aggie!" Anthony. Hanging with a handful of fur in one hand and my knife plunged deep into the flesh of its side with the other, both the Titan and I heard him, found him with our eyes. He was standing at the edge of the trees, terrified. He had peed himself, and though the Call still had a deep grip on me, his fear had caused it to leave him. He was just a little boy, a scared little boy, and the monster wanted his fear.

"Run, Ant! Run!" I screamed at my brother, my twin, my other half, stabbing faster and faster, plunging the knife in. Even as the magic worked and the Titan began to shrink, it was not fast enough. The Titan reached Anthony in a few steps, then he was in its hands, and I was running down the scaly arm, holding onto the spikes there, stabbing its hand, stabbing its fingers, grabbing Anthony's shirt, even as the Titan squeezed and squeezed until—

ZAINE LODHI

I was covered with gore.

I was covered with Anthony.

A monster, probably a Titan—because what else could the graphic death of the other half of your soul create?—began to form in the air beside me. I saw the coalescence of my pain, mottled black and purple and blue, and I screamed at it, slashing out with the same pain that formed it, bisecting the creature with the knife before it could finish forming.

I felt the emptiness in my core, the vessel waiting for magic to fill it, and my spirit was open to the power, but the Titan, the one I had been stabbing and screaming at, was still shrinking. Its fist was coming for me, and I deflected the core magic, redirected it back into the creature that had killed my brother. I pushed the power into it, everything that I originally had and all that was coming to me, shrieking my pain and rage as I did, watching the darkness fill the creature up until it exploded. I fell, far and fast, still holding Anthony's shirt, and when I hit the ground, I lay on my back and wailed at the sky as tufts of fur and magic rained down beside me.

I was still screaming but otherwise catatonic when they found me. I was magicless, clutching my brother's shirt, covered in his and the Titan's blood. They couldn't get me to give the shirt up, to give Martin up, to let them have the creature I had diminished to a handful. They only saw a wad of fabric, barely recognizable as a shirt and the cut, a perfect crescent moon, riding from my temple down to my jawline. It was my only wound, just as Martin was my only souvenir, my prisoner, though I would forget that in the days to come.

When I woke, I was alone in my room. I'd been moved to my bed, but I was covered in bits of Martin and the other monster. The memory stayed with me, reverberating with knowledge of the past.

I coughed and got up, sweaty, my clothes plastered to my body. If you couldn't Hunt, there were other things for you to do; most mage families could barely see, so their eyes were modified, and they were relegated to monster skinning or crafting or experimenting, though a few did go on to be great Hunters. Some mages never entered the business and did other things. I could have done anything; now, I would only be allowed to do one thing.

I heard them talking as I stalked down the hall. Dad stood when I entered the room.

"Okay?" he asked, looking me over. Mom didn't look at me, her gaze on the table.

"Is Ardwin okay?" My voice was hoarse from the screaming, but Dad nodded at my question.

"She is sleeping. There wasn't as much damage done as it looked." Dad shook his head, the anger and disappointment warring for control on his face. "This could have been so much worse. For you to have been hiding that thing for this long—"

He broke off and shook his head again. I looked at Mom, my mouth glued shut. I didn't know what to say to either of them. "I'm sorry."

"It's . . . we all deal with trauma differently," Dad said quietly. He was looking at Mom, as well, but his gaze shifted to me. "We all do."

"Mom?" I asked, waiting for her to look up. When she didn't, I said into the silence, "I remember." I saw the eagerness, the need on my mother's face when her head snapped up. She reached for me and hesitated, not sure if I would share.

I held out my hand to her. "Go ahead, Mom."

"Devon," she almost shrieked my brother's name. We would only live this memory together once. Devon came into the kitchen, alert, ready to battle, but it was only Dad's hand there, reaching for him. Their hands gripped together, and my parents reached for me, each grabbing a hand as I closed my eyes and pulled up the memory of how Anthony had died.

When we came away from the recall, Mom heaved and barely made it to the trash receptacle. Then, she was vomiting and crying. Dad picked her up, his voice a murmur as he carried her to their bedroom. Devon looked at me but said nothing before walking out of the room. I stood in the kitchen alone, feeling lost.

"Take a shower," Devon said behind me, and I turned. He raised an eyebrow and tilted his head. He surged down the hall to his room, and I meekly followed him, stopping halfway to enter the bathroom. I stripped out of my clothes, peeling the fabric away in places, and cut on the shower. The water was hot, and after a moment, I allowed myself to break down. I cried for Martin, for Anthony, for the lost parts of me that had never come off that field.

I heard the bathroom door open, and a soft thump of clothes being set on the counter. When I got out, I saw that it was Hunting garb, fresh, new, exactly my size. I dried slowly, startled when something stretched on my hip. I twisted to look down, and there was Martin, a flat, living tattoo against my skin. Very few Hunters could trap monsters this way, and I had done it without knowing.

"Hi, Martin," I whispered.

I dressed. It was purple, deep purple, a shade that brought out the dark hue of my skin. Hunters could wear any color. I looked in the mirror, at the buzz cut I had worn since Anthony died, at the scar that even magical enhancement couldn't remove. I stared at myself. I was a Hunter.

When I opened the door, Devon was leaning against the wall. He had changed clothes, the golden hue of his leather garb accenting the dark-brown color of his eyes, eyes that were just like Anthony's. He held my knife out to me, and I took it, pulled it from its sheath. I looked at the nicks along the edge, the marks from my first battle.

"I wondered what those were from," Devon said. He hesitated. "We always assumed you and Ant used it to kill the Titan."

"I remember when you tried to give it to me."

"You screamed."

"Sorry," I said.

He shook his head. We were silent. I slid the knife back into its sheath and ran my fingers along the engraving.

"You back?" Devon asked.

I took a moment to answer, considering the return of my memories and the kid I had been seven years ago.

"Sorry I was gone so long." I smiled slightly.

He shrugged.

"Sorry I didn't tell you about Martin."

He grunted. "Wanna Hunt?"

"Yes." I strapped the knife onto my hip, right above the tattoo. I felt Martin purr against my skin, and I shivered with anticipation.

"Don't think just because you took down a Titan at nine that you're going to beat my record."

"I already did."

He shoved me. I didn't know what the future held, but I knew my family would have my back, even when I made mistakes, even when I was foolish. This was my Pack, and I would never keep another secret from them. I looked at Devon and asked, "So, can I talk to you about this new tattoo on my hip?"

"Mom's gonna be so mad," Devon laughed. And I agreed.

The Magic Book of Accidental City Destruction: A Book Wizard's Guide

written by

Z. T. Bright

illustrated by

ARI ZARITSKY

ABOUT THE AUTHOR

Z. T. Bright is an author in deep (like, really deep) cover as a financial planner. He lives outside of Salt Lake City with his wife (who is far more talented creatively than he is), their four perfect children, three ducks, two dogs, and one cat. Yes, it's as loud as it sounds. When not writing or working, he can be found cooking, supporting his kids at their various activities, or enjoying the outdoors—hiking, backpacking, fishing, biking, etc.

Z. T. was the winner of the inaugural Mike Resnick Memorial Award and was published in Galaxy's Edge *magazine in 2021. He writes anything speculative, ranging from sci-fi short stories to middle-grade fantasy novels. Writers of the Future is his second sale.*

"The Magic Book of Accidental City Destruction: A Book Wizard's Guide" was inspired by the power of the internet and social media to both disseminate information and create social divisions like never before in history. It seems to him we all need to examine our relationship with these tools . . . before it's too late (dun, dun, dun!).

ABOUT THE ILLUSTRATOR

Ari Zaritsky was born in 2001 in a small suburban area in Chicago, Illinois. Since childhood, art has been influencing the way he views things in life. Constantly dissecting and analyzing what is around him and asking himself, "How would I draw this?" has led Ari down a creative path.

Pixar's Up *and* Ratatouille *were key to Ari discovering a career as an artist.* Up's *opening scene moved his mother to tears, all without* any spoken words. Ratatouille *inspired his stepdad to pursue culinary excellence because of the phrase, "Anyone can cook." Because both these films moved his parents, Ari set a new goal for himself: to move people through the art he creates.*

Ari has been drawing since his earliest memory. He used to draw only in black and white. He specifically used pencils to shade and draw, which made him steer away from color altogether. Ari's color blindness has proved to be a challenge. However, swimming at the elite level for eleven years, the challenge was nothing new to him.

Currently, Ari is studying at Savannah College of Art and Design, where he is honing his career skills. When he's not at school, Ari is working hard to refine his technical skills and add to his portfolio.

The Magic Book of Accidental City Destruction: A Book Wizard's Guide

I don't usually permit unsupervised children to peruse my stacks. It's one of the Book Wizard Guild's maxims: "Children don't buy books. Adults buy books for them." But I've never been great at following rules, and something about the two young boys that wandered into my magic bookstall intrigued me.

Back then, my stall was merely a canvas stretched over four wooden poles. Nestled tightly in the bazaar just inside the city gates of Archen, my stall had just enough room for my desk and three tables stacked with my magic books. I swept a layer of fine, rust-colored dust out of my stall and into the crowded bazaar, pretending not to notice the boys. What was it about them? I craned my neck, trying to hear their voices over the buzzing of a thick crowd and the click-clacking of mule hooves on cobbles.

Maybe it was the way the books practically cooed like love-struck maidens as the older boy—probably a decade younger than me, around fifteen years old—brushed his fingers across their spines. Maybe it was that the younger of the two—presumably his brother, maybe ten—shuffled around in shoes that were far too big, while the older went barefoot, feet stained maroon with dirt and sweat. Or maybe it was that the younger one reminded me of myself at his age, too mouthy for his own good.

"I thought Book Wizards were men," he said to me.

"Who says I'm not?"

He pursed his lips and narrowed his eyes, glancing from my breasts to my shaved head, then shrugged and bounced over to my children's section—a small stack of moving-picture books. I grinned as he opened the top book.

Wind whistling through tall trees—the kind that can't be found within a hundred miles of the city—could be heard above the din of the bazaar. Out of the corner of my eye, I watched the book's gentle breeze rustle the boy's wild, dark curls off his face. The scent of pine mingled pleasantly with that of the aromatic spice stalls nearby and masked the rankness of mule droppings.

The boy's lips formed a perfect circle as he experienced the magic. "Kadin! Kadin! You've got to see this!"

The older boy, tall and thin with the barest hint of black hair above his lips and on his chin, was studying the cover of the *Book of Truths*, his attention unbroken by his brother's exclamations. I frowned. I'd never liked that book. Many of my books had the essence of dogs, playful and loving. Some of them were like cats, temperamental but affectionate. A few were sly foxes. But the *Book of Truths* was a snake.

The younger brother raised his voice. "Kadin!"

The older boy lurched, as if being awakened from a trance, and peered down over his brother's shoulder. "It's great, Azzam."

But I could see the frown that his brother could not.

"Can I have it?"

"Sorry, Az——"

"Please, please, please!"

"We can't, Azzam," Kadin said, then leaned in closer to whisper something to his brother, as if embarrassed.

"Ugh! You're the worst! Mama and Papa would have bought it for me."

Ah. Orphans, I deduced. As a Book Wizard, it's my nature to marvel at the power of words. The words the younger boy spoke seemed innocent enough. Family members argue. I know that better than anyone. And I mean *anyone*. But if you'd seen Kadin's face, you'd know that those words had the power to cut straight into his soul.

I'd felt that same blade. I knew what it was like to have people who were supposed to love you use words to pick at never-healing wounds. In a way, I envied their brotherhood—it had been so long since I'd had a family—and an overwhelming need to help them preserve their relationship came over me.

I regret what I did next. Truly. It's going to sound heartless and stupid. But I swear it wasn't malicious. A little selfish, maybe, but aren't we all sometimes? And, it broke another Book Wizard Guild maxim: "Never give away anything for free." If I was going to give away a book, it should have been something harmless, like the moving-picture book. It definitely should not have been a book I knew to be a snake.

The guild was pushing the *Book of Truths*, and I wanted to advance in rank. Higher rank meant more spellcrafting permissions. Also, I wanted that book out of my stall, and Kadin seemed to have a way with it—if you can ever trust a snake, it's in the hands of a good person, right? These boys were clearly poor, and if this book could help them make some money, maybe it would ease the stress on their relationship. I had a plan.

"I'll tell you what," I said, picking up the heavy, leather-bound book. "I'll let you have this book now, and you'll pay me back later, with interest."

"What's interest?" Azzam asked.

Kadin looked at his feet. "That's very nice of you, miss, or um—"

"Call me BW." It was the new name I'd chosen for a new life.

"Very kind, BW. But we don't have a way of making enough money to buy this, especially with interest."

"What's interest?" Azzam repeated.

"Ah, but that's the beauty of this book," I said to Kadin. "If you're smart, you can use it to make plenty of money."

"What! Is! Interest?"

"You," I said, plopping the book into Azzam's arms, "need to learn some patience! Open the book."

He did so, groaning under the weight of it. "It's empty?"

I grinned. "Place your hand on the page and ask it what you want to know."

Azzam did as instructed. "What is interest?"

A robust description of the word scrawled itself across the page. The spellwork for the *Book of Truths* made it possible to source any written information that existed among any other book in the *Book of Truths'* global network. I didn't know much about the book yet, as I avoided it as much as I could, but I did know it wasn't omniscient. Just *very* powerful spellwork. Imagine having a massive library at the tip of your fingers— it still required time and effort and determination, but in the hands of the right person, it was a powerful tool.

Young Azzam frowned. "I can't read good."

Kadin didn't bother to read what the book said, stroking his almost-mustache with thumb and forefinger. "Interest is when someone wants to rob you, but in disguise. They give you something now but make you pay more than it's worth later."

I shrugged. "Not quite what the book says, but I don't blame you for your pessimism. I'll charge you a mere five-percent interest. But that's annual. If you're smart, you can use this book to pay me within a month. Cut that five percent by twelve. What do you say?"

It was the easiest sale I'd ever made. I could feel the essence of the book coiling itself around Kadin's heart. Even before he reached his hand out to shake mine, I knew my plan would work. This boy would be a customer forever, and the *Book of Truths* would always help him pay.

I watched them walk away with a pit in my stomach. The essences of the other books went silent, like when you've watched someone make a big mistake, but saying so won't do any good. I didn't know *why* I felt so uneasy. If I had, maybe I wouldn't have given them the book.

Azzam's complaints cut through the noise of the bazaar. "I didn't want that stupid book! Take it back and get the one with the trees!"

I shook my head. Helping these boys might prove challenging with a personality like Azzam's.

Three days later, I sat at my desk in my stall, recording the week's measly sales in my ledger. One book of instant sleep stories—barely even magic, just boring—and two romance novels in which the reader would physically experience the pathos of the main character. I cringed, thinking about what Mahdir would say.

His words scrawled themselves across my ledger.

I surely hope you're only partially through your weekly report. You'll never earn your next rank at this rate.

I huffed. He knew better than anyone that Archen was a difficult city for Book Wizards. That's why he'd left!

I picked up my quill to respond but was interrupted by the unmistakable sound of bickering brothers. I glanced up from the ledger to see Azzam at the stack of moving-picture books. He set aside a few other books as he searched for the one he'd seen earlier. I sensed displeasure from the ignored books, but soon they were purring as Kadin flipped through them.

"Back so soon?" I suspected he would return the book. That would go against another guild maxim—no exchanges or returns, ever—but I'd make an exception in this case. I couldn't saddle a good kid like Kadin with a book like that if he didn't want it. Tension that I didn't realize I was holding released from my shoulders.

Kadin brushed his hands off on his stained linen shirt and pulled out a coin purse, tossing it to me. I emptied its contents onto my ledger. Enough to pay for the book *and* the five-percent annual interest. Weeks ahead of when I thought they'd be back, with more interest than they owed for such a short period of time.

"That was fast," I said.

Kadin shrugged. "Guess you were right about that book."

He wore a shoulder bag today. It wasn't especially nice, just a brown woven satchel, but next to his tattered linen shirt and pants, it looked downright fancy. Kadin clutched the contents of the bag close to his side, and I could almost feel the *Book of Truths* hissing within.

I separated the coins that represented the interest, put them back in the coin purse, and tossed it back to him. I knew what he'd spend it on, anyway. As if on cue, Azzam slid the moving-picture book across my desk, and Kadin tossed me the coin purse again.

The book chittered in excitement. I grinned. For a moment, it felt as if the plan I had conjured the other day had worked on all counts. I had sold a *Book of Truths*, and I knew Kadin would be buying more from me with his new source of income. But most importantly, I hoped this would help the brothers' relationship by easing their financial burdens. Kadin buying his brother a book was a nice start.

As I recorded the sale, Azzam leaned in to see what I was doing. "What's that?"

"It's my ledger. Where I keep track of which books were sold." Perfectly boring to all children and would-be thieves. The perfect place for Book Wizards to house all of the spells that made the books what they were. If you flipped it over and upside down, the pages were filled with letters and symbols that would make no sense to someone without my training, and the ledger was enchanted with a spell so it held unlimited pages. The essence of every magic book across the entire world was housed within.

"Come on, Az, don't be so nosy," Kadin said.

I was about to brush it off like you do when a dog owner apologizes when their pet sticks their nose in your backside. Harmless nosiness, right? But Azzam cut me off.

"Shut up, Kadin! You're not the boss of me."

Kadin didn't respond, moving away as if he'd just disturbed a hornet's nest, pretending to peruse the books.

I couldn't help myself. This little brat needed to be taken down a notch. "Azzam, I have a different book for you. I think you'll like it more."

I keep my first two original spellworks in my desk drawer at all times. One is a simple scrawl on a piece of notepaper I named the "Bookworm." I pulled out the other, a small picture book, from under my desk. It was a prank book.

Azzam examined the cover, graced with exotic animals, meant to elicit a sense of wonder and intrigue. I watched his lips tighten into a grin, and he flipped the book open. The first page of the book showed an image of a large woodland mammal but illustrated from behind as to have a full view of its hindquarters. As he examined the image with a furrowed brow, what can only be described as the sound of a sloppy, wet bowel movement erupted from the book, and I watched a gust of wind from the book push Azzam's dark curls out of his face again. This time, the odor was not so pleasant.

He doubled over, dropping the book and placing his hands on his knees. He wretched and gagged. I doubled over as well, but in a fit of laughter. Eventually, I stood up and wiped the tears from my eyes, peering over at Kadin.

He was not laughing as I thought he'd be. A spike of alarm shot through my gut as I realized I may have offended his protective older brother nature. But no, it was worse.

I could immediately place the look on Kadin's face. It was closer to fear than anything else. Not that he was scared *of* his little brother, or *for* him for that matter, but that he was afraid of how it would make his own life more difficult.

I knew the feeling. Sometimes all you want in the world is to have a good relationship with someone you love. But events outside of your control conspire to make that more difficult. Or impossible, even. I wrote the book on that one. Literally, it's stashed in a trunk somewhere.

Azzam recovered and screamed. He knocked over stacks of my books in a fit of rage, and I could feel them whimpering. Then he glared at his brother, who'd played no part in the prank, with icy cold eyes. "I hate you! And Mama and Papa would too!"

Kadin watched Azzam run off, then looked back at me and

the books strewn across the ground as if he wanted to help me pick them up. He was a good kid. He didn't deserve any of this.

"I'm sorry," I said. "I thought it was harmless. Don't worry about all of this."

Kadin frowned, but nodded and followed his brother. I tidied up and whispered condolences to the books, then looked down at my ledger. Mahdir had scrawled a message after the entry for the *Book of Truths*.

You've sold a Book of Truths? *Congratulations! There may be hope for you after all. I'll have a shipment with more of them out to you right away.*

I swallowed, trying to dislodge a disturbing image of myself neck-deep in snakes.

All ten of the books Mahdir sent me had the same serpentine essence as the other *Book of Truths*. Part of me wanted to keep them locked in a chest. But that seemed irrational. It was what the guild wanted to sell—something about a new wrinkle in the spellwork that they felt would give them a new sales benefit. And maybe they'd realized what I'd done with Kadin—resourceful users of the book would buy more books.

The first person to buy a new *Book of Truths* was Azzam. He barely looked at me when he purchased it, and he didn't come with Kadin. Later, Kadin told me Azzam was using it to learn to read. I was pleasantly surprised about that.

Over the next few months, I didn't sell another *Book of Truths*, but Kadin bought nearly every picture book I had, though I knew they weren't for him. As his apparel improved—new shoes, several brightly colored robes, even some jewelry—the life in his eyes seemed to dim. After weeks of prodding, he finally opened up.

"It's Azzam. I barely see him anymore. He doesn't come to the orphanage. I'm worried about who he spends his time with and how he uses his book to make money."

I nodded, unsurprised.

"The last thing he said to me was that I was being stupid, and the book could make him rich. I'm worried he's hanging around thieves."

"I'm sorry, Kadin. If I see him, I'll try to talk some sense into him." But we both knew I wasn't his favorite person.

"I've got to show him we can work together and make money the right way. If I can show him a better way, maybe he'll stop being such an idiot."

"How have you two been making money so far? Seems like you've been doing all right for yourselves."

Kadin didn't meet my eyes. "Well, I hope you won't be mad about this, but we've been letting others pay us for information in the book. At first, we tried lending it, but it seems like the book starts to bind itself to one person. Eventually, even Az couldn't use mine."

I laughed. "I guess I should have seen that coming. It's a powerful book. That's why it's so expensive. But it does have its limitations. The Book Wizards' Guild made sure to write a line in the spellwork to ensure the book would learn its owner's preferences and only respond to that person after a time. This way, if someone stole it, they couldn't use it. They'd have to buy their own."

Kadin pulled his book from his satchel, laid it on my desk, opened to the latest entry, and turned it to me, pointing. "What about this? Would you be willing to work with me?"

The entry was all about the benefit of diversified sales channels. Using vendors to increase exposure and tapping different markets. In a way, I was a vendor for the guild, so I understood the concept.

Kadin was learning quickly, and I felt impressed. But I had my doubts. Mahdir had moved from the city as he decided he'd never sell the *Book of Truths* here. It was a safe, peaceful city. Not the type of place where magic books sell well. He needed strife, he said.

I wondered if Kadin would just cut into my profits. But I didn't want to be a simple vendor for the guild. I wanted to apply my skills as a Book Wizard and spend my time crafting books. And something inside me *needed* to help Kadin and Azzam. Or maybe I just saw myself in Kadin and needed to guide him, as an experienced practitioner, through the painful process of abandoning toxic family members.

"Let's give it a shot." I held out my hand, and Kadin shook it.

It was only a day before Kadin sold a *Book of Truths*. Kid had a knack for both magic books and sales. He used his own book to understand the tactics of subscriptions and interest, and within a month, all of the books were sold. Mahdir became suspicious.

How are you doing this? Should I be concerned?

It grew like a wildfire. After a year, Kadin and I were swimming in more money than we'd ever dreamed of. Strangely enough, the book sold best to the less wealthy classes, despite its hefty price. But the upper class soon caught on, and it wasn't long before everyone seemed to have one. I moved from my small stall to a three-story shop in the city center with a view of the royal palace and temple. I couldn't keep books in stock quickly enough.

I'd been accepted into higher ranks of the guild and granted access to the inner workings of the business. Kadin was initiated into our ranks as well. On one hand, it was my dream to learn more complex spells and test them out in my spare time. But on the other, I grew more worried about the *Book of Truths*.

To begin with, as I became more familiar with the book's source spellwork, I realized it wasn't *really* passing along facts or "truths," as its title claimed. From what I could tell, it was passing along what others *believed* to be true—whether it was or not. Something about that felt... slimy.

Additionally, the spellwork to tie the books to one particular reader also tailored the information that it presented. For example, someone who *wanted* information about how the movements of clouds were symbols from an almighty deity trying to communicate with us mere mortals would be shown convincing arguments of just that. While those intent on finding scientific answers to the same question would be shown something different.

This wasn't any different from any other time. People have always received information from different sources throughout history and have always had differing opinions. But something about this acceleration of information through the books was worrisome.

Kadin and I held weekly business meetings. We became close. I began to see him as more than a business partner—a friend or even a brother. In one of our meetings, I asked Kadin about Azzam.

His shoulders slumped. "Every time I try to talk with him, he grows hostile. Says I abandoned him to live like an elite without him. I try to get him to work with me, and he just laughs."

"Why won't he work with you? Can't he see you're living more comfortably?"

"Too comfortably, maybe. I think part of it is his pride. But I think sometimes he just *needs* to do things differently than me."

I didn't know what to say, so I patted him on the shoulder.

"Part of me thinks it's the book," Kadin said. "I mean, he's always been hard to deal with, but something's changed in him since he got his book. The group he hangs around with now wrap their books in bright orange cloth and carry it out in front of them when they walk, like it's some sort of statement. I'm not sure I know who he is anymore."

I bit my lip, his words picking at a wound of my own that wouldn't heal. How would I deal with the *Book of Truths*?

After two years, I couldn't live in the city any longer. Due to an ever-increasing demand for the *Book of Truths*, I'd risen to the highest rank in the guild and had learned all the spellwork methodologies, including the ability to edit existing spellwork.

Kadin normally came to visit my home in the arid mountain foothills overlooking the city on a monthly basis. But he was very busy managing many different sales channels, and he'd missed several meetings. I was worried, but he promised me through his ledger that he was fine.

ARI ZARITSKY

Things are a bit mad down here, but I'll come visit soon.

Eventually, he did, and when I saw him riding up the trail on his mule, I ran to him. When I reached him, I recoiled in surprise. He looked awful. His clothes were still very nice, and he was neatly groomed—tightly trimmed chin beard and clean, pulled-back hair—but the left side of his face was bruised, and his lip was healing from a cut.

He assured me he was okay, and I helped him inside and made him some tea.

"There are riots every day," he said, taking a seat at my table. "It's almost hard to avoid them. People are dying, BW."

I sat down across from him and rubbed my face vigorously with both hands. This was why I'd left the city. "And the books?"

"The factions have grown. Everyone carries their books on display in the colored cloth of their faction. Mostly orange and blue. But some green and white too. Churches. Neighborhoods. Schools. Everyone is on edge."

"I've been trying to get the guild to vote on some alterations to the spellwork. But they just laugh at me and say, 'welcome to the real world!' As if this is all normal. I'll keep working on them."

"No, BW. You've got to do more. I know what kind of power you have at your rank. You've got to do something now before it's too late."

"It's not so simple, Kadin. First of all, we're talking about breaking the first maxim. 'The guild always acts as one.' I'd be removed. But we're also talking about our livelihoods! And not just you and me. We'd be changing the source spellwork of every *Book of Truths*, which nearly supports the guild finances on its own. The guild would crumble."

"Are we pretending now that you follow the maxims?" Kadin sighed and took his *Book of Truths* out of his bag and placed it on the table between us. He did the same with his ledger. "I know I'm asking for more than is fair. But I had to try. Good luck with everything, BW. I'm done."

"What do you mean? What are you going to do?"

He shrugged. "Find my brother, for starters."

I exhaled long and slow. "Kadin. I know you want a relationship with Azzam. I want that for you, too. But sometimes, it's just not meant to be. It's not your fault."

Kadin was not one to show much emotion, but his eyes narrowed, and he raised his voice. I'd struck a nerve. "What would you know of it?"

I'm ashamed to say my temper matched his. Or more likely exceeded it. I stood, looking down at him, slapping my hands down on the table. "Do you really need an explanation? Look at me! I'm different from you. I'm different from everyone in that city! And I was told so every day of my life! Why couldn't I just be like everyone else? My clothes were not right. My hair was not right. The people I shared a bed with were not right! Kadin, I saw how Azzam talked to you. I saw how that cut your soul. I lived that pain too. But there comes a day when you have to realize that just because you want someone to love you the right way, and just because they *should* love you the right way, doesn't mean they ever *will* love you the right way. I left my family. You're the closest thing to family I have now. And I'm better off for it."

Kadin placed a hand on mine. "I'm sorry that happened to you, BW. And I'll always be there for you if you need me. Just like I will be for Azzam. I won't just abandon him."

The words came before I could keep them behind my teeth. "Then you're a coward. Or a fool. Or both!"

Kadin stood, tears flowing freely down his cheeks, and turned to leave. Pressing my weight to the table in anger, I watched him mount his mule and leave down the trail toward the city. I spent the night crying and breaking things and drinking strong beverages. Not necessarily in that order.

I awoke to the pain of a skull on the verge of cracking open but managed to clean myself up and start the long walk to the city. I packed several waterskins—not all of them filled with water—and my ledger. Though I wasn't sure I was wrong, I had an apology to make.

It took me most of the day to walk, as I kept no mule. The city was barely recognizable. The bazaar was nearly empty, and there was trash everywhere. Buildings were in disrepair, and people walked quietly in groups with their *Book of Truths* held across their chests.

As I moved toward the city center, it became worse. More people meant more conflict and more destruction. Smoke rose from behind tall buildings. Kadin lived in an affluent neighborhood, which I hoped had been spared some of this mess.

My hope dimmed, as did the light of the setting sun. It seemed the closer I got to his neighborhood, the closer I got to the smoke.

Panic swirled within me as smoke filled my nostrils. I coughed harder and harder as I made my way to Kadin's home. The sky grew darker as I plunged deeper into the smoky streets. The realization that the smoke was emanating directly from Kadin's neighborhood sent icy fear through my gut.

"Kadin!" I called over and over, hoping he'd hear me and we could retreat to a safer part of the city.

But soon, all I could do was cough. I pushed through to Kadin's home anyway but found only carnage. Several homes, including Kadin's, were nothing but crumbled stone and ash. The unmistakable form of charred bodies lay in the rubble.

Barely able to breathe, I ran away from the destruction as fast as I could. Several times I collapsed in a fit of coughing and gagging, and I wondered if I'd pass out and die of smoke inhalation. But eventually, I made it out of the worst of it and found a chunk of broken stone to sit on.

With my elbows on my knees and my face in my hands, I sobbed, watching my tears dot the red dirt between my feet with wet brown.

I didn't know if Kadin's was one of the bodies I had seen. I hoped not. But either way, I felt as if I'd failed him. Failed the city. And even if Kadin lived, I didn't feel confident I'd see him again after our last interaction.

But I owed him something, regardless. In a way, all of this had started with me. Had I not sold him that snake of a book, maybe things would be different. Had I not continued selling the books to others, maybe the city wouldn't be in such bad shape. I had put myself and the guild before the greater good.

Though I still thought Kadin naive when it came to Azzam, it was time to make amends. But could I really do it? I'd spent my entire life dreaming of being a successful Book Wizard.

This wouldn't just be abandoning financial comfort, which I surely would. It would be abandoning a lifetime of hopes and dreams. Not to mention the livelihood of every guild member and possibly the guild itself.

I'd lost Kadin. Could I give up everything else I held dear?

I thought back to the day I'd met Kadin and Azzam. Hadn't all of this started because I was trying to keep their relationship from fracturing? Now the *Book of Truths* seemed to be fracturing the relationships of everyone in the city. Maybe I was already too late, but I had to try.

I opened my ledger from the back, revealing the spellwork of every magic book. I flipped to the page for the *Book of Truths*. I could feel it sneering at me, like it knew what I was about to do. Something I should have done long ago but had avoided out of selfishness.

Then, at the very bottom of the lengthy scrawl of spellwork, I wrote an entry with my first two original spells.

First, the bookworm spell. I isolated it to the *Book of Truths* entry and set it free. It would eat away at the spellwork entered above it, eventually rendering the magic useless.

Then, I wrote an entry for the *Book of Defecating Exotic Animals*.

It would take a little while for the bookworm spell to do its thing, and the sun hadn't quite set, so I used the time to go shopping. While certain sections of the city were in turmoil, the bazaar was still operable. As it wouldn't be long before I wasn't on the Book Wizard's Guild payroll and would be unable to afford deliveries to my mountain home, I bought myself a mule, a goat, a few chickens, and a plethora of seeds. I was resourceful. I'd be able to get by for a while. Eventually, I'd probably need to sell my home, but it would fetch enough to keep me comfortable for years.

As I rode away from the city in the dark, I saw people dropping their books in the dirt and heard cries of disgust. I smiled as we climbed the trail to my home, looking down upon the city below, lit by several large fires within.

Turns out I wasn't as resourceful as I thought. My chickens died within weeks, hardly producing any eggs. My seeds never produced anything but peppers, which were far too spicy to subsist on. My goat gave me milk, so that was nice, but then I had to eat it, which wasn't.

As I finished my last strips of goat jerky and packed my mule for a trip down to the city to see what sort of payday I could get for my home, I heard a clomping of hooves behind me. I turned, ready to fight or run, depending on who approached.

Two dark-haired males dismounted, but I couldn't see who they were from the other side of my mule. I reached into my mule's saddlebag for a knife. I'd been expecting the Book Wizard's Guild to come after me. Maybe this was it.

"BW?" called one of the voices.

The guild wouldn't call me that. It stood for Book Wizard. They knew me by a different name. I dropped my knife and stepped out from behind my mule. It was him.

"Kadin!" I sprinted to him. I couldn't stop the tears. I buried my face in his tan linen shirt, drenching it in tears and snot. Finally, I recovered enough to speak and pinched at his shirt. "Back to tattered linen, I see."

He smiled. "Yeah. Lost everything in a fire."

"Everything except your life. I didn't think I'd see you again."

"You may not have. But Azzam came to warn me there was going to be trouble in my neighborhood. We escaped together just in time."

I turned to the other person. Azzam was taller now, almost a man, but still had those wild curls. "I guess I pegged you wrong," I said, holding out a hand.

Azzam took it. "BW, Kadin told me something about you. That you said he was the closest thing you had to family."

I nodded, tears welling in my eyes again.

Kadin gripped my shoulder. "Well, we were wondering if we could call ourselves your brothers. We may not always get along, but we'll always have your back."

I didn't have great memories of Azzam. But he'd just been a kid. Maybe I could forgive him. And maybe Kadin had been right. Maybe it was more important to always be there for someone, even if they weren't always there for you. After all, maybe they'd be there when it really mattered.

I decided I'd give it a shot and wrapped my arms around my new brothers.

The Squid Is My Brother

written by
Mike Jack Stoumbos

illustrated by
NATALIA SALVADOR

ABOUT THE AUTHOR

Mike Jack Stoumbos is a speculative fiction author, disguised as a believably normal teacher, living with his wife and their parrot.

Mike grew up with three brothers and over forty first cousins, who he enlisted as test audiences (and participants) for his imagined adventures, often reenacted with cardboard props or Star Wars action figures. His love of storytelling brought him to the stage as a musical theater actor, the role-playing table as a game master, and a career trajectory to teach English and theater. In the summer of 2019, however, Mike shifted his writing passion into a priority, and once again became a student: attending workshops, practicing daily, and braving the story submission gauntlet.

Mike's work has since appeared in several collections, including his first pro sale in Galactic Stew and a publication alongside a personal hero in Hold Your Fire: Stories Celebrating the Creative Spark. Shortly after he was named a Writers of the Future winner, Mike's space-opera series, This Fine Crew, was picked up by Chris Kennedy Publishing, for many continuing adventures.

The idea for "The Squid Is My Brother" emerged as a curiosity: how to take something from cosmic horror and make it as endearing as a family member. Even more importantly, Mike wrote this story shortly after the schools had closed due to COVID in 2020 as a young student's first-person account of transferring into a bizarre new environment, fearing the unknown, and learning about humanity.

ABOUT THE ILLUSTRATOR

Natalia Salvador was born in 1985 in Granada, in the south of Spain. She grew up reading, watching adventure films, and playing classic adventure video games that inspired her drawings.

She always liked art and admired book covers and interior illustrations, so it wasn't surprising when she decided to approach that world by studying fine art and graphic design. Her mother always encouraged her and was the one who gave her the final push to pursue a career in illustration.

Influenced by fantasy art and the Golden Age of Illustration, she enjoys creating beautiful images that tell a story.

The Squid Is My Brother

Dear Mother,

Got in my first fight at school today. Wasn't my fault.

Happened in art class. Was instructed how to "draw"—am familiar, not infant. Was given "wildflower." Asked teacher if I could draw something from home biome instead. Raised hand, obtained permission, just like in the vids. (Would have made you proud.) Teacher accepted, said something about "cultural diversity."

Then, was given supplies: markers of limited spectra. Did not object, did not argue. Only invited Brother to change my vision filters. Did not even make a sound!

Brother reached out of backpack, suctioned one true arm against my left temple, then put amorphous arm over my eyes, just like you taught me. Achieved seal, was adjusting vision when heard shriek from nearby table partner. (Perhaps should have used audio filters instead.)

Native Earth girl: "Ew!" and "Put away the *monster*."

I did not understand, neither did Brother, but both felt...hard to explain. Perhaps will learn word, but new concept, never experienced until Earth, and never so strong as today.

Brother retreated, pulled closed backpack.

Put my own head down.

But native Earth girl called teacher, made chirping noises. I didn't listen.

NATALIA SALVADOR

Teacher *asked nicely* that I keep Brother put away. Only, teacher doesn't say *Brother*; says "Xeno-org" like a dirty word, like refuse from science experiment.

I asked why another student, short boy, gets to wear eye filters. Teacher says not to make fun of *glasses*. Children laughed—no, not laugh, *snicker*. Laugh implies joy.

Later, at the recreation break, native Earth girl approached with others. Said something I didn't understand, then snickered again.

When I turned to walk away, she grabbed at backpack, saying, "Don't need backpack for recess."

Felt Brother clench to hold onto my spine, readied my muscles and pumped adrenaline. Brother would have slipped out of backpack to stay with me, but rules about Brother and backpack…

So I spun, held tight to backpack strap with one hand, hit with other hand. Not intended to damage, did not account for added strength from Brother. Not my fault little native Earth girls don't train in variable gravity. Not my fault they weren't taught not to touch or grab other people or their symbiotes.

Had to apologize to teacher, to principal, then to girl when she woke up, then to girl's family. Had to keep Brother completely enclosed in backpack so they would not be offended. Had to apologize again for telling them, "Concussion builds character." No scientific basis for that, just something you (Mother) said once to an ensign; thought it amusing.

Host family had *the talk* with me. Male caretaker insists he's *not mad, just disappointed*. Female caretaker had to explain what that meant. Told me to write a letter to you to tell you *what I'd done*.

Truth: I feel bad about little girl. She didn't know about hole in backpack, or that Brother is always connected to me. Did not feel bad about teacher, principal, or little girl's family, even if they said something about "ambassador" and called you, "Commander Kessler," a hero.

Miss you. Hope you are safe. Glad I have Brother. Not sure if I understand purpose of "exchange program." Perhaps when older...

Love,
Michaela Kessler

P.S. Male caretaker read before I sent. Advised running through grammar program to "fill in sentences."

Declined. No need for superfluous pronouns and articles when meaning is clear. Just like you taught me.

I really hope my second day of school goes better. Can't say I like it though, and it doesn't seem to like me. Me + Earth School = Opposite of Symbiosis. Not that any of the students here would know *symbiosis* if it latched onto their intestine. I wonder if it's just "DC" schools; maybe Cape Carnival is better, sounds more fun. Will have to ask Charlie the next time we call. Charlie is older, probably has more interesting things to study, maybe with kids who are...different.

Still, I wake in the morning, Brother helps my respiration rate change for consciousness. I wash and dress, line up the hole in the back of my shirt for Brother. I eat real eggs from a species called "farm-raised"—I like the eggs, and so does Brother.

I am always careful putting on my backpack. Have to be. The hole is big enough for him, and he can squeeze through a pretty small space as is, but if he's pinched, then I get twinges all down my left side. So I slip on the modified pack, and Brother knows to pull all his arms in.

Brother doesn't object, but I can tell he'd rather be free or in pressure suit. Female caretaker says it's just because it's what I'm used to and that I'll "adjust."

I keep backpack on and open when riding to school. Caretakers know better, don't object.

I keep backpack on and closed in class. Teacher *knows*, but sounds strange when reminding other students, as if not really believing, or not wanting to talk about Brother.

Reading class is annoying, but tolerable. Brother wants to read, upset that he can't join me, and I'd remember better if Brother were there to help me record it. Brother misses seeing, can't see as well in the backpack. And *no*, as I try to explain to caretakers, can't see through my spine; spine doesn't have eyes.

Brother can hear though, better than me, retains vibrations, passes little information, like passing notes in class. Tells me who is snickering, who is whispering. They wonder what happens if I take off the backpack, why I am so tall if I'm so young, whether I have special powers. Mostly, they wonder about what Brother really looks like, and they make shiver noises. Sometimes, I slowly turn to look at them and grin, because they don't think I can hear them, like a real horror villain. Mother would probably tell me that it's not good to do that. She would say, "Don't encourage them."

I don't go out to recess anymore. Teacher lets me stay in.

During recess, I open book to show Brother the pictures. Brother climbs far enough out of backpack, finds my temple, and wraps one arm over my shoulder.

Hear teacher's breathing change to gasping, panting. See teacher clutching at chest—immediately wonder about oxygen intake, but have to remember that Earth is a naturally oxygen-rich world, and that classroom has nonsealed exterior door—(elementary school standard, I am told.) No, teacher is having panic attack. Not medical danger.

Teacher says, "Mica!" (Never asked permission to use short name.) "Mica, put it away." Her voice shakes, her jaw quivers.

I do not mean to cry—not a logical response, not expressing pain, calling for Mother, or purging toxins from body. Just sad. Mother would say, "No use." (Mother would still hug.) But tears come out of tear ducts anyway, go straight down both cheeks, on account of fixed-point gravity.

Teacher's expression changes. She approaches, begins to say my name— Then eyes widen! She stiffens and collapses.

I find this confusing. Meanwhile, Brother finishes collecting tears from my cheeks. Can use the salt and moisture. Natural reaction. Apparently terrifying to teacher.

Wonder if representative of all teachers ...

"I can't have it in my classroom," says teacher. Doesn't lower voice, assumes I cannot hear because separated by wall. Does not understand how attuned Neptunians are to vibrations; obviously, Brother hears.

The chair in the waiting room is deep enough that the backpack has room. My toes scrape the orange carpet as I swing my feet.

"Well, clearly, there need to be some boundaries communicated," says principal in funny voice, harder to understand.

"No other children are allowed to bring pets into the classroom," says teacher.

"It's not a pet," says a third voice I don't place. "We're talking about her symbiote, and she can't just—"

"And we have to look at this like a *seeing-eye dog* kind of thing," interrupts principal.

Third voice softer, understanding, "I think even that is too ..."

"Look," (Teacher) "I can't have it in my classroom. I'm sorry. I can't. I mean, I can't even look at *cooked* squid. Switch her."

"Well," (Principal) "I wasn't able to get her host family on the phone to make anything official. But let's make some alternate arrangements today. Okay? Can you ... check in with her, and ..."

"Sure," (Third Voice).

Teacher and principal exit office, opening door right in front of me. Brother is completely out of sight, but teacher won't look at me. Principal gives a smile. Fake. They both walk away.

Third voice appears at the door, looks down at me, also smiles. Hopefully less fake.

"Mica," he says, "do you want to come in?"

I stand, keeping one hand on my backpack strap, and walk into the office. He shuts the door behind me.

Office is...simple. Not much lighting, all drawers need keys, all cupboards have latches. The one plant is a succulent. Other than the gravity-hung pictures, kind of reminds me of home station.

"It sounds like you had a bit of a rough morning, Mica," he says. He is large, not just tall but broad, not right shape for spacesuit. He arranges a chair that is shorter and gestures for me to sit in it.

I do not object.

"I'm sorry," he says. "I'd like to talk with you about it, if that's okay."

I look around the room. I do not have anything to say yet. Brother frets from inside the backpack—I don't know which of us is more nervous.

"My name is Mister Royce. Do you remember me?" he asks.

I nod. "You signed me up for class."

"I did. Do you know what my job is?"

"Staff sergeant?" I guess.

He chuckles, a friendly kind of laugh. Brother relaxes. "Not exactly. I'm called a counselor, and I have two jobs: one is to register students for classes, and the other is to talk to people if they're having a rough day."

"Oh."

"Now, Mica—" He pauses, changes expression. "Do you like to be called 'Mica'?"

"Michaela," I stammer, giving my longer name. "I don't..." My cheeks get really warm. For a moment I worry I might cry. "Mother and friends call me Mica."

"Oh, thank you for letting me know, Michaela. Is there anyone else here you've asked to call you Mica?"

Clever. He's asking if I have friends yet.

I shake my head *no*. "Just the caretakers."

"Your host family?"

I nod.

"I bet everything feels pretty different right now," Mister Royce says. "It's hard to know what you can say and do, and who you can talk to. Well, you can talk to me. You can ask me or tell me about anything you want, and I won't get mad. I might not be able to answer everything right away, but I won't get mad. Okay?"

I nod again, but don't look right at him. He waits, and I wait, and I try not to cry.

"You know, even grown-ups have trouble saying what they want to sometimes."

I am not sure if I should nod.

"I heard that you're a great writer." He selects a miniature notebook and pencil. "What if you just took some time to jot down anything you're feeling? Like a diary entry, just for you. Don't worry about it sounding perfect or even making sense. Nobody needs to read it but you. But afterward, maybe you'll have some ideas of things that you want to talk about."

He slides the child's tools across to me. Charlie would remind me that I *am* a child, that I'm the youngest of the generational mission. I take the pencil and start writing.

Dear Diary,

"Earth" is stupid name.

"Most advanced species," and decides to call home planet "dirt," "mud," "soil."

All other planets better named, especially Neptune. Even fictional species and home worlds have better names. I bet the extra-solars have better names. Mother will tell me when she gets back from her meeting with them.

I would have gone with her if she had let me. Interstellar travel can't be more dangerous than grade school on planet Dirt.

I worry I will fail *lunch*. I can read, and write, and do a lot of math in my head better than older students, but there is no teacher for lunch, and I can't tell who is the officer of the mess hall. The other students sit in groups, and I can't tell the rules for who sits where and why.

I don't actually need to interact with the mess staff. I bring my own bag, because female caretaker says I need to *ease in* to

American food; male caretaker jokes about me eating military rations.

I don't know if I need to interact with the students. I find an empty table at the edge of the big room and start eating.

Someone approaches me. He is the short boy with glasses who was in my old class, before I got moved.

"Hi," he says.

I do not respond. Perhaps I should have reciprocated.

"Can I join you?"

My jaw drops before I realize he means to share the table. Mother says only Brother can join with me, until I'm old enough to know how adults join—I have theories, will ask Charlie someday.

I close my mouth and nod. Short boy slides a chair to sit across from me. It screeches against the floor polymer, like a docking seal that missed and has to shift and scrape.

"How is Mister Faris? I heard he's chill."

Having no concept of my new teacher's core temperature, I shrug one shoulder.

"You know, people are saying that Miz Lu yelled at you for being from Neptune Station, then fainted when your squid came out."

"What?"

"I think that's kind of cool," he says, then takes a bite. Chews once and resumes, "Kind of like a guardian that shows up to defend you. Do you watch anime?"

"I don't—"

"I can recommend some. Student accounts have a streaming service."

I have a vague understanding of anime, but this is not the most pressing point. "I don't have a *squid*." I say the word like it's something icky, something I don't want to pass over my tongue, but I'd rather spit out than swallow.

"Oh, your…" He pointed at me—no, at my backpack. "Everyone calls them *squids*. Even in the news, they—"

"The Neptunians?" I ask. It's a stupid question. I know that's what he means.

"Yeah, well, my dad says they're not really from Neptune, not originally. That's how they know how to travel." He shrugs. "What do they call themselves?"

I shake my head. "They don't call themselves anything. They don't need to."

"Oh...so how do you know they don't like to be called *squids*?"

I don't have an answer. I take a bite of my MRE.

He does not comment on the packaging.

"You know, my dad says your mom is a hero."

I nod. I'd been hearing that a lot. This place called "Washington, DC" keeps talking about heroes. I'll have to ask Charlie.

Charlie's full name shows up first, with her personal e-contact: Charlotte Campbell.

Then, the live video feed loads in. It shows Charlie's face, and behind her the room. She is sitting at a desk, and she has filled the walls with her posters of ancient rockets and even older guitars. Two of her brother's arms are visible, both draped over her right shoulder.

"Hey, girl!" she says. Big smile.

Makes me feel warmer than thermocoils in a pressure suit. "Hi, Charlie."

"How you doing, Mica? I heard from your host family that you're having a hard time with school."

I nod. A part of me wants to just complain, but another part of me is happy to see her. It's only been days since we last saw each other in person, when we landed in the Florida Sea, but I really miss her. Seeing her feels way more like home than I think even an orbital station would.

"Tell me about it," she says, and looks caring even though she's still smiling.

Charlie is really pretty. Mother calls her "the good kind of pretty." I think it's because of her smile. Charlie's hair is short like mine—more efficient for putting on and sealing up helmets—but she has dyed the front of hers purple. This also makes her look more fun, even though Charlie is practically an adult. She'd had a job called "apprenticeship" back in home biome. She said that this trip to Earth school would be like a little vacation.

"I don't like the exchange program," I begin, and wish I'd started with more context. So I trip over myself recounting the last few days, including the fight, and getting switched out of class, and not feeling like I belonged anywhere or with anyone.

While I'm talking, I can feel Brother starting to tremble. Echoing fear and sadness responses I'd been feeling.

"I'm sorry, Mica. Have you talked to your host family about it? They seem really nice, and they've both been farther than the moon. Oh, and Missus Rasmussen was in Exocorps, just like your mother."

She is right, that caretakers—*Rasmussens*—are nice, but still not like home. Still not familiar with or comfortable seeing Brother.

I chew on my lip. Brother reaches one arm to my neck and applies cooling suction. Obvious sign of tension, sensed by symbiote, visible to Charlie.

Charlie tilts her head to one side. "Sorry, girl. You know, some parts of the adjustment are just going to be hard. Remember Titan Station? Hard at first, but you got through it."

"I guess," I admit. There's a word Mother uses for when you do something because you kind of have to but really don't want to do....

"What can I help with?" Charlie asks and then tries to answer. "We could have calls like this every night if you want, same time. Or if you need any equipment or programs, I can write to the Rasmussens."

"Everyone hates Brother here," I tell her. Not really an answer, I know.

"Oh, I'm sure they don't *hate* your brother, Mica. It's just that—" She makes a gesture with her hands that means she doesn't know what to say. "Look, they don't understand. They haven't really seen or grown up with symbiotes like we have, so it's kind of scary and weird to them."

After waiting the appropriate amount of time for the

transmission, I blurt out, "But Brother isn't scary, and he can't and won't hurt anyone."

Charlie starts to say, "I know that—"

"And he's not a squid!" I finish, yelling it loudly enough that maybe I upset male caretaker downstairs.

Charlie's eyes look concerned. She changes subject a little. "Hey, Mica, you know, you don't have to wait for transmission lag here. We're actually at less than a second delay. It's kind of a cool thing about being on the same planet."

I say nothing.

"Look at it this way: you know about something that none of them do. You are friends with something that scares all of them. You are so brave, and they don't know how to be that brave. Ah!" Charlie holds up a finger to stop me talking as soon as I start to open my mouth—she's right, no lag. "You can't fix that right away. And it's hard. It can be super lonely, girl, but it's only because you are so awesome. You are the single bravest person I know, and you're here on Earth, and representing the Project in Washington, DC. That is incredible!"

"I'd rather be in Cape Carnival with you."

Charlie smiles again. "It's *Cape Canaveral*, sweetie; it's not a carnival, just another city. And..." She shakes her head. "And there was an agreement about where the Neptune Station kids would live—stay. While the team is away. They only get seven of us to spread between the cooperating nations, and it might be as short as a few months, so..." She shrugs. She really doesn't know what to say. "Earth is full of politics. And we need to get through the politics to stay in funding."

Charlie is saying something that her father likes to say. Mother doesn't even use nice words when talking about politics, then she tells me not to repeat those words. I still sort of wonder if *politics* is a bad word. Not enough data.

"I know it doesn't all make sense, Mica. But this is your mission. Your mother is off on a mission—a really important mission, and you have one too. I know it's a lot, but I know you can do it."

I straighten up. I know I'm sitting, but Mother says I've known how to "sit at attention" since age two. I nod to Charlie, who is old enough to look like a grown-up. "Yes, ma'am," I say, like they do on the station—actually, like Charlie says to the staff sergeant. I miss the staff sergeant, too.

"That's what I like to hear." Charlie looks around, then leans in, like she's about to tell a secret.

I know she's far away, but I lean toward my camera too. Brother begins to buzz in anticipation, and I can see Charlie's brother arching one arm.

"And you were totally right for punching anyone who tries to touch your brother. I know Commander Kessler can't answer right now, but she would commend you."

She would commend me! I feel so full and happy that I don't even realize I'm crying again until Brother comes to collect the tears. Mother used to tell me how lucky I was that I always had someone with me to wipe away the tears, that I would never be alone, that I would be cared for by a symbiote that no one on Earth would ever really understand. Mother is second-generation Neptune, first person to even link with three symbiotes at once, so she knows what she's talking about. And I'm third-generation Neptune, and I'm brave enough for this mission.

Dear Diary,

Today was better at school. Teacher-Faris is more "chill" than Teacher-Lu.

Short boy with glasses sat with me at lunch again. His name is Franklin, which he says is better than *Frank Junior*, which I don't get. He is nice, is okay about seeing Brother now, but a little weird about it too. He is also weird about me being two years younger than him and still taller. When I tried to explain that I might be more than that younger because of *time dilation* on my trips to Titan and now Earth, he got excited but confused.

He said his dad (*Frank Senior*) knows about time stuff and is part of X-Force and knows more about the Neptune team's mission. Also says it's dangerous for civilians to be on Neptune Station right now, just in case of "something." I don't know what—neither does Franklin, really. But I see a lot of stuff about the Trans-Solar Project and someone named SETI. And there are cartoon images of Neptunians, of the *symbiotic Xeno-orgs*, but most people like calling them *squids*. Franklin says there's good anime, bad anime, and anime he's not allowed to watch—but that good anime shows Neptunians as good guys. I like that.

Franklin asks about how Brother is connected, why it goes into the spine, if it ever hurts. I get to teach him about it, which is kind of cool.

Mister Royce stops reading the diary entry, sets it down and looks at me. He is pleasant. Also lets me keep the backpack open while I'm in his office. Doesn't flinch at the sight of Brother. Doesn't ask stupid questions, like if he can touch Brother.

Brother gets to stretch and breathe better when I'm here. Right now, is hugging my arm.

"So, Michaela," he says, "does it ever hurt?"

"What? No." I shrug. "Only if someone tries to take him off."

"That would be worse than hurting."

"Exactly," I say. "Mother says it's a dual-edged sword. Symbiote attachment is the best way to keep babies safe in variable grav and with any risk of pressure or temp changes, but it's more dangerous to separate later. Mother was disconnected for three days once, and would have lived if she stayed disconnected, but said it was the worst days of her life."

"I see."

"Charlie says our immune systems wouldn't be able to handle Earth without the symbiote, anyway."

"Oh, yes, Charlotte Campbell. I actually just talked to a colleague about her. She's thriving in the accelerated program. Sounds like a wonderful influence to have. I heard she's thinking of going to Annapolis, which is really close by."

I start to get excited, but Brother notices my wariness and helps keep me in check. "Like visiting soon?"

"No, she's considering it for college next year."

"Next year?" I can feel Brother starting to adjust temperature to compensate for me; I can feel room stop spinning before it starts, dizziness and nausea averted. "But we're not going to be here next year," I tell him. "We're going home. Aren't we?"

Male caretaker does not try to stop me as I run to my room and slam the door. He calls after, "Mica, are you okay?" but doesn't try to follow. Then I hear him say something frustrated that I'm not supposed to repeat.

A little while later, he is on the phone.

"Hi, Nell?" Pause. "No, I think something new happened.... Well, I didn't really get a chance to ask her, but I haven't heard anything from the school.... No, it might be better for her to talk to you. She's just more comfortable with you, that's all.... I'll check on her, but—well, Nell, she's probably listening to everything I'm saying anyway, with the symbiote."

He isn't wrong.

I go to the computer, turn on to try to call Charlie, but she's off-line. Try anyway, but she's really off-line. I input clearance codes, and open long-range communication. Don't care if it's hours delayed or if Mother won't be the first to see it. I can still record and send something. But there's a banner on Neptune Station saying "Not Receiving at This Time." It suggests I send to Io or Titan Station, the waypoints while we can't contact Neptune.

Then, I do the thing the caretakers keep telling me not to do: I go to the search bar. I look for *exchange program* and confirm: not real exchange program. No one exchanged, no one sent to Neptune in our place. I search for *Neptune Station* and the *Trans-Solar Project*. I look for the *symbiotes* and the SETI and the classified things about Mother. *Commander Kessler is a hero*, it tells me, and she is leading a team on a mission made possible by Neptune Station and Neptunians, by symbiotes like Brother, but where she's traveling and how far away and how long is *classified*.

Brother is twitching nervously. Does not know how to help, can only alter endocrine system so much. Cannot rewrite thoughts with chemistry. Tries though. So busy with blood pressure and adrenaline reg that can't even catch tears—

"Mica?" Voice of female caretaker. She opens the door.

I continue search, harder to see though. Am shaking, whole body.

"Mica!" She rushes to me and pivots my chair. "Honey, what's wrong?"

I don't know what I say, and I don't know if I make any sense. I try to tell her about the long stay and it not being a real exchange program, and how I can't contact the station and how Mother is gone—and where is she, and is she coming back.

Then female caretaker says, "Come here," and puts her arms around me. She squeezes me and the being on my back. Brother doesn't mind. In fact, Brother misses hugs.

"What happened?" she asks.

"I just want to go home."

"Oh, honey, I know. I'm sorry we can't make it easier here."

I wipe my nose and look up at her. Nell Rasmussen, female caretaker, is not as pretty as Charlie, and not Mother. But she looks sincere.

So I ask her, "How long?"

She exhales long enough that I know she'll tell the truth, even though she doesn't want to answer. "Honey, we just don't know. Your mother and the Trans-Solar team and all of the Neptunians who went with them—they have gone on a farther and stranger journey than even your flight here. And it's hard to say if it'll be a day, a week, or even months before we hear from them again."

"I miss Mother. And I don't like it here. I don't like wearing the backpack or hiding Brother or having no one understand what it's like to have a *real* Brother, instead of just another kid living near you."

"You know, I'm sure the first people to Neptune Station didn't like it there either."

I give her a questioning look.

"No, really. That was fifty years ago. Almost as old as I am. But that was in the early days of beyond-Belt exploration. Their rockets were *bad*," she said, shaking her head with a grimace like she was about to spit out spinach whose vacu-pack had leaked. "And they even took one apart to make the station. So they were stuck there, and it felt so alone, so dark, and so cold. But if they hadn't stayed there and completed their mission, they never would have met Neptunians and found symbiotes."

Brother has mostly relaxed now. One of his arms is wrapped around Nell Rasmussen's wrist, gently urging her to stay and accepting her comfort.

"They made it work," she says. "And things got better. Your mother is making something incredible happen that only a few people really know about, but no matter how weird it is, she will make it work. And, Mica, you are one of those pioneers. I know that you can make it work too."

Dear Mother,

Avoided a fight at school today. Would have made you proud.

Little native Earth girl, same one, saw me walking through hall this morning, and called out, "Ew! Put the squid away!" Then snickered.

I paused. I walked back to her. Then, took off the backpack, let it drop to the floor, let Brother slide out. Invited Brother with a thought to wrap like he would normally. One true arm over the front of each of my shoulders, one amorphous arm on each side of my neck.

I smiled at little native Earth girl. Her face went white.

I told her, "The squid is my brother." Then, turned and walked away, letting her—and everyone—see Brother, just like we do on the station, out of the hole in the back of my shirt.

They cannot tell me I need to put it away. I am an ambassador for Neptune Station; take my mission seriously.

Don't know where you are, or when you'll be back. Miss you, but I have a mission, too. Will make you proud.

Love,
Michaela Kessler

Gallows

written by
Desmond Astaire

illustrated by
NICK JIZBA

ABOUT THE AUTHOR

Desmond Astaire is a speculative fiction storyteller from Central Illinois, where he navigates the journey of life alongside a devoted wife and forever-loved son. In his other life, Astaire is a senior enlisted leader for a military public relations unit, supervising the training, development, and operations of multimedia content creators.

Astaire's lifelong obsession with science fiction and fantasy was forged as a child in the halls of local public libraries. The addiction was enabled by reading programs like Accelerated Reader and BOOK IT!, and the revelation to write professionally was born after his discovery of Dean Wesley Smith's Star Trek: Strange New Worlds anthology. For these formative experiences, he is forever grateful. Astaire can be found Saturday mornings in Peoria metro-area coffee shops conducting weekly writing sessions and trying to apply Denzel Washington's adage that "Dreams without goals are just dreams, and they ultimately fuel disappointment." Writers of the Future was Astaire's goal since 2017, and "Gallows" is his first-ever fiction publication.

About "Gallows," Astaire says, "The story is about predestination and retribution colliding when a bartender must determine if his customer is the time-traveling tourist an FBI sting is looking for. It was a writing exercise inspired by a Reddit writing prompt, but what made this one especially enjoyable was developing the protagonist's personal vendetta of taking back control of our future by any means necessary."

ABOUT THE ILLUSTRATOR

Nick Jizba was born in Bloomington, Indiana, in 1984, but he has spent most of his life living in Nebraska. He has always spent time drawing, but didn't really consider art as a career option. Losing a safe construction job in the 2008 recession pushed Nick to develop his art into a career. He attended ITT *Tech Institute for game design, focusing on 3D modeling and level design. In school, he ended up doing most of the concept art and sketching for group projects, and that developed into a passion for digital painting. Nick has continued to learn by taking a variety of online classes, taking on the occasional freelance illustration, and working on personal illustrations that he sells at conventions. He is currently working on his first book,* The Sower.

Gallows

Cohenstead is a little nowheresville where High Pass Road meets the Long Tom River in western Oregon. We've only got the Oppenheimer National Energy Laboratory and some basic village necessities, including the dive where I bartend. My customers will call me Gallows, and I am a discerning bartender. Everyone's got a story to hide, and I enjoy stealing it out of them.

March 21, 2022. It's unusually busy for a Monday night, and it makes my heartbeat race. I inhale deep through my nose and blow out through my mouth, and the calming tinge of the nearby pine-tree farm fills my lungs like a good menthol cigarette. *Steady*, I keep reminding myself. *Leverage the facts*. That's what worked in the corporate world, in that other life, which they murdered. *Stay on point*.

There's Pinball, a scruffy hoss in plaid who's collecting beer bottles and clinking the paddles of the vintage pinball machine. Ponytail is sitting stoic and fidgeting with her Tortuga cocktail at a high-top table where she can see the whole room. Newsie Cap is an old-timer who drifts over from Junction City now and then to drink cheap beer and keep the slot machine running. Serious Guy in his serious suit just wanted a black coffee while he worked on his fancy tablet at a booth. Lilly is a spunky woman with a tender smile who elected for a seat and some conversation at the bar.

This is significant because I suspect some of them—or none—may be time-traveling tourists from the future. I have to find out who before they step foot outside the building.

NICK JIZBA

It has to be tonight because tomorrow, the Oppenheimer Lab will be discovering fusion energy, and my window will expire. The FBI is counting on me to deliver bodies.

Yes, I'm on medication, but not for what you'd think. I'm not delusional. Arguably unstable and certainly obsessed, but not delusional. And I'll prove it.

Lilly orders a frosty pint of beer and talks me into ringing up an off-menu fried food sampler. I can't place her accent. It's almost familiar, but *not*. Interesting yet unsettling. It makes my stomach sour.

"Where are you from, Lilly?" I ask.

"Canada, originally," she says, in no maple-leaf accent I've ever heard.

"Oh, yeah? A long way from home, eh?"

"You could say that."

Maybe a century or two?

I always intended my interrogations to start with the crucial question, point-blank and in a tone just coarse enough to disarm a deceiver: "So, what brings you to Cohenstead?"

"Oh, you know. Just passing through," Lilly says bashfully.

Liars. They're all liars.

She's not accustomed to deception. They never are, for some reason. Lilly is especially sweet and flimsy. I know I can lean harder.

"Come on now, Lilly," I say. "I've been doing this a long time. I can smell a good story. What are you really doing here?"

I used to take the nonstop flight from Newark to Buffalo a handful of times a month on business, enough to have a routine down. But Flight 8128 on February 12, 2018, was delayed by two hours, so I ended up spending a lot more time than normal in Terminal C that night. It wasn't difficult to overhear conversations at the airport. Sometimes my coworker and I would do ridiculous voice-overs of strangers' conversations to pass the time. But he had slipped away to the restroom, so I just eavesdropped. Across from me were two starry-eyed college-aged academics interviewing a woman of apparent celebrity about human rights. She had their full attention until the airline called first boarding.

The silver-haired VIP exchanged parting pleasantries and stood to leave. And that's when Tweedledum and Tweedledee saw me. One of them reacted, pretended like we hadn't just made eye contact, and whispered to the other. The other took a glance at me before they began conspicuously bickering under their breath.

"Problem?" I finally asked.

"No, sir, no problem at all," Dee said, backpedaling hard.

Dum disagreed with his companion. "Does the name 'Gallows' mean anything to you?"

Dee slapped Dum hard across the chest.

"No," I said. "My name is David Enzman. I'm sorry, do I know you?"

Dee and Dum continued debating in private. Now they had *my* full attention, and their trepidation caused carelessness in the volume of their voices.

"If it's him, let him get on the plane. Problem solved," Dee said.

"No. We *have* to take him back with us. Remove him from the equation!" Dum argued.

"There were *no* survivors on 8128."

"Exactly. So he wasn't on the plane."

"Or taking him off the plane is the reason he lives because he's supposed to die. I'm not even sure that's him. This is *completely unauthorized*. We're historians, not spec ops."

"But it's goddamn Gallows!" Dum insisted.

It was an understatement to say the pair made me uneasy, so I slipped away to the boarding counter and signaled a gate agent.

"Hey, I don't mean to cause alarm, but those two are acting very suspicious. I think you should probably call security," I said. I handed the gate agent my ticket for the final check-in, and she scanned it.

"That won't be necessary." Dum appeared out of nowhere and flashed a badge. I'd been in enough airports to recognize that it wasn't a TSA credential. "Mr. Enzman, could you come with us for a moment?" he said.

"My flight's boarding," I said. "What's this about?"

"Just come with us, please."

"Absolutely not," I said, turning my attention to the airline employee. "I do not know these people. Please call security."

Dum grabbed me by my arm, and I clocked him with a right hook. Dee lunged for me, but the actual TSA and some county deputies had us all detained by the time we were good and fighting.

They left me handcuffed in a holding room, and I didn't see another person until about two hours later when a Federal Bureau of Investigation special agent with stone eyes and long hair under a baseball cap introduced herself to me.

"And where are *you* from?" Special Agent Burkey asked.

"Redbank."

"What time, chief?"

"I don't know. The officers took my cell phone," I said.

"What time are you *from*?"

"Eastern Daylight Time? I don't understand."

Burkey took the seat across from me to stare me down.

"Your friends in the other room are singing like it's Sunday morning," she said. "I don't even think it counts as an interrogation, really. And we just caught the third one trying to break you all out. The mercenary-looking guy? He's dead, so the other two are telling us everything in exchange for a bargain. Things like your nom de guerre, Gallows. And your headhunter work."

"'Headhunter'? I've never seen those two before in my life. I don't know anything about a mercenary, and I've never heard that name before," I protested. "My name is David Enzman. I am a corporate compliance officer—a nobody. I was supposed to fly to Buffalo on a routine business trip, which I've now missed because of those two jerks. Call my employer, ask him. You know what, better yet, call a lawyer, please. Now."

"Dead men don't have lawyers, Mr. Enzman," Burkey informed me.

"What the hell's that supposed to mean?"

"Flight 8128 crashed at 10:08 tonight. Everyone on board was killed. You were checked in on the flight, so technically..."

101

I was not often speechless. It was a disadvantage in my line of work. But hearing that I should've died that night hijacked every remaining snarky word from my mouth. And that was the least of things stolen from me.

"My . . . partner was on that flight," I said. Hot fire seeped from my eyes and attempts to choke it back only collapsed a dam of sobs. "His name was Adam. Can you check for his name, too, please? Adam Eckart. Please check?"

Burkey let me go on bawling, arguing with the inevitable, for who knows how long, watching, observing. "I'm so sorry," she eventually said, her chiseled eyes yielding some genuine compassion. "You really have no idea what's going on here, do you?"

I imagine my face looked like a child asked to recite memorization on the spot in front of the entire class. I had no answer to give. Nothing even remotely began to add up.

"They said, 'We need to take him back with us,'" I choked out, my mouth dirt on sandpaper. I slammed my cuffed fists on the steel table. "'Take him out of the equation.' What does that mean? Why me?"

"I don't think you'd believe me if I told you. Because I'm not even sure I do," Burkey said. "Either way, we're placing you in protective custody."

"They were going to kill me?" I asked.

"They say they were going to abduct you. To the year 2147."

Loss feels like the terror of waking up in your own bed and not knowing where you are. Or the disorientation of walking into work not knowing where you're going or why. I may have survived Flight 8128, but part of my inner being was killed with Adam. Some people in life are just not replaceable, and what took residence in his void was dismal. Agony. Fury. Retaliation.

They say honor a loved one's memory by cherishing the good times, but memories had never felt more like nightmares, and nightmares had never felt more like real life. I was still having those brutal flashbacks months later on a flight to DC.

"You want to be the good cop or bad cop? Maybe good cop/ good cop this time?" Adam asked me right before walking into the conference room of our next inspection.

This was a trick question. He and I had worked together enough times for me to know that no matter what I chose, he was going to introduce himself to our clientele as a ridiculously exaggerated bad guy. Every single time. And every time, even though I knew it was coming, I would struggle to choke back laughter and have to shift my role on the spot. We probably looked like stoned cartoon characters—he playing a grimacing, stone-faced authoritarian and teary-eyed me, snorting and coughing, trying to introduce ourselves to high-ranking corporate officers we were about to investigate. But we always closed out our cases.

Our department heads saw the dynamic chemistry and consistent results, so they paired us up frequently. We weren't just a good team. We were good friends and real teammates. Adam always knew what rib to poke to disarm any rigid exterior shell I thought I had, and my personality cultivated and appreciated his vitality.

"Hmmm? What do you think?" he asked again. "What about 'good cop posing as bad cop, but deep down really a sensitive cop?'" Adam's brisk and baritone Melbourne accent made every ridiculous proposal sound like a reasonably grand idea.

"I think we should get an apartment," I said.

It had been consuming my mind for weeks. Impulsivity remains one of my self-improvement areas. What felt like eons of lumbering silence prevented me from looking to him for a response, so we stood in front of the closed conference room doors like two fools expecting them to open automatically.

"You sly bastard," Adam said. He slapped me across the back. "Of course we should."

I finally made eye contact, and the proud grin waiting for me said, "Thank you for asking."

"But now's not really a good time to discuss it," Adam countered, "because we have to light these guys up for their hazmat contracts, so I don't think we can really reschedule that."

"Sure," I said, surrendering my own smile. "But I'll be the bad cop. For real, this time."

"Of course," he lied. "Of course."

Turbulence from the FBI jet jolted me away from the memory and incited the sloshing in my stomach. Much of my life between Flight 8128 and Operation Salt Lick felt like hazy snapshots of memories and waking dreams. The therapists called it disassociation due to the post-traumatic stress of near-death. I attribute it to living without a life, without a defined purpose or existence. Dead man walking.

I immediately walked myself through a grounding exercise the therapists swore would alleviate the anxiety. It was just Burkey and I on the fourteen-passenger business jet, and the clouds outside were puffy like mountains of cotton balls. The cabin smelled of refrigerated air. The faux-leather armrests felt taut under my fingertips. The steady hum of the jet's engines was hypnotic. The vodka tasted like comfort.

I think it was five months or so after the crash. I'd just completed inaugural field training at the Federal Law Enforcement Training Centers, and now we were flying to Washington, DC, to begin writing the concept of operations plan for Operation Salt Lick. Intel gained from the two Newark suspects indicated I was a person of interest to the future, so the FBI was happy to leverage me against the seemingly emerging threat. New career. New life. New motivations.

As my eyes came into focus, I realized Burkey was staring at me. Evaluating. Trying to figure out how not all right I was. Was her partner really the investment the Bureau was banking on, or a liability that would crack? Or both?

"What's it like reading your own obituary?" she asked.

"Disturbing."

She'd given me the framed cutout of my death notice from my hometown paper as some kind of dark humor pick-me-up. Too soon.

I now had an immense fear of flying, but the Bureau didn't use private cars for cross-country travel, so I had become quite the connoisseur of preflight self-medication. Burkey flipped through a file folder of my Witness Security Program papers, signing here and there while I lost myself in the view out the window and my nth minibottle of vodka.

"I got word the Marshals closed out your apartment lease. The management ate the 'death declaration' cover story right up. All your stuff should arrive in Virginia by Tuesday," she told me.

"I loved that home."

"I know," Burkey said. She did. "I wish we could've kept you there. But you know we couldn't."

"Yep," I said. "How was Adam's funeral?"

"It was beautiful. It was...very beautiful."

"Good."

"You get to pick your own alias in WITSEC. You really wanted to go with 'David Gallows'?" Burkey asked.

"It's already happened, right?" I smiled at her, poking the bear, reassuring her that my attention was where it needed to be.

"*Please* don't start with that temporal mechanics stuff. I'm an FBI agent, not an elementary particle whatever-ist."

"'Gallows' will be fine."

"Perk up, Gallows," Burkey said. "Today's our big day. We nail this pitch to the Bureau brass, and we may be able to start making a real difference. This will actually change the future."

I drifted away in my stupor, wondering what the time-tourists would be like, where'd they be from, what lives I'd be stealing from them. I felt no remorse then and didn't anticipate I'd feel any when I met my first. They'd stolen my future from me, even if that future was my mortality. It was supposed to have happened, and they'd disallowed it.

And now I'd disallow theirs if the FBI signed off on the counterintelligence program we were about to propose, all in the name of maintaining the purity of our time line by preventing any amount of their interference. I wondered if this would be my life's mission until I met my next natural end. And I wondered how many time-tourists we'd missed over the years before they hit the FBI's radar.

The "Smartphone Woman" from *The Expected One* painting in 1860?

The "Cell Phone Lady" spotted in *The Circus* film in 1928?

The "Time Traveling Hipster" photographed at the South Fork Bridge reopening in 1941 British Columbia?

The "Cell Phone Man" photographed in 1943 in downtown Reykjavík?

The "Coso Artifact" spark plug discovered inside a 500,000-year-old geode in 1961?

How many butterflies had been stepped on already?

How many butterflies would we save?

"Am I allowed to carry the gun in the Hoover Building, or should I leave it on the plane?" I asked.

"As long as you've got your FBI specialist credentials, you can carry anywhere. Just remember your training. Don't pull it out unless it's an emergency."

Burkey set down her folder and stared dead ahead.

"Ah, crap," she said.

"What?"

"I'm going to need an alias, too, if they sign off on this. I'm no good with the code names." Burkey returned to her paperwork after a blank moment. "You pick one," she told me.

It turned out that not all FBI agents wear ball caps all the time. That was just a TV thing. However, Burkey did love her ball caps and *did* always wear one, usually the adjustable-strap type with her hair looped through the closure.

"You can be 'Ponytail,'" I said.

"Fair enough."

Senator Blackcastle of New York was a blunt politician, and it strangely made the October 2018 Senate Judiciary Subcommittee on Federal Courts, Oversight, Agency Action, and Federal Rights debate on Operation Salt Lick more comfortable. I'd seen many corporate goons in his position try to throw their weight around to get out of a compliance grievance. But, like quicksand, the more they struggled, the deeper they sank. Burkey and I had front-row, subject-matter-expert seats to the circus, along with other officials assigned to the FBI's National Security Branch.

First came the attempt at invalidation. "You want us to petition Congress for $1 billion in black budget money to build a ghost town on a bull-hockey basis of time-traveling tourists from the future?" the senator asked. I took silent amusement that Blackcastle's deadpan expression did not offer any hint as to if he was asking rhetorically.

The rest of the subcommittee offered no reprieve as the hearing room fell silent. The FBI National Security Branch's Executive Assistant Director Cubitt spoke up to assume the role of sacrificial lamb.

"The operation would require multiple operating locations across the US for redundancy, sir. So we'd be asking for *several* billion dollars."

Blackcastle's scoff echoed off the walls. "On. What. Proof?"

"Senators, we're entertaining the time traveler theory on the basis of several inexplicable intelligence points," Cubitt said. "The two suspects being held in custody in relation to the crash of Flight 8128 in February have no discernible identities. The credentials found on their persons were fabricated—generic law enforcement replications. Their names don't match up to any government identification numbers, and their fingerprints and DNA have not been traced back to any US intelligence or Interpol database whatsoever. Same for the third suspect shot during an attempted jailbreak in Newark's security holding, whom the suspects identified as a search-and-rescue contingency from the future."

"Sounds like foreign espionage," Blackcastle countered, trying to undercut the argument with the assertion that the simplest explanation was the generally correct one.

"Further, the neurotechnology found embedded in their sphenoid bones is more advanced than any currently existing, to include the research and development of our near-peer adversaries. I'll decline from going into detail unless you'd like to move the hearing to a top-secret classification."

Blackcastle leaned in and doubled down. "Fifteen years ago, you could only talk on your cell phone. Now it's a computer in your pocket. Technology advances. So what?"

Cubitt ignored the appeal-to-ridicule tactic and continued. "Additionally, the two suspects have gone into great detail over the last seven months—in their own words—describing their archiving mission to our past, the time-traveling operations of the future, etc., in hopes of negotiating their release and transit back to the future. These alleged historians have been analyzed by multiple teams of medical, psychiatric, and intelligence agency professionals—including the Bureau's new High-Value Detainee Interrogation Group—and no one can find any evidence of deceit, deception, or mental illness."

Blackcastle's sarcastic laugh sniped the notion out of the air. "Well, shoot, Director Cubitt, why didn't these time travelers just poof on back to the future when they had the chance?" Blackcastle's use of *argumentum ad ignorantiam* logic made me cringe. Cubitt was clearly holding his own in the debate, so a softball punch wasn't going to stop him now.

"Seems these yahoos kinda screwed up from the word 'go' at the airport, huh?" Blackcastle was exhausted. Emotional. Slipping. Losing his composure. "*Never* in all my years did I ever think the *United States Senate* would be entertaining a conversation about marching alleged time travelers to the gallows. *Unprecedented* malarkey."

The thick double entendre landed like an electric shock in my chair.

And it was at that moment that I began seeing Blackcastle differently. Why the desperate swings with logical fallacies? I mean, he was a member of Congress, but his especially passionate level of conviction against the hearing's premise was becoming conspicuous to me. I'd seen this behavior before in my line of work plenty of times when an executive was in the wrong and knew he was losing the fight.

"I think Blackcastle is one of them," I whispered to Burkey. Probably a little too loudly.

"What?"

"I think Senator Blackcastle is a time traveler."

"*Shut up*, Gallows," she hissed at me. "This is not the time."

The nice thing about consonants is that their sound travels, and Blackcastle heard enough of the word "Gallows" for his eyes to not-so-subtly shift in our direction. We locked eyes.

He knew my name. And now I knew he knew.

"The suspects were apprehended during an assault at Newark Liberty International Airport," Cubitt continued, "so they weren't able to physically activate the beacon technology located in their temples. When we removed their restraints in the questioning cell, they were behind sixteen inches of concrete, which reportedly interfered with the beacon signal. We then received a court order allowing us to surgically remove the implants."

"A court order," Blackcastle repeated.

"Yes, sir, a classified FISA order issued under the allowances of the Foreign Intelligence Surveillance Act of 1978, while we attempted to ascertain the identities of the suspects. Our Operation Salt Lick would use the same FISA warrants to arrest and prosecute suspected time traveler 'tourists' by luring them to false-flag historical events staged within our Department of Justice–operated pseudo cities. Utilizing Top Secret Sensitive Compartmented Information classification, no one outside the operation would ever know the nature of the fabrication for all of human history—myself and Congress included. The FISA court and the ghost detainee facilities at the Guantanamo Bay detention camp would take care of the rest until we can isolate the threat."

Senator Blackcastle pressed his fingers into the bridge of his forehead, trying to press out the tension. "You can't charge someone with a crime that doesn't exist, Director Cubitt. The courts cannot rule on a legal case with no standing. Seems I read about that in this document called the United States Constitution. Whose idea was this?"

"Operation Salt Lick could begin tomorrow on the initial basis of several chapters of US Code Title 18. Conspiracy to commit offense or to defraud the United States, agents of foreign governments, major fraud against the United States, for example. I believe the product of our operation would provide substantiating evidence for Congress to criminalize certain future uses of time-travel technology."

"You're being serious, aren't you?"

"Senator Blackcastle, I believe that chronological interference, temporal obstruction, whatever you want to call it, is the preeminent security and intelligence threat to the future of the United States. How can we claim to be 'the land of the free' if our people's very destinies are held at the discretion and will of others—a force that directly affects our children and their children's children and generations to come before they're even born? This initiative is the best, and *only*, option on the table to address tomorrow's threat before it arrives."

Blackcastle waited until the silence became palpable to deliver his final remark.

"This hogwash will never reach the House floor as long as I'm sitting in this chair," Blackcastle said. "And further, I'd like a list of everyone involved in the proposal. I think the ridiculousness of what we've heard here today warrants a fiscal oversight review."

I could already foresee the exact flow and outcome with perfect clarity. Senator Blackcastle would continue nullifying the FBI's presentation, the subcommittee would recess for discussion, and subcommittee chair Blackcastle and his majority party would lead the Judicial committee into denying the funding request—all in a day's time. Time traveler or not, the only way forward would be to remove Blackcastle from the equation. When the subcommittee broke for recess, I waited for him in the halls to do exactly that.

Blackcastle exited the hearing room, surrounded by staffers, but I easily broke in, holding up my FBI identification.

"Senator Blackcastle, may I have just a moment of your time?" I asked. The party froze midwalk. The ID always got everyone's attention. "In private? Just two minutes?"

"Sure," the senator said, motioning his staff forward. "I'll meet you all in my office." The staffers drifted away, and Blackcastle extended his palm. "What can I do for you, Agent—"

"Specialist, actually," I said, shaking his hand. "It's in regard to today's subcommittee hearing."

Every once in a while, the little voice in my head tells me something is a critically dangerous idea. But I've come to learn that I am smarter than that voice, and I ignore it.

"I'm Gallows."

I hadn't let go of Blackcastle's hand yet, and I felt it flinch. His eyes widened ever so slightly, and the muscles in his neck tightened.

"I'm not going to hurt you," I told him. I grasped his hand tighter. "That name means nothing to me. I don't know who I am or what I do in your future, but I don't want it. *I don't want it.* Do you understand? Nod if you understand."

I saw the internal fight in Blackcastle's eyes, the dialogue of terror and debate underway in his mind, calculating the decision of what to do next.

He nodded.

"I can fix that," Blackcastle eventually said. "Just tell me your real name and date of birth. That's all."

"I'll do you one better."

I released his hand and leaned in close and perpendicular to him—blocking the view of the security camera I saw watching us overhead—and motioned to the holster on my belt. His eyes stayed glued on my hand as I removed the 9 mm pistol and handed it to him. Blackcastle's eyes narrowed, his jaw tightened, and I braced myself. The gun was clear of my hands and secured in his for just a moment or two before everything lined up and made sense for him.

"I've been waiting a long, long time—twenty-three years—to smoke you out," Blackcastle said.

"What, are you some kind of deep-cover time-travel special ops? Why me?" I asked.

"Because you're bad for business, and it's getting harder for the industry to sweep you under the rug."

"I don't know what that means," I said.

"You're the pain in my boss's ass that's somehow responsible for travelers going missing across 130 years—including someone dear to *me*."

Blackcastle snapped the pistol's slide back with the lightning velocity of a trained professional. The crack of cycling semi-automatic metal echoed throughout the ornate hall as he leveled the barrel at my forehead and pulled the trigger one, two, three, four times.

Click, click, click, click.

"Gun!" someone screamed.

Capitol Police officers opened fire, and a felled Senator Blackcastle collapsed to the ground into forever sleep before he could squeeze his hands around my throat too hard.

Luckily for me, neurotech was found embedded under his temple by the coroner during the autopsy. From there, his Senate subcommittee was quite amiable to authorizing a classified Operation Salt Lick. The public's extensive cover story said that Senator Blackcastle and I had engaged in a heated posthearing exchange, during which time he snapped and overpowered me, resulting in Burkey's peers labeling me "the dumbest son of a bitch to ever carry a gun" for "accidentally" carrying a service pistol with an empty magazine. But Burkey knew me well enough to see the truth.

"That was incredibly stupid. What if he hadn't taken the bait? How could you have *possibly* known?" she asked me later over drinks at some swanky DC lounge.

"I didn't. There was a chance, and I acted on it," I said. "It's what I used to do in the corporate world. Figure out people's BS and exploit it without them knowing."

"What if he'd killed you?"

"I'm already dead," I said. "2018, 2147, somewhere in between. Who knows? Or maybe I'll live forever."

I swirled the ice cubes around in my bourbon and lost myself in their decay into the oaky liquor. They spun in an orbit of my choosing. My control. My direction.

"Hey," Burkey snapped at me.

"What?"

"You're consumed. All in," she said. "But *why*? Just keep me up to speed. Is your fuel 'retribution' or 'duty'?"

"Yes," I answered, emphasizing the answer with a staring contest.

"Fair enough," Burkey yielded. "Just...reel it in a bit." I nodded my glass to her, and we threw back the rest of the liquor. Burkey grabbed the bill. "So, Salt Lick is going to get green-lit, obviously. Does Blackcastle count as our first catch?"

"No," I said. "I want them alive."

Lilly smiles an embarrassed "you got me" smile that I rarely see during interrogations.

"Business or pleasure?" I ask her.

"I say both, if you love what you do."

Lilly is trained to give nonanswers, and it's enraging me. I need actionable proof before I move.

"Good philosophy," I say. We toast my vodka with her pint of beer. I welcome the soothing burn of the liquor down my throat and the instant wash of relief it gives my brain. I know I have to press harder. "And what do you do?"

Lilly knows she walked right into that one. "Research," she says.

"Oh, yeah?" I ask. I feel my foot tapping under the bar, and I can't make it stop. Better that than my fingers. "Science? Business? Journalism? You're a scientist, aren't you?"

Lilly blushes. "How could you tell?"

"Well, you're too nice to be a journalist or business exec. And I'm a psychic on the side," I schmooze.

That proposition elicits a chuckle.

"Yeah? What's in *my* future?" she says flirtatiously.

"A refill," I say, pulling her another draft. "The Oppenheimer Lab is pretty much the only reason why this town exists. The brains working the supersecret stuff there are most of my regulars. So, what brings you to the lab?"

Lilly narrows her eyes at me. "Well, if I was visiting the lab, I wouldn't be able to talk about it, would I?"

Damn it, Lilly. She's too good, too prepared, and I'm not.

Adam and I used to have once-a-month poker nights with the company's Buffalo crew. Adam was good at cards. Energized but strategic. Played the long game. Took the time to banter the other players off their guard while he assessed the table. I was more of the volatile type of player. Stupid wins, stupid losses.

All in, Adam.

"Word is they're real close to a breakthrough in fusion energy. Know anything about that?" I ask.

"That's supposed to be classified!"

"This bar's the biggest watercooler in town," I say. "Nothing's classified in the town tavern."

I see the debate circling in Lilly's mind before giving way to a fatal flash of excitement with a bit of liquid inhibition.

"Yes, you could say tomorrow is going to be a significant event in US history," she said. "I'd stock up on champagne if I were you." She gives a wink.

A significant false-flag *historical event in US history.*

Gotcha.

"History. Such a fickle thing," I muse. "Hey, you like oldies?"

"Who doesn't?"

"Here," I say, reaching into the cash register for a $5 bill. "Go load up the jukebox. My treat."

"Thanks!" Lilly strides over to the jukebox and selects a handful of songs. My pulse picks up as alternative rock tunes fill the room instead of the golden vinyl sounds of the '50s and '60s.

I have two shot glasses prepared when Lilly returns to the bar.

"Hey, what'd you mean by history being a fickle thing?" she asks. "Kind of deep, huh?"

I ignore the question.

"On me. House special," I say. "Here's to good conversation and good company."

We clink glasses and down the liquor.

"Whooo," Lilly exhales through the fumes in her throat. "I think that does it for me."

"I'm very glad to have met you, Lilly," I tell her. "You know, we don't get a lot of visitors in Cohenstead."

"No?"

"No. We're kind of like an uncontacted tribe here."

"How do you mean?" Lilly asks.

"You ever hear of those pockets of indigenous peoples who live isolated from the rest of the world? They don't even know we exist. But sometimes, outsiders sneak into those communities for research or evangelizing. It doesn't usually end well. The outsider is always discovered, and the community defends itself. You see, outside interference robs them of their right to autonomy."

"You lost me," Lilly says. "Damn, that shot was strong. What was in it?"

"Flunitrazepam."

"What?"

There's a switch underneath the bar. I flip it, and the lights flicker. It takes a lot to power a variable-class Faraday shield, but it was a better alternative than reinforcing every building in Cohenstead with sixteen-inch concrete. Both block electrical signals, just one more stealthily than the other.

I motion Lilly forward as if to tell her a secret.

"You're under arrest for the felony crime of chronological interference," I whisper.

Lilly's eyes flutter, and her face contorts in confusion and panic. They never expect me, and if I do my job right, they never will. With her remaining focus, Lilly taps her left temple over and over again, swaying under the fight with inevitable unconsciousness. She's trying to trigger the neurotechnology to signal an emergency beacon or initiate the trip back to the future. We still haven't figured out exactly how that works. But I do know the neurotech won't work well with the sedative I dosed her drink with, nor the Faraday shield embedded into the walls, ceiling, and floor.

I vault over the bar and catch her before she falls off the stool. The commotion alerts Pinball, and he blows his cover to rush to his compatriot's aid. I grab his collar with my left hand as soon as he gets close and strike him in the face with my right.

Crack! I see Flight 8128 smashing into residential New York state.

Crack! I see Senator Blackcastle signing paperwork censuring the FBI National Security Branch.

Pinball hits the ground, and I twist his limbs into an armbar. Serious Guy is the smart one. He darts for the exit, temple-tapping the whole way. Ponytail fires an electroshock gun into his back with her strong hand, and the time traveler never makes it past the door. Ponytail keeps the service pistol in her other hand leveled on Newsie Cap, who's shifted around to witness the pandemonium. However, in his old age, he is apathetic to anything unrelated to his slot machine and piss-water lager. He's obviously not the party's yet-to-be-seen search-and-rescue agent, so we'll debrief him later and feed him some police sting cover story.

Ponytail and I zip-tie the time travelers and duct tape their mouths. They are angry. Betrayed. Furious. Scared. And they have every right to be. Just like me.

Lilly is half lucid, enough to ask me "Why?" with her mascara-smeared eyes.

"You don't get to interfere with our future anymore," I tell her.

116

"If you ever make it back, you tell them Gallows says 'Don't send anyone else back. If you do, I'll find them.'"

"Hey!" Ponytail objects. "OPSEC."

Dopamine surges through my brain and I have to sit down on a barstool to handle the rush. After all the despair, all the planning, all the training, it still doesn't completely register that this is real and this is happening. We have captured time travelers from the future. When clarity finally seeps back over me, the apex hunter that's replacing the void of loss grasps that this is only the beginning.

Burkey and I put earmuffs and blackout bags over the time travelers' heads before I switch off the Faraday shield and key up the mic concealed under my shirt.

"Control, Echo-2. Echo site secured. The first three are ready for extraction."

Boos and Taboos

BY L. RON HUBBARD

L. Ron Hubbard's remarkably versatile career as an internationally bestselling writer spanned more than half a century of literary achievement and wide-ranging influence. In scope and productivity, it ultimately encompassed over sixty-three million words of published fiction and nonfiction. Esteemed as a writer's writer, Ron was possessed with an unstinting devotion to helping other writers, especially beginners, become more proficient and successful at their craft. He also carved out significant careers in other professional fields—as an explorer, mariner and aviator, filmmaker and photographer, philosopher and educator, and musician and composer.

The culmination of L. Ron Hubbard's enthusiastic commitment to actively fostering the work of new and aspiring writers came with his establishment in 1983 of both the Writers of the Future Contest and the Writers of the Future annual anthology. The anthology is a collection of the winning best new original stories of science fiction and fantasy. It also provides an influential showcase for winners of the companion Illustrators of the Future Contest, inaugurated in 1988 as part of Mr. Hubbard's continuing legacy to the field.

L. Ron Hubbard's earliest work with fledgling writers, undertaken while still in his twenties, was marked by lectures he gave at such schools as Harvard and George Washington University on how to get started as a professional.

As early as 1935, he also began to publish incisively practical "how-to" articles and essays about writing as a craft and profession, which appeared regularly in major writers' magazines. These continue to be used today in writing courses and seminars, and are the basis for the writers' workshops held each year for the winners and published finalists of the Writers of the Future Contest. The Contest has continued to expand and is now the largest and most successful merit competition of its kind in the world.

While the times and markets have changed, many of the challenges writers face are essentially the same. And L. Ron Hubbard's practical advice is as relevant today as when it was written.

In 1936, L. Ron Hubbard served as president of the American Fiction Guild and as a member of that fraternity, he wrote the article that follows, titled "Boos and Taboos." In it Mr. Hubbard challenges the restrictive "taboos" of writing for publications that bind stories in formulaic straitjackets. Urging writers to flout by-prescription storytelling, he describes his own conspicuous success in doing that, with a final, telling reflection on creative energy, sales—and writing stories that will be remembered.

Boos and Taboos

When Ye Editor recently popped up at an American Fiction Guild luncheon, she found me lime punch–drunk against the bar.

Said Ye Editor, "Write me an article on something, will you?"

Said I, "Certainly, on what?"

Said Ye Editor, "'Why You Sold Your Last Story'."

I pondered it for a bit, couldn't remember what I had sold last, and then put the question to two very learned gentlemen of our exalted fraternity.

Said one, "Why did I sell my last story? Well, editors do go blind, you know."

Said t'other, "Why? Because I needed the money."

Said half a dozen more, "Because I needed the money."

Said Ye Editor, "Certainly, but you can't put that in an article. It doesn't make sense."

Well, here it is in an article, but neither does it make sense.

There was reason behind that last sale. Not facetious reason, but actual cold, hard, writing reason. Now that we get right down to the meat of it, the reason I made my last sale a few days ago was the furthest thing from your mind.

I broke all the taboos. Which brings us to the scene.

All writers agree on one thing. Strange but they do—on that one matter. Writing is the screwiest profession man ever invented—as witness our double existence. Writers were originally minstrels, of course, and the minstrels used to wander about sleeping in haystacks and begging their wine, getting paid only in gifts.

We have become elevated to respectability as far as the world is concerned, but we still live that cup-to-lip existence of our long-dead brethren, and our lives, whether we strummed a lyre or a typewriter, are pretty identical.

And every once in a while we like to upset our own traditions just to see what will happen.

So I broke some half-dozen strict taboos and sold the story.

Now, of course, there's a hitch to all this which I must mention, later, even though it smacks of conceit.

But to the taboos. This particular house, in common with the other pulp dynasties, enumerates their taboos in no uncertain terms. But I don't think, after this experience, that they believe them any too strongly.

Their heroes must be strong, virile, upright.

Of heroines they will have none whatever. No love interest!

No first person whatever. All third.

And there were others which I can't name because they would identify the yarn too clearly.

This yarn, not yet published at [this] writing, was told in first person by a gentleman whose deeds smacked of crime. He went to great lengths because of a girl, and was, in fact, entirely motivated by that girl.

Which makes a very unwholesome lesson. Pulp taboos have been handed down, down, down until they bind a story into a narrow, viselike groove, and like water which runs too long in one place, the limited plots are wearing down like stone. In ninety percent of the present pulp stories, tell me the beginning and I'll tell you the end.

All too true. One day an editor told me that, grinding the editorial teeth, little suspecting the answer to it. And so I set out to write a yarn which wouldn't foretell its ending. To do that thing I found out I had to break a couple taboos. I shivered over it as a Polynesian shivers over his own particular *tabus*.

But the story sold. It was just enough out of line to be

interesting, just enough inside to stay in keeping with its brethren. Like a golf shot which slices over out-of-bounds and then sails in for a landing on the fairway.

It is even possible to apply to detective stories—and that, coming from an adventure writer, says a great deal.

These taboos! They're like fetters to a convict—and a writer chained to his mill is enough of a convict already. The story must not be over such and such a length. Well, you get to be an automaton after a while, so that you can write without numbering your pages—as I do—and still arrive at the required length. A sort of automatic alarm clock which shouts, "Ending!"

That's a taboo, to overlength something, but not very serious.

Another taboo consists of virile heroes. Anything but clean-limbed gentlemen with a gat in each hand wait outside. And some of the mightiest stories ever written have been about nervous, anemic, shivering shrimps afraid of their own cigarette smoke. But no, sayeth the pulps, the hero must be lithe, tall, dark and handsome.

The heroine must always be pure as snowdrifts, unsullied, unsoiled, and the greatest worry is about the intentions of the big, bad, sneering, leering, rasping, grating, snarling villain. Dear girls. Most women are married in their mid-twenties. And with all due respect to everybody, the most interesting, witty, quick-thinking ladies are past that age. Dear me, can't we have some really interesting females in pulp?

One outfit puts a ban on anything where adventure fails to go after a reward of some kind. No mental rewards. The clinking clatter of gold and the brittle sparkle of jewels must be in the fore forever. I searched for gold once, twice, but any adventures I might have had, bad or good, dull or interesting, dealt with quantities far more intangible than gold. Esteem, self-respect, loyalty...

Ah, but I'm being too unkind. I could list taboos by the hour and boo at them, showing, of course, my great superiority over mind and matter, demonstrating that I dwell in a void high over all else. But I don't—honest, lady.

My cry is this. Writers are foolish enough, from what they've told me, to believe in a lot of those taboos to their own detriment.

As a consequence, what do we find? The rut, the pit, the cauldron of lost hopes and the rain of sweat. That's a pitiful picture.

A man can clatter out just so much in one pattern before the pattern becomes as solid as a prisoner's bars. Don't argue. I've been through it. It gets so that you can't write anything but what you have written before. You lose all that delightful plasticity of ideas. You are hampered by vague demons who jump up and down and scream in your ears when you fail to place so many words of straight action in a story. You groan at the thought of writing something new, because you know the conflict which will take place in your own head. You'll drown in a sea of already written words, and the tide of youngsters will come up and sweep over you, and Davy Jones, in the form of the reject basket, will swallow your bones forever.

And mainly because of Old Man Taboo.

What courage it takes to break free! You stare at a vision of an empty cupboard. You seem to feel your toes peeping through your shoes; you already listen to the angry words of the landlord as he helps the sheriff toss your writing desk out into the street.

And you remember the taboos, and you know that if you fail to mind those taboos, if you fail to stay walled in and blinded by those ruts, you'll go broke.

And yet, if you don't jar yourself some way, then how will you climb, advance, put markets behind you and see others looming to the fore?

It's a bad spot. About a year into the game, every writer faces it, doesn't quite know what it is, groans and writhes about, and then, when the gentle news is broken—if he has friends friendly enough to break it, to tell him that his stuff is still in one place, that he must advance, for nothing can stand still—he is apt to lose months of work.

The taboos do it. You must mind the taboos, but if you do, you stand quite still for a space and then begin to slide—backward. I wonder how many writers have wrecked themselves that way?

The solution wasn't rammed at me in the cold dazzle of day. It sneaked up on me through black nights of worry. "Damn the taboos!" And I thought about damning them. They were fetters. I couldn't actually face the fact that my stuff was juvenile. How could that be? Didn't I give it my all? And I tried to write for better markets. Markets I knew I couldn't touch. I had to make a break. I felt need of that plasticity of mind which would allow me to do something with a hero besides letting him bump off natives and kiss the girl, and I had to do something with the girl besides letting her kiss the hero and dread the villain.

But the taboos stuck and stuck until I deliberately set out one fine day and sorted out all the taboos of a certain market. Maliciously, I broke them, one by one, stringing out an off-length story.

But the thing retained its stamp. It was, after all, action for action's sake. It didn't live. It wasn't the best I'd done. And so I set out to break more taboos, bigger and better taboos.

For many, many words, I wrote for the wastebasket, and then suddenly I saw a change. Plasticity was coming back. Satisfied and smug, I sat myself down and wrote a yarn and sold it higher than I had ever sold anything before.

The formula to end all formulas had worked.

The whole summation is this. Any magazine, big or small, will take something different, just off their beaten path, if that something is better to their own way of thinking than anything they have purchased before.

"What?" you say. "You mean you have to write twice as good for the same market? You mean you have to spend more time on a yarn? You mean you have to deliberately coax them out of their ideas with quality? Well, to the devil with that!"

Ah, but the glory of it! The feeling that you have done something real! And then those yarns can go higher and still sell lower the second time out. Not that I ever sell a reject, you understand. Oh, cross my heart, never. But you can sell a good piece of cloth to a native who dresses in gunnysacks and palm bark. You can sell a good fast cruiser to a fisherman used to a one-lung sloop. You can peddle can openers to people who open their cans with an axe.

And you can sell a high-class, fast-action, counterplotted, characterized, pulsating yarn to a mag which has heretofore purchased only the action.

It can be done, is being done, and to clinch the deal, unless you're one of those who likes to lie in a rut, [it] keeps you from slopping about in the muddy plain of mediocrity. You'll get rejects, but when you sell, you'll be remembered. Never fear, you'll be remembered.

Give them all their own demands plus everything you want to put into a story. Do it so well that they don't even know their taboos are being broken, and through this, escape from the pit. We'll all be saying, "Well, well, made the awards, did he? Yes, I knew him when."

The Professor Was a Thief

written by
L. Ron Hubbard
illustrated by
MICHAEL TALBOT

ABOUT THE AUTHOR

By the time L. Ron Hubbard wrote "The Professor Was a Thief," more than 125 of his short stories and novellas had already been published in the popular all-fiction magazines of the 1930s. He was a prolific writer in genres spanning adventure, aviation, military, sea stories, thrillers, westerns and even some romance. He started with science fiction and fantasy in 1938. And it is in this field that his fiction is most remembered with perennial bestsellers Fear, Final Blackout, To the Stars, Ole Doc Methuselah, Slaves & Masters of Sleep, Typewriter in the Sky, Battlefield Earth *and* Mission Earth.

"The Professor Was a Thief" first appeared in 1940 in Astounding Science Fiction *magazine—the publication that heralded the Golden Age of Science Fiction.*

The story next saw print in an anthology entitled My Best Science Fiction Story as Chosen by 25 Outstanding Authors *published in 1949. Prolific and well-known editor Leo Margulies compiled the collection. He introduced it by saying they "turned to the writer—or, in this case, twenty-five of the most talented science fiction writers available—for what he considers his best scientifiction imaginative effort."*

The volume included fine stories by famous names in science fiction: van Vogt, Heinlein, Bradbury, Kuttner, de Camp, Hubbard and seventeen others equally distinguished in imaginative literature.

Each author included an introduction for their best science fiction story. L. Ron Hubbard's "Why I Selected 'The Professor Was a Thief'" follows:

> Upon being asked to pick my favorite short story for this anthology I found myself torn between two types of science

127

fiction—the epic, and the down-to-earth sort of thing. For example, to look into Mankind's future without space travel is, in my opinion, to gaze upon a dead destiny such as Wells depicts in his *Time Machine*. The dwindling geographic frontiers hold less and less incentive to the empire builder and demand less and less of strength and courage and imagination in man. The race itself has always depended for its virility upon new worlds, figuratively speaking, and we are even now entered upon an era with our own peoples when individuality and versatility, those base characteristics of the pioneer, are in question when found in a man.

No people become great by codified living; its most important asset is the self-determinism of the individual. And this is impossible under the regimented state which all overcrowded nations must evolve. It is more than an idea that man should go to the stars, more than a dream, more than a piece of imaginative fiction. It is a necessity. Unless he finds new earths for his appetites, new outlets for his lusty talents, all these things will be dead in the dead monotony of a gutted and declined world, barred forever from the stars because initiative was not taken when technicians were brilliant and their ideas new.

However, I do not mean to hold forth on a soapbox. I know there to be other prophets and science minstrels who will point the way and sing man on to the stars. Let me then consider that other, that down-to-earth kind of science fiction story.

"The Professor Was a Thief" may not be great literature. In fact, I am not sure just what great literature really is. A savant I once knew defined it to me as any writing which changed a trend or originated a form. On his authority, then, not mine, this story must be great literature. For it changed a trend. In the days when it was first published all the professors of science fiction were blowing up worlds, creating new universes—making bigger and better cataclysms. My professor had another idea. I thought it rather unique if only because it did not follow an established motif. That is why I especially like this story. I hope you like it too.

L. Ron Hubbard

ABOUT THE ILLUSTRATOR

Growing up in Jamaica, Michael Talbot had a strong desire to inspire and speak to others through art. In 2012 he left his home country to live in the United States and begin pursuing his artistic dreams. He earned his BFA in illustration and graphic design with a minor in animation at Lesley University in Cambridge, Massachusetts, and has since been working as a Boston-based freelance artist on a wide range of projects, exhibitions, and showcases.

Michael believes that all art is interconnected in some facet—informing, complimenting and/or enhancing each other. And although his passion and interest for storytelling are foremost in his practice and craft, he tends to draw from his knowledge in as many areas of study as possible to help strengthen this process. Whenever possible, he uses his rich cultural background from his early life in Jamaica to infuse, improve, and "season" whatever project he tackles, often mixing both digital and traditional media.

The Professor Was a Thief

PREFACE

It was about two o'clock in the afternoon and Sergeant Kelly, having imbibed a bit too much corned beef and cabbage at lunch, was dozing comfortably at his desk. He did not immediately hear the stumbling feet of Patrolman O'Rourke, but when he did, he was, in consequence, annoyed.

Sergeant Kelly opened his eyes, grunted, and sat slowly forward, hitching at his pants which he had unbuckled to ease his ballooning stomach.

His eye was offended at first by Patrolman O'Rourke's upset uniform and then, suddenly, interested. And what sergeantly eye would not have been? For Patrolman O'Rourke's mouth was slack and his eyes could have been used as bowling balls. He ran into a spittoon and heeded its thundering protest and departure not at all. Bracing his tottering self against the desk without changing his dazed expression, O'Rourke gulped:

"It's gone."

"Well!" said Sergeant Kelly. "Don't stand there like a jackanapes! Speak up! *What's* gone?"

"The Empire State Building," said Patrolman O'Rourke.

CHAPTER ONE

No one knew why he was called Pop unless it was that he had sired the newspaper business. For the first few hundred years, it appeared, he had been a senior reporter, going calmly about his business of reporting wholesale disaster, but during the past month something truly devastating had occurred. Muttering noises sounded in the ranks.

Long overdue for the job of city editor, lately vacated via the undertaker, Pop had been demoted instead of promoted. Ordinarily Pop was not a bitter man. He had seen too many cataclysms fade into the staleness of yesterday's paper. He had obit-ed too large a legion of generals, saints and coal heavers to expect anything from life but its eventual absence. But there were limits.

When Leonard Caulborn, whose diapers Pop had changed, had been elevated to city editor over Pop's decaying head, Pop chose to attempt the dissolution of Gaul in the manufactures of Kentucky. But even the latter has a habit of wearing away and leaving the former friend a mortal enemy. Thus it was, when the copy boy came for him, that Pop swore at the distilleries as he arose and looked about on the floor where he supposed his head must have rolled.

"Mr. Caulborn said he hada seeyuh rightaway," said the copy boy.

Pop limped toward the office, filled with resentment.

Leonard Caulborn was a wise young man. Even though he had no real knowledge of the newspaper business, people *still* insisted he was wise. Hadn't he married the publisher's daughter? And if the paper didn't make as much as it should, didn't the publisher have plenty of stockholders who could take the losses and never feel them?—much, anyway.

Young and self-made and officious if not efficient, Caulborn greeted Pop not at all, but let him stand before the desk a few minutes.

Pop finally picked up a basket and dropped it a couple inches, making Caulborn look up.

"You sent for me?" said Pop.

"I sent for you— Oh, yes, I remember now. Pending your retirement you've been put on the copy desk."

"My *what*?" cried Pop.

"Your retirement. We are retiring all employees over fifty. We need new people and new ideas here."

"Retirement?" Pop was still gaping. "When? How?"

"Effective day after tomorrow, Pop, you are no longer with this paper. Our present Social Security policy—"

"Will pay me off about twenty bucks complete," said Pop. "But to hell with that. I brought this paper into the world and it's going to take me out. You can't do this to me!"

"I have orders—"

"You are issuing the orders these days," said Pop. "What are you going to do for copy when you lose all your men that know the ropes?"

"We'll get along," said Caulborn. "That will be all."

"No, it won't either," said Pop. "I'm staying as reporter."

"All right. You're staying as reporter then. It's only two days."

"And you're going to give me assignments," said Pop.

Caulborn smiled wearily, evidently thinking it best to cajole the old coot. "All right, here's an article I clipped a couple months ago. Get a story on it."

When Caulborn had fished up the magazine out of his rubble-covered desk he tossed it to Pop like a citizen paying a panhandler.

Pop wanted to throw it back, for he saw at a glance that it was merely a stick, a rehash of some speech made a long while ago to some physics society. But he had gained ground so far. He wouldn't lose it. He backed out.

Muttering to himself he crossed to his own desk, wading through the rush and clamor of the city room. It was plain to him that he had to make the most of what he had. It was unlikely that he'd get another chance.

"I'll show 'em," he growled. "Call me a has-been. Well! Think I can't make a story out of nothing, does he? Why, I'll get such a story that he'll *have* to keep me on. And promote me. And raise my pay. Throw me into the gutter, will they?"

He sat down in his chair and scanned the article. It began quite lucidly with the statement that Hannibal Pertwee had made this address before the assembled physicists of the country. Pop, growing cold the while, tried to wade through said address. When he came out at the end with a spinning head he saw that Hannibal Pertwee's theories were not supported by anybody but Hannibal Pertwee. All other information, even to Pop, was so much polysyllabic nonsense. Something about transportation of freight. He gathered that much. Some new way to help civilization. But just how, the article did not tell—Pop, at least.

Suddenly Pop felt very old and very tired. At fifty-three he had ten thousand bylines behind him. He had built the *World-Journal* to its present importance. He loved the paper and now it was going to hell in the hands of an incompetent, and they were letting him off at a station halfway between nowhere and anywhere. And the only way he had of stopping them was an impossible article by some crackbrain on the transportation of freight.

He sighed and, between two shaking hands, nursed an aching head.

Chapter Two

A pavement-pounding reporter is apt to find the turf trying—and so it was with Pop. Plodding through the dismal dusk of Jersey, he began to wish that he had never heard the name of Hannibal Pertwee. Only the urgency of his desire to keep going had brought him thus far along the lonely roads. Grimly, if weakly, he at last arrived at a gate to which a Jerseyite had directed him.

With a moan of relief he leaned against a wire-mesh fence

and breathed himself to normalcy. It wasn't that he was getting old. Of course not! It was just that he should have worn more comfortable shoes.

He looked more observantly about him and became interested. Through this factory fence he could see a house, not much bigger than an architect's model, built with exactness which would have been painful to a more aesthetic eye than Pop's.

The fence itself next caught his interest. He fingered the steel mesh with wonder. At the top the poles bent out to support three strands of savage-looking barbed wire. Pop stepped back and was instantly smitten by a sign which shouted:

1,000,000 VOLTS
BEWARE!

Pop felt a breeze chill him as he stared at his fingers. But they were still there and he was encouraged. Moving toward the gate he found other signs:

BEWARE OF THE LIONS!

Pop searched anxiously for them and, so doing, found a third:

AREA MINED!

And:

TRESPASSERS BURIED
FREE OF CHARGE!

Uncertain now, Pop again stared at the tiny house. It began to remind him of a picture he had seen of Arizona's gas chamber.

But, setting his jaw to measure up to the threats around him, he sought the bell, avoiding the sign which said:

GAS TRAPS!

And the one which roared:

DEATH RAYS
KEEP OUT!

He almost leaped out of his body when a voice before him growled: "What is your business?"

Pop stared. He backed up. He turned. Suspiciously he eyed the emptiness.

At last, rapidly, he said, "I want to see Hannibal Pertwee. I am a reporter from the *New York World-Journal*."

There was a click and a square of light glowed in a panel. For seconds nothing further happened and then, very slowly, the gate swung inward.

Boldly—outwardly, at least—Pop marched through. Behind him the gate clicked. He whirled. A little tongue of lightning went licking its chops around the latch.

It took Pop some time to permanently swallow his dinner. He glared around him but the strange change in the atmosphere soon registered upon his greedy senses.

Here the walk was only a foot wide, bordered by dwarf plants. What Pop had thought to be shrubbery was actually a forest of perfect trees, all less than a yard tall but with the proportions of giants. Here, too, were benches like doll furniture and a miniature fountain which tinkled in high key. Sundials, summerhouses, bridges and flowers—all were tiny, perfect specimens. Even the fish in the small ponds were nearly microscopic.

Pop approached the house warily as though it might bite. When he stood upon the porch, stooping a little to miss the roof, the door opened.

Standing there was a man not five feet tall, whose face was a study of mildness and apology. His eyes were an indefinite blue and what remained of his hair was an indefinite gray. He was dressed in a swallowtail coat and striped pants and wing collar, with a tiny diamond horseshoe in his tie. Nervously he peered at Pop.

135

"You are Mr. Brewhauer from the *Scientific Investigator?*"

"No. I'm from the *New York World-Journal.*"

"Ah."

"I came," said Pop, "to get a story on this lecture you handed out a couple months ago."

"Ah."

"If you could just give me a few facts, I should be very glad to give you a decent break."

"Oh, yes! Certainly. You must see my garden!"

"I've just seen it," said Pop.

"Isn't it beautiful? Not a bit like any other garden you ever surveyed."

"Not a bit."

"Such wholesome originality and such gigantic trees."

"Huh?"

"Why, over a thousand feet tall, some of them. Of course, trees don't ordinarily grow to a thousand feet. The tallest tree in the world is much less than that. Of course, the Aldrich Deep is 30,930, but then no trees grow in the ocean. There, now! Isn't the garden remarkable? I'm so sorry to walk you all over the place this way, but I have recently given my cars to charity."

"Hey," said Pop. "Wait. We haven't been anywhere."

"No, indeed not. My garden is only a small portion of what I have yet to show you. Please come in."

Pop followed him into the house, almost knocking off his hat on the ceiling. The house was furnished in somewhat garish fashion and, here again, everything was less than half its normal size, even to the oil paintings on the walls and the grand piano.

"Please be seated," said Hannibal Pertwee.

Somehow Pop squeezed himself into a chair. There was a tingling sensation as though he was receiving a rather constant shock. But he paid it no heed. Determined to get a story, he casually got out his cigarette case and offered Hannibal a smoke.

The little man started to refuse and then noticed the case. "What an unusual design!"

"Yeah," said Pop, and pressed the music button. "The Sidewalks of New York" tinkled through the room.

"Fascinating," said Hannibal. "What delicate mechanism! You know, I've made several rather small things myself. Here is a copy of the Bible which I printed." And in Pop's hand he laid the merest speck of a book.

Pop peered at it and somehow managed to open it. Yes, each page appeared to be perfectly printed. There was a slight tingling which made him scratch his palm after he had handed the volume back.

"And here is a car," said Hannibal, "which I spent much time constructing. The engine is quite perfect." And thereupon he took the inch-long object and poked into it with a toothpick. There was a resultant purr.

"It runs," said Pop, startled.

"Of course. It should get about a hundred thousand miles to the gallon. Therefore, if a car would make the trip and if it could carry enough gas, then it could go to the moon. The moon is only 238,857 miles from Earth, you know." And he smiled confidently. He had forgotten about the car and it started up and ran off his hand. Pop made a valiant stab for it and missed. Hannibal picked it up and put it away.

"Now I must show you around," said Hannibal. "Usually I start with the garden—"

"We've seen that," said Pop.

"Seen what?"

"The garden."

"Why," said Hannibal, "I said nothing about a garden, did I? I wish to show you my trains."

"Trains?"

"Have you ever played with trains?"

"Well—I can't say as I have. You see, Mr. Pertwee, I came about that lecture. If you could tell me what it is about—"

"Lecture?"

"That you made before the physics society. Something about moving freight."

"Oh! 'The Pertwee Elucidation of the Simplification of Trans-portational Facilities as Applying to the Freight Problems of the United States.' You mean that?"

"Yes. That's it!"

"I'm sorry, but Mr. Pertwee does not refer to the subject now."

"Mister— Wait, aren't *you* Mr. Pertwee?"

"Yes, indeed. Now about my trains—"

"Just some comment or other," pleaded Pop. "I couldn't under-stand just what it was all about."

"There's nothing half so lovely as a train," said Mr. Pertwee, almost firmly.

Pop took out his case and lighted a cigarette.

"Would you mind pressing that button again?" said Pertwee.

Once more the worn mechanism tinkled out its music. When it had done, Hannibal took the case and inspected it anew with great attention.

"You said something about trains," said Pop.

"Pardon?"

Pop took back his case and put it firmly away. "You spoke of trains. There may be a story there."

"Oh, there is, there is," said Hannibal. "But I don't talk about it, you know. Not with strangers. Of course you are not a stranger, are you?"

"Oh, no, indeed," said Pop, mystified because he could see no bottle about. "But let's get on to the trains."

Hannibal bounced eagerly up and led his caller through the house, pausing now and then to show other instances of things done very small.

Finally they reached the train room and here Pop stopped short in amazement. For here, spread out at their feet, were seemingly miles of track leading off in a bewildering tangle of routes.

"My trains," said Hannibal, caressingly.

Pop just kept staring. There were toy stations and semaphores and miniature rivers and roads and underpasses and sidings and switches. And on the tracks stood a whole fleet of freight cars in a yard. Engines stood about, ready to do the switching. The roundhouses were crammed with rolling stock and, in short, nearly every type of equipment used was represented here.

Hannibal was already down on his knees at a switchboard. He grabbed up a top hat and plonked it on his head and then beamed at Pop.

"Cargo of strawberries for Chicago," said Hannibal. He threw half a dozen switches. The engines in the freight yard came to life and began to charge and puff and bang into cars, making up a train without any touch from the operator except on the control board.

"That bare space away over there is Chicago," said Hannibal.

Pop saw then that this room was vast enough to contain a replica of the United States and realized with a start that these tracks were, each one, a counterpart of an actual railroad line. Here were all the railway routes in the United States spreading over a third of an acre!

"This is New York," said Hannibal, indicating another bare space. "Only, of course, there isn't anything there yet. Now here we go!"

The freight, made up, began to move along the track faster and faster. It whistled for the crossings and rumbled over the rivers and stepped into a siding for a fast freight to go by, took on water and finally roared into the yard beside the bare space which was Chicago. Here it was broken up and other engines began to re-form it.

In the space of two hours, Pop watched freight being shunted all over the United States. He was excited about it, for he had never had a chance to play with trains as a boy and now it seemed quite logical that they should interest him as a man.

Finally Hannibal brought the cars back to the New York yard and broke up the last train. With a sigh he took off his hat and stood up, smiling apologetically.

"You must go now," said Hannibal.

"Look," said Pop. "Just give me some kind of an idea of what you were talking about in that article so I can mention it in the paper."

"Well—"

"I'll do you some good," said Pop.

"Do you understand anything about infinite acceleration?"

"Well, no."

"Or the fourth dimension?"

"Welllllllll..."

"Or Einstein's mathematics?"

"No."

"Then," said Hannibal, "I don't think I can explain. *They* would not believe me." And he laughed softly. "So, you see, you wouldn't either. Good night."

And Pop presently found himself outside the gate, confronted once more with the long walk to the station and the long ride back to New York.

A fine job he'd done. No story.

Still— Say! Those trains would make a swell yarn. A batty little scientist playing with toy railroads. Sure. He'd do it. Play it on the human-interest side. Great minds at leisure. Scientist amuses self with most complete model road in the world— Yes, that was it. Might do something with that.

But he'd never get far with it.

Trudging along he reached for his cigarette case. He fumbled in other pockets. Alarm began to grow on him. He couldn't find it! More slowly he repeated the search.

Hurriedly then he tore back to the gate and shouted at the house. But the only reply he got was printed on the sign:

TRESPASSERS BURIED
FREE OF CHARGE!

CHAPTER THREE

Pop, it might be said, was just a little proud of having turned out a presentable story where no story had been before. And, feeling the need of a little praise, he finished off his story the following morning and took it to Caulborn personally.

Caulborn, in a lather of activity which amounted to keeping half the staff enraged, pushed up his eyeshade—which he wore for show—and stared at Pop with calculated coldness.

"Well?"

"That story you sent me out on," said Pop, putting the sheets on Caulborn's desk. "You didn't think there was any story there. And you were right as far as news was concerned. But human interest—"

"Humph," said Caulborn, barely glancing at the type. He was, in truth, a little annoyed that Pop had gotten anything at all. When Caulborn had taken this job he had known very well that there were others in the office who had more seniority, more experience, and therefore a better claim.

"You call this a story?" said Caulborn. "You think we print anything you care to write? Go back to the copy desk." And so saying he dropped the sheets into the wastebasket with an emphatic gesture of dismissal.

Pop was a little dazed. He backed out and stood on the sill for seconds before he closed the door. A hurrying reporter jostled him and was about to rush on when he saw Pop's expression.

"Hey, you look like you need a drink."

"I do," said Pop.

The reporter glanced at Caulborn's door. "So he's making it tough for you, is he? The dirty rat. Never mind, Pop, when better newspapermen are built they'll all look like you. Something will break sooner or later—"

"I'm leaving tomorrow."

"Say, look now! Don't quit under fire. You know what ails that guy? He's scared, that's all. Scared of most of us and you in particular. Why, hell's bells, you belong in that chair. We're losing money, hundreds a day, and when it gets to thousands the publisher himself will get wise—"

"I'm being laid off," said Pop.

"You? For God's sake!"

Pop wandered back to his desk. Two other reporters came over to commiserate with him and curse Caulborn, but Pop didn't have anything to say. He just kept on pulling old odds and ends out of his desk, throwing many of them away but making a packet out of the rest.

"You're not leaving today, are you?" said a third, coming up.

"What else can I do?" said Pop.

And he went on cleaning out his desk, looking very worn and old and quiet. He scarcely looked up when Caulborn passed him, on his way out to lunch.

It was about one o'clock and he was just tying a string around his belongings—a pitifully small package to show for all his years in this city room. The phone rang on the next desk and Pop, out of habit, reached across for it.

"Gimme rewrite," barked an excited voice.

"I'll take it," said Pop suddenly.

"This's Jenson. I'm up on the Drive. Ready?"

Pop raked some copy paper to him and picked up a pencil. He was a little excited by the legman's tone. "Ready."

"At 12:45 today, Grant's Tomb disappeared."

"Huh?"

"Get it down. The traffic on the Drive was at its noon-hour peak and the benches around the structure were filled with people. When, without warning, a rumble sounded, the alarmed populace—"

"To hell with the words," cried Pop. "Give me the story. How did it happen?"

"I don't know. Nobody knows. There are half a dozen police cars around here staring at the place Grant's Tomb was. I was about a block away when I heard shrieks and I came tearing down to find that traffic was jammed up and that people were running away from the place while other people ran toward it. I asked a nursemaid about it and she'd seen it happen. She said there was a rumbling sound and then suddenly the tomb began to shrink in size and in less than ten seconds it had vanished."

"Was anybody seen monkeying with it?" said Pop, feeling foolish instantly.

"A chauffeur said he saw a little guy in a swallowtail coat tear across the spot where the tomb had been."

"How many dead?"

"Nobody knows if anybody is dead."

"Well, find out!"

"How can I find out when everybody that was sitting on the steps and all completely disappeared?"

"What?"

"They're gone."

"Somebody is crazy," said Pop. "No bodies?"

"No tomb."

"I got this much," said Pop. "You hoof it back there and get stories from the witnesses." He hung up and whirled to shout down the line of desks, "Grant's Tomb's gone! Get Columbia on the phone. We got to have a statement from somebody that knows his stuff. You, Sweeney, grab an encyclopedia and see if anything like this ever happened before. Morton, grab a camera and get out there for some pictures. Dunstan! You go with Morton and find the relatives of the people that have vanished along with the tomb. Get going!"

Nobody asked any questions beyond a stammer of incredulity. Nobody thought of tearing out to find Caulborn. Sweeney, Morton, Dunstan and others went into a flurry of activity.

"Branner!" cried Pop into the interoffice phone. "Start setting up an extra. We'll be on the street in half an hour. Second extra in an hour and a half with pictures."

"Is this Pop?"

"Yeah, this is Pop. What are you waiting for?"

"Okay. Half an hour it is."

"Louie, get some shots of Grant's Tomb out of the files and rush them down to Composing." Pop pulled his old typewriter toward his stomach and his fingers began to flash over the keys. Hunt and punch it was, but never had a story rolled so swiftly. In five minutes it was streaming down to Composing.

Pop got up and paced around his desk. He rumpled his graying hair and looked unseeingly out across the city room. He had pinch-hit as night editor so often that he did not question his authority to go ahead. And still nobody thought of Caulborn.

Shortly a damp proof was rushed up. The copy boy hesitated for a moment and then laid it on Pop's desk. Pop looked it over. "Okay. Let it run."

The boy loped away and Pop, reaching for a cigarette, again missed his case. Instead he hauled up a limp package and lighted a match. The phone rang somewhere.

"Take it, Pop," said a reporter.

Pop took it.

"Who's this?" said Pop.

"Freeman. Grab your pencil."

"Got it," said Pop, beginning to tingle at the tone of the legman.

"The Empire State Building disappeared about five minutes ago."

"Right," said Pop.

"I'm down at precinct ——. About three seconds ago a cop came staggering in with the news. I haven't had a chance to look."

"Get right down there and see," said Pop. "Grant's Tomb vanished just before you called."

"Check."

Pop put down the phone and dashed over to the window. But in vain he searched the skyline for any sign of the Empire State Building. "Gone," he said. The human being in him was appalled. The newspaperman went into action.

"Goodart," roared Pop, "get a camera down to the Empire State. It's disappeared."

"Check," said Goodart, dashing away.

"Copy boy!" yelled Pop. And into the phone, even while he started the second story, he yelped, "Branner. Limit the first extra. Get set for a second. Story coming down. The Empire State Building has disappeared."

"Okay," said Branner.

"Get some pictures down to Branner on the Empire State," shouted Pop. His fingers were blurring, so fast they raced over the keys.

"New York is going piece by piece," said a reporter. "Oh boy, what a story!"

"Call the mayor, somebody!" said Pop. "Tell him about it and ask him what he means to do."

"Check," said a cub eagerly.

"No such incident in the encyclopedia," reported Sweeney.

"Unprecedented," said Pop. "Lawson and Frankie! You two get cameras and rush downtown to be on hand in case any other big buildings exit. Copy boy!"

And the second story was on its way to Composing. And still nobody remembered Caulborn.

Pop went back to the window, but the Empire State was just as invisible as ever.

"Columbia says mass hypnotism or hysteria," said a girl.

"Get their statement," said Pop.

"Got it."

"Dress it up and shoot it down."

"Check."

Pop walked around his desk. Again he reached for his cigarette case and was again annoyed to find it gone. He lighted up, frowning over new angles, one eye hopefully on the phone.

"Find out how many people are usually in the Empire State," said Pop.

"Check," said a reporter, grabbing a phone.

"Don't try to call the Empire State!" said Pop. "It isn't there!"

The reporter looked silly and changed his call to the home of a director of the Empire State.

Certain that the story would keep breaking, Pop was not at all surprised when Frankie called.

"Pop! This's Frankie. Pennsylvania Station's gone!"

"Penn——! Full of people?"

"And trains and everything!" cried Frankie. "There's nothing there but a hole in the ground. I was lucky, about a block away and saw it happen! You said *big* so I figured Pennsylvania—"

"The story!"

"Well, there was a kind of rumble and then, all of a sudden, the station seemed to cave into itself and it was gone!"

"Statements!"

"A little guy in a swallowtail coat almost knocked me down running away. He was scared to death. Everybody was trying to get away. And right on the corner one of our boys was shouting our first extra. The whole building just disappeared, that's all. People, trains, everything. You ought to see the hole in the ground—"

"Get statements and rush your pictures back here. Don't be a damned photographer all your life."

"Okay, Pop."

"Pennsylvania Station," yelped Pop. "Tim, get this for rewrite. About five minutes ago, Pennsylvania Station disappeared— people, trains, everything. There's nothing but a hole in the ground. There was a rumble and then the thing vanished. Seemed to cave into itself but there is no debris. It's gone. All gone."

"Okay, Pop," said Tim, his mill beginning to clatter.

"Copy boy!" shouted Pop, pointing at Tim. "Pictures of Pennsylvania Station!" He grabbed a phone. "Branner! Keep adding to that extra. We got pictures coming of Pennsylvania Station. It's gone."

"Penn——! Oh boy, what a story!"

Pop hung up. "Angles, angles—" The phone rang.

"This is Lawson. I just heard that Grand Central disappeared. I'll get down there for some pictures and call you back."

"Pennsylvania Station just went," said Pop.

"The hell," said Lawson.

"On your way," said Pop.

"Gone," said Lawson.

Pop reached for another phone which was clamoring.

"This is Jenson again. I been checking all the angles. About a thousand people saw it disappear when—"

"What? What's gone now?"

"Why, Grant's Tomb—"

"Hell, kill it. The Empire State, Pennsylvania and Grand Central have gone since then. Get down here with your photographer."

"I haven't seen him. Did you send one?"

"Get down here. Do you think this is a vacation? Bring in your yarns. They'll just make our fourth extra."

"Okay, Pop."

"Got a statement from the mayor. He's yelling sabotage," said the cub. "He says he's phoning the governor to call out the militia. He says they can't do this to his town."

"Banner for extra number three," barked Pop into the phone. "Mayor Objects. Calls Out Militia. Story coming down." He jabbed a finger at the cub's typewriter. "Roll it out and spread it thick. They'll be half-panicked by now. Stab in a human-interest angle. Make 'em take it calm."

"Check," said the cub nervously.

Pop walked around his desk and again reached for his cigarette case, to again discover that it was missing. "Angles—two men with swallowtail coats—"

Pop whirled, "Eddy! Take this lead. Mystery man seen in two catastrophes. A small man with a swallowtail coat was present today at both the vanishing of the tomb and Pennsylvania Station. Was seen to run across place where tomb had been and collided with one of our reporters just after Pennsylvania disappeared. Got it?"

"Check."

Pop went over to the window. The Empire State was still gone. A thought was taking definite form in his mind now. For some reason he kept harking back to Hannibal Pertwee. Railway stations, cigarette case, swallowtail coat—

Freeman came dashing up. "She's sure gone."

"What?"

"The Empire State. There's nothing but a hole in the ground. There were umpteen thousand people inside and there's no sign of them—"

"Okay! Do me a story about the state of the city—how calm they're taking it. Smooth them down. Third extra on its way and you'll make the lead in the fourth."

"Right," said Freeman. "But you oughta seen that cop—"

"Don't tell me. I don't buy the paper. Write it."

"Okay, Pop."

Pop turned back to his desk. He was so preoccupied that he did not see a dark cloud come thundering through the city room.

Caulborn, with a copy of the first extra in his hands, bore down upon what was obviously the center of the maelstrom.

"Did you do this?" he cried, shaking the extra under Pop's nose.

"Sure. What about it?"

"Why didn't you call me? You know where I eat lunch! How do you know this story is true? What do you mean spreading terror all over the town? How is it that we get a paper out so quick when there's nobody else on the streets? If this is a farce, then we'll be in Dutch plenty. Civil and criminal actions—"

"It takes guts to run a paper," said Pop coldly.

"If that's what it takes, you've got too many. Now we've got to check everything we've printed. If you've got another extra on the rollers, we'll have to kill it and find out if—"

"The third extra is on the street," said Pop.

Caulborn stared, growing angry. "And you took the authority without even *trying* to find me?"

"A story has got to go when it's hot," said Pop.

"All right! *All right!* And you ran this one so hot that you're driving New York into a panic! Get out!"

"What?"

"I said get out!" towered Caulborn. "You're through, finished, washed up. Today instead of tomorrow!" And, nursing his injured importance, Caulborn flung off to his office.

The city room was very quiet.

Pop stood for a little while and then, with a shrug, picked up the package on his desk.

"Well," he sighed, "it was fun while it lasted."

"You're going to take him at his word?" said somebody. "Just because you were smart enough not to wait? He's just sore because you did it so swell—"

"Maybe," said Pop.

"You're going to quit like this?" said Freeman.

"No. Not like this," said Pop.

"Whatcha going to do?" said the cub.

Pop hefted his package. He looked grim.

CHAPTER FOUR

At dusk Pop approached the fortress of Hannibal Pertwee. But this time he did not lean against the fence or spend time in reading signs. True, he could not miss:

BEWARE OF THE LIONS!

but, having seen none on his previous visit, he refused to be alarmed. In fact, he was so unswerving of purpose that nothing short of lightning itself could have stopped him and he had an antidote for that.

At a garage, he had managed to separate himself from five dollars he could ill afford, an electrician from a pair of insulated gloves and the heaviest pair of wire cutters he could carry.

Breaking and entering would be a very serious offense, but he was first going to give Hannibal a chance.

For several minutes he waited dutifully at the gate, hoping that the mysterious voice would again speak. But this time it did not and the house remained as dark as it was small.

"You asked for it," muttered Pop.

Very painstakingly he inspected the latch. Then he donned the rubber gloves and took the cutters and went to work. In a few minutes the gate was swinging open, leaving its latch behind.

Oh, if this hunch he had was wrong!

He marched through the miniature forest down the miniature path and ducked to mount the porch. But there his purpose was eased.

Hannibal opened the door and gazed sadly at him.

"It will be so *much* work to repair that gate," said Hannibal.

"Well...uh...you see—"

"I was very busy. You are Mr. Frothingale from the *Atlantic Science Survey,* are you not?"

"I'm from the *World-Journal,*" said Pop.

"You're sure you are not from the railroad company?"

"Ah," said Pop.

"Well—I am very sorry but I can't ask you in tonight. I am so busy."

"I...er...came after my cigarette case," said Pop.

"Cigarette case?"

"Yes. I lost it when I was here before. I would dislike having to part with it permanently."

"Oh, that is very shocking. Did you lose it here?"

"I had it when I was here and didn't have it after I left."

"Mightn't you have dropped it in the garden?"

"I had it while I was in the house. You don't mind if I come in and look, do you?"

"Why...er—"

But Pop was already shouldering past Hannibal Pertwee and the little man could not but give way. However, Hannibal skipped to the fore and guided Pop into the minute living room.

"I was sitting here in this chair," said Pop, looking under it.

Hannibal fidgeted. "Isn't it lovely weather?"

"Swell," said Pop. "You don't mind if I look elsewhere?"

"Oh, yes! I mean no! I am very busy. Really, you will have to go."

"But my cigarette case," said Pop, edging toward the train room, "is very valuable to me."

"Of course, of course. I appreciate your predicament. But if I had seen it and if I find it— Oh, dear, what am I saying?"

"Well," said Pop, suddenly crafty, "I won't trouble you further.

150

I can see how upset you are." And he extended his hand. "Goodbye, Mr. Pertwee."

Eagerly Hannibal grasped the offered hand. Swiftly Pop yanked Hannibal close to him and gave him an expert frisk. The cigarette case leaped out of Hannibal's pocket. Pop looked at it with satisfaction.

"I wonder," said Hannibal, distrait, "how that got there?"

"So do I," said Pop. "And now if I could inspect your trains again—"

"Well...yes. All right. Just come this way." And he stepped through the door.

Pop was so close behind him that he almost got cut in half when the door slammed shut. There was the rumble of a shot bolt and Pop's weight against the door had no effect at all. He swore and dashed for the hall. Another door slammed there. Pop stood glaring through the walls at Hannibal. Then he got another idea and rushed outside to take a tour of the house. But there was nothing to be seen.

For two hours Pop prowled in the garden. But the night was cold and Pop was hungry and, at last, he had to be content with his victory in recovering his case. He went off up the road in the direction of the station.

Grumbling to himself, he stood on the platform, waiting for a train to carry him back to New York. He could swear that there was some connection between the forest, the miniature car, the trains and the vanished buildings.

"Dja hear about them things disappearin' in N'York?" said a loafer.

"Yeah," said Pop.

"Awful, ain't it?" said the loafer.

"Yeah," said Pop.

"It's them Nazis," said the loafer.

Pop took out his cigarette case. It still contained several cigarettes so, evidently, Hannibal did not smoke. Pop lit up. He was about to replace the case when he wondered if any harm had come to it. He pressed the music button. No sound came forth.

151

"Damn him," said Pop. "Broke it." Well, he could have it fixed. Hannibal, the loon, had probably worn it out.

The train came at last and Pop settled himself for a doze. He could think best when he dozed. But his neighbor wasn't sleepy.

"Ain't that awful what them Reds did in New York? I hear that people are runnin' around trying to lynch all the Reds they know about. Course some don't believe it was the Reds, and I hear tell the churches is full of people prayin'. I'm goin' in to see for myself, but I'm tellin' you, you won't catch *me* walkin' into no buildings."

"Yeah," said Pop.

The train lippety-clicked endlessly, saying the same thing over and over: "Pop's through, Pop's through, Pop's through."

About eight he wandered out of the station to straggle haphazardly uptown. He was trying to tell himself that he was glad he was through. No more chasing fire engines for him. What a hell of a life it was. Never any regular sleep, always on the go, living from story to story. Well! Now he could settle down and rest awhile. Yes, that was the ticket. Just rest. There was that farm his sister had left him. He'd go up there in the morning. Place probably all falling to pieces but it would be quiet. Yes, a helluva life for a man. He'd followed the news for years and now all the stories he had covered were lumped into one chunk of forgetfulness—and he was as stale as yesterday's newspaper. What had it ever gotten him? Just headaches.

Shuffling along, head down, hands deep in his jacket pockets, he coursed his way to Eighth Avenue. From far off came a thin scream of a police siren. Pop stopped, instantly alert. The clang of engines followed, swooping down a side street near him. He raced up to the corner and watched the trucks and police cars stream by full blast. He whirled to a taxi and then paused, uncertain. Gradually he lost his excitement until he was again slumped listlessly. Far off the police sirens and bells dwindled and faded into the surflike mutter of the city.

"Taxi, buddy?"

Pop glanced toward the hack driver. He slowly shook his

head and pulled out his cigarette case. He lighted up and puffed disconsolately. A saloon was nearby and he wandered into it to place a foot on the rail.

"Rye. Straight," said Pop.

The British-looking barkeep pushed out a glass and filled it with an expert twist of his wrist. Pop downed the drink and stood there for a while staring morosely at his reflection in the mirror behind the pyramided wares.

"Fill it up," said Pop.

The barkeep did as bidden. "Ain't that awful about them buildings and all?" he said the while. "The wickedness of this city is what brought it on. Just yesterday I says to a gent in here, I says, 'A town as sinful as this—'"

Pop took out his cigarette case. "Yeah."

"'A town as sinful as this cannot meet but one fate in the mighty wrath—'"

SWOOsssssh!

Pop was jarred out of his wits.

The whole bar had vanished!

The whole bar, complete with tender!

The mirrors were still there, but that was all!

A drunk who had been sitting at a side table looked unblinkingly in the direction of the phenomenon and then, with great exactness, lifted his glass and spilled the contents on the floor. Unsteadily he navigated to the street.

Pop's news-keen mind examined all the possibilities in sight. Was it possible that someone had come in that door and done this? Had Hannibal followed him?

Absently he started to pay for his drink, coming to himself only when he saw for certain that he no longer leaned on the bar. He looked at the floor where the planks were patterned as the bar had stood. And then Pop received another shock.

There was the bar!

About an inch long!

Almost lost in a crack between the flooring!

Hastily he picked it up, afraid of hurting it. He could barely make out the bartender who did not seem to be moving. Pop put the thing in a small cardboard box he found in the refuse and then stowed it carefully in his pocket.

This opened up a wide range of thought and he needed air in which to think. He went out into the street.

Why was he so certain that it was Hannibal? He understood nothing of that man's plans and certainly there were thousands of swallowtail coats in New York City. But still—

This bar had dwindled in size. Was it not possible, then, that the buildings had done likewise? And if they had, mightn't they still be there? He mulled this for a long time, standing at the curb, occasionally hearing the wonder of a would-be customer in the saloon.

"Taxi?" persisted the driver.

"Yeah," said Pop. But before he got in, his abstraction led him to take out his cigarette case and light up. Then he entered the cab. "I want to go to the place Grand Central Station was."

"Okay, buddy," said the cabby.

He pondered profoundly as he waited for lights, and when the driver let him out near the police cordon which had been placed around the hole, he thought he had a glimmering of the meaning behind this series of events.

He paid and strolled along the line.

"Awful, ain't it?" said another spectator.

"Yeah," said Pop. He edged up to an officer. "I'm from the *World-Journal*. I want to examine that hole from the bottom."

"Sorry. Can't be done. I got strict orders."

A few minutes later, Pop was wandering about the hole. The streetlights were sufficient for his inspection and, very minutely, he covered every inch of the ground. Then, finding nothing, he again risked bunions by doing it all over, again without result. He got out and walked away toward the site of the Empire State.

On the way he paused and bought some cigarettes, filling his case. When he had finished he wandered on down the avenue.

But his inspection of the hole where the Empire State had

154

stood left him once more without clue. He was very weary and muddy when he had finished, for it was difficult walking.

He stood once more at the curb, determined to make his inspection complete.

"Taxi?"

Pop took out his case and started to extract a cigarette.

"Tax——"

SWOOssssh!

And the cab folded into itself with such rapidity that Pop's eye could not follow.

Pop trembled.

He shut his eyes and counted to ten.

When he opened them the cab was still gone.

Then he looked more closely at the pavement and stooped down. Here was the cab, a little less than an inch long and proportionate in the other two dimensions.

Pop put it in his cardboard box.

But nobody was near him. Evidently no one had seen this happen to the cab. And if Hannibal had sneaked up and caused it, there had been neither sign nor sound of his approach.

Maybe—maybe Hannibal wasn't guilty.

Maybe New York would keep right on disappearing!

To keep his sanity Pop vowed to complete his inspection. He moved to the next cab in the line in which the driver was dozing. The cabby woke with a start and reached automatically back for the door.

"I want to go to Pennsylvania Station," said Pop. And then, finding he still held the cigarette case in his hand, again opened it to take out another cigarette.

SWOOssssh!

And this second cab was gone!

Pop began to tremble violently. His heart was beating somewhere near his tonsils. With a quick glance around he reached down and picked up the cab and slid it into his box.

"Hey, you," said a loitering cop. "What you doin'?"

"Pi...pickin' snipes," said Pop hurriedly.

"Well, get along."

Pop got without further waiting. It was quite clear to him now who was doing this. Himself! The cigarette case! Hadn't it jerked a little whenever these things had gone?

And wasn't he guilty of murder if these drivers and the bartender were dead?

When he was on a dark street he surreptitiously inspected the case by the faint glow of a shop window.

But there wasn't anything unusual about it. Pop looked around and found a trash can. If this case was doing it, it certainly could make this trash can dwindle. Pop pushed the opening button. Nothing happened. He pushed the music button. Again nothing happened.

He breathed a sigh of relief. Then he was wrong about this. It wasn't his cigarette case, after all. Somebody was following him, that was it. Somebody was sneaking up and doing these things to him. Well! He'd walk around and keep close watch and maybe it would happen once more. When his attention was distracted by the case, this other person— Sure, that was the answer.

Pop, feeling better, walked on to the next avenue. He took his stand on the corner near a large apartment house. This was fair game. And when the other person came near, he would take out his case and then—*bow!*—grab the malefactor and drag him back to the paper for interview.

In a few minutes a fellow in very somber clothes came near. Pop took out his cigarette case and started to open it.

SWOOsssh!

And the apartment building was gone!

Pop was shaken up by the vibration of its going but he did not lose his presence of mind. He snatched the bystander and bore him to earth.

The full light of the street lamp shone down.

He had captured a minister of the gospel!

Very swiftly Pop got away from there, leaving the minister staring after him and then, seeing the hole where a building had been, praying.

By a circuitous route, Pop came back to the hole. He almost broke a leg getting down into it, so steep were the sides. But he forgot that when he found the tiny thing which had been a building. It looked like a perfect model, about five inches high. Pop, hearing a crowd gather on the street, got out of there, stuffing the building in his pocket. There was a sting to the object which was very uncomfortable.

All Pop's fine ideas had gone glimmering now. It *was* the case. It had to be. And to test it out he had probably slain hundreds, maybe thousands, of people. But his news sense was soon uppermost again.

At a safe distance from the site he again inspected the case. He pressed first one button and then the other and still nothing happened. It shook his orderly process of thought. He went on his way, case in hand, and found himself in a commercial street where great drays were parked. He went on. Before him was the waterfront.

A packing case stood upon a wharf. Pop chose it for a test and stood there for some time, pushing the case's buttons. But the packing case stayed very stubbornly where it was.

And then, quite by accident, Pop pushed both buttons at once!

SWOOssssh!

The liner which had been at the pier abruptly vanished!

There was a snap as the after lines went. There was a small tidal wave as the seas came together.

Pop had missed his aim!

He had gotten over being stunned by now. His first thought was to snatch the hawser which had not parted. He hauled it swiftly in. The ship was barely attached to the line. Very carefully Pop looked at the tiny boat, perfect in all details, but less than three inches long. He looked hurriedly about and shoved it into his pocket.

A steward was running in circles on the dock, yelling, "They've stole it! They've stole it! Help, murder, police! They've stole it!"

That "murder" set badly with Pop. He got out of there.

Ten minutes later he was in a phone booth. The night editor's voice boomed over the wire.

"Joe, this is Pop. Look, I've got a bar, two taxis, an apartment building and an ocean liner in my pocket. Stand by for an extra about midnight."

"You—huh? Sleep it off, Pop. And drink one for me."

"No, no, no!" cried Pop.

But the wire was dead.

Pop walked out of the booth, turned around and walked into it again. He dropped his nickel and began a series of calls to locate his man.

"World-Journal," said Pop at last. "I want Barstow of Pennsylvania Railroad."

"This is Barstow. But I've given out statements until I'm hoarse. Call me tomorrow."

"You'll be at the *World-Journal* in two hours if you want your station back."

"Call me tomorrow," repeated the voice. "And lay off the stuff. It ain't good for you." There was a click.

Pop sighed very deeply.

So they wouldn't believe him, huh? Well, he'd show 'em! He'd show 'em!

And he loped for the station.

CHAPTER FIVE

"I won't," said Hannibal, definite for the first time in his life.

They sat in Caulborn's office and the clock said ten. Caulborn had not yet come in.

Hannibal Pertwee showed signs of having been mauled a bit. And even now he tried to make a break for the door. Pop tripped him and set him back on the chair.

"It's no use," said Hannibal. "I won't tell you or anybody else. After what they did to me, why should I do anything for them?"

In the center of the room sat a gunnysack. Carefully wrapped up within it were some items Pop had found occupying the vacant spaces in the vicinity of "New York" on Hannibal Pertwee's toy railway system.

"I'll have you for burglary," said Hannibal. "You can't prove anything at all. What if I do have some models of buildings? Can't I make models of what I please? And they're just models. You'll see!"

"What about those people you can see in them?" said Pop.

"They're not moving. Can't I make people in model form, too?"

Pop was alternating warm and chill, for he knew he was dabbling in very serious matters. Anxiously he looked at the clock. As though by that signal, Caulborn came in.

Caulborn had had a drink too many the evening before and he was in no condition to see Pop.

"What? You here again?"

"That's right," said Pop. "And I have—"

"There's no use begging for that job. We don't need anybody. Get out or I'll have you thrown out." And he reached across the desk for his phone.

Pop's handy feet sent Caulborn sprawling. Pop instead pushed the button.

"Send in Mr. Graw," said Pop, calling for the publisher.

"I'll blacklist you!" cried Caulborn. "You'll never work on another paper!"

"I'll take my chances," said Pop.

Mr. Graw, very portly, stepped in. He saw Pop and scowled. Caulborn was dusting off his pants in protest.

"What's this?" said Mr. Graw.

"He won't get out," said Caulborn. "He sent for you. I didn't."

"Well, of all the cheek!"

Pop squared off. "Now listen, you two. I been in this business a long time. And I know what a story is worth. You're losing money and you need circulation. Well, the way to get circulation is to get stories. Now!"

"I won't," said Hannibal.

On the table Pop laid out the four objects from the gunnysack: the Pennsylvania Station, Grand Central, Grant's Tomb and the Empire State. Then from his jacket he took the bar, the two taxis, the apartment house and the steamship.

"I won't!" cried Hannibal, attempting another break. Once more Pop pushed him back to the chair.

"What are these?" said Mr. Graw.

"Just what you see. The missing buildings," said Pop.

"Preposterous! If you have gone to all this trouble just to make some foolish story—"

Pop cut Mr. Graw's speech in half. "I've gone to plenty of trouble, but not to have anything made. These are the real thing."

"Rot," said Caulborn.

"I won't!" said Hannibal.

"Well, in that case," said Pop, "I'll make you a proposition. If I restore these to their proper places, can I have my job back—permanently?"

"Humph," said Mr. Graw. "If you can put back what this city has lost, I'll give you your job back. Yes. But why waste our time—"

"Then call Mr. Barstow of the Pennsylvania Railroad," said Pop. "You get him over here on the double and I'll put the buildings back."

"But how—"

Again Pop cut Mr. Graw down. "Just call, that's all. You can't afford to run the risk of losing this chance."

"If you're talking nonsense—" growled Mr. Graw. But he put through the call.

Caulborn was licking his lips in anticipation of what he would have done to Pop. What Caulborn had suffered in loss of pride yesterday could all be made up today. He'd show Graw!

It was an uncomfortable wait while Hannibal protested at intervals and Caulborn rubbed his hands. But at last Mr. Barstow, in a sweat, came loping in.

"You called me, Graw? By God, I hope you've got news."

MICHAEL TALBOT

Graw pointed at Pop. "This idiot claims to have your station. He says this is it."

Barstow snatched up the "model" of Pennsylvania. It stung his hands and he put it back. He turned to Pop. "Is this a joke? That's a perfect replica, certainly, but—"

"Look," said Pop, "this is Hannibal Pertwee, probably the smartest scientist since Moses."

"Oh, you," said Barstow.

"So you know him," said Pop.

"He used to bother us quite a bit," said Barstow. "What is it now?"

"Ah, we get somewhere," said Pop. "Barstow, if this gentleman replaces your Pennsylvania Station and these other objects, will you make a contract with him?"

"About his ideas on freight?" said Barstow. "I don't know which is the craziest statement, that you'll restore the buildings, or that anything he can think up will affect our freight. But go ahead."

Pop yanked out a slip of paper. "I typed this. Sign it."

Smiling indulgently, Barstow signed the agreement. Graw and Caulborn shrugged and witnessed it with their names.

"All right," said Pop to Hannibal. "This is what you used to be begging for. You've got it now. Go ahead."

And indeed Hannibal Pertwee had undergone a change. All trace of sullenness was gone from his face, replaced by growing hope. "You mean," he said to Barstow, "that you'll really consider my propositions? That you may utilize my findings?"

"I've said so in this paper," said Barstow impatiently.

Hannibal rubbed his hands. "Well, you see, gentlemen, my idea was to reduce freight in size so that it could be shipped easily. And so I analyzed the possibilities of infinite acceleration—"

"Spare the lecture," said Pop. "Get busy. They won't understand anything but action."

"Ah, yes. Action. May I have the cigarette case?"

Pop handed it over.

"You see, you turn it upside down and—"

"Wait!" cried Pop. "My god, you almost made them come back in here. You want to kill all of us?" Hastily he hauled Hannibal outside, taking the bar and a taxicab with him.

"Now," said Pop, setting them down in a cleared space.

Hannibal caressed the case. "It was very ingenious, I thought. I had been waiting for this very thing. Apparatus would have been noticed, you see, but this was perfect. One can stand on the edge of a crowd and press the buttons, both together, and the atomic bubble within is set into nearly infinite acceleration. It spins out and engulfs the first whole object it embraces and sets it spinning in four dimensions. Of course, as the object spins at a certain speed, it is accordingly reduced in size. Einstein—"

"Just push the buttons," said Pop.

"Oh, of course. You see, to stop the object from spinning we have merely to engulf it with an atomic bubble spinning in four dimensions, all opposite to the first—"

"The buttons," said Pop.

Hannibal turned the case around so that it would open down. He pointed it in the general direction of the tiny taxi.

"It compresses time as well as space," continued Hannibal. "I just release the bubble—"

swooo OOSH!

The taxi increased in size like a swiftly inflated balloon. The *tick-tick-tick* of its engine was loud in the room. The cabby finished opening the door and then turned to where he had last seen Pop.

"What address, buddy?" and then he saw his surroundings. He stared, gulped, looked at the ring of reporters and office men and hastily shut off his engine, shaking his head as though punch-drunk.

"Now the bar," said Pop.

Hannibal pushed the buttons again and, suddenly—
swooo OOSH!

The bar was there, full size.

The British bartender finished filling the glass with an expert twist of his wrist. "And I says, 'A sinful city like this will sooner or later—'" He had been turning to put away the bottle. But now he found no mirrors, only the reaches of the city room. His British calm almost deserted him.

Pop handed the drink to the cabby who instantly tossed it down.

"Now we better not have a bar in this place," said Pop, "if I know reporters. Cabby, you and the barkeep step back here out of the way. Do your stuff, Hannibal."

SWOOssssh!

Click, click.

SWOOssssh!

And both bar and taxi were toy-sized instantly. The cabby began to wail a protest, but Pop shoved the tiny car into his hands.

"We'll make it grow up shortly," said Pop. "Down in the street. Frankie! You and Lawson get some cameras. Freeman, you call the mayor and tell him to gather round for the fun. Sweeney, you write up an extra lead, telling the city all is well. I'll knock out the story on this—"

"Oh, no, you won't," said Graw.

"Huh?" said Pop. "But you said, in front of witnesses—"

"I don't care what I said. I've suddenly got an idea. Who got out those extras so fast yesterday?"

"Pop did!" yelled Sweeney, instantly joined by a chorus.

Graw turned to Caulborn. "At first I believed you. But when I got to thinking it over after I found out how fast they really had come—"

"He didn't mean nothin' by it," said Pop. "He's just a little young."

"Pop," said Graw, "you can't have his job."

"Well, I didn't say—"

"Pop," said Graw, "I've got a better spot for you than that. You're managing editor. Maybe you can make this son-in-law of mine amount to something if you train him right."

"Mana...managing editor?" gaped Pop.

"I'm going to slip out of the job," said Graw. "I need rest. And so, Mr. Managing Editor, I leave you to your editions."

The roof-raising cheer which went up from half a hundred throats about them made Pop turn lobster color. Savagely he faced around.

"Well?" said Pop. "What are you waiting for? We got an extra edition to get out and that means work. Hannibal, you trot along with Frankie and Lawson. They'll help you put them buildings back. And listen, Frankie, don't miss any shots." Hastily he scribbled out the addresses where ship and taxi belonged and then shooed them on their way.

Pop took up the package he had left at the switchboard. He went into the office marked "Managing Editor" and laid his belongings on the desk. He shed his coat, rolled up his sleeves and reached for the phone.

"Copy boy!" he shouted.

"Okay, Pop."

Lilt of a Lark

written by
Michael Panter

illustrated by
BRETT STUMP

ABOUT THE AUTHOR

Michael Panter is an English author and journalist with exceedingly high ambitions and a frustratingly low word count per day. A language enthusiast, he speaks fluent Swedish and is well on his way to learning Italian.

His writing journey began humbly when, aged seven, he penned the sequel to Star Wars: The Phantom Menace. *George Lucas went with* Attack of the Clones *instead. Michael's love for secondary-world fantasy, meanwhile, was fostered largely by Tolkien. In 2018, one of his novellas,* Deathsworn, *won a Watty, Wattpad's highest honour, reminding him that he is good enough, he can do this writing thing.*

"Lilt of a Lark," his first professional sale, tells the story of a hapless musician who has the power to sway the minds of others through song. Droll, witty, and devilishly handsome, drawing parallels between character and author is permissible. Michael currently lives in Stockholm, Sweden, with his partner Jonna and their one-year-old bear cub, Ivar. He is hard at work on a full-length fantasy novel that he hopes will hit bookshelves before his hair goes grey.

ABOUT THE ILLUSTRATOR

Brett Stump is an educator, artist, and illustrator. As a Kansas City transplant in Southwest Missouri, Brett grows fonder of the Ozarks with each passing day. Along the way, he has been dreaming, doodling, and drawing closer to his goal of becoming a freelance illustrator.

Brett creates captivating images, piquing curiosity in all who view them. His works hint at stories and characters which unfold in the viewer's mind. These visual introductions grasp the imagination and create worlds of their own; it is part of Brett's process to entertain how he can tell each story best.

Brett lives just north of Springfield, Missouri, with his wife Kyli, son Shepherd, and daughter Fallon. He enjoys great music, good books, and even better barbecue. When not painting, Brett ingests copious amounts of all three.

Lilt of a Lark

Life was a costly commodity this far north, and the only thing Malk was rich in was poor decisions.

Fortune dictated that he didn't have to choose his bridge. Eleven of them fed into Cathgol, crudely carved and meagrely maintained, all treacherous in their own way on a night like tonight.

Malk took the mountain bridge because he'd taken the mountain road. That it was the most treacherous of them all was a nuance entirely out of his freezing cold hands. It felt better that way, safer somehow.

Back in Heartland, his bunkmates had sung of the wind in the Upper Helm cutting like the voice of a demon. Sulking with a cup of spiced wine in his hand, he'd dismissed the songs along with the hoary hags and the soul-stealing glaciers.

"Preeminent diligence as ever, Malky," he uttered through clenched teeth. He'd still sneer at frosted biddies and icy holes in the ground, sure enough, but he found it mighty hard to now dismiss something that left his woollen cloak feeling like fine silk.

He pulled that cloak tighter about his face and did his best to slump straight in the saddle. An inch too far left, or too far right, and he'd fall.

And keep falling.

A craggy silhouette of dark spires, Cathgol, capital of the Upper Helm, welcomed him like a nest of steel claws. Two sentries manned a portcullis at the bridge's end, bowls of burning oil at their flanks. Laden in pelts, they had as well been bears, though Malk had never seen a bear wielding a poleaxe before.

"Ho!" came the cry. "Who approaches Cathgol?"

Malk jerked stiffly up on his reins as he entered the torchlight, snow swirls dancing their dance to either side, drifting ever downward into the chasm below. "A weary wanderer wanting warmth."

The bigger of the two guardsmen stepped cautiously out onto the bridge. "What be you doing here after dark, *wanderer?*"

"Well...wandering." Malk shook himself rid of the snowy mantle that had settled during the final hour of his journey, a parting boon from higher beings that were surely laughing at him. "That and sliding towards a shivering sleep from which I will never stir. Comprehensively more of the latter at this point."

The guard's face tightened into a scowl. "I meant, what be your business?"

In response, Malk struggled off his gloves, reached down to his saddlebag, and came up holding an instrument of polished black wood. Three feet from tip to base, its neck was a long and slender thing embellished by three golden strings. Its head was carved in the likeness of a songbird. "This is my business."

The guard snickered to his mate; half amusement, half relief. "Just a sleeting bard. A young'un n'all. Must be here for the Count's celebrations."

Malk plucked the leftmost string of his instrument with fingers clumsy from the cold. He winced at the strangled sound it made. *How they expect me to play in such barbaric climes, I will never chirping know.*

"You took the mountain road alone, boy?" the smaller sentry asked.

"Alone...yes," Malk replied absently, entirely focused on twisting the silver screws along the instrument's neck. "Except for Hanna, of course."

"Hanna?"

"My horse."

"You took the mountain road alone on that swaybacked old sow? Are you gritted?"

"Am I what?"

"Mad," the bigger guardsman clarified.

Malk tweaked the highest screw and tried the second string. There was still something dreadfully off. "Mad? No…just exceedingly unprosperous." He plucked the third string and shivered at the twang that rippled forth. "Too tight by half."

"Where be you coming from?" the smaller sentry asked.

"Heartland."

"Heartland?"

Malk returned to the first string and plucked again. "Ah-ha, progress!"

The wind wailed across the bridge, and the bigger guard shivered. "Only rogues and raiders and robbers on the mountain road these days."

Malk smiled as he fiddled with another screw. "Quite right. I met some of them; they wanted Hanna."

"But you isn't raggled?"

"I'm not what?"

"Robbed and or dead."

"I'm not, no. I sang a song for them, and they changed their minds." It had been a close thing in truth. Too close. *I'll be writing the Aviary a ballad when I return south. They'll all hear it. Talon Whistron, Talon Benecbar, the High Ygle himself! One to make their chirping ears bleed.*

Malk tweaked the final screw, held his breath, and ran his fingers across the strings. "There! Now, where were we? Ah yes, weary and wanting warmth." He looked up from his busying.

"You ain't welcome in Cathgol," the bigger sentry announced, eyes hardened by suspicion. "These is perilous times, and we got no want for comely singers and their fancy harps. City's full of them just now."

Malk feigned hurt. "But you haven't heard me play yet. And it's not a harp; it's a cannotina."

"Go back the way you come and play some more for your vagabond chums."

Malk replied first with his fingers, strumming a pleasant chord. *"Rogues and raiders and robbers,"* he began, in a voice rich and sweet as honey.

The bigger sentry snarled. "Right, I'm warning—"

"Rogues and raiders and robbers,
Devils of ditches and dirt,
At the points of their knives, with blood in their eyes,
They demanded his silver and hurt.
Yet our wanderer wandered yet onward,
Unraggled, he came to his prize,
'Twas warmth he sought, and he'd found it, he thought,
For to be turned away was to die . . .
For to be turned away was to die!"

Malk finished with a flourish on the strings. When he looked up again, the sentries were staring slack-eyed. "That was sleeting good," the bigger one said eventually. The smaller one scratched his bearskin cap and nodded enthusiastically.

Malk waved their plaudits away. "Please, my cheeks are already red. Now, about my seeking warmth . . . I wasn't lying earlier when I said I was edging to my eternal end."

The guardsmen looked to each other and then dumbly back at Malk.

He strummed one final chord. "Open the gate?"

The smaller sentry came to his senses quickest. "The gate! Yes . . . right . . . yes. Open the gate!" he shouted up.

The portcullis laboured open. Malk nudged Hanna with his heels and hummed over his work. It was a respectable tune, given the circumstances, though it would need some tinkering if he was to use it again.

The guardsmen still looked like they were stewing over a supremely difficult question. "Which way to the Liar's Lament?" Malk asked as he passed them.

172

BRETT STUMP

"Second on the left and over the bridge," the smaller sentry muttered. "You don't want to play there, though, they're all—"

"Rogues and raiders and robbers...I know." Hooves drummed cobblestones as he entered Cathgol. "That's precisely why I'm here."

The Liar's Lament was further from the velvet-dressed common rooms and canal-fronting wine gardens of Heartland than Malk had ever envisioned himself going. Dirty rushes littered the floor for want of plush carpets, grime decked the walls ahead of portraits of esteemed exemplars, crooks and drunkards stole the places of scholars and tutors. Even the entertainment was inferior; half a dozen artists would vie for the honour of charming an establishment on any given night in Heartland. The Liar's Lament had only a bulky baritone whose off-key offering was better suited to a cattle market. The place was warm—a log-fed hearth held a roaring fire nearby—but when Malk weighed the price of warmth in Cathgol, he wondered if his scales weren't broken.

Couldn't have been an Owl, could you, Malky? Not a Talon nor Thrush? Oh no, you had to be a Lark, wandering the length and breadth of the Org like a feathered fool. He sat and thawed in the corner shadows, chalking up more debts to the Aviary, sipping an ale so thick it was like to choke him as he quietly waited. He'd learned a thing or two about the importance of patience this past year, had Malk. It wasn't his favourite virtue, true, but he'd come to appreciate that he liked making mistakes even less.

So, he waited, and he sipped, watching the locals in their earthen-tone garb drinking like pigs at a trough. They were pale, strapping creatures in the main, with red in their beards, bass in their voices, and features carved from cliff sides. *Rogues and raiders and robbers, without a doubt. But which savage is mine?*

Which indeed.

Talon Whistron had given him a name, sure enough, but the Liar's Lament wasn't the sort of place a man went pressing strangers as to who they were. Not if he liked his guts being on the inside, in any case. *Rezzell. A flowery name for one of these louts.* That in itself was peculiar; Malk hadn't seen flowers growing since before he'd passed Headland.

A light voice cut through his musings. "Now that is a strange get."

Malk raised his eyes. A serving maid stood over him, hands folded over a stained white apron. Slender as a knife, she was the prettiest thing he had seen north of home. "Get?" He tracked her gaze downward.

With his travel cloak drying on the stool beside him, he was a coalescence of conflicting colours to make a peacock jealous. His tunic was quartered green and gold and red and russet; his leggings were here yellow, there blue, sashed with silver and fastened with bone-white buttons. He suddenly understood.

"My mother taught me that life is a song," he said, "and colours are like chords. You can't make a good song from one chord. Rather, you need several."

The maid smiled a pleasant smile. Her skin was only a shade darker than snow, though her hair, cut into a rough bowl around her ears, was the colour of pitch. The cute little nose in the middle of her face reminded him of a button. "That about makes you a walking masterpiece. And not one from Cathgol, I don't think."

"Did my 'get' give me away?"

"Your face did. Tan but not too tan, dark eyes, handsome, and a little pompous, like the gents in those southern paintings. Not so much as a whisker on your chin, either. They say a man's face freezes to stone up here without hair to warm it."

"In Heartland, they say a man's jaw is like his wife: better sharp, best naked."

"You're from Heartland?" The girl's eyes grew wide.

Malk revelled in her awe. The girls back home were laboriously difficult to charm, products of cushion courtesy and silk-bordered surroundings as they were. The girls of the Upper Helm, he guessed, were baser creatures. "Indeed," he told her, rising higher in his chair. "Five days up the Imperial Road to

Gullet. Countless nights thereafter, navigating the narrows of Neckelhaim, a week or so meandering the Mouthambrian Moors, up into Headland, then on to Helm, and finally, well, here."

"But that's almost half the Org. What brought you north?"

"A misunderstanding of monolithic measure." Malk gestured at the cannotina resting across his knees. "In short, I've come to sing a song."

"There's a fancy piece of wood." The maid eyed the cannotina like a cat might eye a sparrow. That was nothing new; it drew looks most wherever Malk went. "There's supper to be had if you'll play for us."

Malk's belly gave an audible growl. "Mine's to be a more private audience, sadly."

"Private?" She gestured to the drunkards at the bar. "A merchant prince? A countess, perhaps? Take your pick." She smiled again, and for the first time, Malk noticed her eyes. One was hazel brown, the other blue, or perhaps even green. He found the contrast appealing.

"I'm waiting for someone," he said.

"There are nicer places to wait. Where did you play last night?"

"In a cave on the mountain road. Not much to be said for the audience, but the acoustics were almost to freeze to death for. I rode into Cathgol this very eve."

The maid raised her brows. "Last I heard, they were turning travellers away after dark. There's trouble abroad in the Upper Helm, don't you know."

He shrugged. "I sang for them at the gate, and they changed their minds."

"And you won't even give us one song? Are you granite?"

"Am I what?"

"Are you *sure*?" she said, giggling.

Malk dipped his head. "Trust me, your patrons don't want to hear my works. Supper would be a fine thing, mind. I tied my horse in the shelter out back, too; she's the half-dead looking one."

"Best keep that between us," the girl said. "The locals will tell you the landlady can be a right hag."

"And does she make the supper?"

"She does not."

"Then I'll take whatever is hot, so long as it isn't fowl," Malk told her. "I don't eat birds."

"And this stranger of yours? I might know them if they're from Cathgol. Perhaps they have a name?"

"Perhaps they do. I was instructed only to meet them here when the Hunter's Moon was at its fullest." Someone had hired a Lark for a job, but that didn't mean they wanted every scullery maid and pot boy knowing it.

"That so? You know, I always heard that southerners were plain as white chalk. You... well, you're not."

Malk flashed the girl his whitest smile. "Lies are like music; spread through the ears."

"I'll take care to remember." She turned on her heels and left him.

Malk watched her until she was lost to the chaos. Perhaps his wisdom would serve her well in this frozen hellscape. *Poor thing, she's wasted amongst these fiends.* He took up his cannotina and silently walked his fingers over the three strings while his imagination explored a path of its own, one leading to deep furs and sweet-scented candles and the myriad oils a man might purchase in Heartland to be applied by soft hands. *Two eyes had she, one brown, one green... the chastest maid I'd ever seen.* Was chastest a word? He would have to look it up when he got back to the Aviary. *Two eyes, had she, one—*

He was abruptly tugged back to the grotty tavern by a hand on his sleeve. Irritated, he glanced at the owner, expecting to see the one he had come here for.

He was met by doe eyes peering down at him over plump cheeks. "Evenin'."

Seven strings. Here we go. "Fret not," Malk said lazily. "I'm not here to steal your songs or your supper."

The bard looked young this close up. Almost as young as Malk. He grinned and thumbed to the spot where he had been playing. "Best o' luck to you."

Malk straightened his tunic. "My apologies. I assumed you assumed me an adversary."

The boy was a sweaty thing, well-fed and red of face under his shock of coal-coloured hair. "Singers of the way are brothers, come what may. Me pa says that. I'm Jeppe Gemstones. Yer lute caught me eye."

"Malk. And it's a cannotina."

"You ain't from here."

"So I've been told."

Jeppe winked. "No beard on yer face. None on mine neither. Got here two weeks ago. Plan was to play my way up the hill in time for the Count's name day."

Malk didn't need to ask how it had gone; the Liar's Lament was at the bottom of said hill.

"Could team up if you like?" the boy said. "You look like you know what yer about. I'm a lousy player, but I've a voice to calm choppy waters. Me pa says that. This were his." He brandished his lute, and Malk saw the three colourful gemstones embedded in its body.

He smiled wryly. "A pretty piece. It would be prettier still if those stones were real."

The comment didn't seem to bother Jeppe. "It's me dream to play for the Count. Me pa played for his pa, see. When he was starting out. I'd do anything to repeat history. Anything in the Org."

"An ambitious aim, but I play alone." Malk looked past the boy. He didn't want to miss his man.

Jeppe slid into the seat opposite, wholly blocking the view. "I'm playing the Upper's Upper Skirt tomorrow. Let's make magic."

Malk tried to peer around him, but the boy simply moved in sync.

"You and me. Birds of a feather."

Have it your way. Malk ran his fingers across his strings and cleared his throat.

"Birds of a—"

The door to the tavern hit the wall with a thunderous crash.

178

The smile dropped from Jeppe's face as the cold of the night swept in, along with a group of three fronted by the largest man Malk had ever seen. *Rogues and raiders and robbers*, he thought, gulping down the last of his ale with a wince.

Malk was no stranger to grand entrances; there wasn't a common room in Heartland that didn't recede into a venerable hush when an Owl or a Talon chanced to pass through unannounced. There was a difference between courtesy and awe, however, and a greater difference still between awe and fear.

The Liar's Lament began to empty out. First a trickle, then a river, soon a flood as the whispers spread and the bodies made for the door. Jeppe Gemstones went with them, quietly and without a second glance back.

Malk was half relieved to see him go. *Brothers, come what may, was it?*

The big newcomer stood like a rocky outcrop, scouring the place with eyes like pricks of ink. He was wider at the shoulders than two of Malk and lent further girth by the shaggy grey pelt he looked to have stolen from an aurochs. In his right hand was a hulking quarterstaff carved from black wood.

Malk stayed where he was, cradling his cannotina, watching curiously as the big man's two lackeys called on the tables and alcoves, forcibly delivering the unspoken message to the few stragglers who hadn't understood it. Malk waited for the Liar's Lament to empty, unseen in the shadows.

When the flock had thinned, Malk rose and strummed the lightest of chords.

The big man's growl as he regarded Malk was like rocks tumbling from a mountain. The wilds of his black beard hid much of his face, but the exposed skin was aged and worn like tired leather.

"Rezzell, I presume?" Malk asked.

"Who gave you that name?"

Malk bowed so low his head nearly touched his boots and offered up his cannotina as though it were a babe. It was a gesture likely wasted on the man-bear, but he would not have it getting back to the Aviary that he hadn't observed courtesy to the letter. That was not how one worked his way back into favour. "My voice is yours, sir. Feed me the song, and I shall play, so long as I deem it fit."

The big man looked at his companions. "Kel, Lem, the minstrel's got scree between his lugs."

Malk smiled dumbly. He had no idea what that meant.

"Raggle him."

He was quite sure he remembered what that meant. He righted himself quickly. "Now, now, fine fellows, there's been a calamitous crossing of, err, strings. I must confess, I like not the way you are converging."

Kel and Lem came on all the same, barrel-chested and thick. One had red hair, the other blond. Both were the same shade of malice. They trapped Malk as though the corner were a cage.

Kel—he of the red hair—reached out his hands to take two fistfuls of Malk's tunic. Lem manoeuvred himself off to the side, his own hands balled into fistfuls of pain. They moved fast for men so big.

Malk's fingers moved faster.

He played a note, and somewhere in the deepest part of his brain, a chord awakened, uncoiled, and slipped forth like an invisible tree root, growing, searching, *building*. It found its target easily enough, and with his bridge secure, Malk sang.

> *"Raggle him, cried the master, and the rats did obey,*
> *They scuttled and scurried on their merry way,*
> *The cheese they'd been sent for was ripe and untouched,*
> *No trap did they see, but they did not see much,*
> *For the cheese they'd be gnawing was seasoned with pain,*
> *And a fistful of flavours they'd nay want again."*

The crackling of firewood could be heard when the last note finally died out, spliced with Lem's muffled groaning as he clutched what looked suspiciously like a broken nose.

180

"Are you sleeting gritted, Kel?" the big man boomed in dismay.

Kel's face had gone the colour of curdled milk under his red hair. He inspected the knuckles that had just crashed into his friend's face. "It weren't...I didn't...I don't..."

The big man turned on Malk. *"You."*

"Me?" said Malk.

"Him?" said Kel.

The big man grimaced. "Who are you?"

Malk cleared his throat. "My name is Malkoriahmavrovianmolossus. Fret not, it's a mouthful even for me, and I'm supposed to be good with words. Malk will suffice; no doubt it tastes better on the tongue."

The big man tried the name in his mouth and found he didn't, in fact, like the taste. He levelled his quarterstaff.

Malk flexed his fingers.

"Enough!" a light voice cut in, keen as a whip.

Malk risked a fleeting glance at the bar. It was the serving maid, she with her mismatched eyes and button nose, innocent and tiny and fragile. *Silly girl.* The oaf would surely crush her if the mood took him. *Two eyes had she, one brown, one green...her skull was smashed to smithereens...* "Fret not, my lady," he called out, "no harm shall befall you."

"Lower your staff, Barrian," the maid urged the big man. "Don't you see? It's *him*, the one who's here to help us. To help me."

Malk pulled a face at the big man. Then his brain caught up to his ears. *"You?* But I thought you were...well, I thought you were..."

"Just a maid?" She smiled mischievously. "Not all lies are like music."

Malk's mouth opened and closed and opened again.

The big man's lip had curled. "Can't be him! He's barely a man; looks green as piss and twice as watery."

The girl moved from behind the bar to stand at Malk's side. "It's him. I wouldn't have called you here otherwise. There's a Hunter's Moon out tonight. Besides, look what he made Kel do to Lem. He's the one we've been waiting for; he's our weapon!"

Barrian glared at Malk expectantly with those beady, black eyes. "That true, minstrel?"

For the first time since he could remember, Malk was at a loss for words. Scrambling for something to say, he stammered, "Someone sent for a Lark. He is I…I am he."

"I'm Rezzell," said the serving maid, who wasn't a serving maid. "It was me who sent for you. They thought me a fool, contacting your Order for help. All of them! They didn't think you'd show at all, but we had no choice. You're our last hope."

The big man's heavy brows had sunk into a scowl. "And you better be worth the waiting."

"Sure he is!" Rezzell answered like Malk wasn't there. "He even got them to open the gates for him! Just like the legends in the tales!"

"Are you a legend, bird boy?"

Malk forced a nervous laugh. "People know my name, if that's what you mean." Technically, that wasn't a lie. Not after the Pauper's Pass, it wasn't.

Barrian lifted his quarterstaff. "They tell you what you're here to do?"

No, they chirping well didn't. Talon Whistron packed me off to the edge of the world without so much as a farewell, a good luck, or a don't die. "Play the tune you are given," the old man had said, "and do not shame us again." Simple enough instructions, to be sure, but something about Cathgol was ruffling Malk's feathers the wrong way. *And what was that she said about a weapon?* "I'm here to play as I can best," he said. "Nothing more, nothing less. But there's protocol to adhere to first. You see, it's every Lark's duty to investi——"

Before Malk could finish, Rezzell burst forward, wrapped her arms around his waist, and squeezed. "Gods bless you, Malkoriahmavrovianmolossus! You came! Say you'll help us get rid of *him*! You'll save us, won't you?"

"Well, I . . . I mean, that depends. I'd have to . . ." *She remembered my name.* "What seems to be the problem?"

The three of them took a long table in the centre of the empty common room. Kel and Lem loitered by the door, the former tapping the wood at his back as he eyed Malk with disdain. *Tap, tap, tap, tap.* Malk could feel the vibrations rising in his brain.

"Could you be a fine fellow and stop that?" he asked, not unkindly.

"I don't take orders from you, *Raven.*"

"He's not a Raven," Rezzell said.

"And be thankful for that," Malk added coldly.

Kel scowled, but the tapping stopped.

Once she'd added logs to the hearth, Rezzell served Malk a bowl of the fare she had talked about. It was supposed to be woodman's stew, he suspected. It tasted more like wood than stew, though, and he doubted the people of Heartland would have fed it to their dogs. Still, ravenous from the road as he was, he tackled it manfully as Rezzell told her story.

Back at the Aviary, he had commonly associated words like "tyrant" and "grief" and "suffering" with the most far-flung borders of the Empire. Of course, he had done so over games of dice, bantering with the sons of Heartland's gentry about unwashed places they would only ever see on dusty maps. Hearing Rezzell venomously spit those same words over ale denser than his bones wasn't half so amusing. By the time she seasoned her tale with phrases such as "overthrow" and "rebellion," any nod to banter had long died its death.

In an attempt to extract some passion from the room—Barrian looked ready to murder the first thing that chanced to come through the door—Malk moved to simplify things. "So, this Count Kerstoff poisoned his lord father and assumed control of Cathgol. I'm right so far?"

"He's taken over, that's right," Rezzell replied. "He imprisoned the Elders of Cathgol first, them whose job it is to look out for the people, and he's passed new laws. *His* laws. The city is succumbed to fear."

Malk stroked his cannotina. *Oh, Talon Whistron, you've gone too far this time.* "You'll forgive my scepticism, but this sounds like an issue for the Imperial Court. I'm more in the minor disputes business, you see: aggrieved spouses; unpaid labourers; lofty lords who—"

Barrian's huge fist came down on the table. "You cost us all the coin we've got and all we could borrow besides. If you're a fraud, I'll—"

"Calm," Rezzell interrupted softly, silencing the big man by placing her small hand over his. "Barrian's village was razed to the ground by Count Kerstoff's men when he refused to let them treble the taxes."

Barrian bristled. "Homes n' hovels can be rebuilt. But those lads didn't do nothing wrong."

Rezzell gave Barrian a look of pity. "The Count took every man and boy from the village. They say he's raising an army to take the Upper Helm back from the Empire."

Malk set down his spoon for fear he'd throw up whatever he put in his mouth. "And no one's stopped him?"

"Folk have been acting all kinds o' strange since he took over." Rezzell chewed her lip nervously. "The castle garrison sweeps the city on the regular to round up his detractors. Anyone who speaks out is plucked from the streets like they weren't ever there."

"On what grounds?"

"Haven't you been listening?" Rezzell asked. "He doesn't need a reason! Cathgol's no longer a place for something as trivial as fairness. Plenty of people tried to stop him in the beginning, but it weren't no use. There ain't many of us left now, just a few brave souls. Common folk, living under the sword. Resisting."

"Resisting," Malk repeated.

"Yeah. We're a resistance, if you like," Rezzell told him.

And I'm your weapon. "Tell me again how I fit into all of this?"

Rezzell stared longingly at the cannotina. "We cause mischief where we can, spreading dissent, reminding people of what life was like before. But it's not enough; they've lost their resolve.

We mean to take back Cathgol, *have* to take back Cathgol. Rally our men, strike at Count Kerstoff himself, remove him before it's too late. We don't lack none for courage, you'll see. Only, we can't fight when the Count is protected by walls and gates and guards."

Barrian grinned. The gesture looked utterly foreign on his face. "That's where you fit in, bird boy. We can't assault him, but we don't have to. Not if we can get in."

"In…as in *in*…as in *into the castle in*…" Malk dabbed at his brow and realised he was sweating. He could ill afford another cock-up; he was meant to be proving he could be trusted, not proving he could incite treason.

Rezzell placed a soft hand on his shoulder and leaned in close. The smell of fresh pine filled Malk's nose. And her eyes…*A man could drown in those mismatched eyes.* "It's the Count's name day on the morrow; he's holding a celebration in the Old Square. Come with me and decide for yourself," she begged.

Talon Whistron's words echoed between Malk's ears. *Do not shame us again.* There would be no greater shame than returning to Heartland with his cannotina tucked between his legs, of that he was certain. The ballads they would sing of him didn't bear thinking about. Even so, Larks had a duty to balance each job as it came. *If I leave on the morrow, I could be home in time for midsummer.* Every second he spent here was a second he would rather spend dicing and drinking expensive wine. *No! Patience, Malky. Remember the Pauper's Pass.* "I…I guess I'll see this Count for myself."

Barrian grunted. "Good. 'Cause I'll break your sleeting wings if you don't."

His waking breath steamed in the morning air. Malk rose stiff as a board and in desperate need of the piss he had denied himself all night for fear his manhood would freeze off. He wondered if it was he that smelled so badly, the pelts that covered him, or the horses he had shared his bed with.

The stable was more dilapidated shed than shelter and not

where he'd expected to spend any night of service in seven lifetimes. Sadly, there wasn't much to be done for the suspicions of men—these particular men were convinced that Malk was going to take over their minds while they slept. To that end, he'd been relegated from the hostility of the Liar's Lament to the ignominy of its back door.

Cursing the Aviary, he sought a corner to relieve himself. Through the holes in the crumbling mortar of the stable wall, he could well enough see that which had been hidden in the darkness.

The lower half of Cathgol looked to be a morass of narrow wynds and buildings huddling tight as whispering thieves. Most were timber and thatch, kissed by snowdrifts and shuttered against elements and eyes both. The city climbed the incline of the rise upon which it had been built, up and up to more respectable lodgings and wider streets, from such heights as Malk guessed the residents spat at places like the Liar's Lament. Prevailing over all was the monstrosity he took to be Count Kerstoff's keep. He could see that well enough, too, perched like an eyrie, its slew of dark spires and twisted towers soaring up into a cloud-speckled sky.

Too far indeed, Talon Whistron. He shook himself dry and strummed his cannotina.

"Cathgol, oh, Cathgol, where rich men are poor,
Where poor men are poorer, and hope is no more,
Where a minstrel may warble, but a bird cannot fly,
Where struggle is truth, and the truth is a lie,
Where one must needs venture when marred by disgrace,
Cathgol, oh, Cathgol, what a god-awful pla——"

The light cough startled him.

Malk spun so fast the cannotina almost flew from his grasp. "Rezzell! G-good morn to you. I assumed myself alone."

The girl wore a simple brown tunic and a warm smile against the chill. She was weighed down by pails of water for the horses yet moved with the ease of a prowling cat. "You've a beautiful voice."

Malk felt his cheeks flush. "Heard me, did you?"

"Just the bit about Cathgol."

"Well, I, err, always start the day with a silly song. Take no heed."

"Did you rest well?"

Well as a blacksmith's anvil. Malk nodded enthusiastically.

"I'm sorry you had to sleep out here. The others...you scared them last night, even if they'd never admit it."

Oh, but of course. They live their lives grovelling to this lord or that, following decrees made by emperors they'll never meet. A handsome fellow with a glib tongue shows up, though, and suddenly everyone's a paragon of independence. "It's quite all right; roofs are overrated things anyway."

Rezzell set down the pails. "They're good men, truly. Some were better than that before this all started."

Malk tried to imagine Barrian as a good man, perhaps poling a boat down a canal in Heartland or offering a ride to a stranded wanderer on his oxcart. His imagination was a vivid one, but it had its limits. "Give them time. I tend to grow on people."

Rezzell looked doubtful. "Kel thinks you're a demon in a man's skin. He's wrapped cloth around his ears to protect himself."

That made Malk smile. "Serves him right. He called me a Raven."

"Some men would take that as a compliment. Isn't a soul in the Upper Helm who doesn't fear Ravens. To hear their song means death."

"Well, he has nothing more to fear from me."

"And me?" she asked playfully. "Between us, is it your beautiful voice I should watch out for? Or that fancy lute?"

Malk lifted an eyebrow. "*Cannotina.* At the Aviary, they teach that sharing secrets is for simpletons."

"Well now, you don't strike me as one of those." Rezzell winked with her brown eye, and Malk's fingers danced unbidden across the three golden strings.

"A Lark without his cannotina is a horse without hooves, a sailor without a ship, a bow without a string."

"A man without a roof?"

Malk chuckled. He felt warmer already.

"I want to thank you again. For answering my call," Rezzell said.

He couldn't honestly claim to have had much choice in the matter, but he wasn't about to tell Rezzell that. "How is it you knew of the Aviary?"

She sidled in closer, inspecting the cannotina, smelling now of ginger and roasted nuts. The scent put Malk in mind of a winter's eve before a Heartland fire. "My pa raised me on tales of the Owls and the Thrushes, the Robins and the rest. The Liar's Lament was his before it came to me. He told me that back when the Empire was great, it were the Larks as kept the peace: Proud Perligovarinian; Bold Bakkahdosyrrian; Ingranideon the Impish. I know them all; they were heroes. Like you."

Pride tickled Malk's chest. His mother had feasted him on those same stories. "I daresay, I don't belong in such distinguished company."

"You being here makes everything possible," Rezzell said earnestly. "You don't understand."

His fingers came alive. "Take me to this Count, and perhaps I will."

They set off from the Liar's Lament with a wan sun climbing wearily into the winter sky. Rezzell led them via pinch-thin alleyways that latticed their way up the hill like sticks in a crow's nest. They avoided the bigger streets, just as they'd avoided the company of Barrian. The big man had complained at that, but Rezzell didn't think it wise to bring him so close to the castle. "You stick out like a splinter from a thumb, even on a day like today," she had said. Malk had to agree, though he pitied the man who would have to remove such a splinter.

In his place, Barrian had sent Lem, and so Malk had to live with knife-like glares being thrown at him for the entirety of their journey. The man's nose wasn't broken after all, but that technicality hadn't softened him any.

It was nearing midday when they finally came to the Old Square, a vast space boxed on three sides by high establishments built in pale stone.

Here, fur-swaddled folk gathered in crowds, a thrum of excitement riding the wind like a vulture waiting to feed. Jesters and jugglers tumbled and tricked their way through the bodies, and vendors hawked steaming spits of meat and poured horns of beer from barrels they could roll over the frost-glazed flagstones. Bards meandered, paining Malk's ears with their strumming, delivering rousing songs of Count Kerstoff's grace and glory. *A tremendous lot of jubilance for a tyrant*, Malk thought. *Though Rezzell did say people had been acting strange.*

"Where's the Count?" he asked.

"Where do you think?" Lem replied, voice thick with scorn. "Behind his high walls."

And high they certainly were. On the fourth side of the square, a colossal curtain wall loomed. Rezzell's gaze settled on something in that direction.

Malk tracked her mismatched eyes to a bulky timber structure that had risen near the gatehouse. A throng of people was slowly thickening at its foot. "What's that?"

"Part of the Count's celebrations," Rezzell answered.

"Then let's get closer to it," Malk said. "I need to see the man properly."

But the girl only wrung her hands and swapped a look with Lem that Malk couldn't have missed. "We can't," she said finally. "There's something we didn't mention last night. Something else."

"Else?"

"We think...I think that the Count might have a wytch in his employ. It'd explain how the people have been behaving."

"A WYT...a wytch?"

Rezzell bit her lip. "It's a messy situation."

Malk scoffed. "I once drank half a cask of wine, fouled my

breeches, and hurled the contents of my stomach over a little girl who tried to help me. That was a messy situation. Messy how?"

Rezzell looked over her shoulders as if to make sure no one was in earshot. "The Count had an older sister," she whispered. "Before. The heir to Cathgol, she was. It was said she dabbled in the old magics that were the way of things in the Upper Helm before the Empire. Her father banished her to the Utter Upper years ago. Now that he's dead, well, it could be that she's come back. If we get too close…wytches see all manner of things, everyone knows that."

Lem spat on the floor. "All manner."

Malk's palms had grown slick on his cannotina. Talon Benecbar had held any number of seminars on the matter of wytches back at the Aviary. As it happened, Malk realised he could recall precisely none of them.

"Just stay close to me," Rezzell said. "And don't draw attention."

She took them to the fountain in the middle of the square, well away from the curtain wall, where a troupe of performers, all colourful jerkins and jingling bells, were entertaining a growing flock. They eyed Malk and his cannotina with suspicion.

"Find another spot," the troupe master, a hook-nosed man with a bulging gut, ordered roughly between acts.

Lem backed away with his palms raised, heeding Rezzell's instruction. Rezzell dipped her head and apologised profusely, but the troupe master shoved her so hard she almost fell over her heels.

Malk's blood rose of an instant. "I rather reckon we'll remain. I'm inclined to play a song, now that I consider it."

"You are thinking this is some flea market competition?" the troupe master hissed.

"Tell me your name, sir, so I know who I'm competing with."

"I am being the Great Grolion of Groyne. My troupe will perform for Count Kerstoff himself this very eve. Be competing with that!"

Malk attacked his strings so hard his fingers hurt.

"Great men, they vie for valour, while lessers vie for coin,
A man can sense the difference, like a pulsing in his groin,
Like eagles do, the great men soar, so the world can see their wings,
Like fleas, the lessers cluster, to lick the heels of kings,
These fleas they jingle and jangle, and profit be their song,
But nothing's great that comes with hate, so be gone, foul fleas,
*   be gone."*

Grolion wasted no time in ordering his performers away from the fountain, much to their surprise. Rezzell looked half-embarrassed as she watched them skulk by.

"I apologise," Malk said. "Far from my finest work."

"How do you do that?" Rezzell asked. "Make people, you know…"

Malk exhaled, and his anger left him. "My tutor, Talon Whistron, says weak minds are made for moulding. A tug here, a push there; some people are easier to move than others."

"But you're just saying words?"

"There's power in *just* words; to steer or support, influence or inspire, hurt or hearten or heal. The cannotina builds a bridge for them to be heard."

Rezzell stared at the instrument again, in the same admiring way she had at the Liar's Lament. "Is it something that—" she broke off, abashed, "that you can teach?"

Lem leaned in, suddenly interested. Malk only sighed. "If I could, I'd be a rich man. I was simply born with a soul full of song."

The crowd was thinning before them, most of its number making their way over to the curtain wall. Rezzell set herself down on the fountain's edge and ran a hand through the water. "Tell me how you came to be a Lark."

"I'm my mother's son," Malk said, but Rezzell's look told him that wouldn't suffice, so he continued. "She was a singer in a travelling troupe, 'twas she who raised me. I used to sing to crowds and return with a hat full of coins, or test rhymes on the jugglers and have them doing all kinds of peculiar things.

191

I had no control of it, you understand, but my mother knew something was awry. When I was ten, she took me to the Aviary for the High Ygle's inspection. I've been there since, striving to serve through song."

"And your father?"

"I never met him," Malk said without sadness. "He was a drummer with the Southern Alliance. He marched with the rebels against the Imperial Army in the Battle of the Splintered Shinn, the same year I was born."

Rezzell sucked in a breath. "The massacre at Shinn. The rebels tried to fight and were slaughtered."

"Yes, well, that scoundrel survived the slaughter. Can't really say he fought, either. He swore to my mother that he never once lifted his sword."

"Where is he now?"

"I haven't a clue. Let's just say he wasn't welcome in Heartland."

Lem sneered. "Didn't lift his sword? Can't have been much of a soldier."

Malk smiled back. "I didn't say he was a soldier. I said he was—"

A deep horn suddenly sounded from one of the castle towers, and in the next moment, the great gate was groaning open. Men-at-arms emerged, rank and file, spears aimed skyward to form a thicket of steel. At their head strode a man in blue furs, the thickness of his beard matched by the ropes of white hair that blew behind him in the breeze.

And he looked big. Perhaps bigger even than Barrian.

"That's the Count?" Malk asked. *Seven strings, what do they feed these people?*

"Captain Otto," Rezzell said. "The Count's uncle and head of his guard."

"Wicked as a rusty nail, that one," Lem said.

Rezzell hissed. "There he is!" She pointed to a straight-backed, keen-featured man riding behind the soldiers. "Count Kerstoff!"

Malk had been half-expecting a gaunt figure, twisted, probably battle-scarred. He had been expecting a man like Captain Otto. The Count, though, looked almost as well-groomed as a peer that could frequent the wine gardens of Heartland. He was younger than Malk had imagined, too. A cape the colour of ice flowed from his shoulders, but his beard and hair were auburn. Cheers went up from the crowd, but the man waved them into silence with a gloved hand.

Behind the Count trundled a cart laden with loaves of black bread. Kerstoff gave a command, and his guards began throwing the bounty into the sea of bodies.

Malk looked to Rezzell. "He doesn't seem that..."

"Evil?" she spat like a tomcat. "Not all lies are like music, remember."

"Right." He strained his eyes desperately, but there was no wytch that he could see. *What do wytches even look like?* Talon Benecbar would know of a certainty.

Then Rezzell's hiss slipped into a gasp. Malk followed her gaze to the gate behind the Count.

The prisoner was a small grey man, half-starved, with irons around his wrists. He cut a stoic figure as he shuffled his way to the scaffold and climbed the steps. The jostling crowd erupted.

With the abruptness of a hammer blow to his gut, it all dawned on Malk; the scaffold, the crowd, the old man in chains. *This is no celebration. It's an execution.*

Rezzell whimpered beside him.

"Sleeting hell," rasped Lem.

"You know him?" Malk managed.

A sole tear rolled from Rezzell's green eye. "Tot. A friend of my pa's. I had no idea it...today...he..."

Malk's knuckles went white on the neck of the cannotina as a noose was fitted. His knees gave a wobble that threatened to steal his balance. In Heartland, they put thieves in the stocks, and Malk had friends who had been publicly denounced for their deviances. This savagery struck a different chord entirely, though, and Malk didn't know if he could stomach its tune.

Below the walls, the Count rode up to the scaffold and looked to be hearing words from his prisoner. *He's pleading for his life,* Malk realised.

He couldn't properly see what happened next, far away as they were, but the gathered drew in a sudden collective breath, and Count Kerstoff sharply wheeled his courser away.

Somewhere beyond the knot of bodies, a drum began to roll. Malk felt energy slowly start to stir within him. It began in his head, then rolled out like a wave across his body. Rising, rising, rising. He strummed a note on the cannotina to give himself something else to listen to.

"Malk..." the word slid lightly from Rezzell's lips, though it was heavy with pain.

Malk hung his head and tried to ignore the drum. He knew what she meant to ask. "I can't."

"But...Kel, last night? And the guards at the gate? You made them do what you wanted."

"Weak minds," he said. "There are too many people here. A truly great Lark? Maybe they could control them all." *But I'm far from one of those.*

Halfway across the square, the drum roll died. Moments later, a trapdoor banged open, and the crowd was lost to a sudden delirium. Rezzell nuzzled her head into Malk's cloak, and his arm was suddenly around her, though he couldn't remember having the thought to put it there.

Back at the Liar's Lament, they nested themselves at the same table Malk had taken the night before. The place was empty and silent as a grave, but for Rezzell's weeping.

Malk wanted to comfort her but didn't have the first idea how. *Perhaps I should sing her a song?* But he quickly decided that was a terrible idea. Instead, he busied himself looking for Lem, who had suddenly made himself scarce. Malk suspected he knew what that meant.

"Tot was a good man," Rezzell said eventually, voice quavering. "A kind man. He carved me a doll when I was a girl."

Malk struggled for something appropriate to say. He still felt nauseous. "He died well," he produced, then instantly regretted it. *Well? He died with a rope around his neck to the sound of a few hundred people cheering.* The sight would haunt his dreams for a long time to come.

"I'm sorry, Malk. Dragging you up here…into all of this. It was a mistake."

"A mistake?"

"It's hopeless. You saw what we're up against."

Her words stung like needles. "If we're talking mistakes, I've a tale you should hear. Ever been to the Innard?"

Rezzell looked up, eyes still wet with tears. She shook her head.

"Well, old Malky here was sent to the Innard to stop a thief who had swindled the Earl of Bowellton. Dull place, the Innard, full of green forests that all look the chirping same. Talon Whistron advised me to track my mark from afar and wait while I shaped a suitable song. You see, it wasn't enough that I simply get back the stolen goods. No, Earl Bowellton wanted a touch of flair, wanted the thief to turn his cart around, take it back, and walk himself down into the dungeons."

Rezzell sniffled. "What happened?"

"Well, in my infinite wisdom, I decided to skip the watching and the waiting. I settled down at a place called the Pauper's Pass and prepared to bamboozle this brigand with a ballad. Alas, my performance fell on deaf ears. Literally."

"Wait, you mean the thief was…"

"As a stone. He escaped, goods and all. Needless to say, Earl Bowellton didn't like that none too much, and the Aviary even less."

"A mistake of monolithic measure…"

"As punishment, they gave the detail nobody would take to the Lark that nobody trusts. The Talons do so love their irony."

Rezzell giggled despite herself. She reached up and wiped her green eye dry. "What's it like there, at the Aviary?"

Malk spread his hands. "Well, it's terribly tedious to tell the truth."

"You said you were good with words?"

195

So he relented and told her all about the Larks and their voices, the Owls and their visions, the Talons and the Thrushes and the Finches and all the rest. He talked at length about the Aviary itself, too; the Ploom Paradeway with its many vibrant colours; the Ygle's Roost, that tower of speckled brown marble that kissed the clouds; the halls and the corridors, the courtyards and customs and characters that gave the place its life.

Rezzell drank it all in as though lost in a daze. It wasn't until Malk's mouth got dry that he realised he'd rambled past the point of coherency. He didn't even think he could remember half of what he had said. *Perhaps it's I who's in the daze.*

"Heartland sounds like a kind place," Rezzell said. "I mean to go there someday when our work is done."

"Why not today?" Malk asked softly. With Rezzell no longer weeping, it was time to ask some questions of his own. "It's warm and safe, and there are places you could get work. Seven strings, I drink in half of them."

Rezzell faltered. "Malk, I..."

"Why are you here, Rezzell?" he pressed pointedly. "You knew there was an execution today and said nothing."

"It's a mess—"

"It could be you up on that scaffold tomorrow, you know. Or ridden down by the Count's men the day after that. For what?"

She bristled. "You said you never knew your father. I admired mine, right up until the moment I lost him. He was one of the first."

"The first?"

"To defy the Count's rule; to be taken one night as though he'd never existed; to disappear. The Liar's Lament was his pride and joy. Now he's gone, decaying in the Count's dungeons for all I know.

"So yes, I knew about today. Every week I go to the square and pray that it's not him I see shuffling out that gate. Maybe you're right. Maybe this is no place for me anymore. But Cathgol's all I've ever known. I won't abandon it."

Oh, Malky. You feathered fool. "Rezzell, I—"

"My pa never stopped telling stories about the Aviary and the

196

heroes of old. That's why I begged your Order for help, even when all the others said I was gritted." For one moment, she looked like giving in to her anger, tears once again glistening in her mismatched eyes. But in the next, she reached out, took Malk's hand, and planted upon it the lightest of kisses. "We need such a hero now, sure as granite. I thought you could be him, Malkoriahmavrovianmolossus."

Malk's fingers began to dance. *Hear that, Talon Whistron? It's the Larks who fill the pages of history. A hero...that's what I was sent here for. And when I get back to the Aviary, well, I'll be a hero there as well, and the Pauper's Pass forgotten. There goes Malky Malk, hero of the Upper Helm. Put a stop to an uprising in its tracks, don't you know?* But before he could get his words out, he felt a giant shadow fall over him.

Malk swivelled, cannotina at the ready. Barrian loomed, flanked by Kel and Lem and a dozen others. The big man thumped the ground with the butt of his quarterstaff. "See what you needed to see, did you, bird boy?"

"And more, unfortunately."

"And? You gonna help us or not? We've had about a bellyful of you and your queer get."

Malk rubbed the neck of his cannotina, mind whirring with thought. *A hero, aye.* "Well, that depends entirely on how many men you can muster tonight."

Barrian grimaced, seeing but not comprehending. It was Rezzell who registered what he'd said. *"Tonight?"*

"Tonight." The way forward was suddenly unfolding in Malk's ears like a masterpiece he hadn't even written. "In Heartland, we give the gift of a surprise for one's name day. If you're serious about this, how many men can you rally?"

"Enough," Barrian said.

"Enough to do what needs be done?"

The big man's beady eyes settled in a glare. "I said enough, didn't I?"

"Good. If I'm to play this song of yours, I have one rule: no one gets hurt. I'm orchestrating a coup, not red carnage. It might be that the Count's men are innocent of any wrongdoing if there's a wytch involved."

"No violence," Rezzell agreed. "We're not like him."

Malk rose. "You have a plan for after? For when the Count is taken?"

"We'll start by emptying the dungeons and freeing the Elders of Cathgol. They'll know what to do next." Rezzell was breathless with sudden excitement. "But Malk, the walls, the guards...how do we get in?"

Weak minds are made for moulding. "I need you to tell me everything you know about Count Kerstoff."

The line of fools was seven strong, embellished by hats and bells and enough patchwork colours to make a blind man's eyes water. The puppeteers waited in front and the jugglers behind. Further back still were the firebreathers, and beyond them the stiltmen, draped in gargantuan cloaks of faux velvet, carrying wooden legs that would make them ten feet tall. Waiting right at the rear in his conflicting raiment, Malk reckoned he blended in just fine.

He watched Great Grolion of Groyne carefully, all the same. The fat man had laughed at him when he'd returned to the Old Square to announce that he'd be joining his troupe.

"Give me a song," Grolion had demanded, a smile on his thick lips and all memory of Malk's earlier song forgotten. "The boys will be playing it as I am kicking you back down the hill."

Another song Malk had given him, and the laughter had been replaced with dull obedience in the man's eyes. He wore that obedience now as he addressed the young guard at the castle's postern gate, boasting how his troupe was the best north of Neckelhaim. The Count, he claimed, was in for a show he'd never forget.

When the talking was done, Malk shuffled through with the rest of them. A few of the others had given him suspicious glances, and one or two had been bold enough to ask his credentials. For the most part, though, they had let him be, too focused on their own preparations to care for the eccentric bard added to their ranks at the last minute.

Night had long since fallen. Outside the castle walls, Cathgol had become a place of eerie quiet, its streets so cold that no one walked them without exceptional reason.

Within was a different story.

The service passage they were ushered into was alive with light, cloying with warmth, rich with the smells of roasted hog. Thereafter, they passed into the outer ward, where noise from the great hall spilt forth and wreaked its havoc in the form of undulating echoes lapping off the walls.

Malk's thoughts went to Rezzell; they'd hardly been anyplace else since she'd planted that kiss on his hand. Picturing her gave him a quiet comfort to hold on to, even if his stomach felt like a bag of eels. *You can't be a hero without doing something heroic*, he reminded himself.

In truth, it was the Count's sister that unsettled him most. Rezzell had said that wytches could see all manner of things. If she saw him and his cannotina coming, he didn't think any song was like to save him. Over and over again had he tried to recall Talon Benecbar's seminars, but they had proved stubborn in their elusiveness. "Conniving creatures, and viciously ambitious," he could recall the weaselly tutor saying, not that it helped him any.

A raucous cheer went up as Grolion's troupe entered Count Kerstoff's pillared hall. The ceiling was high and vaulted, the walls hung with tapestries bearing the crowned helm of Cathgol. A space had been cleared before the dais that was awash with light from bowls of burning oil.

The fools went first, tumbling and rolling, fanning out amongst the tables and benches. Then the jugglers with their knives and the firebreathers after them, sending forth gouts of red flame.

Malk reckoned the guests to number over one hundred. He took them for Cathgol's elite; big burly types with hands like hams and beards a small child could hide in. At least their swords and axes hung from pegs on the walls, beyond reach at a moment's notice.

When the stiltmen lumbered into the hall atop their stilts, a fresh wave of appreciation thundered from the benches. Malk used it to weave his way to the edge of the space before the dais, where he leaned against a pillar, inconspicuous in the chaos.

Count Kerstoff sat at the centre of the high table, dressed in an ice-blue tunic, watching with apparent awe as the stiltmen engaged in mock battles with each other. Captain Otto towered close by him, leaning on a giant axe. He had hard eyes, thick brows, a misshapen nose and weather-beaten cheeks. *This one could be trouble.* But it would not be his trouble. *Perhaps Barrian and he will collide, and the world will collapse under the singular strain.*

A voice suddenly screamed inside his head. *The wytch! Find the wytch!*

But try as Malk might, he could not see any woman who looked like a wytch up on the dais. *There are no women there at all. Perhaps Rezzell was wrong. Perhaps the sister has not returned.*

Grolion's entertainment lasted so long that when the fat man's men finally produced their flamboyant finale and withdrew from the hall so that the feast could begin, Malk was almost relieved.

Almost.

As the servers went about their business and a blanket of noise returned to the hall, Malk stepped to the foot of the dais and cleared his throat. This plan of his would work, he told himself. *It has to. Rather difficult to sing with a noose around your neck, Malky.*

"Count Kerstoff, my lord!" he called. "I wish you good health and better tidings on this most wonderful of days."

The Count glanced down at Malk in surprise. Up close, he was a handsome man, his eyes soft and curious. "Do I know you, sir?"

"I'm a bard, my lord."

"A bard?"

Malk bowed. "The best."

The Count looked to his servants. "I thought the music was to come *after* the food?"

Malk offered up his cannotina before they could answer. Its

three strings gleamed golden in the candlelight. "I've travelled from Heartland. Perchance I may gift you a song to help season your meal?"

The Count studied him thoughtfully. For half a quaver, Malk thought he'd made a grand mistake. Then a cheerful grin spread over the man's face. "A splendid idea."

Malk bowed again and cleared his throat.

But the Count wasn't finished. He raised a hand, and the hall fell into a reluctant hush. "This man has journeyed all the way from Heartland to sing for me on my name day. What be your name, Bard?"

Malk felt eyes boring into him from every angle. "Err... Malko——"

"Shall we have a song from this weary wanderer?" the Count asked the benches.

The roar was deafening. The guests began to pound on the tables, and Malk felt energy pulsing through him. He adjusted his hands and tried to swallow. Only the moisture in his throat had betrayed him. "Ye...yes," he croaked, if only to distract from the drumming.

And his fingers reluctantly began to move.

A biting chill gripped the outer ward, but Malk hardly noticed it under his cloak of fear. The sounds of the feast swept from the hall, yet not so loud as to drown the frantic beating of his heart as he waited in the shadows of a nearby alcove.

Malk had built his bridge, but were its foundations remotely strong? Now that he tried to recollect his performance, he wasn't even sure he'd built it in the right place. There were so many people watching that he might have been *playing* to the wrong person entirely. *Hero of the Upper Helm! You'll be lucky if you're not headless in the Upper Helm!*

Seconds passed disguised as centuries. No one emerged from the hall. The others would be waiting and ready, he knew: Barrian with his quarterstaff; Kel and Lem and whatever bodies they had been able to summon; Rezzell...*Rezzell.* The thought

201

of letting her down at this stage was almost as bad as the grisly death the Count would offer if Malk was caught.

The dungeons, he thought in panic. If he could find them, perhaps he could smuggle Rezzell's father out of the castle. And the Elders of Cathgol, too, whatever good that might do. *A small consolation before I wander into the wild to die of shame.*

Something creaked away to his left.

Malk pushed off from the wall, fingers poised to play. The figure that slipped from a shadowed door wore fine boots that rang on the flagstones as he crossed the outer ward alone. *Thump, thump, thump.* Malk's heart beat all the louder as the man passed by a torch, and he glimpsed the icy-blue colouring of his tunic.

Count Kerstoff strode purposefully to the nearest stair and marched up the steps to the wall walk. Malk's attention turned to the guards at their stations. One by one, they received the Count, first surprised, then confused, then delighted. One by one, they descended to cross the outer ward and enter the hall.

Malk dared to hope. *Those chirping dunces are actually buying it.* He couldn't blame them; if the High Ygle offered him the chance to toast a name day instead of freezing his plums off, he'd have done the same in a quaver.

The walls steadily emptied, the silhouette sentinels abandoning their positions for the promise of wine and warmth. When the last one had made his way into the hall, the Count returned to the door he had slipped through.

Malk was waiting for him. "A toast for your name day," he said, "what a fine idea, your exquisiteness. But what is a toast without friends?"

The Count pondered that for a moment. "Friends?"

Malk strummed a chord, and a heavy twang rippled forth. Sustaining a bridge was easier than building one, and the Count smiled gleefully. *"Friends*, of course."

Malk led him back to the service passage, occasionally sending forth chords, more than occasionally checking their backs for soldiers and steel. The majority of the servants saw Count

Kerstoff and dipped their heads, or else scuttled to get out of his way.

The same young guard stood at the postern gate. He stiffened like a hare before a hawk. "My...lord."

"I wish to see the friends," the Count said. "Open the gate."

The man rushed to heft the crossbar from the door. Yet no sooner had he dislodged it than did a voice sound from the shadows. "Wait."

A second guard stepped forward. This one was an old hand; Malk could tell that just to look at him, grey and stern. *And a problem.* "Is all right, my nobleness?"

The Count furrowed his brows. "I wish to...my...my..."

"He wishes to see his friends," Malk finished quickly. "You heard him."

But the grey guard's eyes thinned. "Friends? Ain't no friends coming by this gate that I know of. We got orders from Captain Otto."

Malk's fingers went instinctively to his three strings, but he stopped himself. He could play for the guard, sure enough, but not without risking his bridge with the Count. "If you'd just open the gate, you'll see."

"Open..." the Count mumbled.

The younger guard removed the crossbar and looked to his superior hesitantly, who in turn stared more inquisitively at Count Kerstoff. "My nobleness, you wish for us to open the gate? You are granite?"

The Count's frown deepened. Malk felt the man slipping away, the bridge between them weakening without notes to sustain it. "Gate?" the Count asked. "Wait...I—"

Whatever he might have said was blown beyond all hearing as the postern gate crashed open. The cold of the night swept in, along with a mob fronted by the second largest man Malk had ever seen.

Barrian struck the younger guard hard with his quarterstaff, knocking him to the floor. Then he levelled it at the older one before he could do anything but gape in dismay. Men followed him into the castle armed with hammers and axes and notched blades. *Common folk, living under the sword*, Rezzell had said, but the only men Malk could see looked used to holding swords, not living under them. They filled the corridor behind Barrian, a ragtag pack of hounds waiting for their master's signal.

Kel and Lem seized hold of Count Kerstoff. The man seemed woken from a deep sleep.

Malk looked at the guard on the floor. "We agreed no violence."

Barrian closed the distance. "Where's the garrison?"

"In the hall, expecting the Count to make a toast. They'll give no trouble now that you have their lord. The castle is yours." *The Hero of the Upper Helm*, Malk reminded himself. It would make for a good song. Indeed, he intended to write it himself.

Barrian came to a stop before him and, in the torchlight, Malk saw something wild in his eyes.

"Where's Rezzell?" he asked.

But the big man only hefted his quarterstaff over his head and smiled that foreign smile.

"No! Barrian, wait!"

The staff came down. And Malk screamed.

"A Lark's best friend is silence," Talon Whistron was fond of saying. "A chalice waiting to be filled when the whole world has a thirst."

Malk wondered if the old man would say the same, sat on his own in a dungeon built into the bowels of a freezing hill at the edge of the world. The thought evoked a pitiful laugh, but when his fingers tried to dance across his strings, they found only air.

His hands still tingled with that massive final release. It was his heart that hurt, though, the way a man hurts when he's lost the most faithful of friends. *That hulking heathen. He smashed it to smithereens ... my poor baby.*

At first, Malk hadn't understood. He hadn't even wanted to understand, so distraught was he in his shock. He'd had plenty of time to digest things as they dragged him feebling and screaming to the underbelly of Count Kerstoff's castle, though. Down into the deep darkness of the earth, into the confines of a cramped cell of cold stone, lit only by a slim candle and sealed by an oaken door ten inches thick.

Barrian had betrayed him. Had betrayed *them*. No doubt he had planned to wrestle Cathgol into his own meaty hands from the beginning, and Rezzell had been naive enough to give him the keys. Kel and Lem and the others had always been his men; that much had been as subtle as a peacock in plume. *Still, you didn't see it. The fool you are, Malk!*

He only prayed that Rezzell wasn't a fool, too, that she had the sense to see the trap that had been sprung. She was a keen girl, that much couldn't be questioned. *But could she ever have expected this?*

Malk pondered that—and his own supreme shortcomings—for what seemed like hours, until his arse cheeks were numb and his back groaned from leaning against the wall. There was no way to mark the passage of time beyond watching the candle slowly burn down. It would soon gutter out, and Malk would be left blind as well as stupid.

"Where one seeks redemption but finds only disgrace," he sang.

"Cathgol, oh, Cathgol, what a god-awful place...place...place..."

His echo taunted him for a time, living on far longer than it should have. It sounded angry and flustered.

Not an echo, a voice! Malk crawled across his cell to a spot beneath the candle where the mortar was ancient, and the slightest of fissures fought to open up between his cell and the one beside it. "Hello?"

There was silence for so long a time that Malk began to edge away from the candle. Then he heard it, gravelly and haggard, and yet without a hint of fear. "Enough of the damned singing."

Malk's heart gave a flutter. "Rezzell's father!"

"What?"

"Your daughter. Her name is Rezzell, yes?"

"Where did you get that name?"

It is him. He's alive! "I'm a friend of your daughter's. Malk is my name. We broke into Count Kerstoff's castle tonight to set

205

things to rights, but we were betrayed. Fret not. I believe Rezzell might have escaped.

"She told me all about you. I know you've been down here for some time. I'm a Lark, see, come to topple the Count and restore freedom. When word gets back to my Order that I've been imprisoned, they'll surely send help."

A lengthy pause followed. "You're the sleeting bard. The one from the feast."

"That's me!" Malk said enthusiastically. Then he frowned. *How could he possibly know that?*

The stranger growled. "I knew something was off. I should have known it was her."

Malk was nonplussed. "Whatever do you mean?"

"This Rezzell of yours. Her eyes are different, no? One brown, one blue-green?"

The chastest maid I'd ever seen. "Yes," Malk said. "Your...your daughter?"

The man sighed. "My niece. And you, Lark, just put a wytch on the throne of Cathgol."

Malk blinked dumbly in the dimness. "I did what now?"

"Elzzler Kerstoff, banished to the Utter Upper for wytchery. I would know, I was there the day my brother sent her away."

Captain Otto. Malk pictured the man as he had been at the feast, clutching that giant axe. *Wicked as a rusty nail*, Lem had said. "You have a false tongue, sir," Malk hissed through the wall. "The Count is a tyrant."

"My nephew is forgiving as a fool, kind to a fault, and trusting beyond even that."

"He...he murdered his father," Malk said.

"Oh? How so?"

"Well, he poisoned him."

"Oh?" The captain sounded almost amused. "Before or after my brother fell down the stairs and broke his old neck?"

Malk shook his head. "Cathgol lives in fear. None may come or go without proper inspection."

LILT OF A LARK

"On my orders. Trouble abroad in the Upper Helm, talk of uprisings and rebellion. We should have known it was her making her move."

Not her. Not Rezzell. "You lie..."

The captain snarled. "Go on then, Lark, prove me a liar."

Malk wandered down the path of his memory. From his arrival, to the Liar's Lament, to the execution. *The execution!* "Count Kerstoff hung an innocent man today. Don't chance to deny it, I was there! Tot was his name, and he was a good ma——"

"You feathered fool!" the captain roared. "Are you blind as well as stupid? Your innocent man murdered three women in as many nights. We gave him the chance to say his last words, and he spat in my lord nephew's face. But you were there... you saw it."

Malk remembered the way the crowd had drawn their breath. "We were too far away. Rezzell said... well, Rezzell said..."

"Go on."

"That the Count's sister was a wytch, and she might be there."

Captain Otto's chuckle was long and loud. "You fell for her and her tricks. Now Cathgol is fallen in turn."

"I didn't fall for anything!" Malk said defensively.

"Think! Did she get close to you? Touch you every time you had a doubt? A hand here, a smile there?"

"She..." *She smelled of pine last night, then of ginger and roasted nuts this morning. Two of my favourite scents. And she kissed me on the hand,* he thought suddenly. *I wanted to send her to Heartland before that.* "No..." Malk heard himself say. "If she's a wytch, why not deceive the Count herself?"

"Her tricks don't work properly on those who already know what she is. She learned that lesson the day she tried to charm her father. She needed a tool she could use."

Not a tool. A weapon. She had been all too interested in his cannotina. *And she made me explain about the Aviary, and my mother, and father. She was weighing me,* he realised. *Gauging my strength and finding my weakness.* It hit him all of a sudden. Elzzler; Rezzell. *I'm supposed to be good with words.* He laughed

207

like a maniac, so loud they could probably hear him in the Liar's Lament.

Then the panic set in.

"The Aviary won't send anyone," he thought aloud. "I'll be dismissed for this! Repudiated like a rogue Raven." *No more expensive wine. No more dice. No more warm beds or nights with oils to be applied by soft hands.*

The captain scoffed. "Dismissed? Elzzler wants the Upper Helm. She'll execute the Count first and then eliminate all other threats. There's a reason we're not in the higher cells with the rest of the garrison. We're going to die, you sleeting simpleton. Down here alone or up there before a crowd."

"I can't die here, you great oaf," Malk snapped. "Oh, the songs they'll sing of my failure! We need to get out!"

"A fine idea. Can a Lark's voice open doors too?"

"It doesn't work like that. Besides, they broke my cannotina." Malk crawled to inspect the door in blind alarm all the same. He groaned. There would be no opening it without a battering ram and several hulking men with several hours to spare. *I truly am done. Without my cannotina, I'm nothing. Just a marauding mess of a man.* He beat out his despair on the oak. *Bang, bang, bang.* Until his arms were weak and his hands sore. Until the energy was buzzing around his body. Rising, rising, *rising.*

Seven strings, that's it. He had told Rezzell that he was his mother's son. For better or worse, he was equally his father's. His voice couldn't save him, but... "Do you know a route out of the castle?"

"Why?"

"A route! One that Rez——that *the wytch* doesn't?"

Captain Otto considered that a moment. "There are ways."

It was enough. "Captain," Malk said, "this is going to sound the wrong side of insane, but do you have a drum in your cell? Something you can beat a tune with?"

"Yer gritted."

"Anything at all?"

Malk heard movement in the next cell. "Half an old chamber pot here. What are you gonna do with it?"

"Survive!" Malk said. "Like my father at the Battle of the Splintered Shinn. He never lifted his sword, see."

"I say again, yer gritted." The chamber pot rattled loudly as it hit the floor.

"A Ruffer! My father was a Ruffer. They scorn them most everywhere, so I never met him. His drum, he…never mind, no time. Just take the pot and beat it on the wall as hard as you can. And keep beating it."

"Are you a sleeting wytch too?"

"You had the right of it before; I am but a feathered fool. But I might be able to get us out of here."

For a time, he heard nothing.

Then, "What's gonna happen if I bang this?"

"Cover your head…or something," Malk said. "Just don't stop."

PANG!

The sound rippled through the wall and awoke the energy in Malk's brain. "Again! More! Faster!"

PANG! PANG!

Malk screwed his eyes shut. He'd always done his righteous best to quiet the energy. He'd ignored it, avoided it, *feared* it even. Now he focused on it.

PANG! PANG!

He felt the vibrations; tingling, alive. They flowed to his fingertips and toes.

PANG! PANG! PANG!

Well past where he'd ever allowed them to go before. To where they became a rumbling. The energy, furious and frightening, demanded he let it out.

He held it in.

PANG! PANG! PANG!

Malk could contemplate nothing else. He was gripping the tail of a lightning bolt, holding up the weight of a thousand skies. And all the while, the energy rose and rose higher still.

Something immensely heavy landed beside him. Part of the ceiling, perhaps. The captain was bellowing from miles away, but the beat kept on.

PANG! PANG! PANG! PANG!

He couldn't contain this force. No one could. Not once it reached its crescendo. It was going to buckle his bones, rip back his flesh, tear him apart. It would...it would...

PANG! PANG! PANG! PANG!

Malk let it out.

The world shrank to nothing for a heartbeat, then exploded into everything. It roared like a beast in its death throe, a surge as unforgiving as it was unstoppable.

When Malk opened his eyes, the cell was dust and rubble. Chunks of bedrock were strewn like broken eggs. The fissure between the two cells had been torn into a gaping hole. Light poured in from the hallway torches outside; the door to Malk's cell had been blown off its hinges without a fight.

Malk peered through into the next cell. The captain stood against the far wall, dumbstruck and covered in dust, half a broken chamber pot in his hand. "What...was that?"

Malk sketched a bow. "Please, don't tell anyone else about that. Or I really will be dismissed."

It had been an easy thing to curse the captain for an oaf with the thickness of a dungeon wall between them. Malk regretted the insult now, as he regretted so many other oversights. *Preeminent diligence as ever, Malky.*

The cellar was the belly of a disused tailor shop at the foot of Cathgol's hill. The captain had said so as they'd made their escape from the castle like rats, scurrying down black tunnel after tunnel. Perhaps he had told him so that Malk knew here, amongst piles of dusty rags older than he was, his screams would be heard by no one.

The veins on the side of Captain Otto's head were thick and throbbing. "I ought to snap your scrawny neck."

Malk raised his palms in a gesture of helplessness. "Now, good captain, I'll have you know I'm a victim."

"A *victim*?"

Easy does it, Malky. "I mean only that I was lied to; bedazzled, beguiled, bewytched."

But the captain wasn't convinced. He was a goliath of a man, formed and frozen like the unforgiving mountains he called home. His eyes cut like shards of pale-blue glass; Malk was butter beneath their gaze. "She couldn't have done any of this without you."

Malk gulped. "And neither can you! If we're to save the Count, you'll need me and my... talents!"

Captain Otto's mouth became a hard line. He was too angered to want reason, but neither did he have a host of options. "If you've an idea, I'd hear it now. It might just save your life."

Malk stalled for time. A set of stone steps were carved into the wall at his right, but he had no idea where they led to and even less idea if he could climb them before the captain grabbed hold of him and pulled off his head.

"Speak!"

"We must discuss our dilemma!" Malk blurted.

"What's to sleeting discuss? Elzzler will execute the Count on the morrow with the whole city watching on. He's as good as dead."

"He can't be!" *If he's dead, then so is my future.* Malk looked again into Captain Otto's eyes. *Then so am I.* "We free the garrison! They'd make short work of Rezzell's thugs."

"We're one and a half men. They're guarded under lock and key. Besides, it's Elzzler we need. We get to her; this whole thing ends." The captain ran a hand through his white beard. "That trick you pulled down there, with the drumming. Can you pull it again?"

Malk shook his head instantly. "I'm not a Ruffer; I have no control over it. I could as easily bring down the whole castle. Count Kerstoff would be just as dead then, and half of Cathgol along with him."

The captain's snarl was a feral thing. "It'd be almost worth it to bury Elzzler."

"You do understand that we'd be in the *wrong* half of Cathgol where that equation is concerned?"

"Then we get another lute? You sang once. You can again."

Malk pinched the bridge of his nose. "That won't work. It wasn't a lute they smashed. It was a cannotina. If I told you how much they're worth, you'd cry. A lute's about as helpful to me as a map to a blind man."

Otto cursed. "Then I should raggle you and have done with it. You know, I heard a story once about a Lark who could change the colour of the sun with a song. What a load o' grit."

Malk rolled his eyes. "Ingranideon the Impish. And he didn't change the colour of the chirping sun. He wasn't even a Lark, people just thought…"

The captain must have seen Malk's face change. "What now?"

Not all lies are like music. Malk glanced about the cellar, at the black rags in their heaps. "I might be able to get to Elzzler. I need to find someone. *We* need to find someone. Tonight."

The captain eyed him suspiciously. "Tell me."

And Malk did.

When dawn finally arrived, it was a beautiful thing, yet on this morn, Malk found he had no songs to sing. For as long as he could remember, he had serenaded himself in times of strife. Without strings to tickle, though, his voice felt an awkward tool, a hammer in the hand of a man trying to dig a hole.

He spent each second courting worry instead. The wheels of his plan were in motion, sure enough, but that didn't mean the cart they were attached to wasn't about to roll off a cliff. It had happened before. *Seven strings, that's all that ever seems to happen.*

The sun was climbing wearily into the winter sky as Malk made his way up the hill toward the Old Square. He was unwashed, unshaved, dressed in dull earthen-tone garb, and tired. So very tired.

He followed the main streets, head down, hood up, and

soon joined a river of people heading the same direction. They nattered to one another of treachery and rebellion, though in four of every five versions, Count Kerstoff wasn't the victim so much as he was to blame. *Rezzell's poison is spreading already, and she hasn't even said a word yet.*

Malk's fingers longed for the strings of his cannotina but were forced to settle for an oaken cudgel hidden in the folds of his musty cloak. "I can't use that," he had protested when it had been handed to him.

"It's easy," the captain promised. "Like raggling a dead cat."

Malk had never raggled any cat, dead or otherwise, but the captain would hear no word of argument.

It was almost midday when he came to the square and saw the bodies packed before the very walls he had conquered the previous night, before the very scaffold a murderer had been hanged from the previous day. The crowd was larger even than it had been then and yet swelling. *Let it grow. That suits us just fine.*

Malk left his hood up. Barrian would be here somewhere, he knew, as well as the rest of Rezzell's hoe-and-sickle soldiers. He could see them sprinkled around the border of the square, holding spears taken from Count Kerstoff's garrison.

Malk pushed, fighting his way through the flock until he arrived at the logjam that was the second row. Here, he was but ten feet from the scaffold and close enough to see the eyes of the men guarding it.

Of Captain Otto, there was no sign. Malk considered that a good thing, even if it did leave him feeling terribly alone. The big man was apparently better at blending in than he looked. Malk only prayed he wouldn't fall foul to any notion of chivalry and ruin the whole thing before the time came.

He turned his attentions back to the scaffold and almost bit his tongue. A stout man with red hair and a hawkish demeanor was standing not two yards away, eyes scanning the crowd.

Kel. Malk turned his head sideways to hide his face. "What's all this about, anywho?" he asked a broad wench beside him.

She spat. "Count Kerstoff's done some treason or other. He's gonna—"

A deep thrumming horn cut her off.

Malk risked a glance at Kel, but the man wasn't interested in the crowd anymore so much as the castle gate. It was yawning open, and from its mouth rode forth a courser. Malk gasped when he saw the rider on the horse's back.

Rezzell had wielded a raw, uncouth sort of beauty, like a wildflower growing on the banks of a murky river. There was nothing raw or uncouth about Lady Elzzler. There was only beauty. Her desires had given over to an ice-blue dress that hugged tight to her figure, and a mantel of white ermine adorned her shoulders. Barrian marched at her side, every inch his master's dog. Malk glimpsed the man's quarterstaff and shivered at what was to come; his bowels already felt like water.

Count Kerstoff cut a stoic figure as he shuffled in their wake, bound at the wrists with irons. His chin was held high, but with his ripped garments and filthy hair, he looked to have spent ten nights in the dungeons, not just one.

Elzzler slid from her horse with feline grace when they reached the scaffold. She took her brother roughly by his arms and marched up the steps. Barrian waited below, glowering at anyone who chanced to look his way.

Whispering broke out amongst the crowd as the Count came to a halt before the noose. Elzzler swept to the front of her stage. "My people of Cathgol..." she began. Malk tuned her out. Instead, he closed his eyes, waiting in anticipation.

And he kept waiting.

His fingers were moving of their own accord, nervously wriggling under his cloak.

"Tyrant!" Elzzler was screaming. *"Grief! Suffering!"*

Malk opened his eyes and looked to the eastern sky. *Now*, he thought. *It has to be now!*

But nothing happened.

A drum began to roll. Elzzler forced her brother's head through the noose and slipped the knot down. Malk's heart dropped into his stomach. "No..." he breathed.

Elzzler stepped back and placed her hand on a lever. The drumming halted. Malk looked desperately again to the east. A dark smudge had appeared against the sky.

Two sounds rippled down into the Old Square.

First came the twang of strings struck furiously by fat fingers. Then a man's voice, deep and loud and proudly off-key.

Heads turned in unison.

A figure straddled the eastern rooftop, swathed head to toe in black. His hood was drawn, his cape long and ragged. His face looked pale and shaven, though at such a range it was impossible to discern any features. The only colour came from the lute in his hands and the three pretty stones in the instrument's body that winked in the sun.

The square fell silent at the look of this ominous stranger. Malk took a deep breath, filled his lungs.

And started to wail. *"Raven! Raven! Run! Raven!"*

Confusion lived on for a few long seconds before the words truly hit home. It was the wench beside Malk who reacted first. She screamed, high and shrill, and panic leapt from body to body like a plague. The crowd began to surge in several directions; mothers covered the ears of their babes; men shoved and fought one another in a bid to win free. The soldiers Elzzler had placed around the Old Square tried to keep order, but they were few, and the mob was many. And all the while, the singing rolled down on them from the rooftop.

Malk held his ground in the chaos, watching, *waiting.* Through the blur, he saw Barrian leading a troop of Elzzler's warriors toward the eastern building. Others among her ranks began fleeing themselves, dropping spears, clamping hands over ears, blind with panic. The figure on the rooftop was dancing now, singing and strumming a tune that could no longer be heard over the cacophony.

A body careened into Malk's back at speed, sending him spinning and tumbling to the flagstones. The world turned upside down. When it righted itself again, he found himself staring at the foot of the scaffold.

Kel wasn't there anymore. No one was; the way was clear.

Malk scrambled to his feet and ran for the stairs. *Wait for the captain,* a voice inside his head urged as he climbed, but he knew that voice was merely singing a song of cowardice. This was his chance; the wytch was unprotected and alone, her men in disarray. Malk drew the cudgel as he took the last step.

Elzzler stood behind her brother, one hand on the hilt of the lever. She took in Malk, and the blood drained from her face, even as her finger rose to frantically point. "Kill him! Kill the Lark!"

But no one could hear her words above the symphony of screams. Folk were drunk on fear. The stranger yet sang on the eastern rooftop, sheltering behind a brick chimney to avoid arrow volleys. Down below, Barrian was attempting to smash down a door to gain access to the building itself.

Malk forced a defiant smile. "Your ruse has been rumbled, Wytch. Your folly foiled. Your—"

Rezzell pulled the lever.

The Count dropped.

"No!" Malk dove hopelessly towards the trapdoor.

He landed at its edge and peered down. The Count was frozen still, as if in midair. His head was yet level with the scaffold, the rope yet slack. For a moment, Malk was dumbstruck.

Then he saw Captain Otto standing beneath his nephew, his great arms wrapped about his legs, keeping him alive.

"Raggle her!" the captain bellowed up.

Malk rose with the cudgel in his hand.

Elzzler's eyes were wide and wild. "You fools!" she screamed down at the square. "That's no Raven!"

"No more than the Count is a tyrant, or you his victim." Malk advanced on trembling legs until he was within range. "Enough, Wytch." The cudgel felt heavy as an anvil, but he managed to get it over his head.

Then something in her eyes stopped him in his tracks.

"Malkoriahmavrovianmolossus...please." Elzzler reached out, and her hand found his chest with the lightest of touches.

Malk frowned. She was an innocent thing, this girl, now that he considered it. Fragile; a little bird with a broken wing needing shelter in a storm. The nose in the middle of her face reminded him of a button. *Some time in Heartland would serve her well. Perhaps I could save her from this frozen hellscape. And what about those eyes? A man could drown in those mismatched eyes.*

The makings of a song came to Malk unbidden. *Two eyes had she, one brown, one green...the chastest maid I'd ever seen.*

He faltered, and his grip loosened on the cudgel. Then a thought occurred to him. *Chastest isn't a word, you feathered fool.*

The cudgel came down. Hard enough to raggle seven dead cats.

Pigeons flew from the rookery tower with the day yet young and cold. There were too many for Malk to count, bound for every major keep in the Upper Helm. They bore word of the attempt on the Count's life and that he was alive and well despite what vicious rumours might have spread to the contrary.

If only I had wings, Malk thought. *I could fly back to the Aviary and shit all over them before I landed.* He ought to be grateful he was returning at all, he knew, and not beside Rezzell and the others in the dungeons, gagged and bound, awaiting trial for treason.

Count Kerstoff had listened to Malk's story in its entirety, occasionally stroking his beard, more than occasionally glancing sceptically at Captain Otto. Upon delivering his statement aloud, Malk hardly believed it himself. Yet the Count had risen from his chair at the end of it and thanked Malk with an embrace and the offer of a warm bed in the castle.

He had slept poorly all the same, tossing and turning through dreams filled with nooses and ravens and broken instruments. Dawn had found him at the window, a fur blanket about his shoulders, longingly gazing south, his fingers strumming strings that weren't there.

He started at the sound of footsteps drumming the flagstones behind him.

"It's true then; you are leaving already?" Count Kerstoff said.

Malk kept his eyes on the sky above the castle parapets. He could yet see some of the birds, far away and moving ever farther. "For better or worse, my deeds here are done, my lord. Heartland calls."

The Count moved to stand beside him, hands clasped behind his back. "You have my leave to answer her, Malk."

Malk gave Kerstoff a bow. With his auburn hair combed fine and the filth of the dungeons scrubbed from his skin, one might never have guessed the man had been in mortal peril. "Mere thanks do not suffice, my lord, neither for your generosity nor grace. They will hear of both in Heartland, I promise you. I intend to write a song."

"I would prefer they be made aware that had things gone awry here, it's they who would have been responsible," the Count said, and the faintest line of anger appeared on his brow. "And that it is not something I will forget."

Malk looked down at his boots. "The blame is mine. If I'd have paid more attention to my lessons and less to my lyrics, I would have seen your sister for what she was. Truly, I seem to be as lousy a Lark as ever lived. Mayhaps I was meant to be a meandering minstrel instead."

The Count's face softened; the anger gone as quickly as it had come. "That reminds me. Your friend, the one who played on the roof? I will need his name."

"He goes by Jeppe Gemstones," Malk said. "I promised him—"

"The captain told me what was promised. He will have a place in the castle until spring. I owe him my life, the least I can do is lend him my hearth."

"He deserves that," Malk said. "Even if your ears don't."

"There's something else." The Count handed Malk parchment, rolled and sealed. "For your superiors."

"Oh." Malk had expected something of the sort. He had survived the swords, but there was power in words. *Power enough to see that I'm never welcome in Heartland again.*

218

"It details how you prevented what would have been the greatest threat to the Empire the Org has seen in over a century; how you successfully deceived my sister into believing you were a feeble-minded creature, one so despicably foolish that he would believe her outrageous lies. Most importantly, though, how you foiled a plot on my life by risking your own, and how you lost your lute in the process."

Cannotina, Malk thought. "Truly, I am terribly thankful, my lord."

"But?"

"Well, see, despite all that, I'm rather pitiful without my cannotina, and the road has no place for pity. Alone, I daresay I'm in for a good raggling."

"Then it is well and good that you will not be alone." The Count placed his hand on Malk's shoulder. "There's an escort waiting by the mountain gate."

"An escort? Like the soldiery kind?"

"Of a sort."

Snow had dusted the ground by the time Malk and Hanna found the right place. There were no soldiers that he could see, just a rabble of unkempt men. Close to the gate, a large man swathed in dirty furs sat ready to stir a pair of draft horses into action.

Where's this chirping escort, then? Malk passed the group over with disdain in his nose. Then he looked again at the oxcart. *Not a large man. Huge.* "Barrian?"

The man on the cart turned at the sound and grinned at Malk. The gesture looked utterly at home on his face. "Bird boy...I, *we*, owe you a sleeting grand apology." He motioned to the group of men. Kel and Lem were amongst them; both gave him abashed nods.

"I don't understand," Malk said.

"Neither do we, rightly," Barrian said. "'Fore last winter, we were tanners and farmers and blacksmiths. Then *she* came to our villages and filled our ears with promises and poison."

"You were under her spell?"

"Aye. Some things I remember bright as brass, not that I could do much about them. Fortunately, the good Count said he knows a thing or two about being under someone else's control."

Malk chuckled nervously. "He did, did he?"

"We've agreed to take you south as far as Headland before we go home. We owe yer that much."

Malk's nose twitched again, and the reality of the situation dawned on him. "Ohhh now, there's really no nee——"

"Nonsense!" boomed Barrian. "Let us be away." He rustled his reins, and the draft horses stirred to life.

Malk groaned and reluctantly fell in beside the oxcart as it rolled into motion.

"You'll be home amongst the other birds in no time," Barrian said cheerfully.

Home. There was a deal of power in that one word. Besides, wine and women were waiting for him in Heartland. *And I'm leaving this dreary hellscape. Perhaps it's not so bad after all.* Malk's fingers danced. He cleared his throat. "Cathgol, oh, Cath——"

Barrian's glare stole the voice from him. "None o' that."

Malk considered grumbling a retort, then thought better. Silence was a Lark's best friend.

The Mystical Farrago

written by

N. V. Haskell

illustrated by

ANNALEE WU

ABOUT THE AUTHOR

N. V. Haskell was born in Texas and has lived across the United States. She writes fantasy and science fiction, and is an amateur historian slightly obsessed with Chinese history and mythology. She has traveled to beautiful places and is fortunate to call a vast array of unique individuals friends, some of whom may have inspired her work.

N. V. credits authors such as Meredith Ann Pierce, Terry Pratchett, and Anne McCaffrey for stoking her imaginative flames as a child and inspiring her to find a voice through writing fantasy. Her first professional sale was in the final issue of Deep Magic *e-zine in 2021. Searching for connection and home in a dangerous world is a favorite theme of N. V.'s, as you will see in "The Mystical Farrago."*

When N. V. is not staring into her computer screen, you might find her at comic cons or renaissance fairs donned in her favorite costumes, reading multiple books at a time, running badly, traveling, or teaching yoga. She currently resides in Northern Kentucky with a great family, a rescue dog with a large personality, and an indignant cat.

After working for many years in health care, N. V. continues to be stubbornly optimistic. She believes that there is goodness in this world if we dare to look for it.

ABOUT THE ILLUSTRATOR

Annalee Wu was born in 1998 in the valleys of Baltimore County, Maryland. Anna was curious about the life around her. She developed a strong interest in the inner lives of fictional heroes and their personal connections to a speculative world. Awestruck by the world of online artists, Anna opened her eyes to art that seemed more realistic than life itself. After many years of searching for the roots of these artists, Anna found a nurturing online community that provided friendship and guidance among people who shared a similar path. She is working hard to polish her work and eventually contribute to the world that inspired her on this journey.

The Mystical Farrago

I stood outside the fading blue and gold striped tent, studying the thinning canvas and fraying edges, a result of time and too much wear. The creatures I passed after entering the exhibition appeared well-tended and healthy, even the charbulls, which can be notoriously spiteful during feeding times. The staff was agreeable, as always, charming the locals with false smiles and flattery. They leaned in to share secrets with some of the more respectable men, while others flirted with doe-eyed ladies. The sharp-edged pink lizards watched me pass, catching my scent with open mouths and flicking tongues, while the triple-headed mandrils lazed in the hot sun, ignoring the prodding of overly curious children.

I did not want to believe the rumors, had wanted to hold on to the echoes of childhood feelings and believe the best of old man Goddard. But, as I entered the tent, there was no disputing the evidence and horrible truth laid before me.

The crysallix was over six feet tall—small for the species— and anchored to a large perch by a golden chain shining around one slender ankle. Her wings shimmered in the dull light of the tent's interior, like an oil slick that morphed from green to purple to blue depending on the angle of light. The pinnacle of those wings arched toward the ceiling canopy while the tips brushed the beige, silty floor. The right wing was missing several large pinions, making it impossible for her to escape easily.

ANNALEE WU

The scent of mountain ginseng and hard nut bread filled my nose—not easily procured with local ovens, the kind only found in the tribal ovens of the western mountains. It reminded me of my grandmother's fondness for the tasteless fare.

The large creature, equal parts bird and human, watched me with glittering, golden eyes. Fine feathers coated her face, hiding any expression. Someone had hastily draped a long swath of linen around her, hiding her breasts and genitals in folds of cloth. I circled her, maintaining professionalism while my stomach knotted. I noted the bloodstains on the linen as Goddard coughed behind me.

I took an authoritative tone, leveling a hard gaze at the ringmaster, who clutched his black hat. "You can't have this here."

The crysallix's eyes flicked between Goddard and me, her feathers ruffling down her spine. There was something wrong, more than the wounds, and though my personal knowledge of the creatures was superior to the average citizen's, anyone who paid admission could see there was something amiss here. How many had paid admission at Goddard's Mystical Farrago to bear witness to her imprisonment and done nothing? How many had she suffered under? If they had seen the creature as equal to human, those who had abused her would have felt the slice of the guillotine. But because her kind did not speak a language easily understood, they were treated as less than. And the only voice she had in this world was when decent people saw wrong and strived to right it, but that did not happen often enough.

Goddard stammered, filling the air with excuses that reeked of falsehoods. They'd rescued her from a smaller carnival that had been sacked in the night. She was the last creature left, he said, and would have died tethered to the wagon that held her if they had not come along.

"How long have you had her?" I opened my notebook, making notations of her condition, documenting all that he said.

"Only a month or two, Lieutenant." Goddard moved closer to me, calloused hands warping his felt hat. He blathered on and, while my pen continued to transcribe his words, I was no longer listening.

She could have shredded him and the rest of the staff with her talons or torn them with her hidden beak. Their ferocity was legendary. Her feet were scaled and thin, but with five three-inch talons growing from her toes that splintered the wood she perched upon. Her arms hugged her torso, hiding the talons that should have been there. But Goddard had probably filed them down. I wondered how he had kept from being killed.

I interrupted the man's monologue, abruptly cutting him off midsentence. "She might have made her way back to her tribe if you had released her when you found her. As it is, you have dragged her leagues away from her native lands."

"She could not have survived on her own, sir. I couldn't abandon her." He brushed the uneven wing with stubby fingers, and she flinched, tucking it closer to her body. "She might have died without me."

The possessive tone of Goddard's voice stabbed a deep discomfort in my chest.

"Mr. Goddard, it is illegal to keep a crysallix. You, being a man of the world, know this simple law. Are you telling me that you did not pass any other tribes that might have taken her? Or any rehabilitation farms?"

His hands continued to worry at the hat while she examined me with discerning eyes. She shifted on her perch, talons and toes crunching the beam that stood three feet from the ground. Large breasts moved beneath the draping fabric as she strained to sit a little taller. I wondered what my scent was to her.

"What have you been doing with her?" I asked. Perhaps it is the quiet language of distant cousins, or the way she stared at me in recognition of another female, or the blood on the fabric. But I knew her story. Every woman knew this story. It did not matter that we did not speak the same tongue.

"Just trying to make a bit of extra coin to pay for her care. She's expensive to feed, and healers don't come cheap." His voice trailed off as I turned on him.

"What were the names of the healers you employed? There are few who understand the species."

He shifted on his feet, continuing the abuse of his sad hat. "They were in the last town...."

The crysallix issued a soft coo, and I met her eyes. A promise settled between us.

"Close the exhibit."

"But..."

"No more shows, no more displays." I gestured to the blood. "No more of whatever happened here."

"Sir..." he stammered, and I was too incensed to correct him.

"I will arrange care for her at the regional exotic creatures' clinic." She flexed her wings slightly as I spoke, strained a little taller, understanding the essence of what was being said. "What tribe does she hail from?"

"I don't know." Goddard's face had gone sallow, but his eyes flashed.

"Where are her leathers? Surely she wasn't naked when you found her." Without the distinct colors of her leathers, it would be difficult to discern which tribe she came from. Though, if we could replace the pinions, she might find her way home.

"Perhaps, sir, if we could come to some sort of arrangement."

There it was again. He did not stop to wonder why I was unaffected by the crysallix, unlike most men. Or why I could breathe her scent and not desire her. For those not exclusively drawn to mate, the pull to her was different.

"Arrangement?" I asked. This was why she had yet to be returned to her tribe—because of bribes and temptation. How many fellow officers had succumbed to it? It was an odd thing to scold someone I'd once revered, but I was not a child, and he was proving my childhood idolizations to be grossly misplaced.

"Mr. Goddard, if you would like to add bribery to your charges, please continue." I wrote in quick, clipped script describing the offenses and tearing off a piece of the triple-layered parchment. "I will return in three hours, and you will hand her over, unscathed, with all of her belongings."

"But I haven't..."

"Three hours. And I will have reinforcements with me. Do I make myself clear?"

Goddard's face puckered, and he spat on the ground. "You little shit. How dare you come into my business and tell me what to do? I remember you. Remember the free tickets and rides I gave you and your friend? And every year I would come back, you would be waiting." He spat again, hitting my boot. "And this is how you repay my generosity? I remember your little friend, too. I remember what happened to her."

He attempted to rattle me by mentioning Judeth, but I'd had years to deal with her loss and would not be swayed. She would have been just as disgusted as I was with the scene.

I shoved the paper into his hands, my eyes never leaving the crysallix.

"When someone demands a kindness be repaid, it is proof that it was never a kindness at all," I said. "Instead, it is a revelation of one's true character." I towered over him, staring into his black eyes until they looked away in shame. "And cover her properly or I'll strip the coat from your back."

As I stepped outside the tent, the crowd continued to mill about. Children ran to the next exhibit, laughing and dripping creamsicles down their dirty hands as well-dressed couples strode by, leaning toward each other adorned in long skirts and tall hats. The air was filled with childhood memories, now forever tainted.

My mouth felt dry with the knowledge there was something here that I was missing, but he would give me only what I could discover on my own. Perhaps the crysallix would speak to me when she was in a safer place. I thought it as likely as being struck by ball lightning on a cold summer day. They were notoriously private creatures, untrusting of outsiders, and, after incidents like this, it was understandable.

They lived in tight-knit tribes in the mountains and valleys to the far west, but there were rumors of other groups nestled in the east and south as well. It was a matriarchal society, with their own written language, their own ways, their own strange foods. They took one love mate in their lifetimes but could breed outside of that relationship and outside of their species. And, according to my mother, those that did not find a love mate continued to attract unwanted attention. There was something about the creatures that drew the gaze of the human male. Perhaps it was the wild feminine, the fierce, winged warrior that defied the male order and gave no unearned respect. Perhaps it was the scent of their pheromones that was used to find a mate. It was said that once love mated, the crysallix ceased the production of their pheromones, but I offer no opinion on that.

I had listened in school as one teacher romanticized them, his tone lilting as he described a lucky meeting with one as several boys leaned forward, entranced. Judeth and I had wondered at their reaction, and it disturbed me in a way I was too young to define. Mother had once said there was a reason we lived so far from town, especially after father died. She said we were always in danger among men.

I often thought of Judeth and considered that if she had been granted even a fraction of the crysallix's strength, perhaps she might still be alive. As it was, I had consigned myself to a quiet life without her. There was nothing more to be done about it. I'd moved away from the Farrago, recalling the way the creamsicles dripped down her knuckles as she tossed her head back in laughter, green eyes shining with affection.

Three hours later, ten officers returned with me, a mix of male and female, per my request. Aggie, the healer who ran the exotic clinic, already stood before the tent when we arrived. She was a short, thick woman with disheveled hair and dirt under her fingernails. Her dress was torn in three places and spattered with what I hoped was dirt. The messenger reported she had nearly knocked him over when she received my request and had beat us to the tent in her haste. When I arrived, she was guarding the entryway like a goose and its nest, preventing any man from entering until they had inhaled a pungent herb that she forced upon them by threat. It negated the effects of the pheromones in the air and would last for several hours.

Aggie's familiar smile warmed me. It was the type of warmth that could settle crying children with a single look. She gripped my hand, daring to pull me in close for a quick hug.

"I was happy to hear from you, *Lieutenant*." She winked. "My Jude would have been so proud."

My cheeks grew hot. "I should have stayed in touch," I said flatly.

She patted my hand. "Life is hard enough without being reminded of our losses." The same softness that Judeth had inherited swam in her eyes. She nodded toward the tent. "Tell me about her."

I conveyed all that Goddard had said, indicating I believed it all to be fabrication. She listened intently, murmuring that he'd probably pulled out the pinions to keep her grounded.

She rubbed her chin. "Why didn't she kill him? Rip his spine through his throat, or sever an artery?" She frowned. "It's out of character for the crysallix."

"I thought so as well. That is why I sent for you." Creatures trusted Aggie. They knew her good intent by her smell. Well, except for the charbull that had taken two of her fingers. But she reckoned he was hungry at the time.

Officer Vinja, on loan from a different department, stuck his head through the flap of the tent. His greased hair jutted in unintentional directions, and one side of his mustache drooped down while the other side curled upward in unnatural cheerfulness. "We have unchained it, sir, but it's fighting our attempts to move it. We can't coax it off the perch."

"Sir?" Aggie demanded, puffing up her chest and scowling at Vinja. Her tone caused the officer to step back in concern. "What do you mean by 'sir'? Have you no eyes to see, nor wits to think?"

"Aggie, it's okay."

But that would not soothe her as she rounded on Vinja. "Well then, I suppose that you might be a young lass? Or I, a neutered charbull? Perhaps that's not an exotic creature at all but a..."

"Aggie, the crysallix." I breathed. She huffed, tossing a few more curt words at him as he opened the tent for us. He mouthed apologies, his cheeks flushed, but I waved him away. He had intended no harm, and it happened too frequently for me to react anymore.

They had clothed the crysallix in a clean dress, tearing the back out to accommodate the wings, but the rest of her was covered. Her wings spread wide, flapping at anyone who came too near as her talons gripped the perch. Goddard stood in the corner, sneering at the officers, who ducked away from each swipe of her hand. Though the claws were too dulled to slice, they could still rend flesh with enough force behind them.

The scent of ginseng and nut bread was thick in my head, reminding me of quiet nights and warm hugs. I knew their scent registered differently for each person.

"You, Mustache!" Aggie waved over an anxious Vinja, whispering into his ear and pointing at the door, which he disappeared through with some urgency.

I should have been the first one in the tent but had stayed back to make sure Goddard didn't run for it. The crysallix watched Aggie with narrowed eyes as the older woman jabbed a finger in Goddard's face and backed him into a corner. I thought she might bite him.

"What have you been feeding her?" Aggie shoved herself into him. Goddard glanced at me, but I offered no rescue.

"Bread and cheese. Sometimes fruit," he stammered.

"Bread!" Aggie rolled up her sleeves, her eyes wide with fury. "She's starving—that much is clear. Bread and cheese aren't part of their diets, you numb-knuckle. They are predators. They need meat—liver and organs—to live. If not, then nuts and specific fruits, but bread? They can only digest nut bread from their recipes, not ours. Are you daft or heartless? Are you trying to kill her?"

"No, no, ma'am. I was trying to save her." His hat lay trampled under their shifting feet. "We found her trapped and injured. Surely you don't think..."

231

"Even I can see that you are a terrible liar, and I don't have the sight." The force of her voice sprayed spittle into his face. "And what did you do with her pinions? Where did you hide them?"

"I don't have them." He stammered, grateful when Vinja returned and she had to step back. Vinja held a large bag under one arm.

Tugging the bag from the young officer, Aggie held a yellow persimmon aloft, making a tutting sound as she advanced cautiously toward the creature. She was whispering as she moved, stopping arm's-length away and offering the fruit to the crysallix as she bowed her head.

Gold eyes flicked from the woman to the fruit, then to me. I nodded, imperceptible to the others in the room, and she swiped it from Aggie's palm. If you have never seen a crysallix eat, it is unlike anything you might have experienced. I would recommend something like a fruit or nut your first time because watching them rend a dove or rodent with their beaks will turn you sour for days.

Her seemingly human jaw opened wide, a black beak extending from the maw, its long point sharp as steel. She devoured the fruit in two bites. Her beak, gleaming slick with juice, disappeared again. Aggie held up another, the scene repeating as a few of the officers shifted uncomfortably. Stepping backward, she continued to coax the creature. She offered two hard-shelled nuts, freshly roasted by the smell of them. The crysallix stepped down from the perch, warily watching the surrounding officers but unable to resist. Aggie produced a piece of jerky, leading the creature through the door, into the bustling crowd of the afternoon.

"We are not done here, Goddard," I said in a steady voice. "I'll be back for those pinions, or I'll be removing something of yours."

I stationed two guards around the Farrago to dissuade any attempt at running. It was a long walk to the clinic. The officers kept the crowd at bay as we moved. Hungering eyes of men that drew too near were met with harsh words and the barrel of a rifle. The frustration of desire as the local men caught her scent and were rebuffed drew angry curses but no violence.

We saw her settled in a large enclosure as Aggie gave her the rest of the food, and the officers returned to their respective stations. I lingered behind, watching her and wondering at her odd behavior.

"What do you smell?" Aggie smiled as the crysallix's beak extended again, tearing through the bag and devouring its contents. "For me, it is the scent of a fresh born babe, my babe. And fresh dirt, with a hint of mint."

"Mountain-dug ginseng and the hard nut bread that my mother baked for my grandmother." A tug of nostalgia crept into my voice. "She smells like home."

She nodded, glancing around to make sure we were alone, and whispered anyway. "How are the feet holding up?"

"No issues, thanks to you."

"And the shoes?"

"Still go through them quickly, but not like I used to. Ever since you trimmed them down, it's been fine. I'll probably need your services in another year when the nails break through again."

"My home is always open to you." She looked satisfied, but her gaze shifted back to the enclosure. "Can you hear her?"

The crysallix flexed and extended her wings, watching us curiously.

"No. I don't know that she will speak to me," I said.

Aggie shrugged. "Don't know that she won't until you ask. Did you see the way she looked at you in the tent? She recognizes kin."

There was a squawk from another enclosure, followed by a louder grunt, and Aggie bustled away, shouting reprisals as she went. I turned to follow when I heard a breath of wind behind me, the whisper of wings. I hadn't considered my proximity to the bars of the enclosure when I turned and stared into intelligent, golden eyes. Greenish blue bristles and filoplumes surrounded her eyes and nose, leading outward to brighter contour feathers. Too much like my grandmother's, but brighter and fuller than mother's had been.

She extended dulled talons in greeting. I hesitated, unsure, before reaching back, allowing my fingers to entangle with hers. She raised her head, sniffing the air before jerking me in close. The sharp beak extended too fast for me to react as she nipped my cheek, drawing a bit of blood before releasing me. It was a bonding ritual. Though I had never experienced one before, my grandmother had spoken of it in her more wistful moments.

I stumbled back as she ambled away and nestled in the soft bedding in the corner. Finding Aggie, I made my excuses and stopped at the station to file my report before heading to my simple apartment.

The crysallix found me in my slumber, lulling me into her dream with a voice as soft as wind. We perched naked in a high tree, the blue-tipped mountains spread around us in a twilight sky. Her name was Nyla, and, like many of her kind, she was a curious creature.

"What are you?" she asked.

"Distant relation," I answered.

She laid a hand on my chest. "I can smell our ancestors in you."

I shook my head. "My ancestors are gone. I have no connection to a tribe. I was raised alone and schooled with the humans."

Her wings stretched wide, matching the iridescence of the mountains before resettling. "But you do not belong with these people. It must be difficult. How do they not see you?"

I swung my legs in the air, explaining that it was not as difficult as it had been for my mother or grandmother, who could not walk down the street without unwanted attention and lived in isolation, devoid of any tribal connections.

Mother began shaving my face at a young age so that I could make trades and sell goods for the family.

"What of your wings?" She cocked her head in a stilted way, leaning around me to eye the fragile, undergrown things.

"Useless, too small to serve any purpose. I keep them strapped down most of the time."

Gently, she ran a tough hand across my cheek. "I can feel the rachis and calamus of the feathers, the barbs trying to sprout. Why do you dispose of them?"

"It is easier for them to accept me if I look like them."

Her eyes narrowed, but I sensed no judgment. Wild creatures understood the motivation for survival in strange environments.

"How do you eat?" she asked.

"Same as you, though my beak is small and weak. I cannot manage the unroasted nuts or hard seeds, but I can eat fish and meat, fruits and vegetables." I shrugged, looking around at the landscape she had brought me to. "Is this your home?"

"It was." Nyla sighed, drawing a single knee to her chest as she gazed about at the mountains. I could almost hear the songs of her sisters crying out to her. She leaned toward me in a gesture of intimacy. "What happened to your mate?"

Not ready to speak of something so painful, I countered, "Why didn't you kill Goddard when you had a chance?"

Her eyes held sadness. "He has something precious of mine. I should have stayed and fought, but no one would have understood. They do not hear me like you do now. So, I left to build strength and restrategize." She laid a firm hand on my shoulder, staring into my eyes. "Will you help me get it back?"

A pounding on my door pulled me from my answer, tugging me from our dream into unwanted consciousness.

I answered the door. Vinja stood on the threshold, hair greased into place and mustache symmetrical in its upward curls. Behind him, the sky was brightening into dawn.

"They're gone," he panted.

"Who?" My muddled brain was still half trapped in Nyla's dream.

"The Mystical Farrago. Durgin and Eads were stationed outside to keep them from leaving, but when their replacements showed this morning, they were gone."

"Durgin and Eads?"

He shook his head. "Dead, skulls bashed in. Goddard took an assortment of creatures and the wagons but left most of the tents."

I rubbed my eyes. "A moment," I said, closing the door and donning my uniform before stepping outside. There was no time to shave off the stubble that poked through my skin. I would have to hope that no one looked too closely.

They'd draped the bodies in white linen spattered brown with drying blood. I did not look beneath, focusing instead on the wheel tracks that led away from town, following the smaller road through the forest. They could be heading north around the western mountains by now, or worse, gone into the deserts to the south. But I doubted Goddard was that foolish.

The hasty departure and abandonment of several exotic creatures made me ponder what he was running from, or running with. While I studied the tracks and dealt with the assignment and care of the abandoned creatures, a message arrived from Aggie.

"I have completed my examination of our guest and need to speak with you. Come as soon as you can."

My mouth was dust as I stared down the road for a moment, deciding my course of action. Issuing orders to the remaining officers and organizing a search party, I specified their route and what to look for. I knew what Aggie would tell me. I knew from the experiences of my grandmother and mother there was only one thing that caused a crysallix to stay with someone they loathed.

It took an hour for me to reach my old home in the woods. Carved between two boulders and shaded by towering conifers, the cave had sat undisturbed for the last five years. Ever since mother had wandered away into the woods, it had sat empty of life, and I had lacked the heart to tend to it. Home was a painful reminder of things lost, and I told myself that I now led a different life and had become a different person. But we are skilled at convincing ourselves of our evolution until the past pulls us back and forces us to deal with those things we never speak of.

It was much like I remembered, perhaps a little mustier and lacking the warm scents of the people I loved. It took thirty minutes of searching to locate grandmother's old trunk, then took me an hour and a half to get to Aggie. Nyla waited for my answer.

"She's had a bantling recently—less than a year, I'd wager. It wouldn't be strong enough to fly yet, and still vulnerable to the elements." Aggie said. The concern on her face was evident, her hair more wild than usual. I imagined the hand-wringing when she realized the situation.

"How is Nyla?"

"Nyla? Aw, that's a lovely name." She crooned before her expression sagged into sadness. "They don't do well when separated from their offspring. Typically they stay together until the bantling begins its first cycle." The expression on my face must have showed my confusion. "Wasn't that true of your mother?"

I didn't answer. I honestly couldn't recall how old I had been when she first left, but she'd come and gone so often after I met Judeth. "Are you saying that all crysallix have a cycle? Even the males?"

It was Aggie's turn to look confused. "There are no male crysallix born, dear. When the cycle comes, they can choose to carry more masculine or feminine traits. Didn't your mother teach you?"

Nyla was sitting up, hugging her knees close, observing us from inside the enclosure. The dress she wore was torn in places, probably ripped by her talons while she slept.

"I have something for you," I said.

Nyla sniffed the air before moving toward us. I pulled the leathers from my satchel, running a hand over their faded blues and greens. There was a heart-worn tug in my chest before I handed them to her. She cocked her head from side to side, wings shuffling down her back as she alternately studied my face and the garments. Crysallixes did not give up their leathers, and it was abnormal to wear another's. I nudged the clothing through the bars. She hesitated for a fraction of a second before clutching them to her chest.

She tore the dress from her back, rending it in long strips, before tugging the leather breeches on and pulling the breast-plate over her chest. The straps crisscrossed between her wings, latching the buckles at either shoulder. The colors were a near match to her feathers. If she wasn't of my grandmother's tribe, she had to be from a neighboring one, and my sadness lessened at letting them go.

Aggie patted my shoulder. "They fit her well. It must have been difficult to part with them. I thought Ardan would have taken them when she left."

"Mother had her own leathers, and these have been hidden away for too long. It seemed appropriate they find a new owner." Nyla smoothed down the pants and tucked the straps under the breastplate edges. When she finished, she stood taller. The wings seemed stronger, despite the missing pinions. "This would have made her happy."

"What about the bantling?" Aggie asked.

Nyla listened, though she did not show it. "I've sent a search party into the desert trails. It won't take long to realize the caravan did not go that way. They are only searching for Goddard and know nothing of the offspring. Hopefully, by the time they return, the bantling will be safely reunited with its mother."

"And Goddard?"

I shrugged, remembering his face when he mentioned Judeth. "His well-being is not my concern."

Nyla stared through the bars, reaching out with her dulled talons. I nodded. She could smell her offspring and track it faster than anyone else could. It was dangerous to smuggle her out of town, a risk to both of us, but it was the only sure way to locate Goddard and the child.

I rented a dapple-gray draft horse, powerful and able to bear the weight of both of us on his back. We skirted the town through old pathways, avoiding the locals. Nyla allowed me to cover her with a cape, but the tips of her wings brushed the haunches of the horse. She was used to being around horses from being in the wagons, but I don't think she had ridden one before. Her arms latched around me as we rode.

Nyla kept her nose angled upward, occasionally opening her mouth to get a better scent, and pointed which direction to turn. It took several hours, but eventually, we found the wagon tracks heading toward the western mountains. The wagon train then split, three wagons heading down the long path to the desert, two wagons continuing on.

Nudging the draft horse to move faster, we followed the trail into the woods. It would be dark in a couple of hours, but the air still held warmth, and Nyla would have an advantage come nightfall.

Two of Goddard's men sat around a small campfire while the old man paced from one wagon to the other, worrying his hands.

Stopping at the far wagon, he pulled back the bonnet before resecuring it and continuing his pacing.

"Relax, Boss. No way they find us, not with the side roads we took," the younger man said. He had the type of leanness that could be misperceived as weakness. He had grown an unruly beard that snuck up on either side of a crooked nose to appear older.

Goddard shook his head. "We rest for a few hours and leave with the first light."

There was a sound from inside the wagon, like a whimper or a weakened chirp. Nyla bristled beside me. The sharp nails of her toes and fingers dug into the ground as we watched and waited. Our horse was a half-mile behind, tethered lightly to a tree and happy for the rest while they'd settled their horses on the far side of the wagons. They had not caught our scent yet.

The other man was older, clean-shaven, but with a face full of scars. He poked the fire, asking, "Is it worth bringing with us?"

Goddard paused, moving closer to the speaker and distancing himself from the wagons. "What are you saying?"

I unlatched the clip on my holster and withdrew the flintlock pistol. It was not as powerful as a rifle, and I would only have one shot before they were on me. So far, I could not see a pistol on either of them, but I suspected at least one of them to have something concealed.

Nyla darted away, skirting the clearing and heading toward the wagon, quiet and quick. I could not have stopped her had I tried.

"All this trouble." The man spat on the ground. "We should cut our losses and be rid of it."

Goddard stormed forward, brandishing a small knife. "Do you know how much money that little thing will fetch us?" The man did not react to the blade being wagged at him. "The foreign markets will pay a fortune for it. I was planning on selling the set by winter, but perhaps this way is better."

The younger man squirmed. "Will it live without its mother?" He avoided looking at his companions. "It seems to be getting weaker."

The blue of Nyla's feathers caught the light as she paused behind the brush beside the wagons, but the men did not notice. To reach the opening of the wagons, she would have to dart into the open, exposed. If they trapped her in the wagon, she would lose the advantage we had counted on.

Goddard turned on the younger man. "They didn't leave us much choice, did they? Stole her away with the food. How was I to know what she ate? It's not like the damn things talk." His face shifted into a half smile. "Nice of that hag to educate me. The little thing ate up half my jerky before it fell asleep."

Nyla slid from the shadows toward the wagon. The rustling caused the young man to turn when I leapt from the bushes.

"Goddard." I leveled the pistol at him, releasing the safety. He paled while the other men started to their feet. "Thought you could escape?"

Goddard sneered as his older companion brought his hand to his hip. "Lieutenant. Didn't expect you to come all this way just for me. You'd think they could better spend our tax money on actual crimes rather than trying to bring in a small crook like me."

Nyla slipped into the tent. A coo echoed from inside. The young man turned again but was drawn back by my words.

240

"I don't plan on taking you back," I said, eyeing each of them in turn. It was a lie, of course. My intention was only to grant Nyla the opportunity to get the bantling and then be on our separate ways. I had not come with murder on my mind.

"You mean to kill me?" He glanced at his companions. "And what of them? You can't kill us all."

"I don't plan on killing them." I cocked the gun, trying to keep my nerves and aim steady. Nyla was taking too long. She should have been out by now.

"Is this about that waif that used to come around with you?" Goddard asked, his face done up in a cruel smile.

My stomach knotted.

"She was a sweet thing, wasn't she?" The smile turned wicked as he spoke. "What was her name?"

The gun trembled with my voice, "Don't."

He snorted, "Jude..."

The explosion from my hands drowned out his speech. The bullet struck his shoulder and he stumbled backward.

Smoke wafted from the gun as Nyla paused outside the tent, a bundle clutched in her arms. Reaffixed purple and blue pinions evened out the symmetrical drape of her wings, catching the light. Her eyes narrowed at the scene before she launched upward, and I knew I would not see her again.

The scarred man leapt over the fire, wrapping his arms around my gut. We landed in a heap of curses and fists, wrestling one way, then the other, as the pistol disappeared into the brush. While I lacked many of the predatory advantages from my lineage, I had enough of their strength to best him.

He grunted in surprise as I flipped him beneath me and pummeled his face. Blood spattered from his nose as bone crunched and gave. But he did not relent. His fist met my cheek as I landed a blow to his ear, and he cried out. He struggled even as his muscles quaked with strain beneath me and, for a moment, I had the better of him.

A sharp hit to the back of my head knocked me sideways. I had forgotten about the younger man. He kicked my ribs, knocking me to the ground as he continued his assault. I gripped his foot, twisting his leg and knocking him off balance while he yelped before the other man was up and joining in. One boot met my ribs, another my stomach, knocking the air from my lungs as I endeavored to rise. They hailed fists and boots upon me as I covered my head and told myself that I could outlast their assault. But blood dripped into my eyes as the world threatened darkness.

"Enough," Goddard said. One arm hung limp, blood dotted the ground beneath his feet. He leveled a small pistol at me as the men swayed beside him, their breathing labored. "You won't be leaving these woods. Maybe I'll feed you to the little crysallix we've got."

He cocked the pistol, and I closed my eyes.

A scream between a hawk and a mountain cat split the air. A flurry of oil-slick wings shot above me as Nyla slapped the pistol from Goddard's hand. Her wings unfolded, knocking one man to the ground. She shredded the face of the other with her talons as she spun.

Goddard stumbled back, searching for the lost pistol as she advanced.

"Please," he begged, holding one hand up. "I was trying to help you."

She stopped, tilting her head as her wings shivered again.

The younger man rose to his feet behind her, a knife in hand. I struggled to reach him, dragging myself on the ground and gripping his leg. The knife glinted in the firelight as he raised it. I screamed her name.

Warm blood pooled onto his boots, coating my hands and splattering my face. The man fell before me, lifeless eyes staring at the sky. White ovals of bone were pulled through the torn gap in his throat. There was a soft gurgling as his last breath struggled to exit and found itself trapped.

Goddard screamed as she leapt upon him. I closed my eyes until his cries ceased, replaced by a sound I knew too well. It was the sound that my mother and my grandmother made when they feasted on ferrets or lambs.

I pressed myself up. Nyla was perched upon his chest, the rest of the scene blocked out by the drape of her wings. Goddard's head lay twenty feet away, expression frozen in terror.

The remaining man watched in horror as his face bled down his shirt. Slowly, he pulled himself to his feet and stumbled into the woods. He would have to seek a healer in the closest village, then tell his tale of the crysallix. A vastly different tale than other men often told. I hoped it served as a warning.

Nyla nudged me awake sometime later, helping me to sit and fussing over my cuts and bruises. Preening me like my mother used to. Once satisfied, she darted into the wagon that our draft horse was now hooked to. She had cleared the bodies away. Long smears of blood led into the trees, and the wheel tracks that led us here had been swept away.

Emerging from the bonnet, she squatted down before me, holding out the small babe to me. Its hands already sported soft talons, slender limbs covered in a dull-gray down with shades of blue surrounding golden eyes. Bringing the creature to my chest, one hand reached my face as I smiled. Nyla leaned close, resting her head on my shoulder with a gesture of pride.

They smelled of mountain ginseng and hard nut bread, of fresh meat and soft down. They smelled of home.

Tsuu, Tsuu, Kasva Suuremasse

written by
Rebecca E. Treasure

illustrated by
NATALIA SALVADOR

ABOUT THE AUTHOR

Rebecca E. Treasure grew up reading science fiction and fantasy in the foothills of the Rocky Mountains. After grad school and two children, she began writing fiction. Rebecca has lived many places, including the Gulf Coast of Mississippi and Tokyo, Japan. She currently resides in Texas Hill Country with her husband, where she juggles two children, two corgis, a violin studio, and writing. She only drops the children occasionally.

Rebecca discovered Writers of the Future shortly after she began writing fiction. She has entered every quarter since, making lifelong friends as a result. Rebecca's short fiction has been published by or is forthcoming from WordFire Press, Air and Nothingness Press, Flame Tree Publishing, The Dread Machine, *and others. She is an associate editor at Apex Book Company and Magazine.*

"Tsuu, Tsuu, Kasva Suuremasse" came about, as many of Rebecca's stories have, from a synthesis of ideas. Research for her sixth novel, a historical fantasy about Napoleonic magic users, combined with a fascination with the idea of animal magic and beloved memories of an "adopted" grandmother from her childhood. The real Emily lived in a cozy apartment across from Rebecca's family and collected dolls.

ABOUT THE ILLUSTRATOR

Natalia Salvador is also the illustrator for "The Squid Is My Brother" in this volume. For more information about her, please see page 76.

Tsuu, Tsuu, Kasva Suuremasse

When Emily buried her son in the icy mud of an unnamed forest in Russia, a fox and a deer came from the woods to help. Martin's chest still seeped blood though his heart had fallen silent; the dark-green uniform which had given him such pride frosted in scarlet rivers. The Frenchman, whose long blade laid bare the heart Emily had nurtured against her breast, lay screaming just out of sight through the trees.

The sound gave Emily strength.

She removed Martin's boots, singing a cradle song in her thin, wavering voice. "Tsuu, tsuu. Kasva suuremasse, kasva karjatsesse." *Hush, hush. Grow bigger, grow to be a herder.*

He had grown to be a soldier, herding death.

Emily rocked back on her worn, cracked boots wrapped in strips of cloth taken from a dead horse's blanket. Martin's musket, greatcoat, and shako were already set aside to be carried back to camp. She'd tied his jaw shut in the old way, grateful his eyes were closed. She clawed at the shards of frozen earth, desperate to make the grave deep enough that the animals, whether they had boots and muskets or paws and teeth, could not ravage Martin.

The buck stepped from beneath a fir, soft brown eyes shining. At first, Emily was afraid. She'd taken a great risk leaving the camp to search for Martin after the battle. Then the buck began to cleave the dirt with his hooves. A fox slunk through a bare lilac shrub, yipped once, then scrabbled at Martin's feet.

Other animals drifted from the woods too: a beaver with a frail sapling to mark the site, a family of chipmunks to dig a pillow for Martin's soft black hair. Too cold to cry, too hungry to wonder at the magic, Emily dug alongside the woodland creatures, grateful for the company and the scant warmth rising from their labors.

Her soul recognized them. These were *väeloom*, spirits in animal form, come to help, drawn by her grief. These were her children: four sons lost to war and starvation and disease. Her husband, her grandchildren, her parents. Of all her family, only one little baby still survived. The *väeloom* brought great comfort. She was not so alone, after all.

At last, only Martin's face remained to cover. Emily stroked his cheek, his eyebrows, and the scar on his temple where a saber had nearly killed him in his first battle.

"Puhka nüüd, mu arm. Näeme varsti." *Rest now, my love. I will see you soon.*

He disappeared beneath mounds of loose dirt, piled on by frostbitten fingers, talons, claws, and hooves. Emily whispered in the language Martin had heard in his cradle, though for the past many years, he had spoken only the Czar's language.

Emily closed her eyes, willing her pain to drift away on the breeze. The *väeloom*, too, seemed to take a moment of reflection, watching her, waiting. The Frenchman pleaded for water, for warmth, for death.

The last, Emily could provide.

Wonderment penetrating beneath her misery at last, she formed a thought, a directive to the *väeloom*.

Kill him.

The fox, fastest, streaked away as a red blur. The buck pounded in his wake, long antlers held low. The smaller creatures cast up puffs of disturbed pine needles as they followed.

The Frenchman's screams peaked, then fell away. Heat surged through Emily, her heart pounding and her hands trembling. She retched, her stomach twisted by her act. She'd followed Martin across Russia, coaching his Polish woman,

NATALIA SALVADOR

Marie, through childbirth and caring for the scrawny infant. Emily had cooked, cleaned, patched up uniforms, tents, and men alike. Her heart had hardened, but she had not fallen into the deprivation of spirit which surrounded her.

Until now.

She shrugged into Martin's coat, collecting his things. His smell surrounded her, musky with a hint of the cinnamon tea he bartered for. Emily turned toward the Frenchman, thinking to bury his corpse as she had Martin's. A penance. After all, somewhere, a mother would hear of his death and weep.

She took a step forward, then shook her head. Let the French bury the French. They did not belong here, these invaders who had taken her last child.

Her legs struggled through the thick undergrowth, skirts catching on branches that snapped in the unseasonable cold. The *väeloom* drifted alongside her. Finally, the meager Russian campfires flickered through the woods, evening's light casting long shadows that danced with the wind. Still, the spirits followed.

Emily turned, taking in their glittering eyes, soft faces. She froze the moment in her memory. *Begone*, she thought. *They will not understand.*

The animals faded into the forest until only the fox remained. It eyed her, nose twitching, eyes twinkling beneath a pale scar across its forehead, just where Martin's had been.

"My loyal child," Emily whispered. "Go. Thank you."

The fox tilted its head back, sniffing the air, and slipped away. Emily stumbled to the campfire's light, the thin flames drawing her in. Would the *väeloom* come to her again? Even one touch of the old magic, an evening surrounded by family, seemed a gift she could not have dreamed of in this wretched life. The price was higher than she'd willingly pay, but in her moment of need, she had not been alone.

Marie, holding the baby at her breast, looked up as Emily approached their fire. The smoldering sticks barely gave off warmth, and the rabbit skewered over the flames had more

249

bones than meat. One of the older women made room for Emily on the fallen log where the laundresses, wives, and whores of the camp huddled.

Marie's eyes took in Emily's glance, her frown. The young woman looked down at the four-month-old baby and gulped, her eyes filling with tears. Blonde, with a thin face made skeletal by hunger and cold, Marie's sincere smile had captivated Martin. Long roads and endless battles had left her blonde hair brittle, her wide lips split and bleeding in the cold. The girl claimed to be twenty, but if she was more than eighteen, Emily was the Empress of France.

"It was quick," Emily said. She held out the shako and the boots to Marie to trade for food or blankets. "The man who killed him is dead. Martin is with his brothers now." The woods shifted; a fox yelped in the distance. Emily drew Martin's coat closer to her, a waft of cinnamon teasing her nose.

Marie nodded, chewing her lip. She would be attached to another soldier by the end of the week. It was the only way to survive. The question remained—would Marie continue to share food and shelter with an old woman? Would the new soldier accept a dead man's bastard? Grandmother or no, everything was scarce.

Karl stirred and whimpered. Marie sighed. Emily took him and, though her throat resisted, she hummed the old lullaby until he settled, blinking wide, blue eyes.

"Tsuu, tsuu..." *Hush, hush.*

Martin had loved her singing as a baby. Later, his boyhood voice joined hers as they worked the fields. Just that morning before the battle, he had sung to Karl, his deep voice filling the space between the trees.

The rabbit was parted out, typical squabbles erupting over who got how much. Emily managed to snatch a thin, gamy piece of leg and swallowed half without bothering to taste. Her stomach knotted around the pathetic meal, aching for more, but she was no stranger to hunger. It would keep her alive. She stroked Karl's cheek, savoring the second bite, imagining rich fat running off the meat, dreaming of the black rye bread that rounded off a meal and packed in the empty corners of hunger.

It was all empty corners now.

Karl's tiny hand, pink and beginning to lose the thinness of a newborn, closed around Emily's finger. He gazed up at her, the firelight dancing in his eyes.

"You are full of fire, little one," Emily murmured. She shifted to a more comfortable position on the log, if such a thing could be found. "Your *vanaisa* Karl was a brave man. He fought hunger and nature instead of the French, but he was a warrior all the same."

Karl smiled, a gaping grin universal to babies.

Emily's heart ached, thinking of Martin's infant smile. She said softly to the babe, "Perhaps you will not have to fight at all."

Marie snorted. "Don't fill his head with nonsense, *vanaema*. Of course he will have to fight. If not the French," she gestured vaguely into the woods, "then someone else."

"Perhaps," said Emily, thinking of the fox. "Maybe the wars will end."

Marie and the other women laughed at Emily before trotting off to satisfy the hungers of their men or the needs of the soldiers. Emily stayed by the dying fire, shivering as night fell over the wood, sharing lullabies and old stories with Karl.

Three days later, Marie abandoned both Karl and Emily, moving into the tent of an officer. Snow had not yet fallen, but the air crackled amongst the woods, sweeping away warmth.

Marie held Karl to her, snot dripping from her nose in a frigid breeze. "He wants nothing to do with the child. Please, Emily—"

"Give him here." Emily had warned Martin about the girl, so young herself.

Marie's arms clung to Karl, then she relented. "I will give you what I can. Someday—"

Emily cocked an eyebrow. "Do not fill his head with nonsense."

Marie flushed and hurried away.

Emily huddled with the baby as the Russians made preparations to pursue the French, who fled the Russian winter and the smoky destruction of Moscow. None would help an old woman and a babe. The army pulled up its boots and slogged away to the south. Searching the abandoned camp, blood and smoke lingering with sharp pine, Emily found blankets, a tent, some cookware, even a rusting sword that would fend off wild animals—but no food.

Early next day, before the sunlight penetrated the canopy of branches, Emily rolled the meager supplies into the tent and strapped it to her back. Karl wailed, encountering the persistent bellyache for the first time in his brief life. Emily knew from experience that soon his whimpers would cease, the hunger as familiar as his mother had once been. She tucked him into a sling against her belly, just as she'd carried his father so long ago in the fields of Saaremaa. Before the wars, before all the death.

They couldn't stay—the blackened crops and echoing farmhouses left behind by the forced evacuations stretched for miles in every direction. Bonaparte's army would go east, to Smolensk and then Vilna. With them would go supply wagons for both armies—the only food in this part of Russia—and so Emily would follow.

Emily picked up her rusted sword and followed after the army. When she reached the edge of the camp, the fox slunk from the woods, peering at her. His bright eyes glittered in the cold winter sun, the pale gap of scarred flesh luminescent. In his mouth dangled a fat mouse, still wriggling. With a crunch, he broke its back and tossed it at her feet.

Emily crouched and scooped up the warm body. She tucked it against Karl's skin under the blanket, her eyes misty. Martin remained, in spirit, to protect her and his son. "Thank you."

Then she closed her eyes; first, to thank the *väeloom* for the food, and second, to press her luck and beg for more.

Milk, she thought. She pictured a babe suckling at a breast,

252

the frothy swirls of creamy milk still warm from a teat. *The baby needs milk.*

The fox tilted its head, ears spread wide and curving to catch the slightest sound. It yipped.

Emily shook her head at her foolishness. If, by some miracle, such bounty had survived the ravages of two armies, the starving serfs would have found it and devoured it by now. She patted the baby's bottom. He was warm enough, she was not alone, and that was better than nothing.

For hours Emily and the fox kept pace; Emily in the ruts of the supply wagons, the fox weaving in and out of the brush. Karl gurgled until his hunger awoke, then he whimpered. The fox—Emily called him *Rebane*, "fox" in the old tongue—howled back at the baby. Before the sun was high above, washing out the tan landscape in a glare so bright it hurt her eyes, Karl had fallen into a fitful sleep.

"Sleep is the best cure for hunger," she crooned to him. "Dream of a full belly."

Midafternoon, Emily forded a small stream, stopping to drink the icy water. She dribbled some into the baby's mouth, and he arched his back, screeching in anger.

Hardened by years of such pain, she forced the lullaby past the lump in her throat and gave him more. "Tsuu, tsuu…" *Hush, hush.*

Rebane drank, lapping up the water. His thirst sated, he scampered into the brush. She changed the baby's wraps and slung him once again across her chest.

Rebane barked off to her right. Emily called to him. Insistent, he barked again. Emily looked to the southeast, where dust from thousands of boots and hooves smudged the horizon. At the camp, she might trade her skills as a cook or seamstress for food. If she did not reach it before sunset, though, they'd be forced to spend another night in the woods. She did not dare approach the camp in the dark.

Rebane barked again. *Come.* The bark was plain to her ears. *Come here*, he called.

Emily slipped and stumbled along the stream bank. Brambles and thick branches blocked her way, scratching her arms and face. The stream widened. Mud sucked at her boots, icy water stabbing into her feet.

A lowing sound met her ears.

Impossible.

And yet, there in a clearing stood a dairy cow, roped to a tree and mooing to be milked. A hidden bounty, kept away from the ravages of the war by dense brambles and luck. Emily kept her meager sword at the ready and crept forward. Rebane stayed back from the animal, his eyes glittering.

Thank you. She nodded to him.

Emily dug out a wide pot from her supplies and sprayed steaming milk into the basin. Placid and grateful, the cow did not struggle. Emily's belly ached for the rich cream, but she took a mouthful, brought her mouth to Karl's, and let the milk dribble in. The milk was rich with fat, sweet and creamy on her tongue. He wriggled in pleasure and gripped her face, his mouth seeking more. When she pulled away, he wailed.

Emily laughed. "You will live one more day, be patient."

Once they were both full of milk, Karl drifted into a more contented sleep, and Emily stood back, eyeing the cow. It had cleared the grass in a circle around the tree. Even some of the bark had been gnawed away. The person who had stashed it here had not returned since the battle. Could she manage to lead the animal? How long before a deserter or a serf or a soldier took it from her? Setting aside the milk pan, she untied the animal and led it to the water.

"That's my cow!" A tall man with a nose like a boiled potato burst from the direction of the clearing. He carried a pitchfork. A serf, by the looks of him, with patched pants and a threadbare shirt beneath a worn coat. Around his neck were two clay jugs.

Emily cursed herself. Of course, the cow had been hidden well from the soldiers, but the man had come for milk. "She was thirsty," Emily said, shifting her grip on the rusty sword.

Goodness was gone from Russia, she knew, and people could not be trusted.

"You stole my milk." The man's eyes were hard—as hard as Emily's own could she see them, she was sure. He stepped forward.

Emily raised the sword. "I have this baby to feed. And the cow needed milking."

"I was coming." He glared at her. "Get out of here."

Emily hesitated. "I'll give you this sword for the cow."

"Don't be stupid."

She nodded. A month ago, he might have taken her offer, with soldiers from a dozen countries rampaging over the countryside, but the armies had gone. If his family was to survive the winter, the cow would be much more useful. But if Karl was to survive the week, Emily needed milk.

"Please. His mother was killed by a Frenchman. His father died at Borodino."

The serf bit his lip. "Our baby starved when the soldiers burned our crops. Give him to me. My wife will care for him."

Emily swayed on her feet. "He is my only family." Her arm tightened on the warm bundle pressed against her, and Karl cooed in his sleep. She'd rather die than abandon him.

The serf shrugged. "Better to be fed and warm than out here. We're good people."

"Never." *Never.* Emily offered the sword. "For one jug, then."

The serf considered. "Toss it to me."

Emily shook her head. "Milk the cow and fill the jug, then leave it and step back. I'll throw the sword into the stream, take the jug, and then you can retrieve it."

He nodded. Emily kept the sword high while he milked the patient animal. She watched him, thinking of the Frenchman's screams and then his silence. When the jug frothed over, the serf capped it with a cork and left it settling into some mud.

Emily sent Rebane an image of the jug, hoping he understood. Her deprivation only went so far. She would not doom the man and steal his cow, but Karl had to survive.

The serf stepped away from the milk. Rebane leapt from the woods and snarled, circling the jug. Emily hurried forward and picked it up even as the serf swore and raised his pitchfork.

"I'm sorry," she said, "but I need this sword more than you do. Thank you for the milk."

"Witch!" The man stared at her and Rebane, his eyes wide.

"Just hungry and desperate, like you." Keeping her eyes on the man, her arms straining against the heavy sword and jug, Emily backed away.

Then she turned and ran, crashing through the brush with Rebane. Karl awoke with a cry. Branches cracked behind; the serf had not given up so easily.

Help me! Emily cried in her mind.

Rebane turned, growling, his teeth bared. Emily pushed through dry lilac shrubs. The man shouted and then screamed in pain. Emily winced but did not turn.

Only when she reached the wagon tracks again did Emily breathe easy. Rebane, blood on his teeth, joined her alongside the road. The serf would go back to his cow. She hoped his wound would not fester, but she'd had to protect her family. Emily took a moment to tie the milk jug to her heavy pack and turned once again toward the path of the armies.

The snow had fallen two weeks ago and now lay thick as a funeral blanket across the land. Emily's fingers were numb, her ears beyond recovery, but the pain could be endured. The sharp cinnamon of Martin's coat had faded, leaving only the empty smell of snow. Rebane stayed by her side, keeping Karl safe, keeping Emily from despair.

The French army dropped gold, silver, valuables looted from Moscow's wealthy houses, and an endless trail of frozen corpses in their wake. Tucked at the bottom of the pack on Emily's back was a pouch full of jewels, diamonds, and rubies from a noblewoman's collection. Just one of the precious stones would make her a rich woman if she survived to sell it.

Emily paused to yank boots off a dead man. Little more than

a boy, but small enough that his boots would replace her own. After tying the shoes on her feet—sighing and wiggling her toes in appreciation of the passing pleasure—she withdrew her sword from the snowbank where she'd stuck it and turned toward the Berezina River.

For a month, she'd trailed the armies, searching the multitude of bodies for food and supplies. Rebane caught mice, and once, a fat alley cat. Emily survived on that and the hard, stale bread she found on dead soldiers, French and Russian alike. She'd replaced her sword three times, now carrying a long steel blade with an elaborate guard wrapped in leather.

Rebane had smelled out a grieving serf who had lost her own babe, but let Karl suckle in exchange for the first rusty blade and the clay milk jug. The second sword—a narrow thing crusted in blood—had been left in the back of a rapist outside Smolensk. Emily had taken a silver tea set from him. Half she'd given to his victim, a young woman who'd taken the teapot and sugar bowl and vanished into a blistering snowstorm. The silver Emily traded in the Russian camps for another woman to nurse Karl. The woman's milk had kept him alive until she froze to death.

Karl babbled against Emily's chest, wrapped in furs and a woolen blanket. Three mice for Emily's dinner provided more insulation. Rebane was a constant shadow now, bound by her lullaby and Martin's love. Rebane's sharp nose and smoldering eyes kept her moving forward, determined to find a place of safety for Karl.

Now the army approached the Berezina River. She slogged through the muck along the wide track of the French army, grateful for new boots, and considered Karl's best chance.

The Russians had blockaded the bridge in Borisov. There would be a battle. Already the cannons and gunfire cracked like frozen branches over the snow. Emily might slip over the bridge with her treasure to leave Russia and death behind her. A bent old woman with a tiny baby would hardly be a threat to either army, and Rebane was at her side. Emily straightened and turned toward the fires of the Russian camp.

Rebane gripped her skirt with his teeth, pulling her to the north.

"The bridge is in town."

He growled and pulled again. Then he scampered ahead, looking toward a forested bend in the river.

Emily sighed. He'd found milk for the baby, after all. Perhaps another grieving camp follower still had milk flowing—the baby hadn't eaten in a day. The snowdrifts clawed at her legs, shards of snow and ice sliding into her new boots. Soon she was under the trees, fir and spruce blocking the worst of the winter. The sharpness of pine needles mingled with the cold emptiness of snow, stinging her nostrils.

Rebane crouched, his ears quivering. Emily stopped, drawing close behind a tree, and peering through the dense forest. Her mouth dropped open. The French army huddled ahead, pressed against a bend in the river. Tattered uniforms, gaunt men, weapons held with careless habit. The French milled around the water's edge, the stiff, empty desperation of dying men as potent as the rushing water and the distant booming of cannons.

Emily crept closer, peering past the dense crowd of starving men. Napoleon had built a pontoon bridge. She admired his determination. Even as Russia and her winter chased him from the north, he refused to surrender. The French would slip away while the Russians guarded the wrong bridge.

Emily looked down at Karl, his dark hair just visible beneath the wraps and blankets that sheltered him. Away from Russia, away from serfdom and war, he could thrive. With Rebane at her side, Emily could protect him.

But first, they had to cross the river.

Emily told Rebane to wait in the woods. Then she shuffled around, emerging near a cluster of shivering women and children near the water's edge. They would be last, of course, after the soldiers crossed. She slipped amongst them as though she belonged, and none questioned her. Who had energy to doubt an old woman? Their eyes were dead already, barely registering her.

All but one.

"Vanaema!" Marie shoved through the crowd. She had lost weight, and wore a bruise on her cheek. "Is that..." Marie reached out for Karl. "He's alive."

Karl heard her voice and awoke, squirming against Emily. Emily drew back. The girl's milk would be long dry after so many weeks apart from the baby. "He is no longer yours."

Marie's eyes flashed. "Give me back my son." The other women drew away, their eyes averted.

Emily shook her head. "I have kept him alive. Make another." She sneered at Marie. "Where is your officer? You sleep with the French now?"

Marie snarled. "He died. I did what was necessary. Karl," she sang in a lilt. "Karl, come to me." Marie reached out and raked her hands along Emily's shoulders, searching for the knot to the sling. Karl began to cry.

"No!" Emily shoved her.

Marie screeched. "Give me my son!" She swung at Emily, fingers clawed.

Silently, perhaps spurred by the rage in Marie's voice, the desperate French broke. The remnants of the army surged across the unstable bridge. Men cursed and grumbled, shoving and striking to reach the other side. The camp followers, too, saw their route clear and pressed forward. Marie's fury was drowned out by the sudden rush.

Emily drew her sword from the fold in her skirts where it hung. "Leave us alone!"

Marie, beyond madness, likely starving, ignored the blade and tackled Emily. Karl wailed in fear. Emily hit the frozen ground, pain sparking from her spine, her legs. Marie batted the sword away from Emily's old fingers.

Karl's terrified cries slipped into the cracks of Emily's hardened heart. Marie's eyes were wild, her breath coming in gasps as she fought for her son.

Her son.

Emily had fought cold and hunger and fear for her children. She'd crossed Russia to protect Karl. Was Marie so different?

Emily's arms tightened over the baby. She hadn't abandoned her children in order to survive. Marie had. She didn't deserve Karl.

Emily had fought for her children. Just as Marie was fighting now. A sharp bark came from the woods, piercing between the struggle. Rebane. Martin's spirit who protected his family. She would not be alone.

"Stop." Emily's heart shattered. "You can have him. Just let me come with you." Emily's voice barely penetrated the cluttered chaos around them. She untied the sling and handed Karl to his mother's clutching arms. Marie whirled, running across the Berezina. Karl's wails faded into the clamor.

"Come back!" Emily stared at her treacherous hands, her throat tight. *Rebane! Join me! All väeloom come to me!*

Rebane slunk from the woods, his ears pressed hard against his head in fear of the men all around, but no other spirits came to her side. Emily struggled to her feet, her heart banging like the cannons to the south, loud and near and full of death.

She had kept Karl alive. *She* had protected him. Marie should have been willing to suffer an old woman at her side. But where was he? Where had she taken Karl?

There! On the second wobbly platform, Emily glimpsed a dark head, a little pink hand. She leapt forward, her knees protesting. The pontoons were rocking, tilting dangerously beneath the stampede of fear. The Berezina, dull gray and pocked here and there by muddy ice, sighed at the minor barrier as it swept south.

Marie overbalanced and fell into the Berezina, her scream taking the place of Karl's, which broke off as they plunged into the choppy river. Karl's tiny body bobbed next to his mother, his chubby cheeks pale against the black water. Emily stumbled into the water with a wail of despair.

The Berezina was frigid. Pain worse than the coldest night dug into her flesh, her legs refusing to lift, her heart pulling her ahead. Teeth chattering, she hummed the tune of her heart, willing her body to move forward.

Grow, grow bigger.

Marie slapped at the water uselessly, mouth clamped shut against cloying waves. Her thin arms lifted Karl above her head, which disappeared for ever-longer moments beneath the water.

A red blur splashed past. Rebane paddled to the baby. He grabbed Karl by the arm and pulled him back to shore. Emily crawled in the mud, refusing the erupting emotions in her chest. *Not alone, not alone,* she thought over and over.

In the river, Marie fell still, her arms no longer slapping at the surface. She drifted away.

Rebane pulled Karl onto the shore. The baby did not move, his mouth wide and his eyes shut. Emily desperately climbed ashore and scooped him up, rubbing his chest, her arms trembling so hard she no longer felt the cold, her stomach so tight hunger seemed a foolish concern.

"Tsuu, tsuu. Kasva suuremasse, kasva karjatsesse." *Hush, hush. Grow bigger, grow to be a herder.*

He wouldn't, not now. The cold silent ground would swallow him, as it had Martin and the rest. All that remained was emptiness. She forced the song through her tears, soothing herself as much as the baby's spirit. She squatted on the frozen ground, holding the baby and rocking.

Rebane shook off. He curled around the baby, thick tail encircling Karl's dark head. Emily's heart grew icy in her chest, but she kept singing. Could Rebane choose? She would lose the link to her past without Rebane, but without Karl, she had no future. Sparkling black eyes found Emily's. Rebane yipped, shivered, and then relaxed completely and fell still.

Karl opened his eyes, a weak wail piercing the air. Emily sang louder, scooping him up and swaddling him in the layers of warmth and protection that had carried him so far. He would live, he would grow. Emily would keep him safe. Rebane's red fur blew in the river's breeze, his eyes dull and empty.

A life for a life.

Emily stood for a long moment, staring down at the thin body. Martin's spirit had protected his son to the last, protected him so he could grow, grow bigger. Perhaps in a safer, warmer world, she could grieve, but the cannon fire grew near, the shouts of battle rising. Behind her, the Russians attacked the French defenders, who would die so their comrades could live.

Emily lifted her chin, turned away, and followed the last stragglers across the bridge. Karl cried as babies should.

The Single Most Important Piece of Advice

BY FRANK HERBERT

Frank Herbert was a reporter and editor on a number of newspapers before becoming a full-time writer.

Although he had been publishing short fiction in various SF magazines since 1952, he became an "overnight" success in 1956 with his first novel, which was serialized in John Campbell's Astounding Science Fiction *magazine as "Under Pressure." (In book form, it's known either as* Twenty-First Century Sub *or* The Dragon in the Sea.)

His career took a major turn with the 1963 ASF *publication of the first Dune story. Since then, of course, Herbert and the Dune stories have become world famous. It can be fairly said that Herbert was the last of the* ASF *"Golden Age" writers. Although those fabulous days had drawn to a close, the sweep and grandeur of Herbert's work during the last years of Campbell's editorship compellingly recall the very best of the* ASF *spirit.*

In bringing classical science fiction to worldwide prominence, Herbert ranks among this field's major contributors. An uncompromising stickler for the kind of storytelling principles that are a vigorous SF tradition, Herbert was both popular and respected.

Here is, to our knowledge, the last essay Frank Herbert ever wrote. He gave it to us with the clear purpose of fulfilling what he saw as a paramount obligation to his art and craft.

Proud of his contributions to the Writers of the Future Contest, as a judge, we had asked him for the single most important piece of advice he would give a beginning writer. Here it is:

The Single Most Important
Piece of Advice

The single most important piece of advice I ever got was to concentrate on story. What is "story"? It's the quality that keeps the reader following the narrative. A good story makes interesting things happen to a character with whom the reader can identify. And it keeps them happening so that the character progresses and grows in stature.

A writer's job is to do whatever is necessary to make the reader want to read the next line. That's what you're supposed to be thinking about when you're writing a story. Don't think about money, don't think about success; concentrate on the story—don't waste your energy on anything else. That all takes care of itself if you've done your job as a writer. If you haven't done that, nothing helps.

I first heard this from literary agent Lurton Blassingame, a highly respected expert on successful storytellers and storytelling. He's a man who's been watching writers' careers and building writers' careers for decades. And I have heard essentially the same thing from many other successful figures in writing; some of the top writers in the world have said it. It is the best advice I can give beginners.

I'd also like to say something about older hands helping newcomers. Like many other established writers, I teach students on frequent occasions and lecture to many other audiences anxious for advice on writing. I'm very happy to be able to lend my help to the Writers of the Future program. From time to time, though, people have come up to me and asked why I want to "create competition" by helping newcomers.

Talking about "competition" in that way is nonsense! The more good writers there are, the more good readers there will be. We'll all benefit—writers and readers alike!

So the other piece of advice I have for newcomers is: "Remember how you learned, and when your turn comes, teach."

The Daddy Box

written by
Frank Herbert

illustrated by
ANDRÉ MATA

ABOUT THE AUTHOR

Even the author of Dune—*the bestselling science fiction novel of all time—had trouble getting published. At first.*

Frank Herbert wanted to be a writer, and though today his name is practically synonymous with worldbuilding and epic science fiction, Herbert didn't start out with a particular genre in mind. He wrote mainstream stories, mysteries, thrillers, men's adventure pieces, humorous slice-of-life tales, and yes, some science fiction.

In his early years, Herbert faced many rejections. His submissions came close-but-not-quite at magazine after magazine. Frank Herbert was an inspired writer with an unpredictable muse. He wrote what he wanted to write, about the characters and the situations that struck his fancy, paying very little attention to the market or the requirements of the magazines to which he submitted.

As a result, his stories were often the wrong length or didn't fit the market. Magazines liked his work but could not use it. His agent also had a frustrating time finding a home for Herbert's work.

And yet he kept writing.

Finally, in 1956, he found success, placing his novel The Dragon in the Sea *with Doubleday, which received wide critical acclaim and made him a writer to watch.*

So Herbert wrote another novel... which he couldn't get published. And another novel, and more short stories, and other novels. He kept trying, with his subjects wandering all over the map, until he finally wrote Dune, *which was possibly the most unpublishable* SF *novel of all, rejected more than twenty times before it was finally released by a house that specialized in auto repair manuals.*

And eventually, that novel made him a world-famous author.

"The Daddy Box" was written for Harlan Ellison's fabled Last Dangerous Visions anthology, following his two ground-breaking Dangerous Visions anthologies. But that anthology was delayed and delayed, and ultimately was never published, so this short story never saw print in either Frank Herbert's or Harlan Ellison's lifetime. It is a compelling, imaginative story that is pure Frank Herbert.

ABOUT THE ILLUSTRATOR

André Mata is a freelance illustrator who lives and works in Portugal. Attracted to the visual arts, he started drawing from an early age, inspired by the stories, movies, games, and themes that kindled his imagination.

After concluding his illustration studies in university, he invested in his independent studies through books, blogs, articles, and tutorials, developing drawing and painting, switching between observational exercises and imaginative work.

Inspired by nature, his main goal has always been the development of imagery that triggers a positive emotional response, weaving realism with imagination.

Working with traditional and digital media, he develops illustrations, paying attention to the light, colors and shapes, while trying to capture the feeling of the moment in a single image.

Influenced by classical literature, the Golden Age of Illustration and imaginative realism, he currently develops work for the science fiction and fantasy field, as well as portraiture, landscape, and animal painting.

The Daddy Box

To understand what happened to Henry Alexander when his son, Billy, came home with the ferosslk, you're going to be asked to make several mind-stretching mental adjustments. These mental gymnastics are certain to leave your mind permanently changed.

You've been warned.

In the first place, just to get a loose idea of a ferosslk's original purpose, you must think of it as a toy designed primarily for educating the young. But your concept of *toy* should be modified to think of a device which, under special circumstances, will play with its owner.

You'll also have to modify your concept of education to include the idea of occasionally altering the universe to fit a new interesting idea; that is, fitting the universe to the concept, rather than fitting the concept to the universe.

The ferosslk originates with seventh-order multidimensional beings. You can think of them as *Sevens*. Their other labels would be more or less incomprehensible. The Sevens are not now aware and never have been aware that the universe contains any such thing as a Henry Alexander or his human male offspring.

This oversight was rather unfortunate for Henry. His mind had never been stretched to contain the concept of a ferosslk. He could conceive of fission bombs, nerve gas, napalm, and germ warfare. But these things might be thought of as silly putty when compared with a ferosslk.

269

Which is a rather neat analogy because the shape of a ferosslk is profoundly dependent upon external pressures. That is to say, although a ferosslk can be conceived of as an artifact, it is safer to think of it as alive.

To begin at one of the beginnings, Billy Alexander, age eight, human male, found the ferosslk in tall weeds beside a path across an empty lot adjoining his urban home.

Saying he "found" it described the circumstances from Billy's superficial point of view. It would be just as accurate to say the ferosslk found Billy.

As far as Billy was concerned, the ferosslk was a box. You may as well think of it that way, too. No sense stretching your mind completely out of shape. You wouldn't be able to read the rest of this account.

A box, then. It appeared to be about nine inches long, three inches wide, and four inches deep. It looked like dark-green stone except for what was obviously the top, because that's where the writing appeared.

You can call it writing because Billy was just beginning to shift from print to cursive, and that's the way he saw it.

Words flowed across the box top: "This is a daddy box."

Billy picked it up. The surface was cold under his hands. He thought perhaps this was some kind of toy television, its words projected from inside.

(Some of the words actually were coming out of Billy's own mind.)

Daddy box? he wondered.

Daddy was a symbol-identifier more than five years old for him. His *daddy* had been killed in a war. Now Billy had a stepfather with the same name as his real father's. The two had been cousins.

New information flowed across the top: "This box may be opened only by the young."

(That was a game the ferosslk had played and enjoyed many times before. Don't try to imagine how a ferosslk enjoys. The attempt could injure your frontal lobes.)

Now the box top provided Billy with precise instructions on how it could be opened.

Billy went through the indicated steps, which included urinating on an anthill, and the box dutifully opened.

For almost an hour, Billy sat in the empty lot, enraptured by the educational/creative tableau thus unveiled. For his edification, human shapes in the box fought wars, manufactured artifacts, made love, wrote books, created paintings and sculpture... and changed the universe. The human shapes debated, formed governments, nurtured the earth, and destroyed it.

In that relative time of little less than an hour, Billy aged mentally some five hundred and sixteen human years. On the outside, Billy remained a male child about forty-nine inches tall, weight approximately fifty-six pounds, skin white but grimy from play, hair blond and mussed.

His eyes were still blue, but they had acquired a hard and penetrating stare. The motor cells in his medulla and his spinal cord had begun increasing dramatically in number with an increased myelinization of the anterior roots and peripheral nerves.

Every normal sense he possessed had been increased in potency, and he was embarked on a growth pattern that would further heighten this effect.

The whole thing made him sad, but he knew what he had to do, having come very close to understanding what a ferosslk was all about.

It was now about 6:18 p.m. on a Friday evening. Billy took the box in both hands and trudged across the lot toward his back door.

His mother, whose left arm still bore bruises from a blow struck by her husband, was peeling potatoes at the kitchen sink. She was a small blonde woman, once doll-like, fast turning to mouse.

At Billy's entrance, she shook tears out of her eyes, smiled at him, glanced toward the living room, and shook her head—all in one continuous movement. She appeared not to notice the box in Billy's hands, but she did note the boy appeared very much like his real father tonight.

271

ANDRÉ MATA

This thought brought more tears to her eyes, and she turned away, thus failing to see Billy go on into the living room despite her silent warning that his stepfather was there and in a bad mood.

The ferosslk, having shared Billy's emotional reaction to this moment, created a new order of expletives, which it introduced into another dimension.

Henry Alexander sensed Billy's presence in the room, lowered the evening newspaper, and stared over it into the boy's newly aged eyes. Henry was a pale-skinned, flabby man, going to fat after a youth spent as a semiprofessional athlete. He interpreted the look in Billy's eyes as a reflection of their mutual hate.

"What's that box?" Henry demanded.

Billy shrugged. "It's a daddy box."

"A what?"

Billy remained silent, placed the box to his ear. The ferosslk had converted to faint audio mode, and the voices coming from the box for Billy's ears alone carried a certain suggestive educational quality.

"Why're you holding the damn thing against your ear?" Henry demanded. He had already decided to take the box away from the boy but was drawing the pleasure-moment out.

"I'm listening," Billy said. He sensed the precise pacing of these moments, observed minute nuances in the set of his stepfather's jaw, the content of the man's perspiration.

"Is it a music box?"

Henry studied the thing in Billy's hand. It looked old... ancient, even. He couldn't quite say why he felt this.

Again, Billy shrugged.

"Where'd you get it?" Henry asked.

"I found it."

"Where could you find a thing like that? It looks like a real antique. Might even be jade."

"I found it in the lot." Billy hesitated on the point of adding a precise location to where he'd found the box but held back. That would be out of character.

"Are you sure you didn't steal it?"

"I found it."

"Don't you sass me!" Henry threw his newspaper to the floor.

Having heard the loud voices, Billy's mother hurried into the living room, hovered behind her son.

"What's...what's the matter?" she ventured.

"You stay out of this, Helen!" Henry barked. "That brat of yours has stolen a valuable antique, and he—"

"China? He wouldn't!"

"I told you to stay out of this!" Henry glared at her. The box had assumed for him now exactly the quality he had just given it: valuable antique. Theft was as good as certain—although that might complicate his present plans for confiscation and profit.

Billy suppressed a smile. His mother's interruption, which he assumed to be fortuitous since he did not completely understand the functioning of a ferosslk, had provided just the delay required here. The situation had entered the timing system for which he had maneuvered.

"Bring that box here," Henry ordered.

"It's mine," Billy said. As he said it, he experienced a flash of insight that told him he belonged as much to the box as it belonged to him.

"Look here, you disrespectful brat—if you don't give me that box immediately, we're going to have another session in the woodshed!"

Billy's mother touched his arm, said, "Son...you'd better..."

"Okay," Billy said. "But it's just a trick box—like those Chinese things."

"I said bring it here, dammit!"

Clutching the box to his chest now, Billy crossed the room, timing his movements with careful precision. Just a few more seconds...now!

He extended the box to his stepfather.

Henry snatched the ferosslk, was surprised at how cold it felt. Obviously stone. Cold stone. He turned the thing over and over in his hands. There were strange markings on the top—wedges, curves, twisting designs. He put it to his ear, listened.

Silence.

Billy smiled.

Henry jerked the box away from his ear. Trick, eh? The kid was playing a trick on him, trying to make him look like a fool.

"So, it's a box," Henry said. "Have you opened it?"

"Yes. It's got lots of things inside."

"Things? What things?"

"Just things."

Henry had an immediate vision of valuable jewels. This thing could be a jewel box.

"How does it open?" he demanded.

"You just do things," Billy said.

"Don't you play smart with me! I gave you an order: tell me how you open this thing."

"I can't."

"You mean you won't!"

"I can't."

"Why?" It was as much an accusation as a question.

Again, Billy shrugged. "The box...well, it can only be opened by kids."

"Oh, for Chrissakes!" Henry examined the ends of the box. Damn kid was lying about having opened it. Henry shook the box. It rattled suggestively, one of the ferosslk's better effects.

Helen said, "Perhaps if you let Billy..."

Henry looked up long enough to stare her down, then asked, "Is dinner ready?"

"Henry, he's just a child!"

"Woman, I've worked all day to support you and your brat. Is this the appreciation I get?"

She backed toward the kitchen door, hesitated there.

Henry returned his attention to the box. He pushed at the end panels. Nothing happened. He tried various pressures on the top, the sides, and the bottom.

"So you opened it, eh?" Henry asked, staring across the box at Billy.

"Yes."

"You're lying."

"I opened it."

Having achieved the effect he wanted, Henry thrust the box toward Billy. "Then open it."

Having achieved one of the moments he wanted, and right on time, Billy went for the effect. He turned the box over, slid an end panel aside, whipped the top open and closed it, then restored the end panel and presented the closed box to Henry.

"See? It's easy."

The ferosslk, having achieved an education node, convinced Henry that he'd seen gold and jewels during the brief moment when the box had been opened.

Henry grabbed the box, wet his lips with his tongue. He pushed at the end panel. It refused to move.

"Grown-ups can't open it," Billy said. "It says so right on the top."

Henry brought a clasp knife from his hip pocket, opened it, and tried to find an opening around the top of the box.

Billy stared at him.

Billy's mother still hovered fearfully in the kitchen doorway.

Henry had the sudden realization that they both hoped he'd cut himself. He closed the knife, returned it to his pocket, and extended the box toward Billy. "Open it for me."

"I can't."

Ominously, Henry asked, "And...why...not?"

"I can't let go of it when it's open."

The ferosslk inserted a sense of doubt into the situation here without Billy suspecting. Henry nodded. That just might be true. The box might have a spring lock that closed when you let go of it.

"Then open it and let me look inside while you hold it," Henry said.

"I can't now without doing all the other things."

"What?"

"I can open it twice without the other things, but..."

"What other things?"

"Oh...like finding a grass seed and breaking a twig...and I'd have to find another anthill. The one I—"

"Of all the damn fool nonsense!" Henry thrust the box toward Billy. "Open this!"

"I can't!"

Billy's mother said, "Henry, why don't you—"

"Helen, you get the hell out of here and let me handle this!"

She backed farther into the kitchen.

Henry said, "Billy, either you open this box for me, or I'll open it the hard way—with an axe."

Billy shook his head from side to side, dragging out the moment for its proper curve.

"Very well." Henry heaved himself from the chair, the box clutched in his right hand, angry elation filling him. They'd done it again—goaded him beyond endurance.

He brushed past Billy, who turned and followed him. He thrust Helen aside when she put out a pleading hand. He strode out the back door, slamming it behind him, then heard it open, the patter of Billy's footsteps following.

Let the brat make one protest! Just one!

Henry set his jaw, headed across the backyard toward the woodshed—that anachronism that set the tone and marked the age of this house—"modest older home in quiet residential area."

Now Billy called from behind him, "What're you going to do?"

Henry stifled an angry retort, caught by an odd note in Billy's voice...an imperative.

"Daddy!" Billy called.

Henry stopped at the woodshed door, glanced back. Billy never called him *daddy*. The boy stood in the path from the house; his mother waited on the back porch.

Now, why was I angry with them? Henry wondered.

He felt the box in his hand, looked at it. Jewels? In this dirty green little piece of stoneware? He was filled with the sense of his own foolishness, an effect achieved by a sophisticated refinement of ferosslk educational processing. Given a possible lesson to impart, the instructor could not resist the opportunity.

Once more, Henry looked at the two who watched him.

They'd done this deliberately to make him appear foolish! Damn them!

"Daddy, don't break the box," Billy said.

It was a nicely timed protest, and it demonstrated how well he had learned from the ferosslk.

His anger restored, Henry whirled away, slammed the box onto the woodshed's chopping block, and grabbed up the axe.

Don't break the box!

"Wait!" Billy called.

Henry barely hesitated, a lapse which put him in the precise phasing Billy wanted.

Taking careful aim, Henry brought the axe hissing down. He still felt foolish because it's difficult to shake off a ferosslk lesson, but anger carried him through.

At the instant of contact between blade and box, an electric glimmer leaped into existence around the axe head.

To Billy, watching from the yard, the blade appeared to slice into the box, shrinking, shining, drawing inward at an impossible angle. There came an abrupt, juicy vacuum-popping noise—a cow pulling its foot out of the mud. The axe handle whipped into the box after the blade, vanished with a diminishing glimmer.

Still clutching the axe handle, Henry Alexander was jerked into the box—down, down...shrinking...

Whoosh!

The pearl glimmering winked out. The box remained on the chopping block where Henry had placed it.

Billy darted into the woodshed, grabbed up the box, and pressed it to his left ear. From far away came a leaf-whispering babble of many angry and pleading voices. He could distinguish some of the names being called by those voices—

"Abdul!"

"Terrik!"

"Churudish!"

"Pablo!"

"James!"

"Sremani!"

"Harold!"

And, on a low and diminishing wail, "Bill-eeeeeeeeeee..."

Having taught part of a lesson, the ferosslk recognized that the toy-plus-play element remained incomplete. By attaching a label at the proper moment, Billy had achieved a daddy-linkage, but no daddy existed now for all practical purposes. There were voices, of course, and certain essences—an available gene pattern from which to reconstruct the original. Something with the proper daddyness loomed as a distinct possibility, and the ferosslk observed an attractive learning pattern in the idea.

A golden glow began to emerge from one end of the box. Billy dropped it and backed away as the glow grew and grew and grew. Abruptly, the glow coalesced, and Henry Alexander emerged.

Billy felt a hand clutch his shoulder, looked up at his mother. The box lay on the ground near the chopping block. She looked from it to the figure that had emerged from it.

"Billy," she demanded, "what...what happened?"

Henry stooped, recovered the box.

"Henry," she said, "you hit that box with the axe, but it's not broken."

"Huh?" Henry Alexander stared at her. "What're you talking about? I brought the damn thing out here to make sure it was safe for Billy to play with."

He thrust the box at Billy, who took it and almost dropped it. "Here—take it, son."

"But Billy was pestering you," she said. "You said you'd..."

"Helen, you nag the boy too much," Henry said. "He's just a boy, and boys will be boys." Henry winked at Billy. "Eh, son?" Henry reached over and mussed Billy's hair.

Helen backed up, releasing Billy's shoulder. She said, "But you...it looked like you went into the box!"

Henry looked at the box, then at Helen. He began to laugh. "Girl, it's a good thing you got a man who loves you, because you are weird. You are really weird." He stepped around Billy, took Helen gently by the arm. "C'mon, I'll help you with dinner."

She allowed herself to be guided toward the house, her attention fixed on Henry.

Billy heard him say, "Y'know, honey, I think Billy could use a brother or a sister. What do you say?"

"Henry!"

Henry's laughter came rich and happy. He stopped, turned around to look at Billy, who stood in the woodshed doorway, holding the box.

"Stay where you can hear me call, Bill. Maybe we'll go to a movie after dinner, eh?"

Billy nodded.

"Hey," Henry called, "what're y' going to do with that funny box?"

Billy stared across the empty lot to the home of his friend, Jimmy Carter. He took a deep breath, said, "Jimmy's got a catcher's mitt he's been trying to trade me. Maybe he'd trade for the box."

"Hey!" Henry said. "Maybe he would at that. But look out Jimmy's old man doesn't catch you at it. You know what a temper he has."

"I sure do," Billy said. "I sure do...Dad."

Henry put his arm around Helen's shoulder and headed once more for the house. "Hear that?" he asked. "Hear him call me *Dad*? Y'know, Helen, nothing makes a man happier than to have a boy call him *Dad*."

Teamwork:
Getting the Best out of Two Writers

BY BRIAN HERBERT
& KEVIN J. ANDERSON

ABOUT THE AUTHORS

Brian Herbert is the son of legendary science fiction author Frank Herbert and has written the definitive biography of him, Dreamer of Dune, *a finalist for the Hugo Award. Brian has also written many original novels, including the Timeweb trilogy, the ecological fantasy* Ocean *(with his wife, Jan),* The Little Green Book of Chairman Rahma, The Unborn, *and* The Assassination of Billy Jeeling. *His earlier acclaimed novels include* The Stolen Gospels, Sudanna Sudanna, *and* Sidney's Comet, *as well as* Man of Two Worlds *(written with his father). Brian comanages the legacy of Frank Herbert and is an executive producer of the new motion picture* Dune *and the forthcoming TV series* Dune: The Sisterhood. *He and his wife live in Seattle, Washington.*

Kevin J. Anderson has published more than 170 books, 58 of which have been national or international bestsellers. He has written numerous novels in the Star Wars, X-Files, and Dune universes, as well as unique steampunk fantasy novels Clockwork Angels *and* Clockwork Lives, *written with legendary rock drummer Neil Peart. He has edited numerous anthologies, written comics and games, and the lyrics to two rock CDs. Anderson is the director of the graduate program in publishing at Western Colorado University. Anderson and his wife Rebecca Moesta live in Colorado, and are the publishers of WordFire Press.*

Together, Brian and Kevin have written over twenty novels and numerous short stories, primarily expanding Frank Herbert's Dune universe, but also on their original SF epic, the Hellhole Trilogy.

281

Teamwork:
Getting the Best out of Two Writers

Writing is a lonely business, but it doesn't have to be.

Some forms of artistic expression are solitary professions, such as a painter, potter, sculptor, musical soloist. You can write alone and tell your story, making every word your private vision. Nobody's going to touch your prose.

Other great art, though, requires teamwork—playing in a band, making a movie or a comic book, being part of a dance troupe. Sometimes that applies to working as a writer, too. Collaborating with a creative partner is an invigorating, rewarding experience that produces stories that are richer, more ambitious, and with a broader foundation than one person can do alone.

The two of us—Brian Herbert and Kevin J. Anderson—have worked together as collaborators for a quarter of a century, writing more than twenty books together for a total of over three million published words—and almost no arguments along the way! It has been a very satisfying experience for us, and playing to each other's strengths has allowed us to create works different from anything we could do on our own.

Fair warning, this isn't for everybody. Not all collaborations work. Sometimes the collaborative process or the prose styles don't mesh, or sometimes two people simply don't have the temperament to work with each other. Bands break up, too. A collaboration is like any relationship—it requires work, compromise, and respect.

The two of us each write our own solo novels as well as our collaborations, but in many instances, the project simply needs two people to do the heavy lifting.

In this article, we'll talk about the reasons for coauthoring a story, and we'll give you some techniques to use and pitfalls to avoid.

WHY WOULD YOU COLLABORATE?

There are many rationales for bringing two writers together on a project. For instance, you might need a coauthor with a particular area of expertise to help you write a certain story, something much more in-depth than just asking questions. Your gritty political thriller might require someone who knows the inner workings of the military or the government. You might find a person who has detailed (and marketable) inside information you yourself don't have, but you are better at telling a story. You could need a coauthor who is an expert in horses, or nuclear physics, or pro football.

Brian's father, Frank Herbert, is the author of the original classic novel *Dune* and the legendary creator of the Dune universe. Frank Herbert passed away in 1986, leaving his science fiction epic unfinished. Frank's last published novel, *Man of Two Worlds*, was a collaboration with Brian, and Brian is now in charge of the Dune canon and continuity, along with two of his father's grandchildren. With his background and expertise, Brian has worked with Kevin, another of the biggest Dune fans in the world, to write multiple international bestselling novels that continue the saga. As coauthors, they share their knowledge in all the nuances and complexities of Dune, with two sets of feet to fill the big shoes that the genius Frank Herbert left behind.

Another reason to collaborate is to build your knowledge and status as a writer. Imagine a master/apprentice-type of relationship, where an established or big-name author takes on a newer cowriter to do much of the work. What an opportunity for someone starting out! In such a case, the well-established author is lending their name, influence, and fan base to sell the book. The new writer gets an impressive credential, invaluable experience, and perhaps even a new group of readers.

Renowned science fiction writer Anne McCaffrey followed this model. She had a stable of apprentice writers that she developed and taught to write continuing books in some of her well-established universes. She would write up a detailed outline of the book she had in her mind, would discuss it with the apprentice writer, and then the apprentice would write the draft manuscript. Anne would polish it, and both names would appear on the cover. This is an excellent opportunity for newer writers if you should come upon such a chance.

Another good reason to collaborate is just to learn from your peers, exchange ideas, and test out writing techniques. When Kevin was just starting out as a short story writer, he found it an enlightening game to throw out an idea and then collaborate on a spec story with one of his writer friends. He would work with other unknown authors (he, too, was unknown at the time), and they would learn plotting tricks, writing skills, sensory description methods, character enrichment. At that point in his career, he had a lot to learn, and so did his fellow coauthors. It also became very clear that while some techniques worked for a certain writer, they didn't work for him—and vice versa.

Brian also collaborated on writing projects, short stories, and a novelette with his friend Bruce Taylor, novels and short stories with his cousin Marie Landis, and, of course, the novel *Man of Two Worlds* with Frank Herbert. Brian also once worked with another writer who was less known than he, and the two of them came up with the plot for a novel, laid the story out in a detailed outline, then proceeded to write their portions of the work. Wisely, Brian took a look at his collaborator's work only a couple of chapters into the project—and discovered that the other writer's work bore little resemblance to what they had talked about. Brian tried to get him back on course, but to no avail—the fellow just would not listen—so Brian ended the

284

project. It was unfortunate because the other writer had a great deal of descriptive talent but could not grasp the importance of working through a plot with a shared vision.

Finally, the best reason to collaborate is because you enjoy it. Brian and Kevin have a great deal of fun bouncing ideas, riffing off each other's suggestions like musicians in a jam session, developing and building a story in directions that would never have occurred to either without brainstorming together. And then sticking to the agreed-upon plot!

COLLABORATION TECHNIQUES

Each collaboration is like a marriage, an intimate creative relationship where you share your deepest details of prose, plot, and characterization. And there are many different ways to approach that partnership.

It's important to play to your coauthor's strengths. For instance, in our team, Brian has a degree in sociology and a wide knowledge of philosophy and comparative religions, while Kevin's background is in physics/astronomy and history. Kevin is particularly good at worldbuilding and action scenes, while Brian adds the philosophical and political depth that is vital to any Dune story. Therefore, when we plot our books together, Brian usually takes the Bene Gesserit or Fremen philosophical chapters, while Kevin will do the space battles or introduce a new alien world. But for fun, we have been known to switch roles, and our writing styles are so similar that readers cannot easily tell who wrote what.

The collaborative method can also depend upon writing style. One writer may love to do first drafts and hate the editing phase; the coauthor could be the exact opposite. In such a team, the "first and final" method works best: One coauthor will do a fast and energetic—but rough—draft of the manuscript, and the second writer will then polish the words into final form.

Kevin has worked this way with several cowriters, sometimes doing the draft part, sometimes doing the final polish. Though it isn't our normal routine, Brian and Kevin together have done some Dune pieces this way, usually when deadlines and constraints in their writing schedules force it upon us.

Normally, however, we rely on the "true collaboration" technique, where we are both involved in every chapter and every aspect of the development, writing, and editing process.

When it's time to start work on our next book, we will get together for several intense days, usually at Brian's house, where we brainstorm the entire novel. In that process, we develop the basic story arc of a trilogy and a more detailed arc for each particular novel, but that is just the starting point. Then, sitting together, we talk and hash it out, taking notes as we go along, throwing out ideas, and developing the novel in detail.

We often break this plotting into various storylines—e.g., the Emperor's storyline, the Baron Harkonnen's storyline, the House Atreides storyline. During these brainstorming sessions, anything goes. No idea is too crazy, and we rely on the other person to talk us down off the ledge if we're going too far afield.

We polish up our notes, juggle the storylines around, and then weave them together. All of the characters and every separate climax must be well choreographed, so the plot and characters put on a synchronized show.

As the story gels, we block out the full, complete outline of the novel, usually 90 to 100 chapters. After that outline has been iterated back and forth until we're both satisfied, we have the same clear picture of the complete story in our heads. Next, we divide up the chapters. Some are obvious picks—we know that this storyline is for Kevin, that storyline is for Brian—then we do a bit of horse-trading to hash out the unclaimed writing assignments. Each of us writes the first draft of exactly half of the book.

When we're done writing our assigned chapters, we stitch them together into a full draft manuscript, and one of us takes the first crack at editing. We smooth out the roughest spots, add missing scenes, fill in blanks we hadn't seen before. We pump up characters and make certain of their motivations, cut out the deadwood. That complete second-draft edit goes to the other partner, who does the same, and sends the third draft back, and so on, usually six or seven drafts until we give it to our test readers, and then do another polish before delivering to the publisher.

We like to compare our technique to a jazz performance, both of us knowing what we're doing, both of us letting the other have solo sections, and in the end, we create unique music. Because the two of us have been doing this for so long, we have it down to a very smooth technique.

On the opposite end of the spectrum is the "round-robin" technique, which differs from the way we do things together. Obviously, we are careful plotters and outliners. Because we're taking a road trip together, we want to make sure we share the same road map, the same route marked, and the same destination in mind.

Other writers, though, are "discovery" writers or "seat-of-the-pants" plotters. They don't like to outline ahead and want to see where the story goes organically. For such writers, a round-robin approach will work better, and it's more of an intellectual challenge. The two writers discuss the basic idea of their story, maybe develop the characters, a few plot points, and then they are off like improv comedians waiting for a prompt.

In that process, one writer will draft the first chapter or scene, then hand it to the coauthor, "Here, follow this!" The other writer picks up the threads and runs for another chapter before handing it back. (Warning, it can easily devolve into a game of one-upmanship, leaving your partner in more and more impossible cliffhangers.) This technique can be fun to test your skill and imagination as a creative writer—or it can also be maddening. Brian successfully used a variation of this technique in coauthoring two horror novels with Marie Landis. After agreeing on a plot, they alternated chapters, with Brian taking #1, Marie #2, and so on.

There are few hard-and-fast rules on how a person should write, but it probably won't be a smooth collaboration if a careful plotter tries to work with a seat-of-the-pants writer, as Brian learned in the ill-fated project described earlier.

The process can also be a lot of fun. In one of our Dune-series novels, we plotted out a scene in which our leading characters were traveling to another star system, and the Guild Navigator—their main hope of survival—ran into trouble, causing the Heighliner to stop in deep space. In the writing process, one of us killed the Navigator, leaving the characters stranded in the middle of nowhere, and then sent the manuscript over to his coauthor, telling him to figure out how to get them out of that mess! (And he did exactly that!)

WHAT DO YOU DO IN CASE OF CONFLICT?

Like child-rearing and coparenting, writing a story together is a very personal process, and you will be exposing your creative vulnerabilities in ways you're not accustomed to—just remember that your coauthor is doing the same. Always make sure that each partner has the same story vision in mind. Otherwise, you'll be working at cross purposes.

Some collaboration instructors suggest picking a "lead author" ahead of time, someone who has the final veto power in the case of a heated disagreement. Writers can argue over something as trivial as an adverb or as serious as killing off a character. If you decide who is the boss ahead of time, when cooler heads prevail, it could help avoid conflict.

For our own part, we have worked together long enough that we've managed to talk everything out and come up with a compromise. In a disagreement, we'll defer to whomever of us has more expertise in a certain area.

Our cross-editing process is particularly designed to avoid disputes. We don't use Track Changes. We don't highlight every word or comma that's been changed. Each of us is a full partner with the complete authority to perform any editing or rewriting we feel is necessary. Of course, if we're going to do anything major—like drastically revising a chapter, changing a plot arc, or killing off a character—we'll pick up the phone or send an email so we can discuss the matter before it's engraved in stone.

Well, we *learned* to pick up the phone, that is. In writing our first novel together, *Dune: House Atreides*, Brian wrote a chapter that followed the agreed-upon plot, but he added some twists and turns in the workings of the chapter. He was quite proud of it. But when he received the manuscript back from Kevin, that chapter was missing, with no comment! Perplexed, Brian retrieved the chapter, studied it carefully, and discovered what he thought Kevin didn't like about it. Brian then revised the chapter and inserted it back into the manuscript on his draft without saying anything to his coauthor about it. When Kevin saw it, he didn't object, and the chapter made it into the final novel. But though we laughed about the incident afterward, it had been the first time we worked together, and we developed a procedure of giving one another heads-ups for major changes.

When we edit each of our Word drafts of the manuscript, the other person doesn't see the changes. We send a clean copy of the rewritten version off to our partner and let him do the same thing, rewriting with complete carte blanche. (Sometimes, but not always, we insert notes in the manuscript.) By the time the novel has gone back and forth several times, Kevin has smoothed out anything that doesn't sound like his prose, and Brian has smoothed out anything that doesn't sound like his. The final result is seamless and clean, written by a collaborative person who is similar to each of us but different in an interesting way.

And even after all this time, we are still extremely close friends!

The true key to a successful collaboration is to respect your partner, welcome their creative input, and accept that not every word is precious or perfect. We have found the collaboration process to be invigorating and rewarding.

As long as you are aware of the possibilities and the pitfalls, try it out, find some synergy with your words, and create new stories you could never have done alone.

The Island on the Lake

written by
John Coming
illustrated by
MAJID SABERINEJAD

ABOUT THE AUTHOR

John Coming lives in Columbus, Ohio, with his fiancée and dog, where he is currently a law student. He writes speculative fiction and has been crafting stories in his head for as long as he can remember. "The Island on the Lake" is his first professional sale. Apart from short fiction, he has been working on completing his first full-length novel. When not writing, John enjoys exploring the outdoors, especially in the Adirondacks, where the ideas behind "The Island on the Lake" first took root.

"The Island on the Lake" takes place in the Adirondacks in upstate New York. The story follows a father's and son's encounters over the years with a mysterious entity that lives near their isolated cabin and deals with time, free will, and inheritance.

ABOUT THE ILLUSTRATOR

Majid Saberinejad was born in 1987 in Qazvin, Iran. As a child, he spent hours every day drawing and painting. Majid has a bachelor's degree in painting from Shahed University in Tehran, Iran. Following university, Majid worked with some small book and magazine publishers and on several mural painting projects.

He loves to portray the environment and its details in all of his work. This has shown itself in multiple ways when it comes to creating space.

He is very fond of the works of great artists, which motivate him to improve his art.

Majid is currently living and working in Marburg, Germany.

The Island on the Lake

SUMMER 2003

My father first took me to the lake when I was seven years old. It was a long weekend in late June when the summer felt young, and the days stretched on like taffy. The first two days we spent swimming and hiking on the old nameless trails around the cabin. On the third day, he took me on the boat, toward the Island.

The sun shimmered off the water's surface, and in the shallows, light streamed down to the lake bottom in golden rays. The wind was constant and deceptive, hiding the sting from the ever-present sun. My neck was so burned that I had hardly slept the night before. I learned to dread the smell of aloe.

"Keep rowing," my father said, nodding toward the child-sized oar he'd brought along for me. "Carry your weight now."

We were out on an old, gray, wooden rowboat that was stored under the deck of the cabin. There had been a snake living beneath the paint-chipped bench that my dad gently pushed out with a broom. Every itch I felt on my skin made me jump, and I'd turn frantically, sure that I'd see the snake wrapping its long brown body around me.

"What's on the Island?" I asked, while I tried to row with him.

He paused. "Well, it's sort of a secret. A secret place that lets you see things."

"See things like what?"

He smiled. "It depends when you go. Today, we'll visit the

292

pool, and you'll see..." My father tilted his head. "Well, anyone you want. If you're curious how Grandma's doing...you can say her name, and the pool will show you."

I nodded and forced myself not to ask any more questions, even though I didn't understand. I remained silent and waited for him to explain, though he never did.

My father looked up and squinted at the blinding afternoon sky. He shook his head and snorted as if he'd heard the punch line of an old joke. But his eyes didn't smile. He sat facing toward me and the creaky dock that jutted out onto the lake from our cabin. Behind his shoulder, growing ever closer, was the Island. It looked small from the dock, but up close, it seemed to loom much larger.

We pulled the rowboat up onto the pebbly shore and my father took a rope out from the front, carefully tying it to a sturdy tree. Out on the lake, a loon call echoed over the water. But here on the Island, everything was muted. Since ours was the only cabin on the lake, silence was to be expected. But I remember only then realizing just how alone we really were out there. The nearest highway was ten miles south, and hardly anyone else lived in between. We were far enough from civilization that we couldn't hear or see anyone else. And nobody could hear or see us.

"Hey." My father grabbed my shoulder and smiled at me reassuringly. "It's all right. Come on."

Pine and smoke scents drifted on the air, and the land sloped gently upward as we hiked on an old trail. I remember having the distinct feeling that the Island's woods felt *different* from the mainland. The ground was harder, with sharper edges. The shadows were deeper and crept toward the trail like stretched arms. The branches and low plants all seemed to sway with a rhythm. Expanding and contracting.

"You know, your grandpa used to take me here," Father said.

"Really?"

"Really." He nodded. "When I was about your age, he

showed me the pool in the summer. And his dad brought him here when he was a boy too." My father looked up again, through the dense needles on the upper pines that surrounded us. "I think fathers have brought their sons here for a long, long time."

I looked around, suddenly unsure of which direction led back to our boat. "All for this pool?"

"It's like I said. A secret. It's...a responsibility too." A forced smile stretched on his face, and he ruffled my hair. "But don't worry about any of that. Today will be a fun day. I promise. OK?"

When we cleared the next rise, the path flattened onto a wide platform where the trees thinned and the ground turned to a soft mossy bed. Twenty feet ahead, smiling on the open trail, was a Woman.

I gasped when I saw her, but my father looked as though he wasn't surprised. She was tall, with smooth brown skin, and thick curly hair that fell around her shoulders. She smiled as we approached, with cloud-white teeth, square and perfect.

"Hello," she said, when we reached her. Her voice was resonant and comforting, like a warm wind.

"Hello," my father said coolly.

"Welcome back, Jim." The Woman turned and held out her hand. "And you must be Pete."

I turned to my father, and he nodded, though his eyes looked strained. I grabbed her hand, which felt warm and soft. She walked forward in slow, graceful steps. Up ahead, behind an overhanging green branch, I finally saw the pool.

The ground opened in an unnaturally perfect bowl of stone, filled with clear water, still like a mirror. The Woman smiled, and let go of my hand before walking back down the path. My father didn't watch her. His eyes focused ahead.

"Who was she?" I asked.

"She's a friend of the owner," my father said. "She helps tend the Island during the summer."

"Why isn't she staying?"

"This isn't for her, bud," my father said. "It's for us."

MAJID SABERINEJAD

My father crouched by the pool's edge and cupped some water into his hand, letting it drip back to the pool between his fingers. "Who do you want to see?"

I looked to the pool, then back at him, still not understanding what he wanted.

"All right, let's start with your grandma," he said. He cleared his throat, and looked right at the center of the water, and in a firm voice said, "Wilma Edelman."

The water shimmered and folded like a fresh sheet. The reflection distorted, mixing and separating the blue and green colors. Then, the image cleared and revealed a yard with a small, tan path leading up to a familiar red door. I leaned forward, reaching my hand out, convinced that I would touch the familiar brass knob on my grandmother's door. But my fingers connected with water and created small ripples.

The pool's view went through the door, and showed a half-lit kitchen, where my Grandma Edelman stood by her old TV. She held a corded phone in one hand and laughed into the receiver. A moment later, she turned, staring right at us.

My father waved at her. "Say hi, Pete." I raised my hand tentatively. My grandmother watched for a moment before turning back to her call.

"She can't see us?" I asked. My father shook his head. *But she looked right at us?* I thought.

"Who else do you want to see? Any friends you've missed since the start of summer?"

"Billy Hoeffler," I said softly. The water churned again, then the pool displayed a view over a dry, yellow fielded golf course. Billy was wearing overly long shorts and a stiff-looking checkered shirt. He marched solemnly behind an older man in a similar outfit.

My eyes widened as I realized just how...limitless the pool was. I could drop in on *anyone*. My friends. My teachers. The President. I remember thinking of the life-sized poster of Allen Iverson that hung in my room back home. Then, a better thought came to my mind.

"Can I ask it to see Mom?"

My father's face darkened. "When you come to the pool in the summer, you can only see what's happening *now*, in the present. Your mom…she's not here anymore, OK? So, there's nothing to see."

I nodded, fixated on something that he kept hinting at. "What happens if we come to the pool when it's not summer?"

My father gave me a half smile. "You're a quick one, huh?"

SPRING 2010

My father and I went to the lake every summer after that first one. Usually, we would go for only a few days. We'd grill out, hike, fish, and watch horror movies late into the evening. And always, on our final day, we'd visit the Island.

Over the years, the unbelievable became normal. I grew accustomed to the Island's strange physical proportions, the Woman, and the pool. We would drop in on family members, and celebrities, or sports matches, and famous museums. Occasionally, my father would ask after people I'd never heard of and take notes in his brown leather journal.

Whenever I asked questions about the journal, or how our family had found this place, or how any of it worked, he would go quiet. So, I stopped asking. And when we got back to land, I felt my curiosity lessen. By the time we'd leave the woods and return home, it was as if everything that happened on the Island was an ill-remembered dream.

When I was fifteen, during my high school spring break, my father announced suddenly that we'd be heading up to the cabin. I'd learned through half answers over the years that every season at the Island was different, though I'd only been allowed up with my father during the summer. But every year, I spent a weekend at my grandma's house in early October. We never spoke about it, but I knew that my father went alone to the lake to see something.

We never talked much on the drive upstate. I learned young that there were things I could and couldn't talk to him about. I stayed busy with friends, and sports, and girls when I had the courage, while he worked long weeks and late nights. We could always find something to talk about. Other places, people, and problems weren't off limits. But when I tried to talk about myself, or him, our conversations grew stilted and awkward. If I tried to bring up the lake, or my mother, the conversation would end completely.

But, during our first night at the cabin that spring, he cleared his throat, and spoke.

"It's beautiful in April, isn't it?" he asked.

I nodded. "It really is." The weather was colder, and all the trees were bare save for the evergreens. But small lilies and wildflowers on the lakeshore had begun to blossom, and the air smelled like fresh dirt and rain. The bugs were viciously hungry in the woods, though they were more tolerable on the water.

But behind all that, I felt as if there was an undercurrent of *tension* that I'd never felt in the summer. It was as if a thousand tightly pulled strings were taut just beneath the water's surface, beneath the land itself, all leading toward the Island. I'd find my eyes drifting toward it when we sat for breakfast at our uneven wooden table.

"You're a young man now," my father said. "And it's time you saw what you're meant to be shown." He clenched his jaw, folding and unfolding his hands before him. "In the spring, the pool shows what hasn't happened yet."

"The future?" I asked excitedly. The prospect brought a million more questions to mind, all of which I silenced. I knew showing too much emotion wouldn't play well with him. Cold, logical, rational thinking. That was the only way to approach a problem to him.

My father waited, studying my expression, before going on. "It can't be changed. Whatever you see, for whoever you say . . . it will happen just the way you've seen it."

A bluebird fluttered by our window and landed on a long bare birch branch, its ashen bark curling back. "Then...is it safe to go? Is it worth it?"

The question seemed to surprise my father. "You don't have to go if you don't feel ready. We're all free to make our own decisions."

Left unsaid was a truth I had gathered from all the years coming here. Every male in our family for as far back as my father knew had chosen to come. They'd all chosen to see the future from the Island.

Fathers have brought their sons here for a long, long time. It was a tradition. A secret. A responsibility. Regardless of what he said, I knew the decision wasn't free.

We awoke early next morning, when the sun was still low in the sky and the water's surface shone with light pink and grape coloring. To the east, tall, dark clouds threatened rain. I stepped into the boat alone, while my father stood on the dock.

"Summer is something we can do together," my father told me. "But looking ahead is something a man has to do on his own."

"Just like when you come in autumn?" I asked.

He recoiled. "Don't talk about that."

"Why haven't you brought me to see her?" I pushed on, feeling emboldened. "If spring is the future, autumn's the past, isn't it? You come to see Mom, don't you?"

He flinched and looked behind me toward the Island.

"I have a right to know," I said.

"You don't have a right to shit," he said in a low, cold voice. "And you have no idea how any of this works."

Without looking me in the eye, he handed me the oars and walked back up toward the cabin, leaving me alone in the cold, wet air. I rowed slowly toward the Island, listening to the wind, and the singing of a distant frog in the brush. Up in the cabin window I thought I saw my father watching me, but then dark clouds engulfed the sun and sent shadows over the house.

The Island's dimensions weren't as distorted now as they were in summer, and after a short time, I was back on the familiar rocky shore. When I went to tie the boat to our regular tree, I noticed that the foliage was different, too. Everything seemed younger, like a new forest after a fire. The undergrowth was teeming and lively, and the trees were thin with willowy strength. Patches of strange purple flowers I'd never seen on the mainland grew in tiny crevasses between the rocks. Budding leaves dripped with moisture and the ground was covered in silver dew.

I noticed immediately that the path was shorter. Even from the shore, I could see the top of the ridge, where I knew the path would flatten near to the pool. I crossed over the ridge, expecting to see the Woman, but instead came face-to-face with a young man with a boyish smile. He was pale with short, slicked-back black hair, and wore brown pants with a dark-green tweed jacket. In comparison, my outfit of torn blue jeans and clunky brown hiking boots felt lacking.

"Hello," the Boy said.

"I...hello?"

He smiled at me again. "You're Jim's son, aren't you?"

My father had never given me strict guidance on how to treat the caretakers we met on the Island, but I'd noticed he always said as few words as possible, if any at all. I nodded at the Boy and kept my lips shut.

The Boy laughed, a light sound that seemed effortless and invigorating. "You two are so stoic." The Boy nodded behind him. "So, training wheels are off. Pops finally agreed to let you come in my season?"

I hesitated, then nodded.

"Don't be too nervous, all right? I remember Jim's first time when he was around your age. Practically lost his nerve and ran home." The Boy put his arm around my shoulder and walked us forward while he spoke. Up close, he smelled like freshly split wood.

"Do you...do you know what he looks at when he comes up here in the autumn?" I asked. My curiosity outweighed my rapidly fading apprehension.

"I've no idea," the Boy shrugged. "But I'm only here in spring.

You'd have to ask the Old Man about that one." The Boy turned to me, a mischievous glint in his eyes. "But you'd be amazed who he asks for when he comes up in the spring."

I frowned. "Does my father visit the Island in the spring?"

The Boy smirked. "All the time."

"Well, what does he ask to see?"

The Boy shrugged. "Everyone. You, himself, and anyone the Island asks him to check on."

"The...that *who* asks him to check in on?"

"Pete, this is all part of the responsibility, right? Jim's given you that pep talk?" The Boy seemed to revel in my confusion, before laughing and slapping my back. "Don't worry about any of that yet. Come on, let's get you to the pool."

In hindsight, I shouldn't have been surprised that my father would sneak up here. And I'd always guessed there was far more to the Island than I knew. But hearing the evidence of it made my stomach feel hollow and dark. I remember some immovable stone settling in my mind, finalizing something I'd always thought. *There are some things a person lives with, and no matter how close you get to someone, those secrets will be yours alone, forever.*

The Boy stopped at the edge of the pool and clapped me on the shoulder. "Have a good time, Pete," he said. "I'll see you later."

"I'm never coming back here," I said to him, willing my voice to sound firm. I felt angry, and betrayed, and at the time I honestly believed what I'd said.

The Boy gave another one of his carefree smiles. "If that's what you decide," he said and waved as he walked back down the path.

The pool was narrower now than it had been in summer. Rushing water ran down from the rock wall behind and caused the pool to gurgle and bulge like a brook after a storm. My reflection was blurry and elongated on the water's surface.

I knew I could have turned around. My father wouldn't have asked what I'd seen in the pool. I could lie and say I'd used it and never have to see anything. But standing over the pool, knowing that the information was right there before me, it wasn't really a choice at all. And if my father used the pool so often, maybe he already knew that I would use it. Maybe he'd waited to bring me here until he was sure I would.

"Stacey Duvorik," I said. I'd start with a future that was less personal than my own. Stacey had been my girlfriend for over a year at that point. She was a girl I'd known since the eighth grade, and though we hadn't said it to one another, I thought that I loved her. It was only years later that I realized that if I had really loved her, I would have hesitated before looking into her future.

The water rushing into the pool churned and created a stable image at its center. I saw Stacey walking in our high school's hallway. She leaned back against a locker, an unreadable expression on her face. Then she peered up and smiled when someone approached her. I didn't know the boy by name, though he looked familiar. She leaned forward, gave him a quick kiss on the cheek, and they walked hand in hand toward the exits.

I turned away from the image, not sure whether to feel embarrassment, anger, or confusion. Behind that, a deeper feeling grew in my chest. Inevitability. My father told me there was no changing what I'd seen. No matter what I did, the future would play out this way.

I cleared my throat. "Jim Edelman," I said in a loud voice, not turning back to the pool until I saw from the corner of my eye that the image of Stacey had vanished.

I saw my father inside the cabin, though he looked years older. His hair had grown thin and gray, and there were new wrinkles at the corners of his eyes. He was writing frantically in his journal, the one that he always kept with him when we were up on the lake. His jaw quivered as if he were about to burst into tears. Then he walked into the closet next to the cabin's bathroom and lifted a loose wooden floor panel, tucking the journal beneath.

I kept watching, but slowly, the image faded. It was only

many, many years later that I wondered how the pool chose which visions to show me. I only gave it a name, after all. It chose everything else. Unlike in the summer, where I felt as if I were using some grand machine, here in the spring, something else was pulling the strings.

All the tension I had felt that whole weekend, all those strings that I could feel pulling toward the Island seemed to tighten and close around me. I could feel something just beneath my feet. Something giant and dense. Expanding and contracting. And It *wanted*. I could feel a million urges and desires, futures and paths. But above all, I knew It was waiting for one last name.

"Peter Edelman," I said, my voice sounding distant and foreign.

The pool pulsed frantically, and the sound of rushing water filled the air. Then the water froze and cleared. I saw myself, dressed in thick winter clothing, standing on the dock. The lake was frozen and snow-covered. I marched onto the lake like some Antarctic explorer, right toward the Island. My future self paused and turned upward, seeming to notice me.

I kicked dirt into the pool, disrupting the vision, and backed away, stumbling on armlike roots that circled out of the wet ground. I sprinted without care back to the boat, nearly running headfirst into the Boy, who was leaning against a tree near the shore.

"See what you were looking for?" the Boy asked.

I glanced back toward the pool, breathing heavily. The Boy pushed off the tree and brushed pine needles from my shoulder. "Intense, huh?"

I shook my head, unable to speak or think. I wasn't sure why the vision caused such terror in me. Maybe it was just the certainty of it. The realization that no matter what I did, or what anybody did, I'd be back here on some cold winter day marching toward this Island. Maybe it was that pulsing beneath my feet, that certainty that *something* was in the Island, and It wanted me here. I felt my throat close, and suddenly the open water of the lake felt like a slowly tightening noose.

I wanted to reject all of it. I wanted to do anything that would ensure what I'd seen wouldn't happen, just to prove I was in control. But I knew it wasn't a possibility. It wasn't a path. It was stone.

I untied the boat, slowly lowering myself onto the wet bench. The Boy stood on shore, hands in pockets, and watched as I pushed off back into the lake.

"Was that the future either way?" I called out as I drifted away. "If I had never looked, would that have still been what happened?"

The Boy shrugged. "I suppose now you'll never know."

Later that evening, when the world around our cabin had grown black and chirping insects pulsed outside the windows, my father and I ate in dim light. He hadn't asked about what I'd seen and didn't seem as if he intended to. We talked briefly about hockey and school and then the conversation stalled.

"What does the Island show in the winter?" I asked, finally.

My father cut the meat on his plate, not looking up or registering that he'd heard.

"I know there must be something," I continued. "If autumn is really—"

"Don't come here in the winter," he said, eyes fixed on his food. "It's not safe."

"Why?"

"Nothing," he said, cutting his food into smaller, and smaller slices. "But you can't ever come here, you understand me? Cabin's not winterized for it and...just don't."

I looked out the window that showed me nothing but my own reflection. I knew the Island was out there, lurking in the dark water.

"What does the Island have you write in that journal?" I asked.

My father reached forward and took a long swig from the green beer bottle before him, but said nothing.

"Why don't we tell anybody about this place, Dad?"

My father looked up sharply. "It's our burden to bear. *Ours.* You hear me? It's a weight that we can shoulder."

"But why do we have to?"

He slammed his fist on the table, rattling our plates and sending my silverware to the floor. "Because who the hell else is going to?"

Autumn 2020

The funeral service was brief and without flourish. My grandma and I decided to hold it at St. Christopher's, though I don't think my father had attended mass there since my baptism. At some point, he had decided to serve a different god.

Two people told me after the ceremony that it was *very tasteful*, which they seemed to think was about the nicest thing someone could say. The cards called the event a celebration of life, which seemed like another charming euphemism of these affairs.

I stayed the night at my grandma's after the funeral, back in Mapleview. My fiancée, Sarah, had been at the church, but she had to return to our apartment in Syracuse right after.

"Will you be all right?" Sarah asked me.

"Yeah. I just don't want to leave her alone."

I shouldn't have worried. Eight different neighbors, with loaded SUVs of food and company, swung by my grandma's house before the sun went down. Late into the night, I was tasked with sorting and re-sorting her refrigerator to make room.

When all the guests had finally left, we sat together in the living room that looked and smelled the same as it had since I'd been a boy.

"Sarah seems wonderful," my grandma told me. "Real, real sweet, salt of the earth."

"I think so, too," I replied.

On the mantel was a faded picture of my grandfather, smiling with closed lips. Beside it sat a new picture of my father.

"It's an unfair world," my grandma said. She hadn't cried during the wake, the ceremony, the burial, or even at the little slideshow one of my father's cousins had put together. But now I saw her cheeks glisten.

"It is," I replied.

"I've lived a good life," she said, "real good one. But it's getting hard losing people."

I put my hand on hers and squeezed it. "I'm not going anywhere, OK?"

She looked at me warily. "I wasn't surprised when I heard what happened," she said. "I wasn't surprised at all. I saw his father walk down that same path, and I knew where it ended. I tried to tell him, but the men in this family are...stubborn." She squeezed my hand back. "Whatever they thought they had to carry...you don't have to."

The death was ruled an accidental drowning. It had been a windy, fierce day on the lake, and my father had been drinking. He texted me, hours before it happened, and I knew something was wrong. It had been almost a year since we'd said more than a few words to each other. It was a brief message, and when I called him repeatedly after, I got no response.

It's a poor inheritance I pass to you.

I called the nonemergency for the county shortly after, and they promised they'd send someone up. They found him floating facedown near the edge of the dock.

The day after the funeral, I left Mapleview with a promise to my grandma that Sarah and I would return for Thanksgiving. I went back to Syracuse, and for a few days, settled back into normal life. Soon enough, though, I felt a familiar pull. Northward, the cabin on the lake sat unattended. The Island called to me.

The next weekend, I responded.

A dense mist hung over the lake like a cloud. Fallen leaves floated lazily on the water's surface. The fall colors on the trees were muted. Oranges like fading fire, and reds like dark apples. All I could hear as I rowed to the Island was the splash of my oar hitting the water, and the cries of lonely birds left behind.

It took me thirty minutes to reach the Island, well over twice the time it took in the summer. The Island was massive now, longer than I'd ever seen it. Depleted trees stood proudly on the shoreline like a bulwark. Sitting on a thick fallen tree was an older man with gray and red hair, in an old corduroy jacket and dark-blue jeans.

He watched me while I hopped out from the boat and tied the rope to a maple tree with pumpkin-orange leaves. When I finished, he pushed off his knees and groaned. He stopped two paces from me, and we waited while a thin wind blew over the lake. The Old Man held his hand out, and I shook it.

"It's a pleasure," the Old Man said.

"Sure," I said.

I let go of his cold, calloused palm, and studied the long trail leading inward.

"Why did you come here?" the Old Man asked. "What's the purpose of remembering, reliving things we can't change?"

I frowned at him, waiting for him to say something more. The other caretakers had never started a conversation in this way. "We look back at good memories all the time," I started. "It's why we take pictures, make home movies."

"Fair enough," the Old Man said. "But you didn't come all this way for happy memories."

"I don't know...we look back so we can learn from the past, avoid the same mistakes."

The Old Man laughed and wagged his finger at me. "I knew you'd say that. I knew it. I've heard that before, believe it or not." He turned and began shuffling up the path, and I kept stride beside him.

"I presume you've been visiting in the spring?" the Old Man asked.

"You presume?"

The Old Man shrugged. "I have better things to do than spy on my siblings."

I eyed the Old Man. "Yes, I have," I said eventually. "Every spring since the first."

The Old Man nodded. "I expected as much. There's nothing as tempting as what's behind the next door, eh?"

"I haven't asked it about everything," I said, picturing Sarah's face smiling in my head. It helped that I met her in early June, when spring was already past. We fell together so naturally and easily that it felt like reconnecting with an old friend. I'd followed the Island's guidance about where I would go to school, which friends I would keep, which planes to take. Ever since my first visit, I had become obsessed with its visions. Obsessed, resentful, and obedient. I asked it about everyone. Everyone except Sarah. Something told me the moment I said her name, I would erase some wonderful, closed door that held a universe behind it, and replace it with something settled.

In keeping the Island from Sarah, I also promised myself that I'd keep Sarah from the Island. I knew that she'd believe me if I told her, maybe even without having to see it for herself. I told myself I was sparing her from harm. There's nothing she could do to help me, anyway. And while I was hurt, and angry at all the secrets my father had kept from me, I agreed with him on one thing: this was our burden. It isn't meant to be shared.

It took us an hour to reach the pool. Like the other caretakers, the Old Man walked back down the path to leave me alone in the late afternoon light. The water was black, and unrevealing, like an impossibly deep well.

I had a million things I wanted to see. Before me, I presumably had all of human history. But the names I ended up speaking were familiar ones. Jim Edelman, my father. Ellie Edelman, born Ellie Miller, my mother. I watched them dancing when they were young and then carrying around a baby I knew must've been me. I watched my mother working in an office with coworkers and friends I'd never met and then watched my father cry at her grave.

Hours later, when the sun began to set, I felt a nudge on my shoulder.

"You should be getting back," the Old Man said.

I flinched, then turned to him angrily. "And why is that?"

The Old Man looked down at the ground warily. I followed his gaze and listened. I had been so absorbed with the pool that I hadn't noticed the rising, steady noise from the Island. It was like a low wind blowing, or the hum of some ancient machine. The longer I listened, I could make out long cycles to the sound. Expanding and contracting. Like the slow breaths of something massive.

The Old Man and I half jogged back to the boat, and by the time I reached it, the sky had turned black. When I undid the rope, the Old Man grabbed my arm.

"Don't come back in the winter," he said. "With your father dead...Its eye will turn to you."

I nodded, though I knew it was a promise I couldn't keep, and pushed the boat into the black water.

WINTER 2020

Sarah and I were watching some old science fiction movie when the fight started. It was something she said that had set me off, something so innocent and meaningless in hindsight that it's laughable. But it reminded me of the Island, and my father. Before I knew it, we were fighting about half a dozen unrelated things, boiling beneath the surface. And though I knew it was my fault, I felt too stubborn, too pulled apart to apologize.

"What the hell is going on with you?" she demanded at one point.

I was standing across the room from her, my hand pulling hard at my hair. I felt a pressure in my throat that made it hard to swallow, hard to breathe. And I wanted to tell her. I wanted to tell her so badly everything I had seen, everything that had happened. But I didn't. Because I was afraid. Afraid of what she'd think. Afraid that it meant I wasn't strong enough to carry this thing on my own. And I was afraid that even if she could have accepted it once before, I had waited too long, and revealing it now would be revealing that I'd withheld part of myself the entire time I'd known her.

So, I said nothing. I walked out of our apartment and sat in the snow-covered car. On the way out, I grabbed a jacket that her brother had left at our place the weekend before. I looked down at the gray and red sleeves and started laughing, since no other reaction made any sense.

I recognized the coat, because I'd seen myself wearing it once before, a long time ago, on a snowy morning at a frozen lake. I came back in that night and slept on the couch. In the morning, I left before Sarah woke up. In the early Saturday snow, I drove north.

I reached the cabin before noon, but the sun looked like it had already given up for the day. The sky was gray and white, with drifting flakes of snow twirling sideways to the ground. I could see my breath inside, though I didn't bother to set the fire. I wouldn't be in here for very long.

I walked toward the closet and stared down at the loose floorboards. I had checked the spot years before, wondering if my father's journal was there, but had found nothing. I was too preoccupied to even remember when I had come up in autumn.

The panel was cold and heavy, but it slid out from the floor with ease. And right beneath it, as if someone had placed it there only moments before I arrived, was my father's journal. Oil marks lined the spine where some other hand had once held it for many hours.

Written on the pages in neat, orderly pen was my father's handwriting. There were fifty or more pages filled, front and back, in his small, precise hand. Names, dates, descriptions of people I'd never heard of. Some pages bore instructions.

Tell Anderson Sewell that nine years isn't enough.

Send letter to Anna Carter with a picture of Bill Carter.

Bump into Morgan Cooper at grocery on 11.16.11 and offer to pay for her cart.

310

The instructions continued line after line, some random, while others bordered on the unsettling. I flipped to the last entry, hoping for something, anything that would explain it all. Part of me expected a note from my father, left specifically for me. But there was nothing. The second half of the journal was left white and blank.

I slid the journal into the wide zipper pocket of the coat that belonged to someone else and put the floorboard back. I sat alone in the cabin for a while, straining to see the Island through the frost-tinted windowpane. Later, I'd question how much of that day was predetermined. Did I choose this for myself, or did the Island lock me into this road when it showed me my future? Maybe the cycle had started long before I'd ever come along. Maybe I was the last car on a train that had been coming here for generations. With all that baggage and conditioning, perhaps it didn't matter whether I chose the path if I was being prepared to walk down it all along.

I walked for hours on the frozen lake. The snow had picked up, lowering my visibility to ten feet or less. At one point, I felt something watching me. I stared up into the blank clouds and remembered. Eleven years ago, I'd watched this happen.

Ahead, behind swirling snow and ice, shadows of hunched dead trees formed. I nearly tripped when my boot hit a snow-covered rock raised above the flat lake surface. I blinked in surprise and looked around at the land buried beneath the snow, rising from the ice like some sleeping giant. I had reached the Island.

Up ahead, standing atop a drift of snow, was a little girl in white. She had shoulder-length pale hair that looked translucent white at some angles, and pale blonde at others. Her face was oval shaped and childlike, though as I grew closer it looked aged and wrinkled as well. Her eyes shimmered between youthful, infant-like curiosity, and aged resignation. She could have been my height, or much, much smaller. The more I stared at her, the more discordant her features grew.

"Welcome back," the Girl said. Her voice was layered, one tone light and ringing, one deep and cracked. Both cold and emotionless.

I stuck a gloved hand into my coat pocket and fumbled inside before holding up the journal. "What is this? What does it mean?" My voice was hoarse and dry. Cold air invaded my throat.

The Girl's eyes flicked to the book, then back to me.

"Why did you have him do all of this?" I pressed on.

Her face was blank and unchanging.

"Well," I yelled, "if you expect me to keep doing this, you're out of your goddamn mind."

The Girl cocked her head. "This is the burden, Peter. *Your* burden. It doesn't matter how you feel about it."

I threw the journal toward her feet. It spiraled in the air before implanting into the snow. The Girl's eyes remained fixed on mine, my little act of rebellion meaningless to her.

"Come," the Girl said, and turned away. I only hesitated for a moment.

I walked beside the Girl, who sometimes looked like an old woman, for a long time. So long that the distant sun passed its zenith and began a quick retreat into the horizon. When my fingers had gone so numb it hurt, we reached the pool.

The pool was frozen over, without a flake of snow accumulated on its glassy surface. I walked up to the edge and gazed down to see a hazy reflection of myself and the Girl.

"What does it do?" I asked.

The Girl turned to me. "You haven't figured that out yet?"

I took a hesitant step onto the ice. I had put hours of thought into what the winter months would show me. Though I wouldn't admit it to myself, I had suspected for years what I would find. It was part of the reason I had decided to come, despite all the reasons not to. I walked toward the center of the pool and took a deep breath.

"Jim Edelman," I said. For a moment, nothing happened. No break in the pool's surface, no sound or motion. Then I heard a faint shift behind me.

"Hey Pete," my father said.

I turned to find him standing on the ice. He looked younger than I remembered him.

"You...it's..." I started.

"It's good to see you too," he said with a sad smile.

"Why'd you do it?" I asked.

My father's face tightened, and he looked past me, toward the cabin, where they'd found his body. He wore an outfit I'd seen him in a million times. A red and black flannel, with worn khakis. It looked surreally out of place next to the half-dozen layers I had on.

"I was so tired," he finally said. "I just wanted...I needed it to be over. And I wanted to see her again."

"Have you? Seen her?" I asked.

He shook his head and turned away. I looked down at his reflection in the pool's surface, and suddenly saw a line of men stretching out from behind him. I saw my grandfather, and behind him, my great-grandfather. Down the line it went, father and son.

"You're stuck here," I said. "When you died, you didn't...go wherever she's gone to."

My father turned to me and gently grabbed my shoulder. "Don't call for her," he pled. "If you say her name, It can see her. It gains influence. Even now."

I pulled away and took a step back. "Why did you get involved in this...why would you bring *me* into this?"

"It told me It would kill you, if I didn't," he said. He spoke with the conviction of a soldier defending his actions.

"It? What the hell is It? And how could you listen? You let this place ruin your life, let it ruin mine too," I yelled.

My father frowned. "It's the only way, Pete," he said. He grabbed my shoulder again, and despite everything else, I felt some base part of me comforted at the intimate contact. It was the most I could remember us touching since that spring afternoon that felt like a lifetime ago.

"It's the only way," he repeated. Then he was gone, along with the row of reflections behind him. The Girl stood by the pool's edge, staring at me. She had the journal in her hand.

"This season, you may rest," she said. "But in the spring, it must begin. You will have a list of names to check in on, and my younger brother will give you instructions on what to do with them. The same will follow for the summer and autumn. You won't need to visit again in the winter unless It requests you."

I looked at the journal and grimaced before pushing by the Girl. I marched ahead quickly, not glancing back at her or the pool. Over the next ridge on the trail, the Girl stood in the center of the path, her statuesque face slightly pulled in annoyance.

"Don't force Its hand, Peter," the Girl said. "My siblings will ease you in, it isn't—"

I pushed past her again and put my head down. I saw the sun drop and send weak white and yellow rays to mimic a sunset in the west. I had hours of travel to get back to the cabin, but if I could just—

The Girl was in front of me again and grabbed my arm with a strong, bony hand.

"This is your last warning. If you don't agree, It will confront you," the Girl said, a hint of fear creeping into her voice.

"It? What is It?" I demanded. The Girl said nothing. I ripped my arm from her grip. "I don't want anything to do with this, OK?"

"It's too late for that," the Girl said. "You've looked in the pool in summer and used Its arms. You've looked through the pool in autumn and used Its memory. You've looked through in spring and used Its eyes. Did you think there was no price for that? Did you think your debt wouldn't be called upon?"

The Girl's strange, flickering, ageless face looked at me in confusion, as if I were the one not making sense. But there was no more time to argue. We'd reached the Island's shore, and without another word, I marched out onto the ice, back toward the cabin.

I made it ten minutes before I heard It. Under the ice, something moved, and the whole world seemed to distort around me as if the very air was recoiling. Beneath my feet, the ice buckled

314

in a rhythmic expansion and contraction like slow breaths inhaled and exhaled. The wind picked up, cutting snow and ice into my face. When I opened my eyes, the gust had cleared the snow from the ice in a fifty-foot circle around me.

Then, in the fading light, I saw It beneath the ice. A shadow stretched out, formless and in motion. Larger than the cabin or my apartment complex back in Syracuse. It rose from the depths of the lake and pressed Its dark body against the ice, while I stood there frozen. The ice cracked and shattered in a thousand places, and I started screaming. I took one step and felt my boot fill with cold water. With my next step, I went straight through the ice, into the bitter water, and fell toward the thing stretched out beneath.

SPRING 2021

Lightning cut through the sky behind my window. One. Two. Three seconds later, thunder rolled forward like a heavy door bouncing shut. It was a warm night, one of the first in months, so Sarah and I had gone to bed with the window partially open.

She had been sleeping before the last loud boom of thunder made her inhale loudly, and I felt her shift in the darkness on her side of the bed.

"You awake?" she whispered.

I nodded, then realizing she couldn't see me, said, "Yeah."

"Bad dreams?" she asked.

"Yeah," I repeated.

The nightmares all started the same. I was back out on the lake. Sometimes alone, or with my father, or even Sarah. In the dream tonight, I was drifting on the old rowboat. I looked around, panicked, cursing myself for coming out here alone. I rowed as fast as I could, straining to get back to the dock, which seemed to pull back from me as I moved toward it. Then, I felt It beneath the water. And before I could scream, or move, It pulled me under.

Then, the visions start.

It always showed me variations of the same thing I saw when It had pulled me beneath the ice in the winter. I see my own dead eyes staring back at me. I see Sarah, and my grandmother, and my neighbors, and friends. I see my coworkers and the mailman. I see every living soul that I know. And I see all of them dead.

After It pulled me under the ice, I woke up back in the cabin, the leather journal sitting squarely on my chest. I'd half convinced myself I'd hallucinated my entire experience out on the Island.

But then, back in Syracuse the next evening, the first night-mare came. I awoke on our couch screaming, flailing as I fell to the floor. Sarah was at my side immediately, and like that, our cold war ended.

Since then, the nightmares and sleepless nights had become part of our routine.

"Do you want to talk about it?" she asked. Lightning flashed our room dark blue and purple.

"No, I'm OK," I replied, as the hammer of thunder fell.

Sarah reached out and touched the side of my face. "You know that thing we talked about...earlier this week? How I asked you to think if that's something you'd want, and you said you needed time to think about it?"

I nodded. Of course I knew what she was talking about. It was all I could think about since she'd mentioned it.

"Well...have you thought about it?"

"I have," I said. "It's something you want, right?"

She sat up on her elbow. "It's something I want with you, if you want it too. Stop avoiding the question. Do you want it?"

I pushed myself up to be level with her. I had prepared a thousand different ways to say no, ever since she'd mentioned the possibility of us having a child. I'd rehearsed it in my mind. I could use rational excuses like money or youth. I could lie and say I never wanted children. I could argue for why our lives would be easier without them. But looking into her eyes then,

I knew there was really only one reason why I was petrified by the idea. And I didn't want it to have any sway over me any longer.

"Maybe I do," I said.

"Maybe?" she repeated, and I nodded. She snorted and gave me an annoyed smile. "Maybe, he says. Wonderful."

"It's a strong maybe," I replied.

"Uh-huh," Sarah said, and rolled back over. A moment later, she reached back and touched my arm. "I can work with a maybe."

It was somewhere between midnight and sunrise, when I finally gave up on sleeping, and went to sit at our kitchen table. The storm continued outside, whipping rain against our screen door, swirling up chunks of cold dirt. In my right hand, I held the leather-bound journal, half its pages empty, waiting to be filled. In my left, I held a lighter.

I still hadn't told Sarah about anything that had happened. Maybe one day. When I was braver. When I felt like I had gotten a handle on this on my own. Maybe. But tonight, I'd finally grown the courage to do something else. I wasn't sure what the Island could or would do to me if I failed to visit before the end of spring like It demanded. Perhaps all Its threats would come true, and whatever power lurked under the water's surface would unleash hell on everyone I loved. Perhaps I had already damned myself to linger in the frozen pool with my father, and all those before us, when I died. But that was an inheritance I refused to pass on any further.

I had the foresight to disable the fire alarm before I started ripping pages from the book and lighting them one by one. Eventually, the journal was just a leather husk that I walked outside and threw into the dumpster beside our garage.

I sat at the kitchen table and listened to the storm. I thought of my father, and of Sarah, and of the unknown future we had ahead. And I waited for the morning to arrive.

The Phantom Carnival

written by

M. Elizabeth Ticknor

illustrated by

XIAOMENG ZHANG

ABOUT THE AUTHOR

M. Elizabeth Ticknor is a gender-fluid writer and artist who shares a comfortable hobbit hole in Southeast Michigan with her Wookiee husband and their twin baby dragons. An avid reader of science fiction and fantasy, Elizabeth also enjoys well-written horror. The authors who have inspired her include Douglas Adams, Ray Bradbury, Orson Scott Card, Neil Gaiman, C. S. Lewis, Chuck Wendig, and David Wong. Her other interests include drawing, painting, and tabletop role-playing.

Elizabeth is a winner of the Baen Fantasy Adventure Award; her short fiction also appears in Fireside Magazine *and an assortment of anthologies by Flame Tree Press, Air and Nothingness Press, and WordFire Press.*

Elizabeth introduces her story with this: "The first story seeds for 'The Phantom Carnival' took root almost two decades ago, when I read Riding the Rails: Teenagers on the Move During the Great Depression, *by Errol Lincoln Uys. The thought of train-hopping teenage hobos stuck with me for years. I originally wanted to write a historical romance in the vein of the 1992 film* Far and Away, *but I couldn't seem to get it down on paper; every time I tried, I felt like the story was missing something. In the end, I replaced the romance with a platonic friendship and added a speculative element, which caught my interest far more thoroughly. Once I determined what Alice and Dog-Faced Dan were running from, the rest of the story fell into place in short order."*

ABOUT THE ILLUSTRATOR

Xiaomeng Zhang was born in Chengdu, Sichuan, China, in 1990. He has always had a keen interest in art, but science fiction movies captured his imagination, and he began to imitate scenes and characters he saw in those films.

He attended the Academy of Art in San Francisco to conduct his own comprehensive art research. It was a valuable opportunity to meet creatively talented artists with similar interests. After graduating from university, he worked in animation, video game development, and as a graphic designer.

His love for digital painting is reflected in his creativity. He uses his spare time to paint and study different styles of artistic creation. In the subsequent work, his ideas often brought unexpected effects for his company.

His work has been presented in several art magazines.

Xiaomeng continues to innovate his artistic creations and provide his freelance clients with high-quality illustration services.

The Phantom Carnival

Moonlight bounces off the tracks of the St. Louis railyard, refracts off train engines, and dances over the puddled remnants of the day's rain. I avoid the light as best I can, creeping from shadow to shadow, and tug my newsboy cap tight against my skull. Work's dried up in town, so it's time to catch out for someplace new. I hate riding the rails. In town, I can safely be myself: Alice, the freckle-faced girl with short-shorn caramel curls. Out here, I have to pretend to be somebody else: Al, the dirt-smudged boy perpetually in need of a haircut.

Dog-Faced Dan slinks alongside me. He doesn't need to work at hiding like I do; his lithe form is practically one with the darkness. Most people would find the sight of Danny's long-stretched face and wolflike teeth unsettling, but to me they're oddly comforting. He's the one who hauled me into a boxcar my first night out, who taught me how to protect myself, who glamoured my eyes so I could see the truths most people are blind to. I owe him everything I have—which is my life, mostly, but isn't that the most important thing anyone has when you get down to brass tacks?

Danny taps my shoulder with a claw-tipped hand and points to a train crawling out of the station, halfway across the yard. "That's our freight, Alice. Race you!" He dashes ahead before I can argue.

I weave through the yard, trying to stay hidden. I don't mind if Danny beats me—the magic pumping through his veins leaves

321

him faster than me on my best days—but I can't afford to miss that train if he catches it. Dangerous for anyone to ride the rails alone at night, let alone a sixteen-year-old girl. I can pass for masculine when I have to, but I'm always better at it when I'm playing off Danny's manic energy.

A barrel-chested man in a suit steps out from between a pair of trains, the space between them pooled with shadow. Has to be a railyard bull—he's dressed too fancy for a hobo. He bolts toward me, arms and legs pumping like well-oiled pistons. I give up hiding and dash for the train, coat flapping in the wind. The local bulls are notorious for brutalizing anyone they catch riding the rails without a ticket, no matter their gender.

The bull's true nature becomes clear when he dashes into the moonlight. His square jaw, handlebar mustache, and well-muscled body are nothing but a glamour to hide bark-like skin and knotted wooden limbs. I'd figure him for a lot louse like Danny if it weren't for his milky-white eyes and slack-jawed expression. He's a carny. Every carny has those same dead eyes. Terror curdles my stomach. Bad enough to be caught by a railyard bull—getting dragged off to the Phantom Carnival is a one-way ticket to trouble. Danny says that the grifters—the monsters that run the Carnival—kidnap people and eat their memories like candy.

The train picks up speed as I rush toward it. I take a deep breath and leap for the ladder on the back of the caboose. The ladder glows blue. Must be made of iron. Danny didn't like that, I'll bet—and the railroad bull won't either. I catch a rung and pull myself up. It doesn't burn me like it would a lot louse or carny. If Danny hadn't taught me about the Carnival, I'd be a scrub like anyone else.

The carny grabs my left leg, his hand tight as a vise, and pulls me back down toward the tracks. Panic lances through my stomach and I scramble to hang on.

Danny jumps off the roof of the caboose, lips curled in a canid snarl. "Let go, you stupid bogey!" He tackles the carny and sinks a too-wide mouthful of teeth into the big lug's right shoulder.

The carny roars with pain. His grip loosens.

I take advantage of the distraction and lash out with my right foot. My heel batters the carny's jaw, then slams full-force into his eye socket. He lets out an agonized bellow and crumples onto swiftly receding train tracks, clutching at his ruined eye.

I clamber onto the roof and swivel around in a panic. "Danny!"

Danny vaults off the carny's back and dashes after the train with an energy I could never replicate. He scrambles up the ladder, palms sizzling from the iron's touch, and tumbles onto the roof beside me. His chest heaves with peals of laughter.

I shudder and stare at the tracks. We're moving fast enough now that they rush behind the train like a river. "That was too close."

"Are you joshing me? That was great."

"I almost got taken!"

Danny's laughter tapers off to a chuckle. He rolls to his feet. "Don't worry, I wouldn't have let him get you. Even if he managed to haul you off to the Carnival, I'd hunt you down before they fleeced you." Before they stole my memories.

I narrow my eyes and wrinkle my nose. "What makes you so sure you could?"

"Because I'm me." Danny's face splits in an ear-to-ear grin, jagged teeth gleaming in the moonlight.

I roll my eyes. Danny's confidence is infectious, but sometimes his head gets too big for his shoulders. "Let's find somewhere to hunker down. It's cold up here." Wind stings my face; damp air numbs my fingers.

I wonder at the brazenness of the carny who tried to snatch me straight from a railyard as we hop from the caboose to the next car. The ever-rising number of kids desperate enough to leave home in search of work is making the grifters bold. They've sent carnies out to abduct people from trains and hobo jungles. Danny's even seen a few lurking in big city alleyways. Worst part is, there's no one we can ask for help. Most people are scrubs, unable to see through the grifters' glamours—and how are they supposed to notice the uptick in missing persons when the whole country's mired in a depression? Folks just up and leave home every day, and you never know who's coming back and who's gone forever.

Danny and I scale boxcar rooftops until we spot an open door up ahead, a yawning black opening in the side of a car. Swinging over the side of an open boxcar is dangerous, but so is clinging to the roof of a rushing train. All it takes is one ill-timed tunnel to suffocate you or knock you off your rooftop perch. Best we get inside.

Danny swoops over the side and into the car. My chest tightens with jealousy as he sticks the landing; it isn't fair how easy this sort of thing comes to him. I don't envy him and the process he went through to acquire his tricks, but the gifts and glamours the grifters wove into his flesh almost make up for the memories they took from him.

Almost.

I grab onto the roof's edge and slide my legs off. Wind pulls at them like a swift-moving current. It reminds me of the time my parents went on vacation to Montauk when I was six years old. I snuck off while Mama and Papa were touring the lighthouse and fell off a rock into the ocean. I floundered back to shore, but I've been afraid of swimming ever since.

I'm still searching for footholds when a particularly violent gust tugs my whole body sideways. My hands slip. I scrabble for purchase but there's nothing solid to hold on to—I slide off the roof with a shriek. My heart hammers in my chest as I anticipate the agony of slamming into the track and tumbling under the wheels. If I'm lucky, I'll only lose a leg. If I'm not lucky, I'm dead.

A pair of hands snatches me out of the air. Not Danny's, they're far too large. And furry. Why are they—

My knees bash the lip of the boxcar door as the stranger hauls me inside. I bite back the yelp of pain that longs to burst free. When I'm on the road, I can't afford to be seen as a girl; I need to fit in, just one of the boys. Anyone who says boys don't cry is a liar. I've seen loads of tears since I first caught out. Even so, I can't afford to raise suspicion.

As my eyes adjust to the dimness of the boxcar, I spot half a dozen silhouettes. The boy who dragged me into the boxcar is a lot louse. His glamour is stocky and well-muscled, the hardworking farm-boy look. His actual body is massive, bigger than most grown men. He's covered head to toe in thick white fur like a yeti, but his features look mostly human. He's got big brown eyes, warm and inviting.

I glance around the car and my eyes widen. There are seven people including me and Danny, and I'm the only one who isn't a lot louse. One boy shimmers amethyst-purple in the moonlight, like the inside of a geode crystal; another has skin so pale I can see clear through to his veins, his organs, even his skeleton. The last two look like twins—at the very least, their glamours are identical—but one's true form has skin like crusted lava that spider-webs with red-hot cracks every time he moves, while the other looks to be made of living ice. They're holding hands. I'm amazed the ice-boy's hand doesn't melt in his twin's fiery grip.

The yeti checks me over for injuries, eyes brimming with concern, hands exploring far too much of my body for comfort. "You okay there, kid?"

I grunt, assume my most masculine voice, and pull away before his hands reach my chest. "I'm fine. Just scraped up."

Danny sidles up, interposes himself between me and the yeti, and gives his most fiercely charming smile. "Easy there, friend. I appreciate you catching my little brother and all, but he doesn't much like to be touched."

The yeti arches an eyebrow. "He's your brother? The two of you don't, uh, look that much related."

"He's adopted."

I affect a glare in Danny's direction. "*You're* adopted."

Danny chuckles and throws his hands up as if in surrender. "We're *both* adopted." He glances around the room, takes in the crowd. "Don't worry. He looks like a scrub, but he's savvy." He tugs at his over-large, pointed ears with claw-tipped fingers.

The yeti grins. "Good to know." He sits in the boxcar's door frame and dangles his feet over the edge. "I'm Earl. And you are?"

Danny drapes an arm over my shoulder. "Dog-Faced Dan. This is Al."

The walking geode crystal speaks up, his voice strangely breezy. "Short for Albert?"

I shake my head. "Just Al."

Danny gestures at his fellow lot lice. "Seems like bad luck, so many of us bunched up in one place."

Earl grunts. "The twins have been together forever. The rest of us met in boxcars or jungles. Figured there was safety in numbers. Where are you two headed?"

I shrug. "Nowhere particular."

Earl smiles. "We're headed to Chicago to catch the World's Fair. 'Century of Progress' and all that. You two should come along—I hear it's quite the show."

I shiver despite the tight press of people in the boxcar and shake my head. "There ain't going to be work there—nothing worth having, anyway. The Fair's been open for months. All the best jobs are bound to be taken."

"There'll be food, at least," Earl says. "Food and company and stuff right out of science fiction novels." He leans in toward Danny and whispers, "Plus, there's supposed to be a back-alley doctor there. Someone who can bring back our memories."

Danny's ears perk up like an overexcited puppy's. "Where'd you hear that?"

"I met a yegg in Los Angeles. Looked human, but he was savvy as all get-out. Said he used to be a lot louse, but the doc cured him—got his memories back and everything."

Danny lets out a low whistle. He leans close and whispers in my ear. "I'm thinking we ought to head toward Chicago."

My eyes narrow. Something about Earl's story doesn't add up. Danny and I have been traveling together for almost a year, and in all that time I've never heard of anyone being able to reverse the grifters' handiwork.

I glance skeptically in Earl's direction. "This yegg, how do you know he wasn't joshing you?"

Earl smirks and tousles my cap, smushing it down on my

short-cropped curly hair. "Relax, kid. I can smell a grifter a mile away."

My whole body tenses. I hate being patronized.

Danny pushes Earl's hand away, gently but firmly. "He don't like being touched, remember?" Earl shuffles back a few steps; his expression turns sheepish. Danny turns to me. "I get why you're nervous, Al, but if this is real, I *need* it. You don't know what it's like, living like this."

I bristle. "I can't go home any more than you can!"

"At least you know you *have* one." Danny's ever-present grin fades, tainted with long-buried sadness. "You remember your parents. You remember your name. Dog-Faced Dan isn't my *real* name—it's just a placeholder. My memories are patchier than the coat I'm wearing, and I want them back."

"I thought you wanted to make *new* memories. You're always talking about seeing new places, doing new things—"

"Just because I want to make new memories doesn't mean I want to give up on the old ones." Danny pulls me into a hug and presses his forehead against mine. "Please. I need this, and I'd rather do it with you than without."

Oh, God. If I say no, he's going to do it anyway. He'll leave me to ride the rails all on my lonesome. The idea of trying to find someone else to watch my back makes me sick to my stomach. Who else could I even trust with my secrets? Some boys might do me right, for sure, but how would I know them from the ones that would take advantage of me in a heartbeat?

I bite my lip hard enough to draw blood. The copper-penny flavor floods my tongue, grounding me back in reality. I can't lose Danny. I don't *want* to lose him. "All right." I take a shuddering breath and nod.

Danny pulls back and lets out a whoop of triumph. Earl gives him a friendly embrace. The other lot lice welcome him into the fold as well, cheering and circling around him, pressing close in their excitement. Earl backs off and sits in a corner of the boxcar, letting the others do the talking now that he's got his way. His posture is relaxed, but he watches everything like a hawk. His

327

gaze never strays far from me. Seems he doesn't trust me any more than I do him.

I want to be happy for Danny, but part of me is even more afraid of what might happen at the World's Fair than of riding the rails on my own. Who will Danny be once he gets his memories back? How much will he change? Will he want anything to do with me? What if he changes from someone who accepts me for who I am into someone who will take advantage?

I sit in the corner opposite Earl and wrap my coat as tight around me as it will go. I want to believe Danny will always care about me, that he's good right down to his core, but no amount of coats or blankets can warm the chill of fear that's wormed its way into my heart.

Chicago bustles like a fresh-shook beehive. The World's Fair sprawls between 12th and 39th Street, filled with Art Deco and Moderne-style buildings painted in a riotous rainbow of colors. The streets are jam-packed with all kinds of folks: fancy-dressed couples strut through the streets in bolero jackets and puff-sleeve blouses; families with hand-sewn, heavy-patched clothes gawp at the finery surrounding them; dirt-smeared children slink through the streets, sucking on striped candy sticks.

What stands out most to me are the smiles—sometimes even grins, all the way up to people's eyes. That's not a common sight these days. I've been staring at the scars that run through the heart of America since Papa lost his job at the car factory and we had to move into one of those ramshackle Hoovervilles. Seeing this much happiness fills me with hope for the future of our country—for *my* future, even. I haven't dared to hope like this since I ran away from home.

Neither hope nor joy finds Earl's pack of lot lice. They remain stern and focused, scouring street after street on the hunt for their doctor. Danny keeps to the back, faking calm, but he's on the alert, eyes and ears swiveling like he expects to see carnies around every corner. I keep pace with him, arms wrapped around my chest.

Danny glances down at me. "You all right, Al? You're looking mighty low." I wish we were alone, that we didn't have to pretend. I like it better when he calls me Alice.

"It's a lot to take in, is all. So much color. So much noise." Not many lot lice, though. A place like this, I'd expect to see at least one in a hundred, maybe even one in twenty, but Danny and his new friends are the only ones wandering the streets.

Danny chuckles. "I like the bustle. It feels comfortable. Familiar."

"Maybe you were a city boy, then?"

Danny shrugs. "Maybe. I just know I like crowds."

Earl falls into step beside us. "We've found something." He shepherds us to an alleyway entrance glamoured to look like a wall stretching between two buildings. On the other side of the illusion, at least thirty lot lice are lined up in front of a navy-blue door. A broken board mounted above the door frame has the word "Doctor" scrawled on it in chalk.

The hairs on the back of my neck prickle. This feels *wrong*. I grab Danny's hand and squeeze. He squeezes back and whispers, "I know."

I suck in a sharp breath. "Then why?"

"Because it might be real." Danny takes a spot in the alley. I huddle beside him, trying to ignore the sick feeling building up in my stomach. Earl sits behind everyone else, big enough that he blocks the exit. The alley is officially full.

The door swings inward and a woman in a nurse's uniform peeks through. Her grandmotherly glamour contrasts with the youthful glow that hides beneath. She surveys the gathered crowd and smiles. "The doctor will see you now." She beckons the fish-man at the front of the line. "Come in. Come in."

One by one, the lot lice enter the doctor's office, but nobody leaves—not through this door, anyway. A couple of people start to get second thoughts and shamble back toward the exit, but Earl talks them down and convinces them to resume their places in line. The muscles in my back coil tighter with every lot louse that walks through those doors—it gets to where I can barely move.

The twins enter at the same time. That just leaves Danny, Earl, and me. I shiver so hard that Danny drapes his coat over my shoulders. It doesn't help, not really, but I appreciate the gesture.

When it's Danny's turn, I walk up beside him. The nurse shakes her head and waves me off. "Not you, dearie."

My brow furrows. "You let the twins go in together."

The nurse smiles sadly. "The twins were both lot lice."

Danny scowls. "Al's savvy."

The nurse shakes her head and says, "Savvy isn't enough, young pup. This one doesn't need treatment. He should go back home, where he came from."

I jut my jaw forward stubbornly. "Don't have a home. Danny's the closest thing to family I've got."

Earl comes up behind me. His hand is so big it envelops my entire shoulder. "You heard her, kid. You're not welcome here."

I shrug his grip off, nostrils flared. I don't care if he's twice my size; I won't let him intimidate me. "Keep your paws off me, you big greaseball!"

Earl smacks the side of my head against a wall hard enough that my ears ring and spots flash before my eyes. I collapse like a rag doll, eyes wide.

Everything seems to happen in fits and flashes. Danny howls in protest. Kneels before me. Strokes my hair. Whispers words that don't make sense to my addled brain.

A massive paw lands on Danny's shoulder. Earl tucks Danny under one arm. Danny bites and kicks, but Earl's fur is too thick. He hauls Danny through that doorway like a writhing toddler and slams it so hard my teeth rattle.

The door vanishes. That hastily written sign clatters to the ground and lands at my feet.

I spend most of the winter on my lonesome, wearing Danny's coat over my own. It smells like him at first, a weird mix of dog fur and autumn leaves, but eventually all that's left is road dust and my own sweat. I think about going home every night, but then I remember how skinny Mama was getting and the frown lines etched into Papa's face. I can't burden them with an extra mouth to feed—they've got enough to deal with on their own.

I work when I have to, but mostly I keep to myself. Danny always said that if I don't want to get outed as a girl, it's best to only speak when spoken to, and I can't bring myself to get close to anyone else. I only trusted him with my secret because he trusted me with his.

Carnies crop up more often as the weeks drag on. There's one on every train, sometimes more. Some pose as railyard bulls, but more ride trains like hobos, making friends with lonely kids in boxcars, wandering off with newfound friends and never coming back.

The fear of getting stolen grows so strong, I avoid anyone wearing a glamour. Most of them are probably lot lice, but the only way I can tell for sure is to look at their eyes—and if you get close enough to see a carny's eyes, odds are it's too late. I trade three loaves of stolen bread for an iron pocketknife at a hobo jungle outside of San Diego. It weighs heavy in my pocket, but I keep it with me always; the blade's blue glow is strangely comforting. Lot louse or carny, iron hurts them all the same.

Two months after Danny was taken, I'm catching a freight out of San Antonio when I spot Earl weaving through the yard. The white-furred giant slinks into a refrigerator car three trains over, glancing around like he's afraid of being followed. My chest tightens with rage, terror, and a deep longing for revenge. Earl stole Danny from me—I want to take something just as important from him.

That refrigerator car, though...I hate refrigerator cars. If the door shuts with you inside, you're history. More than one gaycat's climbed into a reefer, gotten locked in, and frozen to death. They're good places to hide, though, if you're bundled enough to survive the trip.

I pull Danny's coat tight around my shoulders, pop the collar, and stalk toward the reefer. My fingers slide into the pockets of Danny's coat, find that pocketknife, and clutch it like a lifeline.

Just before I climb in, a fiery glow catches my eye. Lava-boy emerges from the shadows and charges at me. I dodge, but the living ice sculpture catches me in a full-body tackle. His eyes, once brilliantly blue, have gone cold and milky. He's turned carny. I scream and flick open my pocketknife. He slams my hand against the ground over and over with grim efficiency. The blade slips from bruised fingers and clatters between a pair of railway ties.

Lava-boy rushes past me, into the reefer, and tackles Earl into the side of the car. Earl lets out a loud grunt, then hurls Lava-boy against the opposite wall. The whole car shakes from the impact. I thought they were friends—why are they fighting?

Ice-boy turns his head toward the reefer when Lava-boy hits the wall, a puzzled expression on his face. I take advantage of his distraction and fumble for my knife. Rock—rock—blade. It's sharp enough I cut myself on it, but I don't care. I grab the wooden handle with my bloodied hand and take a swing at my attacker, slicing into his arm. He howls with pain. The wound blisters and blackens. He backs away before I can cut him again, clutching at his now-useless arm, and turns toward the boxcar—just as Earl throws Lava-boy at him. The two carnies collapse into a heap.

The train starts moving. No time to second-guess my instincts. I dash for the reefer car, squeeze past Earl's hulking form, and scramble inside.

Earl studies me for a moment, then glances back toward the doors. He doesn't recognize me. I don't know whether to be relieved or offended. He hovers near the boxcar entrance until the train is moving too fast for the twins to climb on. Then he scoops a tattered bindle off the floor and leans against a wooden wall, eyes haunted.

I brandish my pocketknife menacingly. "Hey, Earl."

Earl flinches at the sight of the iron and tilts his head inquisitively. "How'd you know my name?"

The lack of recognition on his face infuriates me. "You dragged a friend of mine through a magic door a few months back. Danny." His expression remains confused. I roll my eyes and clarify, "Dog-Faced Dan."

His brow furrows. "You're that savvy brat. Albert?"

"*Al.* Where is he? Where's Danny?"

"Back at the Carnival, if he's lucky."

"How's that *lucky*?"

"If he's still there, they ain't finished fleecing him yet."

My thoughts grind to a halt as I struggle to process Earl's statement. "But—he's a lot louse, he's already been fleeced." Then again, so were the twins. The memory of Ice-boy's milky gaze makes me shiver.

"A lot louse is just a carny who managed to escape with some of their memories intact. The grifters like to finish their meals. Time at the Carnival don't pass the same way it does here, though—they might not have finished with him yet."

My cheeks grow hot; my grip on the pocketknife tightens. "Why didn't they fleece you?" I want to punctuate the question with my blade, but I keep my hand steady.

Earl sighs. "I made a deal with the grifters—I'd bring back their lost toys in exchange for keeping my brainpan intact. They tried to back out of the bargain once I held up my end, though. I gave them the slip, but they've been after me for weeks." Earl laughs darkly. "Deal or not, I'll bet they fleece everyone in the end."

Part of me feels sorry for him, but the rest of me says he deserves it. I refuse to let the pity sneak onto my face. "I need to get Danny back. I have to get him out of there before—" I can't bring myself to finish the thought, let alone the sentence.

"Good luck with that, kid. You don't even know how to find the Phantom Carnival, let alone get him out."

"No. But you do. You know how to get in *and* out." I shift my blade so the moonlight glints off it. "And you're going to show me how."

I'd rather arrive at the Phantom Carnival over-armed than under-prepared, so I sneak into a dump and collect everything that glows: a screwdriver with a half-rotted handle, the mangled inner workings of a typewriter, and a pair of rusty sewing shears. Earl said the grifters have the same weakness to iron as carnies and lot lice, and I plan to take full advantage of that. I wrap the screwdriver's handle with cloth so it's easier to grip, twist the typewriter pieces into caltrops, and break the shears into two long blades. Then I sharpen everything until the edges gleam in the moonlight.

Once that's sorted, I head to the nearest dead-end alley and draw an outline of a door on the wall in chalk. I cut the top of my arm and smear a bloody handprint where the doorknob should be. I swallow the lump in my throat and say, "My bindle's packed. I'm ready to walk the midway." After a moment to steel my nerves, I knock on the wall.

Emerald-green wood kisses my knuckles. A door that wasn't there a moment before swings inward. A grifter stands on the other side: twice the height of a man, rail-thin, dressed in a pinstriped suit with a tailcoat and a black top hat. Skeletal fingers stretch out like spider legs, ending in razor-sharp blades. A shadowy smudge clings to the place where its eyes should be; its shark-toothed grin stretches from ear to ear as it steps aside and motions for me to walk past.

I step onto the cobblestone midway of the Phantom Carnival, heart pounding, teeth clenched. The grifter lets me pass without issue. Earl said the ones guarding the doors are always friendly—until someone tries to leave.

The air has a strange, metallic tang. The sky is black—no moon, no stars, not even any clouds. Strategically placed gas lamps light up row after row of buildings, tents, food stands, and carnival booths. Colors blaze so vividly they make my eyes hurt—this place makes the World's Fair seem pale by comparison. But the shadows are also deeper, the buildings taller and leaner.

Carnies man booths and stands, resembling everything from wood or stone statues to bizarre combinations of human and animal anatomy. They wave and grin at passersby, but their empty stares make me shiver head to toe. There are a few humans here and there, but most everyone walking the midway is some degree of lot louse.

Tucked away at the end of an alley, much like the street where

I first saw it, is a familiar navy-blue door. The word "Doctor" is written above it in that same hasty scrawl. I pull the pocketknife out of my coat, steel my nerves, and knock.

The old-but-young nurse opens the door. I push my way inside, shove her against a wall, and press the knife against her throat before she can say boo. Her flesh sizzles at the blade's touch, but her eyes aren't hollow—she's still got memories left. I snarl, "Where's Dog-Faced Dan?"

Her lower lip quivers and her eyes dart back and forth while she parses my question. "Down the hall. Seventh door on the right."

"How can you do this? How can you help the grifters hurt people?"

Eyes wide, she whispers, "Some folks are better off not knowing who they used to be. The grifters glom onto people who are hurting and take the pain away."

"The grifters take *everything* away." I shove her aside, drop the knife back into my pocket, and rush off to find him. The hall stretches weirdly. The farther I go, the taller and thinner the doors become. The seventh door on the right is twice my height, but so slender I have to turn sideways and squeeze to step through. It opens, not into a doctor's office or waiting room, but onto a forest of thick, tall redwoods that stretch along a grassy embankment. From this side, the door stands solitary in the open air, almost like a tree in its own right; its frame is adorned with ornate carvings of wolves chasing rabbits, mice fleeing snakes, and eagles snagging fish in their talons.

Holes have been dug out beneath some of the redwoods on the embankment. Roots act like wooden bars for the earthen cell Danny paces in. It takes me a moment to recognize him. His dark hair blends into a fresh coat of fur that covers his body. He has a tail now—a big, bushy thing that dangles down to his knees. But it's definitely Danny. I know the face under that fur, I know those eyes. They're still dark, still human—still *his*, at least for the moment.

I get as close as I can, press against the bars, and whisper, "Hey, Danny."

Danny flinches and whips around to face me, claws and teeth bared.

I drop the shear, back up, and hold my hands out to show I'm not a threat. It's been months since he saw me last. I'm covered in road grime, I'm skinnier than I used to be—it makes sense he wouldn't recognize me immediately. "It's okay, it's me. I'm going to get you out of here."

Danny's brow furrows. "Who are you?"

My heart lurches in my chest. It's not that he doesn't recognize me—he doesn't *remember* me. Blood drains from my face as I try to cope with the devastation. "I'm—I'm a friend." There'll be time for proper introductions later.

I cut at the redwood roots barring Danny's escape with one of the shear-blades. It isn't made for sawing, but it slices through those roots like butter—right up until one whips out like an octopus arm and twines around my legs. A second root latches onto my wrist, holding my hand in place.

A grifter snakes out from between the trees, dressed in a bizarrely proportioned doctor's coat, with a stethoscope draped around its neck. Its facial features are just as muted and indistinct as the others of its kind, but a head mirror gleams on its forehead like a single, unblinking eye.

Danny whimpers and scrambles into the deepest corner of his cage. My joints lock up, legs trembling so hard I can barely stand.

The grifter approaches me, crouching down until its horrific approximation of a face is inches from mine. "What do you think you're doing, little boy?" It tastes the air with a snake-like tongue. An impossibly wide grin spreads across its face. "I beg your pardon. Little *girl*."

My stomach clenches. I've gotten good at passing—the idea that it can just *know* like that is unsettling. "I'm—I'm taking Danny home." I slip my free hand into the pocket with the iron pocketknife, but keep the weapon hidden.

"Who? Him?" The grifter points at Danny and tilts its head. "He *is* home. There's more of my world in him than there is of yours."

XIAOMENG ZHANG

My temper flares. "Only because you took it from him!"

"I take pain and give peace. I turn people into living works of art that know nothing of the ills they once suffered."

"They don't remember the good things, either."

"Any memory can be painful, child." It sniffs the air again. "All your memories, my pet, even the sweetest ones, have been tainted with grief. I can smell it. I could absolve you of that grief, of that pain."

I shake my head. "No! It's mine. You can't have it."

It studies me for a long moment, then says, "I'll let him free if you give something of yourself in return."

Why is it bargaining? This has to be a trick. "How do I know you won't just take all my memories and finish him off for dessert?"

"Memories taste sweeter when freely given. Besides, it's best not to overindulge."

I swallow hard. "How much do you want?"

"A day, perhaps. Two, at most. Idle moments here and there."

It's lying. I *know* it's lying. But if it gets close enough, I can cut it. I take a shaky breath, slide my hand inside the jacket to grab the pocketknife, and nod.

The grifter slithers close, right hand extended. I flick the pocketknife open and swipe at the grifter's arm. It bats my hand aside, knocking the blade from my fingers, and plunges a finger into my forehead. It doesn't hurt—if anything, it feels euphoric. My memories burn bright and glorious, more potent than ever before.

Then bits of myself begin to vanish at the speed of thought. The grifter's not taking whole memories, not yet, but it's taking *names*—every instance of my name, thought, heard, or spoken. It doesn't just take my parents' names—it takes their faces, blurred and smudged as if I were looking through a dirty lens. Then the name of my hometown and any memory of how to get there. It's too much, he's taking too much—

I scramble for the screwdriver hidden in my other pocket and stab it into the grifter's right eye socket. The grifter jerks back and *howls*, flailing in an attempt to shake the tool free without touching it.

I snatch the second shear-blade from its makeshift holster and fight the searing pain in my hand long enough to stab it into the grifter's heart. The skin around its chest wound blisters. Those blisters erupt into boils, then massive, cancerous knots that spread through its torso, down its legs, and up its shoulders. The grifter's swollen body explodes in a spray of black ichor, sending my weapons flying. The screwdriver pierces my shoulder tip-first, but what makes me *scream* is the iron searing my flesh like a red-hot cattle brand. The shear-blade stabs into the ground at Danny's feet.

I pull the tool out of my shoulder by the cloth-wrapped handle and chip away at the roots that bind me. Once I pull free, I wrap the shears' handles in tattered remnants of the grifter's coat and cut the final bars of Danny's cell. I try to ignore the way my skin shimmers, pearlescent, as I motion for him to leave the cage. "Come on, Danny. I know the way out. I'll keep you safe."

He hesitates, staring at the grifter's still-bubbling remains, then studies me for a long moment, nostrils flared. He breathes deep, lets out a jagged sigh, and steps out of the enclosure.

The first thing Danny does when we slip back to reality is complain about the cold, so we head for the railyard to catch a southbound train. No specific destination in mind, not yet. Just somewhere warm. I study my features in a puddle as Danny peruses the railyard. The pearlescent sheen isn't limited to my arms—every inch of my body shimmers in the moonlight. My hair glimmers with every movement. No more caramel curls. They're white as bone, now.

Danny finds an open boxcar and ushers me inside. We tuck into a dark corner and sit together, pressed tight for warmth. Danny gives me an awkward smile. "Thanks for getting me out of there."

I force a smile in return. "No problem." I'm lying, of course. It was a problem, will *always* be a problem, now and forever. I've

339

lost enough of myself that I'll never be able to go home—but he's lost even more than I have, so I can't bring myself to complain to him about it.

"What's your name?"

I bite my lip. "I don't remember."

"Me either. Guess we're even." He leans back against the wall. "You called me Danny?"

I nod. "You used to go by Dog-Faced Dan, but I always liked Danny better."

"Danny it is. We could call you Pearl, if you want."

I wrinkle my nose. "What kind of name is that?"

Danny chuckles. "The same kind of name as Dog-Faced Dan."

I shake my head. "No, I want something—simple. Boyish. It's not safe to be a girl on the road." My throat tightens. "You taught me that."

Danny thinks for a minute. "What about Jack? Short for Jacqueline. Besides, Jack's the hero in all the best fairy tales."

I weigh the name in my mind and nod slowly. "That'll work." I hold my breath for a long moment, then ask the question I've been dreading. "What are you going to do now?"

Danny shrugs. "I'll probably just keep drifting. I know how to survive out here—it's everything else that's muddled. What about you?"

"I'll be doing the same. I couldn't find home anymore, even if I wanted to." My fingers pluck at the lining of Danny's coat.

Danny gives me the side-eye. "We could stick together, if you want. Look out for each other."

My breath hitches in my chest. "Really? I wasn't sure you'd want to—I mean, you don't know me from Adam."

Danny laughs. "You know more about me than I do. I'd like to get acquainted again." He holds out his hand and gives me a caring smile. Good right down to its core.

I take his hand and squeeze it, fighting back tears. "I'd like that, too." The grin that spreads across my face isn't forced this time; it's massive, the kind of smile you feel in your eyes. Danny

340

and I may have lost important parts of who we were, but maybe we'll be able to find out who we *are* together.

I drape Danny's coat over our chests like a blanket and we snuggle in for the night. It's not comfortable, exactly, but it feels more like home than my patchy memories of a house and a bed. Part of me misses having a family, but it's more of a vague longing than something sharp and poignant. Really, at this point, Danny and I *are* family, and that helps in some strange way. We owe each other everything we have—which is our lives, mostly, but isn't that the most important thing anyone has when you get down to brass tacks?

The Last Dying Season

written by
Brittany Rainsdon

illustrated by
JEROME TIEH

ABOUT THE AUTHOR

Brittany Rainsdon grew up as the only girl in a family with four brothers. She's reversing that trend with her own children—four girls and one boy. In 2010, Brittany graduated from Brigham Young University-Idaho with a bachelor of science in nursing. She has worked in both medical/surgical and rehabilitation specialties, although she currently enjoys working as a stay-at-home mom.

Throughout childhood, Brittany wrote many poems and stories but lost her spark upon entering college. After having her third child, she sought a creative outlet, and her passion for writing reignited. Once she found the Writers of the Future Contest, Brittany decided to enter every quarter until she won... and after sixteen consecutive entries, she did.

Brittany's first published story appeared in Deep Magic, *spring 2021, and was republished in* The Best of Deep Magic Volume 2. *She was published in* Writers of the Future Volume 37 *as a finalist and now in* Writers of the Future Volume 38 *as a Contest winner.*

Brittany lives with her husband and children near the Snake River in Idaho, where she swears it looks like a wintered Narnia for nearly half the year. She has many pairs of fuzzy socks.

About her story, Brittany shared the following: "After a dramatic health scare, I reflected much on what mattered most to me—as well as my greatest fears. My biggest concern wasn't actually dying, but leaving my children without a mother. This concern, coupled with musings on the value of life, spawned the characters and ethical dilemmas within 'The Last Dying Season.'"

ABOUT THE ILLUSTRATOR

Jerome Tieh is a Singaporean digital illustrator focused on creating immersive worlds.

Although he initially entered Maryland Institute College of Arts seeking to get a degree in game design, he found himself enthralled with illustration—be it preproduction visual development or postproduction promotional art. He soon found himself dedicating most of his time to illustration—while still focusing on the entertainment industry.

Jerome's works span from posters to concept art to motion graphics and UI mock-ups. Since 2020, Jerome has been interning for UX Is Fine as a designer/motion artist, which he hopes will give him further insight into the inner workings of the video game industry.

The Last Dying Season

My womb-daughter danced on the graves of ghosts, twirling atop the ruined steps of the Neet temple our colony had crushed six years before. Her long, black hair flared around her like a skirt and her blue eyes gazed at the dimming turquoise sky, innocent and unaware we were spending our last days together, or to be more precise, her last days. My life—my consciousness as Edrei Muller—could always be reuploaded into another body.

"Wooma, watch me!" Nadia's five-year-old voice echoed off crumbled stone pillars.

I didn't respond as I made my way inside the temple ruins, reading my scanner and comparing the information on it to my current location. I needed the final piece to the puzzle. The heartsplant. If there was a way to save this dying world—and therefore my daughter—it would be in that bit of life.

"You're not watching!"

I glanced at Nadia, who was hopping on the cracked steps with one foot, then the other. "I see, Nad. Give your wooma a minute, okay?" I squatted beside the collapsed entry wall, brushing away dead ticlus leaves to read an encryption. Could they have hidden it here?

I ran calloused fingers over the carving. My face twisted as I translated the ancient Neet: *Engrisa, orosa, uvteka.* The Neet mantra: Enlighten, uplift, overtake. How ironic. I imagined the free Neet with their clicking mandibles, their many barbed legs,

JEROME TIEH

their shiny silvery exoskeletons. They had been graceful and wild and incredibly dangerous—which was why Prima, our leader, had ordered the last survivors chipped and enslaved after their first molt, a process in which human consciousnesses overrode their own. And as those Neet grew, we forced their bodies to labor, but these Neet never were as graceful, as dexterous, as *beautiful* as the free ones had been. In some ways, it felt an incredible waste. Because after all we'd done to conquer this world, we were going to lose it, too. We'd been overtaken, just like the Neet. Only we couldn't blame anyone but ourselves.

The sharp clatter of a skidding stone caught my attention, and I whirled to see Nadia in the center of the room, scrambling up the back of a hollow Neet exoskeleton, reaching to touch its broken pincers. She grinned, acting as though she knew how to ride one.

"Nadia, get down from there. It isn't safe."

Nadia pouted, her lower lip wobbling as if I'd yelled a curse, but she slid off and sulked to the opposite wall. A few moments later, I heard the steady *thunk* of her throwing rocks. I grimaced as I moved to the dead plants. The information hidden in those was usually more promising than physical carvings, anyway.

My reputation as a botanist and geneticist on Earth had landed me this opportunity to colonize and have myself uploaded onto a mind chip. They'd lured me with the program's promise of eternity: *You'll live forever, endure and explore. You'll be doing something that matters. You'll live to see and BE the future.* I hadn't imagined the future would taste so sour.

But the recruiters had been right. On Kalefe, I *had* discovered things that mattered. My studies proved the Neet weren't primitive. Though they had no computers, no sleek spaceships or war machines, they'd utilized plants in ways we never had. Flowers and vines were their technological hardware, storing entire libraries of data in a single seed, leaf, or flower's DNA.

But this leaf held no new information. I crumpled it to dust.

I'd spent the last four years scouring every Neet temple, every burrow—but none of their technology adequately explained why the planet had turned, why our crops would no longer take, even after I'd altered their genomes with our EVEE ship's CRISPR technology. I'd tried splicing Earth plants with the indigenous ones. It had slowed their demise, but it was still upon us, as if the planet had a mind of its own, claiming a slow sort of vengeance for our killing and enslaving the Neet. And in their plants, there were references to something called the dying season. Surely we were living in one now, but I had no idea how bad it would get or if it could be stopped.

Worst of all, Prima was threatening to evacuate us soon—but there was no cryo wing on the EVEE ships that bore us here. Embryonic Vessels for Expansion and Exploration. There had been enough room for frozen embryos, basic supplies, and the memory chips of a thousand of Earth's brightest to guide the first generation through colonization. As a primary colonist with a mind chip, my memories could be saved on the ships, and I would be reuploaded into another body once we landed on a more suitable planet.

But Nadia would not be. None of the two hundred children would.

Small hands tugged my sleeve. "The tenders say the Neet are just bugs...but they built this. How? It's beautiful."

My lips twitched. The temple *had* been beautiful. Before the bombings, it had looked like a cross between a spiral seashell and a mud dauber's nest, smooth sand-colored stone spiraling upward with a few spaces between the lower columns. And above, the wild plants of Kalefe whispered through an intentionally open ceiling. But now it was crushed. The cracked ceiling had crumbled, and sharp rocks gouged upward where pillars had snapped. The ground was littered with rubble.

"The Neet used to be different," I said, bending forward to sweep a stray hair out of her face. "And their temples *were* beautiful. But both the Neet and their wild plants were dangerous. We had to be cautious. We still should be." I pointed to a frail kardish vine that hung from the temple's crumbling ceiling, its purple leaves withered. "If that wasn't dead, it would choke us for touching these. You'd need fire to scare it off." I gestured to my torch, which I'd abandoned on the ground near the entryway encryption. "Kalefe protected its own."

"And we're going to fix it!" Nadia spoke proudly, but then she caught my expression and her brow furrowed. "What's wrong?"

I leaned against the wall, rough rocks poking into my back. "I had hoped to find the heartsplant here, Nad. The Neet brought their children to it after their first molt. The Neet didn't just alter plants for lighting, defense, and other advantages. The Neet worshipped them. And if there are any answers left to find, they'd be in the heartsplant. Records show they grew it in this temple, but I can't find it."

Nadia frowned. "Then I'll help you. What does it look like?"

I picked up a stick and drew in the dirt, describing the prickly plant that looked almost a rosebush, but with teethlike protrusions in the center of midnight-blue flowers.

"I know where that is." Nadia tugged my arm and pointed at the exoskeleton. "There!"

She couldn't really know, but I put on the best show I could, scrambling for my torch as I swept forward. "Stay back." I warned, feigning seriousness. "I'll keep this close in case it attacks."

But as I advanced, my heartbeat quickened. Beside the exoskeleton were the snapped remains of some sort of structure, and centered under it, a crack. As I crouched closer, an intoxicating musky scent poisoned the air, and a small vine protruded. My stomach leaped, and I held up a hand, halting Nadia, who was too much my shadow. I approached on my own. Was it alive? The plant shrank as I advanced, reacting to the flame the same way the kardish vines did, but a prickly blue flower opened, glowing. Why had I not seen this plant and Nadia had? Neet young had been brought to the heartsplant. Was there a connection?

My mind chip blazed, a message flaring. It was from Prima, transmitted via the satellite that orbited Kalefe. *Gates close in one hour, Edrei. I'm sending a Neet to transport you. Report to my quarters upon your arrival.* I cursed. She'd be wanting to discipline me for taking Nadia beyond colony walls, but how could I leave my womb-daughter behind, knowing these were our last days together? Our last moments...

"Wooma?"

I let out a shaky breath. "Prima wants us to come back. The sun will set soon and the gates will close." I flexed a hand. "But first..." With a pair of clippers, I carefully plucked a petal and then retreated, dropping it into the scanner. I held my breath.

"Wooma, was I right?" Nadia peered over my shoulder, excitement dancing in her eyes.

"It *is* the heartsplant," I spoke softly, scanning the information as the history of the Neet spilled across my screen. And as I scanned and searched, a burning hope filled me.

Starships. The Neet had come here on living starships that still slept underground. A plan formed as I read the rest of the information, heart bursting at the chance to save my daughter, to watch her grow. I didn't care if Prima wanted to discipline me today. After seeing this, she would agree. The heartsplant changed everything.

Dirt plumed the air as Nadia and I rode the sleek back of the enslaved Neet. The wind slapped with a salty grit that stung our lips, clogged our noses, and whipped our hair as we huddled into the high necks of our coat collars. We galloped without a saddle, the Neet's many legs whooshing as it glided over ravines, weaving between dead helfi trees and shriveled shiga bushes. The extensive emptiness of the wild seemed to swallow us as Nadia rocked against my chest. A future lost...

The dwarf planet Kalefe was supposed to be our new home, our escape from a dying world. For a time, it had been. I still remembered the rush I felt the day I was reborn. Fresh from the birthing hatch and uploaded into the body of an adult female, I toured our colony, gawking over the outer wall at the glowing uras vines, the rippling tendril-like leaves of the shiga bushes, and the towering red helfi trees that grasped heavenward like living earthen skyscrapers. Four-winged yaris birds screeched as they flew and Kalefe's two moons were bright white specks against a cloudless turquoise backdrop.

I shouldn't have been reckless, but upload had made me giddy, and the robotic tenders hadn't been able to stop me from rushing out to explore. I groped waxen leaves, swept my bare hands and feet across the soft moss floor, the brittle bark, and inhaled the musky floral scent of a world unknown. So unlike the barren Earth I had fled, Kalefe was beautiful, alive and strange, full of hope and wonder.

Yes. We'd been born to a most beautiful future. One we went on to tear away from the Neet. One that would be torn from us as well.

The Neet stumbled and Nadia let out a startled scream.

"It's okay, Nad."

The Neet righted itself and I wrapped my arms around her, as if my presence alone could keep her safe. Her knuckles whitened as she gripped the hard ridge of the exoskeleton where the Neet's neck met its thorax.

Bring us to the south gate. I sent the message via my mind chip.

The Neet's mandible clacked.

Nadia stiffened against me, unfamiliar with the primitive communication an enslaved creature was reduced to using. Because although a human consciousness bubbled inside the Neet, a defect in the programming prevented its direct communication.

"Wooma, are we almost home?"

I gazed up the ravine where the stone walls softly sparkled against the fuchsia and green light show of the setting sun. "Don't you see it?" I lifted her head, turning her to look.

I felt her muscles relax as I kissed the back of her head. The familiar cluster of stone buildings shot skyward near the colony's center. As the original settlement, it remained an impressive feature, but the buildings were largely abandoned this time of year.

Stop here.

351

The Neet clacked its pincers and halted outside the gate. I slid off first, then helped Nadia down. Without a second glance, the Neet shifted around the corner and burrowed down a hole, probably already on another assignment.

"That was fun, Wooma."

I smiled. Children weren't usually allowed into the wild and certainly not on the backs of Neet. But given the circumstances… I ruffled her hair, brushing a finger against crunched-in leaves. I wrinkled my nose. "You need a bath."

"Only cuz you made me see nasty plants."

I shook my head, but grinned.

As we walked through the gate and under the shadow of the colony walls, a chill slipped through me. The cranking gate descended in a clamoring cacophony, but the silence that followed allowed even our whispering footsteps to echo. Gripping Nadia's hand, we advanced farther, making our way through the surface structures. After dark, cold spread quickly, and it was far easier to maintain temperatures under a thick layer of stone and soil. Storm season drove everyone underground. In some ways, it felt as though we'd already evacuated.

We twisted around the last alley and descended into the tunnels. Trailing the ceiling above us, uras vines flickered, dying with the rest of the Neet's vegetative technology, and a pungent stench filled our nostrils. Heaviness settled in my chest. We passed corridor after corridor, some branching off, some collapsed from early conflicts with the Neet. Discolorations marred the cold stone. We may have taken their tunnels, but we had never seemed to be able to scrub the stain of Neet ancestral blood from the walls. I still could detect faint scents of their acrid ichor.

"Head home, Nadia," I whispered, gesturing her down the hall. "I need to see Prima."

"Are you going to tell her about the heartsplant?" Nadia's eyes sparkled, still energized from her trip to the temple.

"Of course. You made a wonderful discovery today. You should be proud."

She smiled and dashed down the hall, dark hair flowing behind. My heart seemed to leap after her.

Edrei, report to my quarters.

I frowned and made my way deeper in the tunnels, then tapped the door made of ticlus plant. Sluggishly, it retreated into the wall.

Prima motioned me inside. Silently, I crossed the threshold. She sat at her desk, a simple structure made of hard steel. Her gaze stayed on an open holo, studying; so I studied her. Prima's four plaited braids had bits of silver woven through natural red, the leadership decorations glinting under the diminished uras lights. Her jaw tightened and then smoothed. She was cold and strong and beautiful. But so much more. This slim, muscled body hosted General Pallavi Bhatt, the same mastermind who had concocted interstellar travel via embryos and mind chips a hundred years prior; though here she wasn't an Earther chasing interplanetary adventure and immortality. She was Prima, our leader who had ruled during the conflict with the Neets, and she had personally yoked the last free one six years ago. She was legendary.

Prima finally moved to look at me, clearing her throat. "You took your daughter with you to one of the Neet temples today."

I nodded, though it wasn't a question.

"I asked you not to."

"You didn't *order* me not to."

She raised a brow. "Do I need to?"

Heat surged up my neck, angry words dying to be spoken, but I swallowed them. "No. I already found what I needed. But you must read it."

Her brow creased as I handed her the tablet with the heartsplant information. She hooked it to her computer, uploading the information onto her holo, and began scanning again. After a moment she stood, eyes darkening as if the information disturbed her.

I kept still, fingering the trio of dark braids that hung against my back, rocking on my heels and waiting for the chance to

speak. She had to understand. We could save our children. *All*
of them.

Prima finally met my gaze, cocking an eyebrow. "You
were recruited for your expertise on plants and genetics. Not
archaeology or linguistics. Are you sure abou——"

"Yes." My heart fluttered against my ribs. "This information
was in the heartsplant. It was the Neet's most sacred plant.
I knew if we found it, we'd find the answers we were seeking."

"In living spaceships?"

"Yes." I smiled again, gesturing at the holo. "They're hiber-
nating underground. Don't you see? We can bond with them,
just like the Neet did. It's why the Neet brought their young to
the heartsplant at first molt. To bond them to their spaceships
in case they needed to leave."

"If that's true, then why didn't the Neet leave?" Prima pursed
her lips. "When they lost the tunnels, they should have."

I hesitated, enthusiasm ebbing. "Perhaps . . . perhaps they had
no place left to go. No resources to support transport."

"That is still a problem for us." Prima handed me back my
tablet. "Our stores are spent."

"No." I stood a little taller. "If we stretched our supplies,
we could last at least another storm season—and we have
coordinates to other potential worlds. It's not the same as the
Neet. If we ration an——"

"And what, Edrei? You want me to load up these alien
starships—which we do not know how to run—with children
and hope we arrive at another planet before they starve? That
isn't merciful. It's cruel."

"And leaving them here isn't cruel?" My voice cracked.

"She isn't even your blood." Prima shrugged, but the glassiness
of her eyes told me she knew it still hurt. "She was your womb-
child. Nothing more. But enough. I didn't call you here to
discipline you. I called you here because I need to alter your
chip."

I clutched the tablet to my chest. Was she going to erase me
then? "Why?"

Prima's face fell flat, but she reached out a hand, as if in sympathy. "We wrote a code for situations like this. You shouldn't have to feel guilty."

"I don't understand. Situations like..."

"What we did to the Neet." She gestured to the holo. "Hard choices. With immortality comes the burden of eternal guilt. It is, at times, insurmountable. But that guilt cannot be allowed to consume you, Edrei. You are a valuable asset to our mission, but your emotions must be bridled so we may achieve our goals. With this code, I can enter your mindspace and cull out the memories that hinder your judgment. You can start over. Your daught——"

I recoiled. "You want to destroy my memories of Nadia?"

"I intend to unburden you."

She held up a chip, set it on her desk, and pulled cords from a drawer that could connect to the port at the base of my neck. She spoke softly, "I need you to forget about the starships. The storm season is nearly upon us and once they hit, we won't be able to get past Kalefe's atmosphere. We'll be stuck here—all of humanity—and I won't risk that kind of destruction. I need you to put this life behind you and look to the future. I've already retired half of the enslaved Neet."

A shiver rocketed through me and a sick feeling settled in my gut as I imagined the still forms of the enslaved Neet rotting in the tunnels. What would Nadia think? If Prima had already started retiring them—I shook my head. "You act like we're the only survivors left of humanity, because we have had no communication with the Earthers we left behind. But there's still time, we aren't that despera——"

"Do you think this is the first time I've utilized that code?" Prima raised an eyebrow.

My mouth dried, as if I'd swallowed cotton, my mind groping for the memories of my past life. But the images were indistinct, untenable, like trying to hold sand in a sieve. Had I once had a family on Earth? I felt I did, but—

"Sometimes sacrifice of the few is necessary for the many.

I will not allow the last of humanity to die because there is a small chance we could save a few more. We have enough embryos on our ships to try again. And we must." She stood, holding the chip.

"No." I jerked backward.

"No?" Prima's face reddened. I'd always walked a fine line, pushing back when I disagreed with Prima, but I had never disobeyed a direct order. She took a step toward me. "Guilt robs life, Edrei. Even an immortal one. Nadia's memory will hold you back—and therefore, it will hold all of us back. The last of humanity is counting on us to succeed. These are hard choices, impossible choices no one should have to live with. Please. Don't make this harder than it already is."

My chest heaved. "I—I don't want you to do it. I can handle it."

"You can't *handle* it." She stepped forward again. "And this isn't a choice you get to make."

"Stop. . . ." I fumbled backward, nearly knocking into the ticlus plant. But as I held up my hands, I knew I couldn't stop this. All I could do was end things on my terms. "I don't want you to do it. But if you give me the code, I can do it myself. I—I *will* do it myself." I held out my hand.

Prima stared for a moment. Her eyes glistened as she dropped the chip into my open palm. "There won't be room for you on the ship if you don't erase those memories. If you can't—"

"I can." I made a fist.

She nodded. "We leave tomorrow, before the storms have a chance to come in. I'll send a tender to watch over Nadia tonight. Say your goodbyes if you must, but the sooner your memories are gone, the lighter your burden will feel. You are dismissed."

Once in our private quarters, I sent Prima's tender away. I didn't want to lose these last precious moments with my daughter, even if I wouldn't remember them. Because she would. Guilt stung the back of my throat as I crouched next to Nadia's bunk. The mattress squeaked as she rose to squeeze my neck.

"Wooma, I had fun today." Nadia lay back, and I slid the scratchy blanket under her body, binding her into a cozy cocoon.

"Thank you for helping me." I touched her cheek. "I wouldn't have found the heartsplant without you."

Nadia wrinkled her nose. "It smelled funny at the temple. Does the wild always smell like that?"

I grimaced. "No. It used to smell...clean, I guess. Like rain."

"Or snow." Her eyes shone brightly. "It will start snowing soon, I'm sure. We could make a snowman. Promise me we will?"

"Nadia..." My throat thickened. How could I tell a five-year-old goodbye?

"Wooma, what's wrong?"

I shook my head, blinking fiercely. "Nothing. I just, I love you." I bent forward, kissed her cheek and stroked her hair, inhaling deeply. She still smelled of soap from her bath, but a bit of Kalefe lingered. "I love you so much."

She leaned forward, rubbing her nose to mine. "Love you more!"

Every night she'd said that to me and every night I'd argue back. But this night, I felt too guilty to argue. This night, her words felt much too true.

I left the bunkroom for the living area and collapsed into my hard-backed chair. My throat felt as if I'd lodged a pebble in it, but I breathed deep and opened my hand. The tiny black chip weighed in my palm as I considered my options. If I didn't erase Nadia, I'd be giving up more than an opportunity to study another planet. I'd die. And though I felt responsible for Nadia, didn't I have a greater responsibility to the program? To the future of humanity? What was the memory of one little girl worth? My stomach roiled, acid burning the back of my throat. I hated myself for considering, hated the atrocity I was committing, but as my guilt grew, it only solidified Prima's reasons for ordering the memory wipe. I couldn't live like this.

And I didn't have to.

Taking another deep breath, I flipped on my tablet, inserted the chip, hooked a cord to the port at the back of my neck, and closed my eyes.

My mind buzzed with the events of the day, and I imagined my brainwaves as little bumps in a road, the mark of a concentrative, if not slightly disturbed, beta state. But to access my mind chip, I had to disconnect from myself. I inhaled and hummed, focusing on disengaging, increasing the amplitude of my brainwaves while slowing their frequency and reaching for the meditative calm of alpha state. Deeper still, I let myself melt, slowing the frequencies further, until I wasn't thinking of waves at all and my body seemed to disappear.

My consciousness refocused as darkness lifted, revealing my bright white Earther home. I had entered theta state—and therefore the physical manifestation of my mindspace. I stepped forward.

A breeze whispered through twin oaks that flanked the front of my house, and the painted blue door gleamed in yellow sunlight. I twisted a brass knob and entered, hands flexing and unflexing as I crossed the threshold. The house smelled of cinnamon and spices, and a crackling fire roared in its grate, spitting sparks and smoke up a brick chimney. These were added accessories, a mere setting, and not an executable code. But the pictures *were* executable.

Bitterness flooded my mouth as I studied the photographs lining the mantel, images I could touch to relive. Nadia's birth, her first tooth, teaching her to read and write. A new one hung near the window of our trip to the temple today. I shook my head. These would all have to go, but it wouldn't be as easy as pulling them from the wall and shoving them into the fire. I needed an executable function for that. I hardened myself.

Where was Prima's code?

It would be a physical manifestation here too, and I searched the house for something out of place. I found it in my bedroom. A long, sleek sword with a tasseled pommel rested on a mahogany wood dresser. Heart hammering, I picked it up, turning the cold instrument over in my hands to read the encryption on the blade.

Prima's code.

Gripping the leather handle, I strode into the front room, determined to make this quick. Prima had been right—guilt was already plaguing me, but as I stared at the pictures above the fireplace, all I could hear was Nadia. *I love you more.*

I shuddered and ran to the mantel, touching the picture of her birth. A shock burned through me as I relived the moment of ecstasy when I'd first held her wriggling pink body against my breast. I'd never felt so proud, so in love, even though I'd been warned not to. She was a beautiful baby, and though I'd been offered tenders to take her, I'd brought her home.

I moved to the next picture, one where Nadia had brought me to school, proudly exclaiming her wooma could fix the school lights because I knew how to work with plants. She'd been wrong—the schoolhouse was above ground at the time and all the plants on the surface were the first to go—but her pride in me had never diminished, despite my failing to fix them. And her example had taught me not to give up on her, to keep going, even when it felt impossible. Trembling, I stepped back, then brushed a hand on the memory of today, reliving Nadia's excitement and innocence, her dancing on the stone steps. My chest caved. It was beauty and innocence that made life worth living, that gave me hope for humanity.

Gasping, I stepped backward. I dropped the sword and clutched my aching chest. This was wrong. Deleting my memories of Nadia wouldn't cleanse me of guilt. Sure, it would delete the memories that elicited such emotions, but it would also steal the education that accompanied them—everything she'd shown me of what I needed to change in my life. Everything that made me more.

Because Nadia *had* changed me. And if I couldn't save her, the least I could do was preserve her memories in mine.

But there is *a chance to do more than remember.*

The words of hope burst through me. Hands shaking, I kicked open the ottoman and dropped the sword inside, as if Nadia were here and I needed to hide the evidence of my betrayal. The sword thudded against the bottom of the ottoman, shifting papers and discarded notes I'd not had time to sort through for deletion. I slammed the lid shut.

Jerking myself from theta, I woke again in the hard-backed chair of our dim underground quarters. Sweat circled my armpits, slicked my hands, but my breath came in fevered chills. Nausea gripped me as I rushed to Nadia, touching her cheeks and warming her hands. How close I'd come to not appreciating her face. The thought sickened me.

"Nadia?" I whispered. "Child, you must wake."

Nadia rolled, peeling open her eyes with difficulty. "Wooma, I'm tired."

I shook her again. "You must get up, Nadia. We're going on a treasure hunt!"

Blinking fiercely, she jerked upright, the sheets sliding from her chest. "For what?"

I tapped my tablet. "A Neet spaceship."

We slipped from the colony under the light of Kalefe's twin moons, opening the gate from the inside. Once outside the stone walls, we navigated a steep ravine while the moons played hide and seek, peeking between the naked branches of helfi trees.

I clutched Nadia's hand. Tangled masses of dead and dying vegetation scratched against our clothes as I navigated us through the desolate wild of Kalefe and back to the Neet temple. At night, it felt eerie to stand under the trees, as though we were walking through a skeletal graveyard, the bones of a planet laid bare, the stench sterile.

Nadia stopped, wrapping her arms around her chest. "Wooma, are you teasing? Is there really a spaceship here?"

"Yes. But we have to go to the temple first."

"Why can't we ride a Neet? That was fun."

The image of Neet carcasses rotting in the tunnels flared. I didn't answer.

Overhead, gray clouds overtook the first moon, bringing a fresh wave of darkness and cold. The ground leveled, and I scanned the next downward drop, clutching a gnarled branch for balance. Was it this way or...? The dark made it difficult to navigate, and a bitter breeze whistled through the ravine again, raising gooseflesh on my neck. Minutes later, specks of blue-tinged snow flecked against our cheeks, icing our hair with crystals. Nadia's little huffs of condensation were a soft metronome in the silence. I clutched her hand tightly, trekking over snapping branches, cursing inwardly. The storms were upon us early.

"Wooma, I'm tired. And cold. We should go home."

"I'll carry you." I picked her up and nuzzled her face into my neck. Her nose prodded my heat and her chilled fingers dug under the back of my coat collar, but her breath was warm. I stroked her hair with numbed fingers, running them through unbound locks. Worry twisted my stomach. The weather was changing quickly. Would Prima leave without recovering my chip? I shook my head, focusing on the present. Where was the temple?

There!

I recognized the path as my eyes traced the winding shape of a dried riverbed to the collapsed building.

"I see it, Nad." Limbs trembling, I broke into a run. Icy air burned my lungs as I pounded forward, dried vegetation crunching, rocks skidding. As I raced into the ruins, darkness enveloped us, our footsteps echoing as I searched for the exoskeleton that had stood over the hidden heartsplant. I fumbled with a flashlight— I'd not brought a torch this time.

"I don't like it here." Nadia lifted her head, nose red. "Wooma, there's no ship."

I shushed her. "The ship is buried elsewhere. But first we must communicate with it, wake it up." I set her on the ground.

She jammed her hands into coat pockets, black hair slicked against her forehead. "They talk?"

361

"They communicate. Not talk." I knelt, running a hand under the dead Neet, finding the crack and then movement. The heartsplant was still alive, still here. My heart beat furiously.

Nadia trembled. "How do they communicate?"

The vine lifted at the sound of Nadia's voice. I pointed at the prickled vines and toothy flower as she shrank back. "According to the data from the heartsplant, we can form a communicative link by touching it. This will make it possible for us to board the spaceships."

"I don't understand. Touch it?"

I raised an eyebrow. "You'll have to let the flower bite you."

Nadia's eyes went wide. "I—I don't want to."

"Nadia, please." I didn't want to force her, but how could she comprehend what was at stake? I stroked her hair and whispered soothingly, "I'll be right here with you, making certain you're safe. I'm doing it, too."

Her eyes shone with tears as she sniffed. "Why did you bring me here? I want to go home."

"We can't yet." I swallowed. "Not together anyway. Not without doing this. I—today was our last day."

Nadia sat silent for a moment, but when she spoke again, her words were a spear of ice to my chest. "I already knew, Wooma. The tender that came today said you and the other woomas are leaving soon." She scuffed the ground. "I didn't believe it. Called it a liar. But you lied to me about fixing Kalefe."

"I didn't lie."

"Then you lied about leaving."

I dipped my head, cheeks burning. "I'm not leaving, Nadia." I squeezed her hand. "Not ever. But we have to do this. Together, okay?"

She stared at the flower, biting her lip. "If you do it with me, then I can."

I rubbed her arm. "Together then."

I approached the plant with her small hand in mine. The glowing flower opened, midnight blue dazzling in darkness.

"It's beautiful." Nadia's eyes widened.

"It is." I squeezed her hand again. "Now, on the count of three, we reach for the flower. One...Two..."

As we made contact, an intense current flowed through me.

At once, I knew I had done something wrong.

There was nothing but blackness, no sense of time or direction. Nadia's hand still clutched mine, the only physical sensation here, but though I called her name, there was no answer. And there was something else, something...foreign. I breathed slowly, clearing myself of fear, willing Nadia to do the same. This was a mindspace—an unfinished one.

In the early days of learning to access my mind chip, it had been like this, a meandering black nothingness. My oaks, the little white home, the rooms within it, had been painstakingly constructed through concentration on brainwaves. Navigating blackness was harder than opening a physical front door; but it was still possible to build something new using meditation and by concentrating on brainwaves.

I roused calm, humming away my fear, my regret, and focused on the amplitude of my brainwaves to enter theta state, encompassing Nadia as well. Still black, but there was ground now, a surface underfoot. I struggled, lowering the amplitude again, and the blackness dissolved.

Disoriented, I stumbled. Nadia fell beside me, trembling. It was as if a blindfold had been ripped from our faces. A sharp musk filled my nostrils, and as I squinted, I recognized the scenery as the spot we'd stood in moments before—the wrecked temple now smooth and clean, the ceiling coated in healthy kardish vines. In the center of the room, where the exoskeleton had lain, was some sort of towering trellis made of white stone. And peeking between the wall's dauber-like pillars, lush trees and bushes whispered. Outside, a gurgling river lulled. Birds chirped.

"Wooma?" Nadia squeezed my fingers as I helped her stand. "It *is* beautiful."

"As beautiful as it once was." My heart squeezed. "But then it must also be dangerous." I raised a brow as something caught my eye. "And something's not right."

Carved into one of the pillars was a blue door—my blue door. As I scanned the room, scattered pictures of my daughter were displayed throughout the temple. I turned, noting the upended ottoman, my mahogany dresser, and a crackling brick fireplace behind the trellis.

This mindspace was transposed over mine.

Suddenly there was a clicking and scuttling. I stiffened. The sound was unmistakable as the smooth scamper of the many-legged creatures we'd taken Kalefe from. A free Neet. I shoved Nadia behind me, but there was movement above.

"Get down," I whispered as the kardish vines descended, though they did not attack. Yet.

"We've waited too long for someone pure." The voice rattled through me and Nadia shrank behind.

"What?" A chill rippled down my back. This should have just been a data deposit.

The kardish vines shot forward, looping around my daughter's ankles and yanking her upward. "Wooma!"

"Nadia!" I screamed, grappling for her hand, but she slipped through. The vines curled her into the ceiling as I ran for the trellis to chase her upward, but I leaped and missed, slamming my head against the cold ground.

"Nadia, it isn't real." I yelled. "Find your body, bring yourself back to your body. Concentrate."

But she didn't move, the vines wrapping around her, cocooning her as a spider does its prey.

"Nadia!"

"She cannot hear you."

More clicking echoed through the temple, a rattling of pincered feet against stone. I swirled in time to see the Neet advance. My hands flexed, searching for a weapon but finding none. The Neet slowed, then stopped in front of the trellis, its sharp pincers snapping maybe six feet from me. Its silver exoskeleton and spindly legs mirrored the light of my fireplace as blank black eyes bored into mine.

"Your corrupt technology has ravaged Kalefe and stolen the Neet."

It clacked its jaw, but the voice didn't come from the creature's mandible. It didn't seem to come from the Neet at all, but from vibrations around me.

"You are a memory of a world lost, speaking words of nothingness. Let my daughter go."

"We do not speak nothingness. We are the true rulers of Kalefe." More clicking echoed. "The *gods* of the Neet."

"The gods?" I shivered. "You're code an——"

"We are entities within the heartsplant." The Neet's mandible clicked and drew closer, smelling of that same sickly floral musk that lingered at the temple site. "We are not Neet. We invigorate the bodies of those presented to us. Those that are pure, as the Neet were. We enlighten, uplift—"

"Overtake." I finished the Neet mantra as the magnitude of my error dawned.

"Yes." The Neet shifted form, morphing into a replica of Nadia. It smiled strangely; her eyes somehow as blank as the Neet's had been. "We join and adapt with those unbound, those pure, but you cannot be enlightened, Edrei. Your mind chip has made that skinsuit unfit for occupancy. We would have taken it if it were. Once our presence is downloaded into your Nadia, she will bring us more hosts."

"No!"

"It is only fair. After all, you stole our Neet, corrupting the young ones with your selfish technology."

My hackles rose, cheeks burning. "Nadia won't help you. Release her."

The creature cocked its head, speaking solemnly. "Feel for her hand in the physical world. She is there, physically. But her mind remains trapped here. She is lost to you." The creature pointed up at the bundled kardish vines and a chill rushed through me. "Just as the Neet were taken from us." Black eyes flashed dangerously.

"You should have listened to your Prima. You should have run while you could and escaped. But even now, your starships are malfunctioning, unable to withstand the attack we've forged thanks to your unsanctioned *intervention*."

I stepped backward. "What attack?"

The creature smiled. I hated the way that smile looked on my daughter's face, a look of amusement much too adult and condescending. "When you snipped our flower today, it is true, we revealed some of our secrets, but we also embedded a code. It will ground your ships, and even if your Prima can overcome it, she will not be able to launch them before the storms are here. You will remain on Kalefe and your entire species will succumb as we finish our dying season."

"Dying season?" I recalled the reference, but there was more meaning behind it, surely.

The creature grinned. "A dying season is a time of intentional planetary death, necessary to purge unworthy inhabitants from Kalefe's surface. We send out signals, speak to the plants and animals, forcing them to sleep until the unworthy species succumbs. But life will return. After your species is defeated, we will quench the signal and restore Kalefe to its proper order and beauty." It paused. "And then, since your ships are grounded, we shall have our newest hosts. The worthy ones."

My blood chilled. This was why our crops didn't take. But the heartsplant was wrong. "Humanity will fight."

"The Neet believed they could fight us, that they would never submit." The creature quirked an eyebrow. "But they did. Every inhabitant falls to our rule. And now your daughter—"

I shook my head, nearly choking. "She's a child, an innoce——"

"We all do what we must to survive. Have you forgotten your own words?"

A vine shot from underground, twining up my legs. I fumbled to peel it off, but as I made contact with the plant, hot images sizzled, like boiling water being thrown onto skin. I clawed at my eyes as if I could stop the images, but they flooded. Exoskel-etons smeared with blue-green blood strung up against the base of a half-dozen helfi trees, the burst of bombs and tunnels caving, fireworks and laughter as temples toppled, and the shrieking mourn of the soft-bellied Neet young who were hunted down after their parents. Even their eggs were crushed beneath brutish boots. I closed my eyes, shaking my head.

These weren't my memories. But they weren't any less real; the pain of the Neet rocketed through me and I shrank as the enormity of their destruction roiled in my gut. These hands that now cared for a child, that worked with plants and studied fields, had once burned them, cut down Neet colonies and left screeching alien babes to wallow in the poison pits. I'd bombed their tunnels, toppled their temples. I hadn't been just a botanist or a geneticist. In these memories, I saw my face and knew I was a murderer. And more than that, I'd been the one to tell Prima to enslave them so we wouldn't "endanger" the ecosystem. We needed them, I'd known, but hadn't understood why.

I cowered. How many times had I allowed Prima to purge me of guilt?

"Your Prima claims that absolving you of guilt is necessary for progression." The creature stepped closer, and the vines fell away. The images faded. "But without conscience, courage becomes cruelty. See what you have done? Your kind has refused to atone for its evil and therefore is allowed to languish in barbarism."

My hands shook, and my voice trembled. "What do you want?"

"We need new hosts." The creature spoke simply. "Have you not been listening? Those who have been chipped are corrupted by your technology. We could hold their minds for a time, but the battle for control is too great and eventually those minds go mad. Under our influence, your daughter can lure other children here, but we need adult bodies. Male bodies, as well as female. Your EVEE ships are capable of producing them, growing hundreds of thousands. Fully formed. Perfect for hosting. But we lack the passcodes needed to take advantage of your machinery. You must help us."

I clenched my fists. "I refuse."

The creature's voice lowered. "What if we were to release your daughter? To give you access to the Neet spaceships so you may escape together? You could start a new life."

I stiffened.

"Give us the passcodes to the EVEE ships, and we will release your daughter. We will absolve you of your crimes and allow you safe passage."

My gut twisted as I searched the mindspace, the pictures of my daughter, the smooth pillars, the wriggling vines, the white trellis. Nothing here could aid me. I needed help and more time. I spoke quickly, "I have them at the colony. I can bring them. Release my daughter, and I will."

The creature shook its head. "No. Your mindspace is transposed over this one. The codes are accessible." It moved beside the trellis, gesturing to my blue door carved into the stone wall, but there was no way I'd let that creature have free rein within my mind. My thoughts jumbled as I groped for a plan.

Beside the trellis, shadows danced, a fire crackling softly. The fire.

Without thinking, I pushed past the creature and dove, thrusting my hand past the grate and yanking out a burning stick. I brandished the fire, embers glowing angrily, but there was no warmth to the stick—no executable function to the code.

The creature laughed. "As you told your daughter, this mindspace isn't real. That fire is nothing more than a pretty accessory, as easily put out as a thought." The creature snapped its fingers, and the fire sizzled to ash.

Fear clawed up my throat, and I stepped backward, stumbling over the dresser and then the ottoman. Its lid flipped off and papers tumbled out, along with...the sword. I swooped forward, grabbing the leather end.

The creature laughed again, stopping to pick up the papers, sorting through them. Its eyes danced with amusement. "You would have made an interesting host, Edrei. Too bad you are tainted." It eyed my sword and snapped its fingers . . . but nothing happened.

The fire might have been for show, but the sword was not.

The creature's brow knit, moved to snap its fingers again, but before it could, I lunged. The creature rolled, shedding the skin of my daughter and transforming into a Neet, claws clattering against stone. I swiped the sword, slicing at a front leg as it retreated, squealing though I'd not made contact.

I advanced, pushing past the ottoman. Grasping with pincers, the creature threw the dresser at me, but I batted it away with the sword, not caring as the pretty piece of furniture disintegrated. But then it threw a picture. Instinctively, I held up the sword, but when it made contact, something inside me shattered and the memory, whatever that picture had held, was gone. I recoiled as the Neet barreled forward.

It slammed me against the ground, and the sword clattered away. I stretched out my arm.

"We will take the passcodes by force. We can occupy your mind, control it, if but for a short time." Its voice vibrated through me as the Neet hovered above, lowering its clacking mandible toward my face. The musky scent smothered me in blackness as I strained, feeling for the sword.

My fingers connected with the tassel. I pulled it in, twisted to get a proper grip, and then blindly shoved. The Neet's underbelly gave a sickening squelch as I buried the blade to its hilt. The blackness dissolved, and the Neet came back into focus.

With bulging eyes, its body flashed, changing from Neet to Nadia, and then to other companions we'd lost during our conflict. I pushed myself upright, backing away. The creature shimmered and shifted again and again, fumbling, clawing at the sword with fingers, then pincers, then other appendages of creatures I'd never seen. How many species had fallen under the spell of the heartsplant? Then all at once the eyes went still, the body faded, and my sword clattered to the ground. I scrambled forward and grabbed it.

Heart smacking against my ribs, I turned, spotting the bundle that held Nadia. If I'd killed the creature, the vines should have released her. But they held firm. Which meant the entity within the heartsplant wasn't dead.

"Fool. We are not one but many."

I fumbled with the blade as vines shot from the ground, from the walls. I sliced fast. And as the vines dropped, they disappeared, having made contact with my blade. But some sneaked past, blazing images across my skin before I hacked them away. Shrieks filled the air, a vibrating hum that ripped through me, then grew gradually silent. The heartsplant entities *were* dying—all of them stored in this single plant, a thousand memories and lives.

I glanced upward, where Nadia's consciousness still hung above the trellis—where that wicked entity cocooned itself around her silent form, still in the process of downloading. I had to release her.

Leaping onto the trellis, I caught the lowest ridge in the smoothed stone, then pulled myself upright and climbed. Vines undulated angrily above me as I situated myself, gauging the jump to the ceiling. But as I poised my sword, ready to leap, a whisper rattled through me.

"You know nothing but destruction. So destruction you shall have, losing not just your daughter, but your memories as well...."

Movement sputtered below, and my gaze flickered away from the bundle that held my daughter. It had tricked me. My pictures of Nadia were gone, but as I gazed back at the vines, I saw them huddled together, a shield of memories blocking my path to the heartsplant. The sword could slip through the pictures, but it would take them as well.

Hot anger boiled in my chest as I raised my sword.

"If you kill us, you deserve the destruction that awaits. The suffering and starvation. You will watch your daughter die. Helpless. We have enacted what will become our *last* dying season and so purge all life from this world. All to purge it of humanity. Of the evil that is you."

Evil. I flinched. *Evil.* I gripped the sword as I stared upward, ready to shred what was left of the heartsplant entities. But in the twisting vines, the desperate voices, the despicable act of sacrificing a child, I saw something familiar…myself. My mistakes. These Neet gods, the heartsplant, they were me. And they were right to label me a disgrace. My hands shook, my grip on the sword loosening.

Because even if I didn't remember what I'd done, I had still done it. I *had* destroyed this planet. I'd killed the Neet. I'd enslaved the survivors. And in so doing, I'd forced Kalefe into a dying season, one which would compel us to abandon our children.

Would remembering prior guilts have changed my actions? My eyes misted as I thought of the heartsplant burying the stories of hosts past. They remembered and yet they'd still gone on, doing what they felt necessary to survive. I couldn't know how I would react if the past had played differently. The only actions I could change would be what I would do now. What we would both do.

"You're right." I lowered the sword. "I have known nothing but destruction and I have faced no retribution for it. But neither have you. My daughter is innocent, as the Neet were innocent. If anyone deserves to be enslaved, it is us."

"We will not be enslaved." The voice roared in my ears. "And you are unfit, corrupt. You cannot be enlightened."

I lowered my head but kept my gaze on the vines. "Because of my mind chip, yes, it would allow me to fight for control. But what if I were to *let* you in? What if we were to work in harmony?"

"You lie. You who steal and then forget. You who—"

"Being able to recall crimes has made no difference in your actions. I understand now. Forgetting cannot change the past. But remembering and doing nothing is an equally great sin. Only forgiveness can change our path, trust that will lead us to a brighter future."

"And you believe you deserve our forgiveness? Our trust?"

I raised my shoulders and glared at the vines. "Do you deserve the Neet's?"

Silence filled the temple.

"Let my daughter go. Take me. Use me to communicate with my Prima and negotiate a better life for your people—for both our people. You have no better option. And neither do I."

The vines undulated again, slower, as if uncertain. Then they lowered, unraveling from Nadia slowly as it laid her on the temple floor. She didn't move, but then her body faded from the mindspace.

"She is alive and will wake shortly."

I nodded and the vines descended, hesitating to touch. My muscles flexed as I lifted my arms in acceptance, anticipating a scalding, but as the vines brushed my skin, a tingling sensation spread. The vines continued, snaking around my body, and the knowledge of a thousand lifetimes flooded. Suddenly, I knew what Prima meant when she claimed eternity held guilt.

The plants felt it too.

Remorse.

Eternity dwelled within me as I stared up at the ceiling of the wrecked temple. Nadia stood over me, rubbing my face. "Wooma, please. Are you okay?"

The heartsplant within did not fight for control, allowing me this moment to be a mother. Slowly, I sat up, clutching my burning skull. It was crowded in this mind, but there was room for both of us, so long as we didn't fight. I shook my head. "I am fine."

Nadia shivered as I pulled her to my chest. Her lower lip wobbled. "I—I don't remember what happened."

We put her in a trance. It felt like a dream. The heartsplant's voice vibrated through me and somehow our connection helped me recognize the pulses it was continuing to send out, a calming message to Kalefe that the dying season was to end.

"You are safe, Nadia." I smiled. "Everyone is safe."

"The tenders said you were leaving me. That I'd be...alone." She sniffed, pulling back. "Did I...did I tell you before? I was mad. I was scared."

"Prima wanted me to." I ran my fingers through her hair. "But she was wrong. We don't have to leave Kalefe. Not on alien spaceships, the EVEEs, or anything else. Kalefe has endured its last dying season, and once the storm season ebbs, life will start anew. Better than before."

"Really, Wooma?"

I cradled my daughter in my arms and stood, staring past the ruins and at the dark shadow of the colony, a small blip on the horizon. We'd scarred this land. And we would fix it.

"I promise."

Nadia's face brightened, and as a bit of snow fell from the sky, she wondered aloud about snowmen and angels and the many seasons of life that lay ahead.

We had much to change in this world. And though I knew there were pains and regrets we would surely face here, when I looked into Nadia's innocent eyes, I saw the future as she did.

Bright.

Alive and beautiful.

Full of hope and wonder.

A future we could finally embrace. Because it was *ours*.

The Third Artist

BY DIANE DILLON

Leo and Diane Dillon met while attending Parsons School of Design in New York. After graduation, they married and chose to blend their talents, working together as one artist; the beginning of a career that spanned fifty-four years.

Being interracial, they dedicated their career to be inclusive of all races and cultures to reflect the world we live in, especially those who were rarely represented at that time in the early 1950s.

As a collaborative team, they produced many styles and techniques inspired by art ranging from ancient Egypt to the Renaissance, from the secessionist movement to Japanese prints. Despite the versatility of style, their art remained recognizable as the Dillons' work. Although their work is diverse in style and subject matter, each project bears the hallmark of clean, precise lines, painstaking attention to detail, innovative use of color, and warmth of characterization. The Dillons' art has been described as "magic realism."

Leo and Diane especially enjoyed illustrating fantasy, myth, folktales, and science fiction. They are most known for their children's book work and their innovative science fiction work.

Among their many awards are two back-to-back Caldecott Medals for their children's book illustrations for Why Mosquitoes Buzz in People's Ears *and* Ashanti to Zulu. *Leo was the first black artist to receive the Randolph Caldecott Medal. They received the Hugo Award for their Ace Science Fiction covers and the World Fantasy Life Achievement Award. They were also inducted into the Society of Illustrators Hall of Fame.*

To quote the Dillons, "Art in its many forms has survived over the ages to inform us of lives long gone. Art inspires, lifts our spirits, and brings beauty to our lives. We pay homage to it and the people who created it."

They would say their greatest creation is their son, Lee, who is also an artist.

The Third Artist

Leo and I were born in 1933, eleven days apart, 3,000 miles apart on opposite coasts, and from different worlds. Leo was black; I was white—at a time when it was illegal to be together in many states.

From the time we were young, we both knew we wanted to be artists although we didn't actually know what that meant. My parents supported and encouraged me even though girls were not encouraged to have careers at that time. Leo's parents were not too eager to encourage Leo because they couldn't imagine he could make a living as an artist. Fortunately, Leo's father had an artist and poet friend, Mr. Vollman, who saw Leo's talent and encouraged him.

We met in 1953 at Parsons School of Design and that is where our story begins.

Our relationship at Parsons started as competitors, admiring each other's work before we actually met. I started a semester later than Leo. I saw his work pinned up on the wall on my first day and knew this was serious competition. Leo later told me he saw the piece I had on my desk and felt the same way. We were majoring in advertising and had the same classes. By the second year, our friendship became more serious although we tried to hide it, not knowing if we could be expelled, or worse, but before long the other students knew. To our relief we were not confronted in any way about our relationship, although one of the instructors told Leo he would have a problem being hired and another instructor told me he didn't like to teach talented girls because they just got married, so it was a waste of time teaching them. That didn't discourage either of us.

Our classes consisted of advertisement assignments, life drawing, design, silk screen, photography, and type design. Parsons concentrated on the creative part of illustration. There were no business courses. We were told we would learn the business side when we got our first job. Business and art were like oil and water, not mentioned in the same sentence in the '50s.

When we graduated from Parsons, Leo easily found a job at a publisher for a men's magazine, and I got a job at an advertising agency. Nine months after graduation, we decided to marry despite discouragement from friends on both sides. Leo's parents were accepting but worried that we would have problems; it could be dangerous for their son. My mother was not enthusiastic but tried to be accepting. My father had died before I got to Parsons, but I believe he would have been supportive.

Our first apartment on 106th Street and Second Avenue was a railroad flat, three rooms plus a bathroom—an eat-in kitchen, a middle room, which would normally be a bedroom, and a living room. The rooms were small, about eleven feet by twelve feet. The middle room was smaller since the only closets in the apartment were in that room. The middle room became our studio. It barely held our two drawing boards and taborets that contained our supplies. The living room included a convertible couch that opened into a bed.

I quit my job to become a housewife. Leo kept his job but brought extra work home from the publisher that I worked on with him. After almost a year, Leo was not happy with the nine-to-five routine or commuting on the subway and wanted to freelance. I agreed. Unfortunately, we didn't have the savings to support that decision and the next few years were difficult. With a weekly salary we could budget the money for rent, food, and travel. Freelancing was actually starting our own business.

Since we had taken no business classes on keeping accurate records or how to negotiate, we learned the hard way. There were times in those early years when we forgot to bill for a job we had done, or worse still, billed for a job twice—which was especially hard, also embarrassing, when the client discovered the error and asked for the money back after it had been spent. When a job came in, we accepted it, and when the finished art was done and delivered we waited, sometimes for two weeks, to hear if there were any changes before asking how much we would be paid. Clearly not good business sense. I'm happy to see art schools now include business in their curriculum.

At first, when we made an appointment with an editor or art director, one of us would take the portfolio in. If they gave us work, we finished the pencil drawing, then the other one took it in for approval before starting the finished art. We made sure they knew we were interracial, hoping to avoid any uncomfortable scenes. Other than a few jaws dropping, or surprised expressions, there were no unpleasant occurrences in the publishing world. We never knew if we didn't get a job because of who we were.

Now that we were freelancing, the steady weekly paychecks no longer came in. There could be weeks or even months between jobs or checks. We made appointments with advertising agencies and publishers to show our portfolio. The portfolio had mostly original art with only a few printed pieces. It consisted of everything from type design to full-color magazine illustration. We were unknown. The reaction was either "I like your work, come back when you've had more experience" or "There are too many styles and techniques here. You should have a specific style so it is easier for us to think of you when we are looking for an artist." We solved the portfolio problem by making three portfolios, one for magazines, one for book covers and book design, and one for album covers. We also called ourselves Studio Two for a while hoping that clients would accept the various styles and techniques, thinking there were others in the studio as well.

In the late '50s when we began our career, there were no personal computers, no internet, no cell phones, no websites. It was a different world. It was important to be in New York, where most of the advertising agencies and publishers were. Also, there was no FedEx. Today, an artist can work from anywhere in the country.

There were times freelancing when we had no work, when the cupboards were bare, and no checks were due. Once we were reduced to biscuits and tea for breakfast, lunch, and dinner for three days. During these early times, Leo's father, who owned his own truck, would "drop by" on his way to a delivery to bring a bag of groceries or something he had made for dinner the night before. He had been a chef in the West Indies, and he made some delicious food. Leo's father also asked Leo to help him with a delivery sometimes and insisted on paying him for the day. We never asked his father for money, but he must have known we could use his help. Only after work was coming in steadily, we noticed "Pop" wasn't dropping by with food anymore and then we realized what he had been doing. My mom was working to support herself after my father died and wasn't able to help.

Those days were hard but endurable, knowing there was a goal and a reason for the sacrifices. If we hadn't had the Dream, it would have been much harder, and we might have given up and gone back to staff jobs. When we had steady work, we looked back on those days fondly and felt grateful Leo's dad was there when we needed the help.

When there were more published pieces in the portfolios, clients could see we were reliable and experienced and gave us more work. Remembering the hard times, we took everything that was offered from type design to textbook work, book jackets to album covers. We managed to overcome the client's objections to our many styles and techniques; in fact, I think that was why we were offered such diverse assignments. If the client asked for a particular style, we considered their request but if we felt another style worked better, we did what we felt was best.

Once the client saw the finished art, they often said, "That's just what I wanted," even though it wasn't what they'd suggested.

Techniques and style were our way of expressing graphically what we wanted to say, much like words are to a writer. Why would we want to limit ourselves? We experimented with techniques and mediums, some we had never done before. We worked with all the usual materials as well as clay, marbleizing, carving in wood, we developed a stencil technique we called frisket, used melted wax, and even did a cover in crewelwork. We also tried working on many surfaces, including paper, wood, silk, plastic, canvas, and acetate. Experimenting with materials was stressful but exciting, even when things didn't go as planned. The disasters taught us to be flexible and inventive.

One example of that is when we were given a map to illustrate for *Time Life*'s series on the Great Ages of Man. It was a map showing the cradle of civilization. We decided to do it in clay on a base of wood. We nailed chicken wire to the wood to hold the clay. The map was completed. It was due the next day, so to speed up the drying of the clay we warmed the oven, turned off the heat, and placed the map in the oven overnight. The next morning when we opened the oven door, the map had cracked into many, many pieces. We were in shock. We had to call the art director. We told him things were going well but we needed a few more days. Happily, he agreed to give us a little more time. Now we had to figure out how to save the job. There was no way we could remake the map. We took the pieces off the wood, carefully cutting the wire, keeping the pieces in order, then gluing them back together onto the wood. When it was done we filled in some of the cracks but found that the cracks made the map look more ancient so we left some. We hadn't planned for cracks, but in the end the map was even better.

Flexibility was important when working together and as illustrators. Being flexible was a learning experience over time. Being competitive, we knew having separate careers would be a problem, so we thought it would be safer for the marriage to join talents and work together. At first, when we discussed what we had in mind for a job, we might agree verbally but when one of us started the drawing, the other was surprised because they'd envisioned something different. We realized each of us had different pictures in our minds even though we were agreeing. That could lead to an argument. To solve that problem, we made small thumbnail drawings while we were talking, to show what we were thinking, which helped. Our final drawings, to size, were detailed, not sketches, so we both had a guide to follow when passing the work back and forth. Even with the detailed drawings, changes happened when the image was traced down for the finished art and the painting began. When we passed the art back and forth, we learned to accept what was done when we got it and to continue from there instead of trying to change it back to our own vision. Over time we developed trust and the process became smooth, so we rarely disagreed about the work in the later years.

The advantage of working together was a second pair of eyes. When something wasn't going right, the other could take the work with fresh eyes.

Working at home in our studio, we were more isolated than if we had a staff job. In the late '60s, after a little over ten years of freelancing, we joined the Graphic Artists Guild. That was an education in the business of being an artist, finally. We learned that we should be selling the use of our art but not the original. In 1901 the founders of the Society of Illustrators had gone to court to fight for the right to get their originals back from the client and they'd won, but by the time we graduated from art school in the '50s that knowledge was lost. Many clients kept the work. The guild campaigned against work-for-hire agreements that freelancers were asked to sign. Work-for-hire meant that any company that hired us owned the artwork even though we weren't an employee with any benefits. Legally, if an artist is a hired employee of a company, the company owns whatever he or she creates, and in return the employee gets benefits that include things like vacation with pay, retirement benefits, etc. So, for almost fourteen years we had not even asked for our original art back.

The Graphic Artists Guild, or GAG, also published the *Pricing & Ethical Guidelines Handbook*, or PEG. The PEG had information about how to negotiate, ethics for the artist and the client, pricing, contracts for artists, and other helpful information for freelancers. The guild still produces the handbook, and it is available on the internet now.

The fact that we could get our art back was important. When starting out we had no idea our art was worth anything. As we developed a reputation and became known, our art had value and collectors began to purchase our work. That made a huge difference in filling those gaps when no checks were coming in.

Not long after we joined the Graphic Artists Guild, we joined the Society of Illustrators. It was formed to promote and exhibit the art of illustration; it included lectures, educational programs, and juried competitions. It was also a social meeting place for artists where we met and made new friends and compared experiences with clients and prices for work. Being members, we also learned more about the business of illustration, and we were no longer so isolated. In 1981 the society was established as a museum.

We had been working for about twelve years and were established when we were asked to teach illustration at the School of Visual Arts. It was the late '60s during the psychedelic period. We heard about classes where students were drawing on long sheets of brown paper and then wrapping themselves in the paper, or students were asked to sit and stare at another student as an assignment. Weird conceptional assignments that had little technical information. We wanted to teach materials and technique. The head of the department felt that concept was more important—that once an artist had an idea, they would find a way to express that idea. We prevailed and taught the basics. We taught for seven years. Our classes were full because the students were hungry for practical information.

We taught two days a week but spent the day before

preparing the lesson and the day after recovering, so, in reality, we were spending four days. At that time work was coming in steadily and we were working day and night, sometimes all night, to meet deadlines.

We contemplated starting a studio but didn't want to be managers or involved with the business side of running a studio. We were happiest sitting at our drawing boards doing the work, so, we finally gave up teaching, but we were the better for the experience.

Starting out, we could never have imagined the career we had. Because we were freelancing, we had accepted whatever came to us, which led us on a path that we could not have planned. Every new job was different with new challenges, new problems to solve, and it was never boring. Our stubborn refusal to specialize opened us to many different assignments for young adult and adult book covers, magazines, textbooks, album covers, and posters. Eventually, in the later years, we became known mostly for children's picture books and our science fiction work.

Our preference of subject matter was fantasy, myth, and science fiction rather than technical subject matter. Technical illustration was a challenge and was rewarding, but fantasy, myth, and science fiction gave us more freedom to create and invent characters and worlds. Children's picture books gave us many pages to tell the story. We imagined what happened between the lines of the manuscript and even added our own statements. An example of that is *Why Mosquitoes Buzz in People's Ears*. The West African tale was an animal story. All the animals played a part, but we noticed the antelope only had a small part, he was only sent to fetch another animal. We decided to make him more important, showing him on several pages smiling out at the reader and on one page he is up front and center. Also, there is a little red bird watching the play on every page, an observer like the reader, and on the last page when the story is over, she flies away. She was not in the manuscript. As long as we were true to the manuscript, there was opportunity to add our little side statements.

DIANE DILLON

In 1977 we were awarded the Caldecott Medal for our illustrations for *Why Mosquitoes Buzz in People's Ears*. We had to give an acceptance speech at the American Library Association's annual conference that summer. This was a new experience, speaking to hundreds, if not thousands. Even if Parsons had offered public speaking, we most likely would not have taken it, believing we would never be speaking to audiences. Now we found ourselves traveling around the country speaking, usually with a slide presentation, at bookstores, libraries, and universities.

During speaking appearances, we were often asked how we worked together. We never divulged our process because it was divisive. In any case, passing the work back and forth made it difficult even for us to know who had done what. Some people asked, how could we give up our individual identities? Our identity was what we called "the third artist," which created something that was different from what we would have done separately. We were one artist.

It was not so unusual for artists to work together. In school we admired Alice and Martin Provensen's work, a husband-and-wife team. In art history we learned that many artists had studios with assistants who painted backgrounds, drapery, or were specialists that painted the architecture. Those artists included Michelangelo, Rembrandt, and Rubens. In our times, one good example is Jeff Koons.

Our son, Lee, worked with us on many assignments as he grew older. We hoped he would be an artist, and we encouraged him, giving him his own drawing board and art materials when he was very young. Later he took classes at the Art Students League, School of Visual Arts, and New York Academy of Art. His interests were in painting, sculpture, and jewelry. He preferred fine art rather than illustration, although he could have been part of the third artist if he wanted. We also felt grateful we were able to raise Lee ourselves, since we were working at home.

Looking back on our career, we were lucky to have worked at home doing what we loved. It wasn't always easy, but it was

384

rewarding, challenging, even with moments of euphoria, when everything was going smoothly. We often heard the statement that art is fun. Maybe to preschoolers who had no limitations, no manuscripts to interpret, no research, or those annoying deadlines. The closest we got to "fun" was near the end of a job. In the beginning, there was the anxiety of looking at a blank page and wondering what we were going to do. During the process if problems came up, we had to solve them. It could be fun when all we had to do was refine details, add highlights, and we were ready to say, "It's done!"

A Word of Power

written by
David Farland

inspired by

BOB EGGLETON'S
THE MAMMOTH LEADERS

ABOUT THE AUTHOR

David Farland introduces "A Word of Power" with this: "Over the past few years, I've had a lot of people ask if the Writers of the Future Contest accepts flash fiction or short shorts. We do. In fact, we had a short short as a Finalist for this book, and we had another last year. So, when I was asked to write a story for this volume, I thought it was a great opportunity to bring in a flash piece about magic, and wonder, and longing for home. Enjoy!"

For more information on David Farland, please see page 1.

Sadly, this is the last story David Farland wrote. He finished the edits just a few days before his passing.

ABOUT THE ILLUSTRATOR

Illustrators of the Future Contest winners created the art for each story in this volume with one exception. Here, David Farland wrote a story to accompany the cover art created by Illustrators of the Future Contest Founding Judge, Bob Eggleton.

Bob Eggleton is a winner of nine Hugo Awards and twelve Chesley Awards, the 2019 L. Ron Hubbard Lifetime Achievement Award for Outstanding Contributions to the Arts, and a 2015 Rondo Award in Classic Horror, as well as an award from the Godzilla Society of North America. His art can be seen on the covers of numerous magazines, professional publications, and books in science fiction, fantasy, and horror across the world including several volumes of his own work. He has also worked as a conceptual illustrator for movies and thrill rides.

Of late, Eggleton has focused on private commissions and self-commissioned work. (The latter was the genesis for this year's cover art.) He is an elected Fellow of the International Association of Astronomical Artists and is a Fellow of the New England Science Fiction Association. He has a minor planet named for him by Spacewatch, 13562bobeggleton, and was an extra in the 2002 film Godzilla Against Mechagodzilla.

Bob is currently completing paintings for an illustrated version of King Kong *celebrating the ninetieth anniversary and a large Clarke Aston Smith book. He recently finished essays for a new book,* The Art of Frank Kelly Freas.

Bob has been an Illustrators of the Future Contest judge since 1988. He has participated as an instructor for the annual workshops and as an art director for previous anthologies.

About the cover painting, Bob said, "My idea was taking this older work of mammoths and merging it with these new elements, humanoid robots exploring a past earth. Or is it someplace else? That is for you to decide.

"I feel privileged to have worked with David Farland on his last story, and so dedicate this cover art to him and the memory of his life."

A Word of Power

*W*hen you are the wise woman of a village, Fava thought, *people believe you know everything. They want your counsel when there is an argument about who killed an aurochs—the one who threw the first spear into its gut or the one who finished it off. They want you to heal festering wounds.* This morning, Tchupa had come crying copious tears, pleading for Fava to bring her husband back to life. Fava had to explain that doing so would require greater magic than she had. She could only provide a tea made with blue bergamot flowers to give Tchupa courage and to numb her grief.

Now this!

Fava was busy in her small hut made of mammoth tusks, covered in hide. She'd been grinding roots to make a tincture to prevent wounds from festering when Thantok rushed in. He was a brute with a soft gravelly voice and brows so deep his eyes peered out beneath his sockets like smoldering blue fires. Thantok stood panting in the doorway, out of breath, and said, "Trouble!"

He loved to bring bad news. He stood propped by his spear after a long run, hair shining red in the sunlight. Clamshell bangles on his wrist gleaming like bone. Thantok held the unwelcome news on his tongue as if it tasted delicious, but before she could ask more, he explained, "They are stealing our mammoths, all of them!"

For a hundred generations, certain humans had poached from

the Neanderthals. The Bear Clan and Rhino Clan were gone, like so many others. Her Mammoth Clan had fled north to escape, abandoning warmer climes. But some newer human tribes were hungry, slinking about, feasting on other people's meals—not like the Neanderthals.

Each Neanderthal Clan had stuck to its ancient territory, taking sustenance from their totem animals. Most clans harvested meat for food, fur for warmth, and bones for weapons. They did not hunt another clan's totems. This kept harmony among the Neanderthals. Fava's people had maintained peace with some human tribes, but this new one ignored such boundaries.

Other hunters raced up behind Thantok and a dozen gathered there.

So, some humans were stealing their mammoths. She imagined them—weak creatures painted in red mud with their long spears, and she smiled.

"Mother Kwaw will not allow it." Kwaw was the matriarch of the last mammoth herd, far older than any Neanderthal and wiser than any human. She knew how to avoid their pits and spears!

Thantok grinned, eager to deliver more bad news. "It is not humans that drive the mammoths. It is something terrible. It is men made of metal like this—" He pointed to an ingot of silver Fava wore on a thong around her neck.

She frowned. Metal? Men of metal—neither Neanderthals nor humans?

"They do not really drive the mammoths," Thantok warned. "The herd merely follows them."

When you are the wise woman, everyone comes for counsel, Fava thought, but deep in her chest, despair welled. She knew much, but she did not know everything. Even the oldest who had lived a lifetime could not know all.

Some things she did know. She knew how to talk Mammoth. She had learned it from the wise woman before her. "You are destined for greater things," the old woman had said when Fava at eight had mastered the first call. Fava had learned to reproduce mammoth words by trumpeting and swaying and pretending to flap her ears.

Over time she'd learned to speak with the matriarch mammoth, Kwaw, whose name meant "Grand Mother" in the tongue of the Clan. Mammoths were wiser than other mastodons, as wise as Neanderthals. It was the Grand Mother who gave permission to take an old member of the herd who was dying or feeble. In return, the Clan honored the mammoths and protected them from other predators—both wolf and human.

"I will talk with Grand Mother," Fava said, perplexed.

"Take your magic!" Thantok urged. "You may have to kill these men of silver."

Fava raised her brows in disagreement. It was too soon to talk of war, but he was right. She might need magic, real magic. She might need to speak a Word of Power to crush these creatures.

She reached out around her and pulled magic from the air, invisible filaments that felt like spiderwebs wrapping her arms, binding her heart. When she'd gathered it all, the Word of Power crouched in her throat like a cat in a tree, ready to pounce, and she nodded to the hunters. "Let's go."

The journey to the hunting fields took many hours of running. The whole village followed, even mothers with babes. It was a long run, even for Fava and her Neanderthal Clan. Along the way, she kept gathering magic, focusing on a great Word of Power. Would she slash the silver men, or crush them, or make them grow heavy and fall through some ice? What was the best way to destroy such creatures? Was there a way?

An icy wind blew from the glaciers that crawled along the valleys, chilling the sweat on her forehead, making her lungs burn. Even though the grass was lush and flycatchers fluttered about snapping up crickets and mosquitoes, the sun seemed sickly as it dropped for the day. It died a solemn death as if it would never rise again.

Fava worried. Other clans had passed away, become no more. Why not hers? Had these silver men brought a disaster that she could not recover from?

Some among the group suggested that they "go back" to the warm lands in the south. Though, Fava knew that life is like a river and only flows one way. *There can be no going back.*

When darkness crept up from the shadows to swallow the land, she spotted the first sign of the intruders. There was a tall, silver tree, higher than the hills in the distance, catching the last red rays of the sun.

"They came in that," Thantok said, pointing his spear. "It is a boat that sails through the skies!"

Thantok had not warned her of this. *Always withholding more than he reveals.* Fava felt awed by the intruders' power.

As the Clan raced through a valley between icy glaciers, they came upon metal men marching through the dusk.

They did not look evil or craven. They were shiny and walked beside the mammoths like friends, neither driving them desperately from behind nor leading them as a mother duck guides its hatchlings. The Grand Mother herself led the way.

Fava stopped, wondering what to do. *Should I try to crush the metal men?* She did not know how much energy that would require. She would have to focus hard to drop boulders on each man with pinpoint accuracy. She bent her will, began to form the word "Crush!"

Let's try the easy way first. She stood and swayed from side to side, her hands low and waving like a trunk, then reared her head and trumpeted in Mammoth, "No follow!"

Grand Mother halted. The silver men stopped.

Grand Mother trumpeted, "We go!"

Fava's eyes followed Kwaw's trunk wave toward the sky ship.

Fava wanted to argue, to urge the mammoths to stay, but to her surprise, the silver man beside Grand Mother raised a metal staff in the air. A small golden light issued from it. The man spoke in perfect Mammoth, trumpeting, "Come!"

The word hit her with such force, Fava staggered. It was like being hit by a fierce wind from nowhere—both compelling and remarkably gentle.

BOB EGGLETON

She imagined rocks hurtling from the gloom and crushing metal bodies. She prepared her spell. She glanced around—the ice cliffs above! She could call down boulders of ice!

Fava prepared the Word of Power, but the silver men spoke faster, "Come!" Though it was but one word, in Mammoth it held layers of nuances. *Come, my friend. Join the herd. Be at peace.*

They raised their staves, and the golden lights shone like glowing eyes in the dusk, and suddenly light filled her mind.

The heavens darkened instantly, and she saw stars, more than she'd ever imagined. Fierce, piercing her heart.

Come to the stars.

At once, she recalled her mentor's voice promising, "You were meant for greater things."

She beheld the metal men's designs. They had not come to kill the mammoth. They had come to rescue, to lead them to a new home, far away, and now they were calling her, too.

In her mind, Fava glimpsed a distant world, one where pastures grew green and thick.

A new home in the stars. A better place than she'd ever imagined.

She realized it was a Word of Power greater than others, more potent than any weapon she could imagine. "Come!"

To the stars, my friends. Lay down your weapons and come.

The Greater Good

written by
Em Dupre

illustrated by
JIM ZACCARIA

ABOUT THE AUTHOR

Em Dupre's present incarnation largely believes she was born on the wrong planet and writes all manner of speculative fiction, with or without permission. "The Greater Good" began in Orson Scott Card's literary boot camp in 2013. She has been published in Daily Science Fiction *and won the first prize for flash fiction in the UA Anthology* Obvious Things.

About "The Greater Good," Em says, "I've always been interested in the concept of justice and knowing that the world may change, but humans and their base desires remain the same. I often wondered if there had been one adult in Lord of the Flies, *how would that have affected the outcome? And how could we implement hands-on guidance in a speculative future?"*

ABOUT THE ILLUSTRATOR

Jim Zaccaria was born and raised in East Boston. Jim has worked varied jobs in graphic design—first as a printer, then a print buyer, and then as a graphic designer specializing in book cover design. His work has won acclaim from Bookbuilders of Boston, The New York Book Show, and the Boskone Art Show. Also, his work has appeared in the annuals from Bookbuilders of Boston and Infected by Art.

Much of his daily work is book cover design for publishers and independent authors, though he feels the pull toward image creation. Over the last several years, he has started to build his portfolio and exhibit at various conventions, squeezing in new art every chance he gets.

Jim has been drawn to the arts from an early age. Music is an

*immense inspiration for ideas, and much of his work is influenced by
a song title, lyric, or mood. Other subjects that motivate and spark
his imagination are mythology, poster design, and artists working in
imaginative realism. Most of his art is produced digitally, and he sees
that as a perfect medium for commercial works. He also enjoys working
in traditional methods as well as blending digital and traditional.*

The Greater Good

Capt. Belen Kaleri usually confessed his indiscretions during our mandatory disclosure sessions. I'd watch him pick at the crisp-pleated gutters of his midnight-blue uniform pants as though plucking remorseful guitar strings. Ashamed perhaps because I knew that one who was charged to lead so many was weak in the most common of human ways. I wouldn't waste my breath reminding him that the needs of the body have little to do with duty. Shining a light into the black chasm of an old, divisive conversation would lead us to the same dead end. The captain didn't know his verbal admissions were necessary to direct the computer to where the memory was placed.

We sat back-to-back in the low light of the closet-sized room that served as my domain, intimately tethered together by the reconciliation helmet. Hidden in plain sight, adjacent to the library on the civilian sublight ship *Eudoxus*, disguised as a mere therapist, I held counsel. Restricted to an arm's-length distance, I had guided generations of colonists as they studied, dreamed, imbibed, and fornicated their way through the constellation Ophiuchus and beyond. We rippled through the five dimensions of space, a curved shadow in the periphery, spiraling on invisible strands headed to Gliese 1214-b, some forty-two light years away.

The captain and I both led the ship in our own distinct ways, but we couldn't be more different. The captain was a man of about forty but tracked much younger and had the dubious honor of belonging to the last generation of the Earthborn.

JIM ZACCARIA

His smooth face had few lines, likely because he seldom smiled. I had the impression that he was carved from stone and then dipped in wax, the true solidity of his character hidden beneath such a thin veneer. He sat ramrod straight, supported by his concrete spine, rigid from duty and purpose.

My masculinity, on the other hand, seemed more of a limpid afterthought. Despite my full head of dark hair, no one had ever called me handsome. The words I heard to describe me were quiet, intelligent, and probably homosexual. I had the face of a man, but my body was slight, like a lanky boy that had only just hit his growth spurt. I worked tirelessly to maintain my wiry physique for no other reason but to adhere to the ship's strict fitness requirements. But my true purpose required a higher standard and protected me as well as a suit of armor.

"You have no reason to worry, Counselor Parrish. We both agreed it was a one-time thing."

Unvarying, he uttered the same feeble phrase as if saying it aloud would temper the bitterness of this new moral infraction that I would once again have to consume. Who was it this time?

"Name?"

"Junior botanist Chenan Luek."

I recognized her immediately. Soft-spoken, Korean ancestry, blue hair—she had to see me twice in the past for growing synthetic recreationals. Unlike the captain, the woman wasn't married. I tagged her file, summoning her for an appointment tomorrow.

Linked together, my mind followed the gentle bond to prod at the captain's neurals and subsequent interconnections. With a practiced thought, I thoroughly coaxed his will to relax. The helmet numbed his scalp, and a sound like a slow exhale could be heard.

"What are you doing?" His loud words slurred from the gas that the helmet seeped into his lungs. He spoke over the piped-in mellow piano that mitigated the distant vibrations in his head. The captain never sounded like this before. "Are you eating me?" His voice drifted as if far away.

I chuckled at the ridiculous thought. "Only your sins."

Of course, there were rumors about me. Asexual single males usually provoked such dubious attention, although the inference to cannibalism was a new spin. If anyone had bothered to ask, I would quickly assure them that the only relationship I needed was my work. "Anything else that you need to tell me?"

Abruptly the captain was sitting upright, fighting the chair, fighting our connection. "Then how do I learn?"

The helmet automatically corrected itself by releasing more gas, and the captain returned to his previous limp state. This very same thought had always been a conflict for me. Humans learn through mistakes. Was I halting their progress? Their maturation? At the bottom of that nagging feeling, I knew it didn't matter because this existence was temporary. It was not for me to understand. Unsettled, I cautiously continued.

The moment lengthened between us as he searched his recent past for any transgressions that would interfere with the harmonious atmosphere on the ship. With the skill of a seasoned tracker, I followed his thoughts as they wove in and out, hiding only to reappear once again. In the helmet, the flickering pulse of light on the overlapped holograph of his brain grid dulled to a steady somber gray, except for three offending points glowing with a crude glare.

Targets marked; I channeled the true function of the reconciliation helmet, an apparatus that long ago, someone nicknamed the "Redeemer." I concentrated the purifying gleam into his brain. I know from my training that his saliva slickened as though his tongue was now coated in dense oil, and I heard a sound like cutting into a juicy pork chop. And there's a point in the ritual where Capt. Kaleri is unable to move. In that hallowed juncture, we combine almost into one being, a single mind inhabiting two distinct bodies. A gentle pressure, like a finger caressing our brains, the hallucinatory smells of dried petals as my mind circled his thoughts, the blissful warmth that passed over us both as my Redeemer cored away his memory, then I drew it into myself.

And as his feelings surged into me, my heart joined the captain in a shared beat, and I tasted their sweaty passions, their heated desires, our heated desires, as we kissed all the way into Chenan's suite. Something in my chest clenched in partial envy but mostly awe. Deliciously, she opened to me like a dew-laden jasmine flower, and sweet rhythmic waves spread through my limbs, an aching joy saturating my senses.

But these relationships are not mine. These lives I absorb are spectral experiences forever out of reach. Even I cannot measure the sacrifice I have made for the *Eudoxus*. Not for the first time, a cold twinge of jealousy lodges itself in my chest like an icicle. Their underlying corruption becomes a part of me, and for the greater good, the captain loses all. And I gain nothing.

Some report headaches afterward, forgetfulness, perhaps a temporary loss of motor function, or a taste of phantom cabbage. I myself wallow in feeling deflated as the once-vibrant tang of their experiences is orphaned in my memory.

There were lengths of time when the steadfast captain would complete his duties while balancing his love of casual liaisons with responsibility. Reminding the crew through his exemplary behavior that fraternizing with colonists was strictly prohibited. But the bells of temptation rang from every corner of the ship. Desire seethed like heated cats, single-minded in driving lust. When the captain began nightly prowls through one of the ship's thirteen different biocosm habitats in a baseball cap and ripped jeans, I knew to be ready.

In the beginning of his tenure some twenty-five years ago, I used to beg him to come see me and douse the match before it lit the fuse. Clenched as tightly as a boxer's fist, he refused. Nowadays, I quietly wait for the inevitable moment when the burden of guilt instigates hyperactivity in the ventromedial prefrontal cortex, which is when all privileges are revoked until a mandated visit to me. Captain or colonist, the requirement is the same.

My office door slides open to a wood-paneled room, empty

except for the brooding carbon-colored recliners in the center. I enter from a private passageway that leads from my compartments when the tingle alerts me to their seated presence. I am the only one on the ship who knows that these are biotic interrogation chairs. In our comfortably low seats, the living material restrains our bodies. Then the reconciliation helmet channels my focus into that irritated portion of their brain that burns with guilt. Living cables mummify our faces—soft as cotton, dense as steel, with connectors that link our minds. From the outside, the reconciliation helmets emerging from the chairs look foreboding, ominous—but the peace they grant makes the process all worthwhile. The first prototypes looked like old lead diver helmets, but the ones I use are sleek and serious.

My visitors relieve themselves of their burdens: stealing, lying, cheating, rampant ambition—all the tiny little missteps that would normally require punishment, tribunals, time in the brig. Which in our limited space would then lead to judgment, resentment, alienation. I am necessary, the peacekeeper of the floating dispossessed.

The cables retracted and Capt. Kaleri blinked uncertainly at me. A visible fog lingered in his eyes, and I knew his thoughts were having trouble sticking. Inside my head, I heard and felt his indiscretion join the other voices filed throughout my mind.

"Why did I come to see you?"

"You were inviting me to dinner."

"Yes, of course," Capt. Kaleri said with a thin smile, "Jem and I would love to have you at our table."

I had not yet been born when the signal burst through the newly erected lunar South Pole communications telescope, Icarus. Beamed across the galaxy through the infinite black ocean of electromagnetic radiation, the easily detected static message repeated at perfectly regular frequencies. The Earth Mother news feeds chronicled the broadcast and its unknown creators as possible threats, causing world governments to ramp up the technological war machine in preparation. Anyone with a pirated copy of the transmission was directed to delete the possibly contaminated signal.

While the world's governments fought over the proposed location for building a data prison of sorts where they would quarantine a single isolated machine and unpack the message, Gunner, an amateur cryptologist from Luna Settlement Gamma, deciphered how to unlock the detailed information.

The decompressed knowledge flung itself out over Earth's atmosphere, where in moments, a symphony of images and a rainbow of sounds simultaneously waterfalled onto every available television, handheld, and billboard screen on the planet: circular hovering art that collapsed upon itself, moving pictures of a breathtaking sun-stippled city, with even buildings and rising lights spiraling outward in the comforting shape of the golden equation.

A collective silence blanketed the transfixed world when a cuneiform message scrolled by. The accompaniment of thunderous music quivered the emotion centers of our cerebrums. Then hints of the alien technology, a form of communication that used quantum entanglement. Contained in the modulated intrapulse frequency amid the outpouring, an invitation of sorts, like a student exchange program with schematics for a toroidal ship to take us there.

The white button-down shirt I chose hung a bit on my lean frame even with my normally strong posture, but the black formal jacket covered it up nicely. I hummed Beethoven's Ninth to myself in anticipation of being in company this evening while sweeping a quick comb through my hair and blending the sprouts of gray I'd had since my teens. My long fingers banded the psicom against the two small bony protrusions behind each ear, allowing the ribbon to pulse data into my visual lobes, syncing me to the heartbeat of the ship.

The three thousand star-bound passengers were only vaguely aware of my presence. Almost leprous, I parted the crowd, shunned for a reason that, like a thief, constantly slips their minds. The entirety of my being ached with the resulting loneliness.

The Primatores warned me of this during my years of training—the discontinuance of my believable existence. They called it *cessation*—a side effect of repeated helmet use, along with the suspension of aging that scientists could never quite explain. Everlastingly thirty, with a thick carpet of hair and an unlined face, I possess a close-to-infinite life span, until we reach our destination in approximately five generations or a hundred years.

My quarters were bachelor comfortable, complete with the closest approximation of a davenport that I could find. All sorts of entertainment were merely thoughts away; each psicom connected to Earth Mother reels, newly captured space casts, music that spanned eons. In addition, the *Eudoxus* had its very own theater, galleries, artists, and immersive collaborative simulation that could be accessed only from the virtual stacks. I'd redecorated a decade ago, which amounted to no more than printing out a new duvet cover and changing the walls from a dark blue to a hazy twilight. Although florists delivered a fresh arrangement weekly, it did little to minimize the aura of Spartan sterility.

It was tiring to be forgotten, especially compared to the rest of the ship's whirling vitality. But I knew in the deepest region of my soul that this journey would not succeed without me to keep the calm, salve the stinging wounds, and protect the multitudes.

Few who live on the *Eudoxus* have escaped without seeing me at least once in their lifetimes. There is no way to live confined on a crowded starship without being maddened by covetous feelings, whether they be for berth size or romantic partners. My visitors complained of disruption by professional jealousies or sibling rivalry. It's human nature attempting to fill what is missing by theft, to gamble what you can't afford to lose, or to cover up any cracks with subterfuge, wanting, craving what you perceive is being denied.

Temptation on the *Eudoxus* was a bruised longing that no one ever spoke about. It persisted like cancer, attacking both righteous and weak. It nagged like a tiny splinter of glass in the calloused part of the foot. And in the normal way of society, people pretended not to notice.

Deeply rooted desires sufficiently starved turn to anger. I averted the further cycle by enforcing scheduled leisure time coupled with a bit of exertion to clean out the most tormented of heads. For the resistant, I usually mandated taking an aerial for a spin or biking through the desert biocosm. In extreme cases, forcing a divorce from the cause of such unrest and shifting the offender to a new part of the ship cured the problem.

Compulsions, on the other hand, were a different beast altogether.

In one of the five fully automata-run, three-tiered public dining rooms, the ship, for the entirety of a week, paired a human cook with a randomly selected restaurant as a requirement to maintain their food preparation skills. Of these, a favorite chef was chosen to prepare the captain's monthly formal dinner, consistently the most sought-after event. The lively affair, held in a private dining room beyond the main concourse, stood in profound contrast to the usual bleak vastness reflected outside the portscreens. I attempted to dampen my delighted grin at being included, containing it as a mere look of passive amusement.

Instead of music, the captain preferred the deep insistent rumble of the far-off wind from the moody vacuum of space. And for background entertainment, starlifting had already begun on the nearby blue supergiant. A stoic parade of gleaming copper collectors first laser-cooled then purified the gases before their transfer to fuel storage tanks.

Days before approaching, the ship's radiation shielding had automatically thickened as the fusion propellant expanded and hardened, protecting us from the deadly particles. As I sipped my rosemary greyhound, the raging monstrosity flared across the aqua-shifted backdrop, hurling village-sized cosmic fireballs of blue hydrogen and helium.

Jem, the captain's wife, exuded arctic elegance. Her snug dress with flowing sleeves caught more than one officer's eye. She was a woman of about forty-five with a full face and a laugh like trickling honey. I was treated to quite a few jealous glances as I found my place card to the right of hers. She presented herself as an agreeable person except when the conversation turned to the futures of engineering or linguistics. In those instances, she lashed out like a mercurial force of nature, weaponizing her words, laying waste to any opposition with a flimsy opinion.

From the boozy way the lavender martini enveloped her words, I could tell this was not her first or even second drink of the evening. The sharpness of her green eyes belied her drunkenness. Like most off-Earthers, whether born among asteroid or moon settlements, she was ferociously resilient. With no Earthly attachment and black skies being the norm, the confinement on the ship made her blossom like only someone who had never touched foot to grass could.

Jem's visits with me usually consisted of displaying her shame at loving her professions more than her husband and children, a sentiment that needled her roughly every two years—unlike the shades of violent sexual proclivities that I retarded every few months or so.

We sat at the far end of the long table, opposite her husband's place. From my angle, I noted how Chenan's eyes flirted madly with his, needing acknowledgment that she no longer found. A misstep on my part not to consider the captain's audacity in waving his dalliance like a victory flag. With my psicom, I summoned her file forward and banded it for immediate holding.

Not five minutes had passed before the mediators arrived, and Chenan was making her apologies. Head to toe in simple suits of navy blue, mediators were my apprentices. From their few, I would choose a strong understudy like myself, someone with an inherent sense of responsibility.

If Jem had any inkling of her husband's affairs, I had no proof.

"Counselor Parrish, Minister of Governance, I've stopped being surprised by your name intruding on our dinner parties. One of these days, you will have to tell me how like clockwork, you manage to wrangle a last-minute invitation. If I didn't know any better, I'd say it was blackmail."

"You know how I dislike honorifics."

"Whenever you're around, Adrian," my name sounded jagged on her tongue, "I can't help but feel uneasy, as if we're all back in grade school and someone is about to get in trouble."

"Perhaps the cook."

Her tepid laughter came easily. Too easily. "The watcher in the weeds, the sentry on the wall."

Fixing my green eyes on Jem, I gave her an easy nod unbothered by her baiting. "Ahh. You read Fentrell."

"Not for many years."

We got lost in that careless conversation that happens so often when the party relaxes enough. I recognized the faces in my immediate vicinity, both colonists and crew. I knew them all more than they knew themselves. Near me sat Lieutenant Yari, an enlisted laser communications engineer who lied to overcompensate; Electra, an Australian-born agriculturist and dental surgeon with a secret fetish for the teeth she examined; Zachary, one of the many geochemists and planetary scientists, who had urinated in more than a few cups of coffee; and Friedrich, a physicist and stand-up comedian with stolen jokes. I let myself drift, swollen with emotion, hands braided together, pleased as the chatter streamed into a rushing waterfall of words, laughter, and drink.

And then I had a curious epiphany: that if not for my intercessions, we wouldn't be having this lovely dinner. Yes, we would still be in space—I couldn't take proper credit for that. Ever since Earth Mother had heard the slow sequence of long pulses detected at the lunar South Pole, a race to the far galaxies was inevitable.

But I *was* responsible for the civility: truncating vicious gossip, blunting anger, and stopping every overindulgence. Shaping

407

a society, guiding it to perfection. On this ship, there was no higher power.

I was chewing my garlicky mushrooms and vatted chicken with newfound vigor when across the table, Dr. Sadegh, whose nose was sharpened by stark Iranian ancestry, slackened his jaw. His eyes fixed forward, glazing over as his psicom received a full sensory communiqué.

He stood to attention, followed shortly by the captain, then finally me.

The system had worked flawlessly, like a rare diamond, for the last thirty-eight years of our voyage—which was why the body on the floor came as such a surprise.

Noor Acharya lay dead in the light field of the VR simulation stacks, discovered by cleaning automata. Emergency protocol dictated medical personnel were to be summoned first. Despite Dr. Sadegh's fondness for voyeurism and hidden cameras, there was no one on this ship I would trust more in a medical emergency.

The manufactured gravity from the spin of the ship was purposefully lower in this sector for maximum game immersion. The stacks were reminiscent of a dormitory. Players lay in bullet-shaped capsules that seamlessly locked their psicoms into the simulator. Nearly floating beneath the glass enclosure, they were kept sufficiently hydrated while the servers pumped heart-throbbing, somatosensory, hyperrealistic adventures straight into their brains. Noor's favorite game most recently had been Darktide. At my request, mediators used the override to gently wake, then sequester the other players.

The captain stood behind me as we looked at the woman curled up before us. Her lowered lids partially hid the two black holes of her dilated pupils, fixed at a point in nowhere as signs of strangulation darkened into a deep maroon necklace around her throat. Her shoulder was shrugged upward, resting under her left cheek as if she were about to doze off into sleep.

This was not the first time there had been a death on *Eudoxus*.

There had been three fatalities from a minor explosion near the Earth Mother communication array, one death resulting from a toxic leak, and three suicides. Suicide was merely a function of random variability. Already we had four fewer than previously expected. Factoring in optional life extension through organ cloning, at an average of one death every seven years, we had another good fifty years or so before age-related natural causes began their culling.

The cleaning automaton nervously spun on its vacuum treads, the cyclone in its canister whirring in starts and stops as it looked for a way around the mediator blocking it from completing its normal routine.

I looked toward the nearest mediator guarding the scene. "I'm going to need the microlens footage from the automaton and the contents of its bin."

"Why would anyone want to kill a mountaineer?" Wrinkles formed between the captain's brows as concern drew his face down. He brought his hand to cover his mouth, digging his thumb into his cheek.

He doesn't remember, but he had known Noor once. She was his first act of infidelity on the ship. Their affair happened shortly after we stopped the two-year acceleration toward Tau Ceti to drop our first civilization package. She opened for him like a lotus, her dusky body a panther in the sultry jungle night.

I shook away the memory and tagged all the files of the present mediators. Although their vows supposedly prevented the need for reconciliation, the strangled corpse reminded me that the unstoppable force of human nature did not always flow in an honor-bound direction. Having word get out that there was a murderer on board would not be good for morale.

"There will be panic," Capt. Kaleri said.

"When has a simple accident caused anything more than concern? Return to your guests," I responded calmly. We both knew that there was no need to cause further alarm by his absence.

"Keep me updated." The captain paused as if he was about to

say something more but instead performed an abrupt about-face, leaving me alone with my conclusions.

I have my own memories of Noor as well. She was the first in a handful of couples required to submit to an involuntary divorce because of a tendency to assault her husband during arguments.

I turned to the attending mediators milling around the room. "What do we know?"

Of the small group, a young man, whom I recognized as Luddy, stepped forward. Author, historian, and a much-too-regular visitor to the semi-underground casino. He would never ascend the hierarchy to make it past mediator. His closely cropped hair revealed his tense face.

"The victim's VRecreation entry was recorded yesterday at—"

I cut him off with a raised palm. "We will refer to the unfortunate as 'colonist' or 'passenger.' And how could she have been here since yesterday? Isn't there some sort of enforced time limit? Could it be that the capsule malfunctioned?" I personally had never used the capsules for anything more than immersive teaching in the athenaeum.

"According to the logs, colonist Noor Acharya entered the VRec area, where she joined the sector's ongoing multiplayer game."

"Who else was there at the time?"

Luddy sent a file of over three hundred names, which danced in my vision. "They were all in full dive at least once between today and yesterday."

I tipped open a link and combined my psicom with Noor's. Light crossed light as I dropped into a soundless oblivion. The black became a tunnel that carried me through a whooshing, hollow digital storm.

Abruptly I found myself in a medieval village with Noor's body lying limp in fetal position on the cold stones of a decaying castle while a jaunty lute played a melody in the background. NPC merchants shouted to me to check their new weapon stock as unconcerned players ran past her lootable corpse on the way to a quest. Armed guards slew rabid monsters that somehow made it past the defensive wall, causing a hot spray of blood to blast my face. My character's fist tightened automatically, and my feet took on a default fighting stance. Disgusted, I left the simulation, wondering how people could be entertained by a realm filled with brutality.

Invoking my title as Minister of Governance, I flicked orders at my mediators to seal the VREc area and had the body transferred to quarantine. As we'd never had a crime of this magnitude nor expected one until landfall, there was no known procedure.

Consulting the post-flight psicom library resulted in a trove of detective sims and instruction on proper police procedure, which dictated that I use a forensics automaton at the scene and then notify and question her kin. Engineer, photographer, and closet bulimic Teah Martin repurposed a common maintenance machine with the program as advised, and less than five hours later, the report nagged at me from the periphery of my attention.

The well-monitored ship traced Noor's last two days with the unsettling precision of a sniper with a victim in its sights. Two days ago, she had conquered the climbing wall in the sports sector with a small class of junior-level mountaineers, taken a shower in the locker room, and dined in the tiki bar with two colleagues from the astrohydrology department who had just purposely failed a planetary-mission operations simulation. After liquor and laughs, she entered the VREc and never walked out. Other players who came and went never gave her capsule a second look. The faultless footage answered no questions.

The trash cylinder, too, offered very little in the way of clues, DNA from hair and skin that could have come from anywhere on its route or anyone who had played immersives that day. And the microlens footage just showed exactly what I had seen myself: the automata rolling into the room during the lowlight hours, suctioning the floor and UV sanitizing the off-line capsules that registered no psicom activity such as Noor's. The capsule itself had been serviced only by maintenance automata and in no way differed from any other on the ship. Upgrades to the multisensory program trickled in nonstop from the central software command, and there was no decision-making authority to treat one capsule differently from another.

Forensics automata recorded her cabin search and the catalog of all items. Noor Acharya had resided on the seventeenth deck of the capital quarter, which curved around the inner circle of the ship. It was the most metropolitan of all the places to live and desperately sought after. She didn't have a cabin—Noor had lived in a suite, one of the few accommodations that didn't share a bathroom.

According to her records, Noor had grown up in an asteroid-mining colony in the belt, living hand to mouth in a hollowed-out rock, extracting precious metal from captured S-types before the water and organics on their C-type homes ran out. It was probably the reason she studied astrohydrology, concentrating her whole mind on a resource so necessary but so scarce. She and her team were responsible for maintaining and improving the current atmospheric and terrestrial ship environments. Noor had been chosen for her personal drive—internal motivation with a grounded, deep sense of purpose—just like all the other accepted candidates.

But unlike some of the other colonists, her purpose seemed to have waned as she fell victim to the excesses of the ship. From the looks of things, all of Noor's earnings of onboard credits were paid to the ship's additive manufacturing machines, AM machines for short. Her cabin was overburdened with fabricated furniture modules so modern that her chairs resembled torture devices. A large telescreen with a bay window looked out over the flashing lights of the spinning core and the captured asteroid used for streamlining terraforming.

It came as a bit of a surprise to me that she was one of those off-Earthers who worshipped all they had never experienced. She must have been one of the anxious firsts to see what new styles, fads, hard research data, and breakthroughs came over the tight-beam laser transmissions—though by now, they must be decades, scores, and soon-to-be eons out of date.

Alternately, her daughter Raye, who felt responsible for her

412

parents' divorce, had a room with the soft feel of a warm soul. Not because of the pale gray pillowy walls that must have once kept out the sound of her parents fighting, but because pictures of daughter and father hung everywhere. Camping with him in the tundra biocosm, her very first hand-started fire, playing the violin while he covered his ears in mock pain, her big trophy at winning the survivalist games. Nothing seemed out of place except the one conspicuously hidden lock of hair that tested as belonging to her father, Chris Felgentreff, a survivalist, and consummate thrill-seeker who also had a mastery in picotechnology.

Raye was part of the first generation that grew up only on the ship. She studied Earth as if it were a history lesson and chose instead to focus on computer science, specifically on upgrading the factory modules that were designed to fuel construction in a new colony. Currently, she was fine-tuning a program to construct additional support vehicles and, perhaps in the future, even new modules for the *Eudoxus* itself.

I closed out the file but left open the picture of Noor giving a thumbs-up from the top of the climbing wall with Raye by her side. Both grinning, they looked closer to sisters than mother and daughter. Besides this one photograph, there was nothing else they shared.

While she never remarried, Noor had remained in a closely monitored, committed relationship with one Edgar Segundo, a human performance and limitations instructor with skills as a flight surgeon. Dr. Sadegh notified the next of kin for me, as I had no reason to pry into their lives.

The plausible story was that Noor had an undetected clot that caused an embolic stroke while gaming—a fantasy that I decided to sell to Capt. Kaleri.

The portscreen on the far wall behind his desk dominated most of the captain's ready room. It looked down toward the night-side of a tidally locked planet drifting into view. One hemisphere lay half-frozen in perpetual dark, while the other, half-scorched in perpetual light. Occasionally, he spun his chair just enough to see if the astrohydrologists had been successful in setting off enough shockwaves to dislodge the ice shelf. Communication packets occasionally chirped their progress.

Capt. Kaleri gulped his coffee and muttered something to the navigator via psicom. Unused to being summoned, then ignored, I focused my attention through the glass partition separating us from the bridge with its unbroken circle of glowing screens. Their electric radiance bathed the faces of all who sat before them. The captain cleared his throat as a signal for me to continue.

"The bruising most likely came from the coagulation," I offered in the way of explanation. It would have been easier to simply erase the whole troubling situation from his mind, but nothing about seeing a murdered body had caused any more than fading ripples in his calm. The alarm bells remained silent, which meant my hands were tied. The reconciliation helmet couldn't excise what it wasn't programmed to find.

"We both know those were fingerprints," he fumed, letting out a breath it appeared he'd been holding for days. "It's shocking to know the first real infraction on this ship was murder," the captain said as he made it a point to order a recount of the limited supply of secondary support weapons to his bosun, in case any were missing. "Instead of trying to lie to me, you should be finding who did this. Until we make planetfall, I am well within my rights to impose martial law."

Gray smoke was rising from somewhere on the planet's surface.

"Only in the event of my demise." I could smell the drops of fear coming off him despite his granite composure. He was scrambling for a way to regain what he thought was control instead of the supervisory role he truly filled. "That would certainly be a memorable entry in the history books," I said, knowing his ego would fill in the ominous blanks all by itself.

Capt. Kaleri bristled, hanging a glare on me as tight as a noose. "How about this for incentive? We're not going any further until the murderer is identified and dealt with."

"It should only be a matter of days for this problem to resolve itself."

"And if it doesn't?"

I crossed my arms and leaned back comfortably on his leather couch. All I had to do was wait for the murderer to feel the inevitable guilt of his or her crime and come to me seeking atonement.

On the portscreen, the ice on the planet began shifting.

The system by way of psicom integration had scanned everyone aboard and come up zeros. A week later, my chair remained empty of the perpetrator, and for the first time, I questioned what the world had done in allowing this voyage to go ahead. My confidence frayed.

The captain stalled in our acceleration, and even the hydrologists began to question why. Sitting down at my communication panel, I tapped out a report to the Primatores, not so much expecting an answer that wouldn't come for years but to put what I knew into perspective. Sighing heavily, I lay my head down on the blinking panel, opening my eyes to Noor's psicom that Luddy had given me a couple of days ago.

Psicoms were genetically locked to the user, but the tech automata had cleared it of any outside manipulations. It looked no different from mine, except for being on the head of someone who was murdered. Without thinking, I removed my psicom and replaced it with Noor's.

With the psicom's security disabled, Noor's cyber footprints were like coal-covered boots in snow. The onboard algorithm had already sorted her mail which held nothing interesting. I curled two fingers and called forward the innocuous-looking reel icon blinking in thin air. A twist of the hand yessed the internal recording of her gameplay.

I tipped open the link, and light crossed light as I dropped into a soundless oblivion. The black became a tunnel that carried me through a whooshing, hollow digital storm.

Instead of the medieval village, I appeared outside of a ruined

415

fort guarded by floating eyeballs with laser beam protection. With sword and magic shield ready, I, as Noor's character, waded in alone. With a twitch, I sped up the playback. There were hours of melee carnage. I could smell the animal stink, feel the sickening warmth of monster blood and barely lift my weary sword arm if not given enough time to rest. Sometimes the events led to her death only to have her being reincarnated in the medieval town before repairing her gear, paying for protection spells, and setting out to rinse and repeat.

When the pack on my back grew heavy with loot, we entered a doorway of moving light that brought us to what looked to be a mage tower in the desert. Here she was jumped by shadow bandits, and one wrapped its hands around my neck and squeezed. I could feel its dark hands tighten around my throat, damage numbers drifted upward, large and red. Immune to my sword attack, the creature's grip tightened, my eyes bulged, guttural cries dribbled from my mouth, and darkness swam in my tunneling vision.

I yanked off the psicom and heard it clatter to the floor. The sudden movement shot a twinge through my bicep in an echo of the muscle remembering that a short while ago, it was needed to hold a weapon. At my feet, Noor's psicom looked as dangerous as a rattlesnake. Not bothering to pick it up, I made a triangle with my arm and rotated the shoulder in its socket, trying to loosen the stiffness. Martial weapons, highwaymen, slogging through the sticky wetness of bodily fluids, how could anyone think this was fun?

That shadow creature didn't feel like a normal part of the game. "Is there a way to log onto Darktide remotely?" I spoke aloud.

The auditory pickup on my panel typed out a response: *players do not have that capacity*.

"Who would have that ability?"

Game designers if we were near Earth.

"What about *Eudoxus*'s system engineers?"

416

The onboard system itself sees to the management tasks of all games, specialized and otherwise.

"Such as?"

Character designs, quest updates, maintaining the sensory feedback, and simulation integrity.

"No. I mean what are the other types of games?" I fought to keep the exasperation out of my voice.

Military, medical, the usual specialized training games to provide the players with both specific and hyperrealistic scenarios such as hostile environments, lack of oxygen, carrying the wounded while tired and on foot. . . .

The words on my panel stared back at me as more possibilities filled the screen, waiting, it seemed, for my mind to glean something from the stark responses. At least I now understood the haptics leading to the evolution of Noor's neck bruises. But what didn't make sense is why the sensory feedback would be set that high. Or why she would be killed in the first place?

I thought for a minute before asking out of curiosity, "Who decides the level of sensory response?"

The program.

Which meant that some unknown person had altered the VRecreation game heuristics to use deadly force only on her character. I was going to need to see the in-depth server logs.

My own psicom unit warbled, and I warily placed it on. Dr. Sadegh's hawkish face appeared in my visual cortex.

"Counselor," he said, "when am I permitted to release the body? Her daughter has been quite insistent that she be allowed to find closure in her mother's passing."

At that moment, I felt the shadow killer slipping away like sand through my fingers. Queasiness twisted my stomach. What was most confusing was that none of the colonists selected for the mission had manifested homicidal tendencies, as far as the screening in intense simulated environments had detected.

These were curious, knowledgeable scientists, agriculturists, civil administrators, logicians, and intrepid adventurers with

417

superb genetics and exemplary health. A chosen few selected from the moderately sized pool of physically and mentally disciplined applicants or investor-extended invitations were then put through rigorous tests to measure the possible future psychoses that have a way of developing in all societies, regardless of pedigree or conditioning.

Their great names would forever be written in the annals of history and space exploration, in addition to the perpetual grants to the families and relatives they had been forced to leave behind. But as it sat, there was a murderer on board who felt no shame. As sole justiciar, it was my sworn duty to bring this deviant to heel.

"Counselor?" Dr. Sadegh's worried face filled my mindscreen.

Whoever had done this must have had a motive, but not even the past month of surveillance footage of Noor going about her days could suggest it. Perhaps there was another way.

"You have my permission."

The small recycling service was held at one of the nondenominational sanctoriums that embraced only the positive aspects of past religions. The airy space was filled with mourners. I sat behind the lectern facing the rows of the bereaved, listening to their tearful acknowledgments of Noor's contribution to life on the *Eudoxus*. I casually called up details about each of them.

No one had known about Noor's nasty blackouts when drinking tequila that left her a stumbling, angry mess with hot, smelly breath. My mind brought up loud, violent assaults in which she attacked Chris like a punching bag as he backed into the bathroom, arms crossed in defense. Red scratches striped his face as he clutched his cracked sternum from where she kicked.

I noted that Chris sat in the far back, his face drawn as he leaned forward and wept into his hands. Taking away his memories of how he got hurt had left him ignorant of why they had been forced to split.

A little while later, I stood next to a sobbing Chris, who held his daughter's hand as automata lowered Noor's mushroom spoor–infused body into the floor, where the internal system would carry her to the biocosm of her choice and give back even in her death. The memorial would continue at The Apothecary, one of Noor's favorite haunts in the forest region.

Hidden in the back of a coffee counter behind a heavy black curtain was a speakeasy, styled after the Prohibition era. The automata bartenders wore lab coats, and the dark, fabricated wood shelves held garnishes like specimens in old apothecary jars. The bar itself accessed your psicom and wrote out a prescription for a curative.

Chris had a full tumbler of rum but hadn't touched a drop. Fortunately, he did not have the same temper as his ex-wife. We sat near the fake brick wall, shadowed in the moody lighting. His eyes said he still hadn't forgiven my decision. But as was in his nature, he simply accepted it.

"She wouldn't have wanted you here," Chris mumbled.

"An aspect of the job."

"Breaking up happy homes is not much of a profession." Chris emptied his glass in one long swallow, then bent forward, groaning slightly in pain.

"You don't look well, Chris."

"What business is that of yours!" he bit back. His mask of anger collapsed, returning to the drawn look. "I'm sorry. I'm sorry. I didn't mean it."

He was confused, but if he had known the truth, he would have been thankful. To me, the rest of the mourners looked like puppets placed in a scene, reminiscing about a woman none of them ever really knew.

"We were supposed to be having a wedding, you know. Not a funeral. Not this. Raye was so happy."

"Congratulations are in order, I see." I placed a reassuring hand on his shoulder. "There would be nothing better than to go ahead with your wedding and celebrate life. If Noor's stroke has taught us anything, it's to live while we can."

"Not my wedding, our daughter was supposed to get married.

She called off her wedding to Stavros a couple of months ago, right after I got out of the hospital. I was laid up for a week with a grade-four punctured liver. Even Noor came to visit me there."

A week? That was odd. "You weren't released the same day?" The medical bay stored multiple samples of all inboard blood for transfusions as well as undifferentiated stem cells, which were used to grow new organs or tissue and comprised the main component of regenerative injections.

"A freezer in the lab destroyed my stem cells. They were going to use Raye's, but there was some sort of mix-up. They excised three-quarters of my liver."

The playback of Raye and Noor in the hospital three months prior was anything but ordinary. While Noor hovered over Chris's bedside, a doctor pulled Raye aside. The surveillance footage in the office she brought her to had no sound due to doctor-patient confidentiality, but Raye's darkening eyes and gritting jaw said enough.

"I apologized for the lab's mismanagement." Anastasiya, a young researcher who used to stalk a Canadian astrophysicist and glassblower named Ethan, leaned forward as she typed into the system. Glowing green letters appeared on the screen.

"What happened?"

"You heard about our bunk freezer?"

I nodded.

"Well, to expedite Mr. Felgentreff's treatment, I asked his daughter if she would donate her stem cells, to which she agreed. But her stem cells were a genetic match for the captain's DNA, not her father's. We must have gotten their tissue exchanged somehow. I searched for any additional errors, but it appears it was only a one-way mistake. I took more samples from Mr. Felgentreff. He's going to have to wait an extra month but—"

The chair screeched on the floor as I abruptly stood. "I appreciate your time."

Anastasiya returned to clicking on the keyboard as I left.

I entered one of the motorized gridcars, transparent automated lifts that traveled horizontally and vertically in consistent two-deck loops. The gridcar accelerated to the left. I stayed on as we passed the municipal buildings, light glinting off the steel and glass. The strata of the *Eudoxus* surrounded me, swallowed me, made me a part of its whole. Such an ugly business in such a beautiful place.

Sometime between Noor's death and now, I had become too old, a ghost already many years gone. I had cut out only part of the problem without the sense to double-check physical results. Noor had been pregnant with the captain's child and had not known.

With a thought, I brought up the surveillance of Raye during the time of her mother's death. It appeared she had received notification at the very moment her mother logged into Darktide. Then she had leaned back into her chair, fingers typing away on the invisible symbols of a laser-light keyboard, psicom strategically absent.

I knew now that I would never find a remote user logged into the server; she had surely wiped the evidence. But I also knew that I would never allow anyone to use this technology again. I banded Raye's file, summoning her to my office immediately.

As I waited, these sad conclusions taunted my uneasy mind, directly opposing my dull yearning to sleep this whole dirty business away. I sensed a creeping restlessness bleeding into my thoughts. These recent actions were a new, sad beginning of sorts, the first sacrifice in the raging war I fought against human nature. I had never felt more alone.

This crime was my fault, but I wouldn't let it ever be repeated. And when I could find the time, I would shed a tear for my part in fathering the first murderer on the *Eudoxus*.

Suddenly a wrongness overcame me as static filled my head, and my psicom spontaneously connected to an anonymous link. Light crossed light as I dropped into a soundless oblivion. The black became a tunnel that dragged me through a whooshing hollow digital storm until I materialized on a rocky shoreline, neck immobile and wrapped in a chokehold with my head

421

simultaneously being pushed forward against the thin arm crushing my throat.

Untrained in combat while fighting to stay calm, I inched my fingers around the arm that cut off my oxygen supply as I concentrated on the distant dull sunlight, which failed to pierce through the thick murk of sour clouds that represented the sky. The surrounding landscape resembled an open sore weeping burnt-orange dust that seared my lungs as I fought for my life. Lightning realization told me that Raye had somehow hijacked and thrust my psicom into what the neon red jumpsuits we wore confirmed to be a training simulation.

Acidic waves crashed on the shore. I felt Raye wince as the misting water stung our skin, and we both coughed as the moist, churning air burned through our sinuses. As I heard her hacking in my ear, I realized that we could both be hurt! Raye had panicked, and this attack was poorly planned.

Afraid of the caustic tide, Raye shuffled us back away from the coastline, her grip loosened enough for me to collapse to my knees, gasping for air, and pitch us both forward just as another wave broke and the seawater raced to the beach. We both grunted in pain as the cold sulfuric liquid touched our skin. A larger, more threatening wave crested, and Raye scrambled to the safety of the sand.

Death surrounded me, forward and back—either way, I was lost. I chose to retreat into the water, eyes tearing and teeth clenching. Ankle, knee, then waist-deep, farther and farther from her reach, trying in vain to access my psicom all the while. I felt no response. Raye had me trapped.

"First rule of survival," she yelled from safety as I wiped my face with the only dry part of my sleeve, "Anything can be your enemy. But you wouldn't know that since you aren't one of us."

Everywhere the water touched set my skin to flame; the tide tugged at me, threatening to pull me under, and I held fast even as I choked with every breath. My training in nonviolent communication taught me to keep Raye talking so that she might realize the error of her ways, but I felt completely unprepared for this.

"You've been so careful up until now. Unfortunately, I have no reason to participate in landfall exercises." I shouted above the unceasing roar of the turbulent waves as I bit back a scream. *This is only a program, my psicom is still attached.* I clutched at the thought of the emergency channel, hoping that although I couldn't tell, it continued to respond as usual.

"Boredom, perhaps? And why not? Your clearance surpasses even the captain's. I always wondered who masqueraded as law enforcement on this ship." The dark points of Raye's eyes held me in their ice. "Any last words? Too bad this was your first experiment with alien landfall. Too bad the heuristics were set too high, must have been a glitch in the programming. I'll fix it as soon as we're done."

The jumpsuit stuck unpleasantly to my body as the world dimmed to a single point of unbearable pain. I heard myself howl animallike and desperate. When I caught my breath, I confessed the hardest truth I could, "You killed an innocent woman! Your mother had no idea who your true father was. She was in a dysfunctional relationship that only brought harm, so I took that memory from her, and for that I'm sorry. I'm the one you wanted. You should have killed me."

A spike of doubt slashed through the smug expression on Raye's face. For the first time, I saw fear and knew that the deep connections of these clouded emotions now left a trail of guilt that I could follow. Truth had shown me the way.

The receding tide sucked at me violently as a colossal new wave formed, rearing up overhead. Her fear now cycled to a golden triumph. I screamed out in anguish as reddened skin sloughed off in the energetic motion of the water, "Executive Override 4112120332!" There was no way to tell if the command worked. Maybe it was too late.

When the freezing water descended, I expected an agonizing doom, but it covered me in such a cool and quiet relief that

I didn't struggle as the liquid silence closed over my head and swept me back into my office.

Raye was still shouting as the mediators locked her in the chair, but I could only concentrate on the residual red echoes rising through my scabbing flesh.

"Who are you to decide anyway? You're no better than we are. You sit there judging and passing sentences. Maybe I killed the wrong person! But who judges you?

"WHO JUDGES YOU?!"

Sitting on my side of the Redeemer, raw and exposed, the machine targeted the proper constellations of guilt in Raye's blizzard of memories, shining on the encepholograph. I ate her sin, though I logged off uncertain if I'd consumed it all.

Despite my victory, I felt lost, and for the safety of the ship, she couldn't remain. Raye was dangerous and possibly contagious. Unable to find a solution, I volunteered her to be the first human tester for cryonic sleep. I looked at Raye as if seeing her for the first time, lying in the cryochamber. Tears froze on her cheeks as her body grew solid. I knew I should be lying in the cold, next to her. Me and all my kind.

Heavy with my leaden burden, I slumped, face in hands—a remorseful statue, unable to straighten. After the disquiet of a tensely protracted moment, I marshaled enough will to activate the panel and transmit the results of this tragic investigation.

"In conclusion, the Redeemer doesn't always work as intended because it leaves intact the underlying intention for the person's bad actions. Upon promotion, perhaps the next counselor, with your help, will find a way to adjust the machine's programming and include the catalyst for such behaviors in their search to be removed as well. Regardless of the Primatores' approval, I will begin training my successor." My fingers swiftly brought up the files of the five most promising mediators and placed Dapeng at the top of the list. I briefly wondered if he would remove my memories. And once retired, would I still be responsible for what I didn't know?

For the Federation

written by

J. A. Becker

illustrated by

ARTHUR M. DOWEYKO

ABOUT THE AUTHOR

J. A. Becker lives in Sydney, Australia, with his wife, two kids, and an annoying miniature dachshund. He writes sci-fi, mystery, and action-adventure stories primarily for himself, as none of them have landed anywhere. That is until now. J. A. wrote "For the Federation" as a way to show his son that despite a world of rejection one should keep trying. Never, ever, ever, ever did J. A. expect his story to win. Nor did his son.

J. A.'s work is heavily influenced by Roger Zelazny, Knut Hamsun, and the man himself: L. Ron Hubbard. Of particular note is Hubbard's "Devil's Manhunt," probably the best short story ever written in the action-adventure genre. This work inspired J. A.'s love of the genre and the idea of writing stories that put people on thrill rides.

J. A. enjoys reading, writing, board games, and spending time with his wonderful family—not the dog, though.

ABOUT THE ILLUSTRATOR

As a scientist (computational modeling of drug design), Arthur M. Doweyko has authored 140+ scientific publications, invented novel 3D drug design software, and shares the 2008 Thomas Alva Edison Patent Award for the discovery of Sprycel, a new anti-cancer drug.

He writes and illustrates science fiction, fantasy, and horror. His debut novel, Algorithm, *garnered a 2010 Royal Palm Literary Award (RPLA) and was published by E-Lit Books in October 2014. His second novel,* As Wings Unfurl, *took first place as Best Science Fiction (Pre-Published) in the 2014 RPLA competition and was released in 2016 by Red Adept Publishing. Many of his short stories have been honored as finalists in RPLA competitions, as well as achieving Honorable Mentions in the L. Ron Hubbard Writers of the Future Contest. He has published* two short story anthologies (My Shorts *and* Captain Arnold), *both of which have garnered awards.*

Besides science and writing, Arthur has maintained a lifelong love of art. From copying comic book covers at an early age to illustrating science fiction and fantasy themes utilizing various media, including oils and digital art, Arthur has always found the time between experiments to pursue his artistic dreams and share his visions of a future unbounded.

He lives in Florida with his wife Lidia, teaches college chemistry, and happily wanders the beaches when not jousting with aliens.

For the Federation

The night terrors started and that's a very bad sign, apparently. But, honestly, what the hell do they know? Not a damned thing, if you ask me.

I'm frenzied and worthless, kneeling beside Sam, singing to him, holding his little body down to stop him from hurting himself.

He's totally gone, eyes black and swinging his arms and screaming in a life-and-death battle with the little monsters in his head.

I shake with rage and choke back my tears. I want to reach into his brain and pull the little blighters out and crush them between my razor-red fingernails, one by one. And then I want to punch Craig as hard as I can in his square, strong jaw for bringing us here to this not-even-partly-annexed-stinking-swamp planet. And for bringing us to that fetid bog where they crept into Sam's ears on little sticky legs and wrapped themselves tight around his brain. And for the Federation doctors who don't know anything about anything!

Drawing a deep ragged breath, I hold it and hold it and hold it till it hurts. Then I blow out the poison in a long, steady stream.

I can't let hate destroy what I have left. There's still time for my seven-year-old baby boy, maybe.

The bedsheets are like a boa constrictor around his skinny throat. I untie them and futilely whisper over and over how much I love him. And how I will save him. Whatever the cost, my baby boy Sam, I will save you.

A five-car convoy careening down a dusty road is a target. Might as well have a flag flying on the roof that says, "Federation Council President, Craig Benson, Inside."

"Beth, *my dear*, how else do we get there?" Craig asks, turning his square head around in the passenger seat to address me.

"A jump ship?" I reply acidly, not at all liking that *"my dear"* routine of Craig's. I stroke Sam's head, but he pushes my hand away and turns his golden face to watch the foliage blur by the window. Better now. All forgotten, I guess.

"They'll pull that down," Craig says. "Anything they can see, they can pull down."

"Well, isn't that some kind of monumental screw up," I say. "Land a whole Federation Regiment on an annexed planet for pacification, without even knowing that the natives can kick your ass. What kind of lamebrain made that decision?"

He doesn't say anything, just turns back to the road.

Low blow, that. I know it was his decision. Everything to do with this disaster was his decision.

"And so who's this second-rate quack we're going to see this time?" I ask.

I've got to dial it back, but it just keeps bubbling out.

"Retired Colonel Max Benson," Craig replies. "He was a doctor in the biotech corps."

Retired? We're really dredging the bottom of the barrel now.

Their sky is the color of ash, yet their trees are almost neon green. How is that possible? And their suns are two perfect red coals, high up in the horizon. Devil eyes glaring at us.

Hands down, it's the vilest backwater planet I've ever set my boots on.

Despite the red ocean between us, I still love Craig. It sickens my heart right now, but I do. I have to remember that the weight of 250,000 Federation lives and all the lives of this planet's inhabitants are on his shoulders. And Sam's too. I'm just a gun you point and shoot, but he's got the weight of a world to carry. It's easy for me and crushing for him.

Sam suddenly straightens, points out the window, and babbles incoherently.

He stopped talking a week ago, which is another very bad sign according to the ancient Federation scouting report we managed to dredge up from the archives.

Not much there, of course. Just a couple dispatches about a scout that came down with brain parasites that the nanoes couldn't expunge. Apparently, his head swelled and blew like a watermelon four weeks after he stopped talking. I can't believe they actually put that into the report; it's more color than you'd expect from grunt scouts.

And then I see all too late what Sam is babbling about.

Five of them step out from the trees.

You can barely tell them apart from the trees. They're like walking willows, bark arms and stick legs and bristling heads of ivy. Is it any wonder why we underestimated them?

Grabbing Sam, I jam him down hard beneath my seat. Then I grab Craig by his big, stocky shoulders and yank him into the back with us and pile him on top of Sam.

Both of them squeal and squirm, but they're no match for my enhanced strength.

"Jump!" I order the driver and he rams his foot down on the pedal to vault us into the barren ash sky.

But it's too late.

The two-ton, black-armored car running the van splits apart like a piece of wet tissue and a dozen Praetorian Guards, kitted to the nines, come spilling out and skip across the dusty earth.

At that velocity, they're dead—my little implant calculates.

Our engine screams, but all we do is come to a slow stop. Our car's shimmering black hood buckles as if some invisible giant is sitting on it.

I'm out and firing my sidearm at the snap of a finger.

Impact round catches one right between his wooden teeth and he blows apart beautifully.

The car behind us leaps into the air as if it were chucked by some mighty hand. Then it comes apart and twelve little men sail into the ash sky.

I catch another on the side of his head and that turns him into a cartwheeling ball of fire that skitters into the neon jungle.

Then I and the open car door I crouch behind are seized by some unseen hand and tossed away. We sail maybe two football fields in length, then I twist fluidly around and land on my feet while the door shatters on the ground behind me.

At exactly 999.3334 feet away, I take aim and catch another right where his balls would be and he's sawed in half.

The Praetorian Guards have set up a box perimeter around our car and are firing. They're not accurate though. Bullets and explosions rocket all around the remaining Willows, but nothing touches them. I file a note away for more scenario training for the guards. Scenarios I will run personally.

Running now, quickly closing the gap between me and Craig and Sam. My heart is still at rest, and I haven't broken a sweat yet. Still, even at this age, I amaze myself.

Twelve black armor-clad Praetorian Guards standing in front of our car suddenly blast apart like bowling pins and scatter into the sky.

Running, I jump fifteen feet into the air toward them and straighten into a perfect arrow with my handgun as the tip, and I take aim. I am death on a lightning bolt, and they have no chance whatsoever.

Sam steps out of the car and into my line of sight. Midair, I twist sideways and re-aim around him.

Then I feel a gentle hand on the back of my neck, which presses down and steers me headfirst into the earth. The impact snaps my neck, and the world goes dark.

Some internal clock somewhere inside me is broken, so I've no idea how long I've been out.

I shake my head to realign myself.

A foiled assassination attempt on Craig five years ago shattered my spine. The hard-mercury replacement has partially liquefied and nearly reformed the crack in my neck.

There's no danger. We're back at the base. I can tell from the cold steel walls. And Craig is still alive, or they would have put a bullet between my eyes for failing to protect him.

A startled thought rockets through me: *Sam! Is he OK?*

I pause and consider that train of thought.

Truly, I am a monster, not a mother. My last thought should have been my first thought.

I snap up to a sitting position and they're both at the end of the steel table.

Sam, untouched. Golden hair falling over his eyes. Not a scratch on his seven-year-old slender frame. And Craig, a tall, square gorilla with a deep, bloody gash across his forehead. That, I realize, was from me when I jammed him beneath the seats.

It's not a reunion written for the movies.

Sam doesn't move. I lug my bleeding, broken form with a dozen tubes attached to it across the table to put my arms around him. He doesn't hug back. His eyes are black, and those nightmares are now visibly bubbling beneath the skin of his forehead.

It is so hard to see an enemy an inch from my face and I can't kill it. It breaks me.

"Beth, they assure me you're OK." Craig says, putting his long arms around us. "You're going to be fine."

His heart rate is elevated. Body is rigid. Stress cracks splay from the corners of his blue eyes. Very unlike him.

"Are you OK?" I ask.

"Why the hell are you thinking of me right now with you nearly destroyed on the table! Stop thinking of me! I don't deserve it." And he suddenly backs away. Sam makes some screeching noise and covers his ears, leans into me for protection.

Shock cascades through me. Never once has Craig ever yelled at me. Despite being through hell together, he always maintains his game indifference.

"I'm sorry," he says. "I'm sorry." He touches Sam's shoulder, who shies away from him.

"There's another wrinkle that's presented itself," he says to me.

"And what, pray tell, can be worse than this Imperial screw up?" I ask.

"I'll just come right out and say it 'cause it's so insane," he says. "Sam has apparently developed the ability to do what they can do."

It doesn't register. Or I don't let it.

"What in the living hell are you talking about?" I ask.

Craig leans in, takes Sam's slender shoulders in his massive meat hooks. "Sam, buddy. Can you go watch the vids while Beth and I talk?"

Wordlessly, Sam walks over to a chair and sits. He flips on a vid screen and the algos recognize him and start playing his favorite show.

"You didn't see it," Craig says. "Sam stepped out of the car, reached his hand out, and the earth rolled up beneath the Willows' feet like it was a carpet. Then Sam made a throwing motion and the whole ball—two tons of earth, grass, and trees—was hurled away. I don't know how far they flew or where they landed. They became specks on the horizon."

I let that new intel soak in my cerebellum. I lie back, the dozens of tubes connected to me rattle and clank on the metal table. I squint against the overhead lights needling into my eyes.

I don't know what to make of it.

"The balance of running this situation out here has become a little more challenging now," he says.

Not registering his meaning, my hands ball into fists and lightly pound the table.

His massive hand engulfs my bare foot, and he gently squeezes it.

"You want a bit of the Federation's attention," he explains. "Just a bit of it, so they give you what you need to do your job. But if you fly over the radar, you suddenly become of interest to the higher-ups."

"And Sam doing this...this thing, is flying over the radar?" I ask.

"Yes. Some general somewhere will want to own this. Probably, General Mackinaw, as he's weak and being forced out and he's been snooping around. Desperation has no boundaries. It's nothing for him to send a regiment of his own to claim this place and all the powers within it. Claim whatever it is that Sam has. It'll elevate him tenfold in the eyes of the council."

Cold terror coils in the pit of my stomach. It's all I can do to stop myself from leaping off the bed and kicking something to oblivion.

"This is just a game?" I spit. "He's...he's just a..." And I stop to look at him, my son, blankly watching the vid screen. He hasn't eaten since it happened. He's become a whittled stick with thin arms, and I can see his ribcage poking against his T-shirt.

He's unique to begin with. Royal Bodyguards like me are forbidden to have children. And men like Craig, Council Presidents, are chemically castrated from birth, so they've nothing more important than the Federation to think about.

And then this miracle. This madness. This upending of our design and purpose.

"It's all a game," Craig says, squeezing my foot painfully. "And you're losing sight of that. You're forgetting that the moment you stop thinking it is, is the moment you lose your edge."

Hurts now. He's almost breaking it. I look to Sam and I can't scream.

"You've been distracted, unfocused. More concerned about Sam than your job. And that can get all of us killed. Me. You. Sam. And everybody here."

A sob swells in my chest, but I don't let it out. I bite it back, and I don't kick his hand away from crushing my foot either, 'cause I deserve it. He's right. I am an unfit killer and an unfit mother.

"I've contained this for now," he says. "The news hasn't spread. The only ones who know are the guards that were with us, and I immediately put them out on patrol with complete radio silence."

He releases my foot. Smiles deeply. Those square teeth are brilliant white.

"They're fifty klicks out, northwest from the base, and are due back in an hour. It would be awful if something happened to them and they couldn't make it back to report what they saw."

I nod and begin pulling the tubes from my body. I am a gun, and he's just pointed and pulled the trigger.

Then I stop as some mad little thought flutters in my head.

"And Sam?" I ask.

An almost imperceptible flush of crimson crosses his face. Then it's gone just as suddenly and he's a cold wall again.

"I have thought of everything. An old friend, a highly decorated bioengineer, is surreptitiously on his way here with a dozen of his crew. They will get to the bottom of Sam. You don't need to think about it."

Sam raises his cherub face from the vid screen to smile at me. Eyes sunken deep in starving sockets.

"I'm sorry, Craig. I wasn't doubting you. I was just..."

"There is nothing to be sorry about," he says, cutting me off. "Just don't fail us—me, the Federation, and Sam—again."

Fifty klicks out, they're all dead.

Even with my enhanced vision, I stumble about in this land's inky black midnight. Not a star. Not a moon. Not a peep of light.

Their twisted corpses litter the trees. I find phaser burns on their armor. One has their head neatly separated from its body. Some kind of energy sword, from the looks of it, 'cause the neck is cauterized. Another has a perfect hole burned through the center of his forehead.

And as I'm bent over, admiring the marksmanship, I turn my head ever so slightly and that's what saves me from having it cut off.

The killer doesn't make a single sound. Just creeps up and slices at my neck with an electric-blue blade, which crackles a centimeter by my neck.

I roll and roll and then I'm up on my feet and firing. But whoever it is, they're gone.

Then a foot fills my face and I fly back about ten feet from the blow and slam up against a tree.

Through the bloody haze cascading over my eyes, I see who it is.

It's me.

A younger me, fresh out of the academy. My stars, how striking was I?

Six feet, perfect proportions, wonderfully curvy hips, full lips, and short bobbed blonde hair. Though I can't see them, her eyes are flawless jade green, like mine.

Concubine, assassin, and bodyguard, all perfectly bio-assembled into one.

And not a single scar or bruise blemishes that perfect, creamy white skin of hers.

She's impossibly fast, like I used to be, and closes the distance and slashes that electric-blue sword of hers.

I duck and the tree I'm slammed up against is neatly severed in two. It goes crashing down behind me with a tremendous boom.

"Pretty good for a birther," she says, as she pops my head up by kneeing me hard in the face.

I killed a girl in college for calling me that once. But that was a long time ago.

Somehow, she's disarmed me in all of this. VibroKnife. Sidearm. And my rifle. All neatly stripped away without me noticing.

My god, was I good.

She spins neatly, flawlessly, and back-kicks me in the stomach, knocking the wind out of me.

My right-cross is a long time coming, and she easily dodges it, catches me by the wrist and flips me onto my back.

And she's so perfectly like me that before I can even move, she drives her sword straight through my abdomen and into the ground. Staking me to the hard earth.

Her mission is to kill, obviously, 'cause she doesn't utter a word before she pulls out her sidearm, takes aim, and fires.

Only the inexperience of youth would have left me alive. A mistake I would never make twice.

I drag myself along the ground, leaving a thick trail of blood behind me.

There were words burned into my mind that give me courage in times like these.

I am nothing but to serve, and to serve, I become everything. For the Federation, for my Liege, my life I pledge to thee.

But they give me no comfort now.

There's a med-kit in the guard's bag who had his head severed. I struggle with the catch. So simple, but my fingers are all thumbs.

Have I been retired? I wonder as I fumble. *Is she my replacement?* It would make sense. It's expected when I've failed so often and lived well past my prime. And a birther, too. No more excuse necessary.

My hand shakes, and I drop the injection gun. My fingers can't close around the handle to pick it up. A continuous stream of liquid pours from my red nails.

Craig set me up? Or was she General Mackinaw's? Or are they both working together and I'm in the way?

It's all possible.

Craig isn't bred to love like me, he's bred to think, to plot, to plan.

Or am I exactly where I'm supposed to be? Not a mother. Not a killer. No longer a concubine. No more an assassin. I am a sad, broken gun with no one to pull the trigger. A useless thing and Craig made the right decision to replace me. For this world and for its lives, and for the Federation that depends on me, I am nothing now.

Like a tidal wave, these thoughts wash through me, ripping everything from me and leaving me raw and bare.

I throw up whatever's left in my stomach, then hate myself for the gut-wrenching pain it causes. My body convulses electrically. Needles stab through my eyes. I've been hurt before in battle, but nothing like this.

There're more tears cascading down my face than I've cried in this lifetime.

I can't hold it all in my head. I can't see through what to do or who to kill. There's no place for me anymore. No Craig. No Federation. No reason...

Then a thought strikes a gong in my head that shatters everything in my mind.

Sam.

He is the finger on my trigger—and he is the reason to pull it.

Everything else doesn't matter, just him. My boy. My impossible boy. I am gobsmacked by this revelation, and I shake from the pleasure of this new purpose.

Suddenly, I find I can grasp the medi-gun and I jam it into my arm and pull the trigger. Nanoes stream in and start painfully weaving my flesh back together; almost hurts more than when it was torn apart. Through the mind-numbing pain, I pull a thick silver bandage out of the bag and wrap it around my waist. It inflates to cut the bleeding off. Then I tend to my little wounds like a pianist playing the piano, my fingers flitter about on their own accord.

There's a dead, elite army scattered in these trees around me.

Ammo. Guns. Grenades.

Enough for whatever Sam needs.

"We were so beautiful together," I whisper. "You the brain, and I the hand. They wanted to make you a general because of us. No higher honor for our pairing. Do you remember?"

Craig is dead asleep beneath me. Nestled snug in our bed. His guards lie in the doorway, broken. Very poor training. I blame myself.

I slip the hypo-needle out of my bag without waking him, then lean in close to his face and put the point to his thick, pulsing carotid artery.

437

Still, he sleeps, eyes frantically searching for answers beneath his lids.

I know it's conditioning. I know it's genetic. And I know it's orders. But no matter how it's come about, I still love him. That part of me I just can't kill.

A quick jab and he's out.

I unfold my black stiletto and get to work, neatly slicing off his index finger.

I pull the guards inside the door and lock them in.

In twenty hours Craig will wake up with the worst headache of his life and Sam and I will be long gone.

Like a rat, I scurry through the air ducts. I easily pounce on the remote droids in the vents and put my stiletto through their eyes to disable them.

Then a finger on a door and it opens.

There's more than I expected in Sam's room. Seems the highly decorated bioengineer is already here. Sam is out on his bed and hooked up to five different machines. A long lobotomy-like laceration across his forehead nearly makes me cry out.

I slip inside and gently close the door behind me.

He is so impossibly thin beneath his sheets. He's barely there.

Now I know why they can't take them out. On the monitor, I can see them in his head. They're far more active than I realized. They look like black leeches squirming through the tender folds of his cerebellum. His head is a wriggling ball of them.

I carefully shut off the monitors so as not to set off an alarm. Then I gently unhook the wires and tubes coming from him.

He doesn't stir. He's in a mild medical coma.

I have no plan but rescue. After that, it's anybody's guess. For the first time in my life, I'm running without a full battle strategy. There was no time for anything else.

I gently lift him up off the bed and I can't help but pause for a moment to hold him in my arms. I listen to his struggling breaths and smell his wonderful scent. I should have done this every single night before bed. So many regrets.

Then we're out and down the corridor, easily slipping past the guards, as I know the exact timing of their patrols.

And then a finger on the hangar's bay door, and here is where it gets tricky.

There's over three hundred jump ships, cars, tanks, and cycles in here. It's going to be nearly impossible to sneak one out undetected.

We're moving toward a black-armored car when she appears on the hood of a tank, steps off, and lands gingerly.

Unbelievable. She didn't take me out with a rifle the moment I stepped in, which she could have easily done. And to boot, she's unarmed, except for the electro-sword, which catches blue fire as she switches it on.

She thinks she can take me out and reinstate her reputation in the process. I know her mind.

Was I always that arrogant? I wonder. Or that stupid?

I let inexperience guide her into imagining I'll only defend now that she's got the upper hand. I lash out unexpectedly.

Shocked, she just has enough time to pivot and my stiletto sticks into her collar bone instead of her neck. I use that stunned moment to leap into the air with Sam nestled in my arms and kick her twice in the face with my hard, black boots.

She tumbles backward, her sword skitters across the black iron floor.

Bad luck though. Twelve thunderboots stomp in. Somebody had alerted the guards.

A finger on the jump jet's door panel and it swooshes open. I've just enough time to lay Sam down before she gets me.

She plunges my stiletto into my back and the blade breaks off on my hard-mercury spine. I would never have let poetic revenge lead me like that, even at her age. I would have sliced off the top of my skull with the sword and been done with it.

I place my two hands on the jump jet's cargo bay floor and I double-leg-donkey kick her in the face.

She turns the momentum of that devastating blow into back-flips and lands perfectly beside her sword. She does the splits, retrieves her sword, and scissors herself back up to standing. All in one fluid motion.

I'm dead now. I see that.

Strength, speed, and youth are still more than a match for cold, hard experience.

"Mom!"

I turn. Sam is sitting up. He reaches his hand out and electricity crackles around me. My younger me is midair now: sword straight out, legs back, in a perfectly executed fencing flèche that will skewer my head like a toothpick through an olive.

Then she's gone. She, the troops, and two hundred of the tanks, jump ships, and armored cars are scooped up and thrown through the hanger's back wall with a world-ending crash. The force of the wind tears at me, tries to suck me out along with the mess.

Then stillness. I watch them disappear into the backdrop of the black night.

I don't hear them land.

"Mom!"

His hand clamps down on mine. His eyes are squirming black.

He says that word again to me, *Mom*, a word I don't deserve, and then he falls back and dies.

The jump jet touches down beside the swamp and I leap out with Sam in my arms. The devil eyes peek over the mountains and light the horrid day.

"Please!" I scream. "Somebody help me! I know you're out there!"

Nothing but silence returns to me.

"Please! I know you can help me! You're the only ones who can!"

For the first time in my life, exhaustion buckles my legs and I collapse by the swamp side.

He's not breathing, but those things in his head are still squiggling around—a sure sign Sam is still alive.

"PLEASE!"

My scream echoes across the scum-layered swamp and bounces off the moss-covered trees.

Then I see them emerging from the quaggy gloom.

It's the first time I've actually seen them up close. They aren't made of wood. It's a brown carapace, and it doesn't cover everything. There're spots of soft white flesh that shine through. The hair isn't ivy, it's lichen-covered vines.

"Please! I know you can understand me! Please help me! My son. He's sick. They went into his head! Help him!"

They tower over me, obscuring the devil suns.

Their unblinking black-stone eyes rain indifference down at me.

"Please!" I grab one by what I think is his knee. "Please!"

Sam's head rolls about lifelessly in my arms.

"He's the only thing worth anything to me. I'll do anything."

Their voices are a kind of high-pitched chittering, and my embedded translator has a hell of a time adapting to it.

"Gone. Soul fled. But for his children, there's still time."

An ocean of tears fills my throat, I choke them back.

"I don't understand!"

A jump jet screams far off in the distance. They can't be following me. I've disabled my transponder. There's no chance they can find this one swamp in the billions that pimple this planet.

"He has passed," one of them chirps. "But his children have a chance. Our children too."

"Children?! Are you saying those leeches in his head are children?"

Revulsion turns my stomach in knots. Were my gun in my hand, and not in the jet, they would be in charred, bloody pieces.

"His children. Our children. We start as such, then become us. Into the waters now for their lives."

There is too much to think on and none of it good. I've failed so terribly I can barely allow myself to breathe. My tongue fumbles for the catch in my false back tooth.

"Please," one of them warbles. "Please. It's soon. For your son. For him."

I wade out into the swamp water carrying Sam in my arms. He's so light he floats right on the surface. His body parts the scum before us, leaving a bare wake behind our passing.

I take him out till I'm waist high, then I kiss him on his wet, cold cheek and let him go. The swamp water closes over his face as he sinks down into the murk.

They get theirs and I get mine. The catch in the tooth is tricky, but I can manage. A little leverage with my tongue and my mouth will turn into a foamy volcano, and I too will rest in the murk beside him.

Suddenly, stars sparkle in the dark waters beneath me. Eight, nine, no, ten little pinpricks of light blossom into being. They're alive and circle about me, chasing each other playfully between my legs.

They've hatched. Their serpentine skin brushes up against mine as one darts by my leg.

I must be mad.

It's all built up and I've snapped loose from the few pieces of foundation I had left. Every tenet broken and I am adrift in a fetid, scummy pool filled with brain-sucking leeches. And the maddest of all is that I love this. They duck and flash about my legs, rubbing up against them, which sends waves of pleasure tumbling through me. I feel at peace. At home. Alive. And for the first time in my life, I feel free. Free from the Federation. Free from Craig. Free from me.

I lie back in the waters and bob on the surface with my offspring tickling about me.

I am mad, mad, mad, and I love it.

Then a voice shatters my blessed peace.

"Beth! You are categorically Section 8. Completely, mentally unfit for service."

Abruptly, I stand.

There she is, in all my perfect, proportioned glory, standing on the edge of the swamp. Blue sword sheathed by her side. The

Willows have evaporated back into the swamp. The glowing lights below my waist have dissipated. But they are there, I can feel them lightly nibbling at my arms.

"I am so disappointed," she says. "You are a killer of worlds. Revered at the college. I've studied your exploits. And when I got this assignment, I was actually scared. I expected to find Shiva the Destroyer herself."

Perfect red lips pout and foolish hands fall on curvy hips.

"But I've found only you," she continues. "This mad, whimpering, insane thing. I don't want them to find you like this, too. It's too embarrassing for our line. I'm going to do this for you."

Now I know she'll never make it. I know this. She's not me in the least. She's arrogant. Foolish. Overconfident and will always be so, no matter what hard lesson life teaches her—she will never learn.

I walk carefully back to the water's edge, not making any quick movements to alarm her or the brood.

"Craig is out and my General Mackinaw is in," she says diffidently.

And that's how they tell you that someone that you love is gone. And I, being her, know how excited she is at this open-world now at her feet. Fame. Glory. The Federation. And everything else be damned.

I climb out of the water, dripping with slime and stench.

She backs away from me, draws her sword, and charges it.

"You are right," I say. "For the glory of the Federation, you are right. I have fallen. I have betrayed my love. I have birthed a child. I have let my duties suffer. And I have failed the Federation. There is nothing for me in this life any longer."

I slowly lower myself to the ground on all fours. I extend my head out and bare my long neck in offering.

And like the ambitious fool I know she is, she goes for it.

"For the Federation!" she shouts and brings her crackling blue blade down on nothing.

With her head next to mine, my red razor fingernails split her throat with a flick of my wrist.

ARTHUR M. DOWEYKO

Popping up with her over my shoulder, I launch her end-over-end into the swamp.

She gurgles and screams as bubbles boil in the water about her. The whole swamp roils alive.

I look away and stare at the devil eyes till silence falls.

It's too hard to watch yourself torn apart.

The Federation doesn't stand a chance.

There's me, the leader, my boys, the soldiers, and a whole nation of warriors with unimaginable powers.

For the Federation. For the freedom. For the Willows. And for my sons.

At my command we lift the entirety of General Mackinaw's base into the ash gray sky and eject it past the stratosphere of our planet.

Psychic Poker

written by

Lazarus Black

illustrated by

TENZIN RANGDOL

ABOUT THE AUTHOR

Lazarus Black (he/him) is an American author of genre fiction living under the shadow of a Pacific Northwest volcano with three Goddesses: his wife and two daughters.

"Psychic Poker" is Lazarus's first sale, but hardly his last. It juxtaposes poker, the synthesis of probability and human behavior, with psychic powers, the solution to both probability and the chaos of free will. What if every player is psychic? What if no player has an advantage? What if their lives are at stake? But the strength of the story is in the reluctant main character: Tyson Young, a middle-aged Aussie with an acute wit.

Lazarus writes from life. His stories are inspired by the diverse communities he has lived in, plus friends and family across the globe. He specifically attacks stereotypes and reinvents tropes to reflect authentic experiences that are sometimes stranger than fiction. He once earned a free funeral until the mortician learned his name was Lazarus and a good laugh was had by all (bystanders included). A true lover of learning, Lazarus has traversed North America dozens of times, has been a professional artist, advertising creative, software developer, database designer, epigrapher, executive, educator, inventor, game designer, pool hustler, heathen clergyman, machinist's apprentice, glass blower, scholar, actor, many other roles, and now published author of fiction.

He hopes you enjoy "Psychic Poker" and look forward to reading more from him in the future.

ABOUT THE ILLUSTRATOR

Tenzin Rangdol was born in 2003 in the small city of Dharamsala, India, situated at the edge of the Himalayas. Tenzin was infatuated with the art of drawing when he scribbled his first cube in grade school. He went on to dedicate himself to drawing and improving with pencil and charcoal in sketchbooks and newsprint paper. With a traditional foundation and education from the internet, he explored digital painting and expanded his narratives and illustrations. He currently lives in Silver Spring, Maryland, and is soon to graduate from Albert Einstein High School. Tenzin intends to pursue a career in freelance illustration and continue to learn and explore the art of creating immersive narratives and worlds.

Psychic Poker

N*o one is supposed to know what I do.*

The envelope lies torn in my lap, teetering on my knee as my belly threatens to push it off like a jealous cat. I sit in my caravan, behind my dinner table slash desk, enjoying the Mooloolaba Beach breeze through my window. Australian climate's fine. Blue sky. Yellow sand. Ugly shirts. It's not a glorious life, but I make the most of it. I'm that kind of legend.

Caravanning lets me travel where I like and avoid people I don't like. And mail from people I don't like. I don't like mail. I don't read mail. I barely email. And I almost tossed this one in the bin with the rest. But the addressee was too specific:

To Mr. Tyson Young, The Best Psychic in the World

The letter flutters in one hand as the plane ticket sticks in my other. Questions tick over in my mind, but the most pressing comes out my lips.

"Who mails anything anymore?"

The whole setup is a taunt, of course. And the taunter worked hard to hide themselves from seering. People believe all sorts of rubbish, like psychics can learn things about a person by touching something they've owned. This had been computer printed, computer addressed, computer postaged, but not trusted to be opened if it'd been computer delivered.

Fortunately, you don't have to be psychic to be smart. Even without reading, I knew the letter declared one of three things: Mr. Anonymous believes too hard in the power of psychics, wants some sort of scientific proof that I am one, or desperately needs one now.

It's all bloomin' three.

Dear Mr. Young,

Please accept this invitation to participate in the first annual Psychic Poker Tournament.

There is no fee.

You will be provided with ten million Chinese yuan to buy your seat at the table. Play until you win everything or lose. Six seats will be filled by invitation only.

I check the exchange rate on my phone and whistle. Sixty million yuan converted is twelve million bucks.

This is both a challenge and an experiment. There will be no media or fanfare. Your only reward will be all the money you win and the personal satisfaction of defeating five other psychics.

Please find your airline ticket to Honolulu included.

I look forward to learning if the World's Best Psychic is named Tyson Young.

No signature.

It has all of the hallmarks of a legitimate scam: it promises everything is free, gives me almost no time to think—let alone pack—before my flight, and the personal note strokes my ego and pokes it at the same time. Nice touch.

Hell if I'm going, though.

I like anonymity. Not just because of the folks begging me to tell their future, but because of blokes asking how I've married three times. Sometimes, we lot like pretending we can't see what's coming and just live it. Hope and pessimism are our yin and yang.

Today I'm a pessimist. If some rich guy thinks he can lure me out of hiding so he can prove psychics exist, he's gotta be dreamin'.

My phone is about to ring. So, I fold the letter, drain a glass of single-malt Starward, and pin down one with the other on the table. One lonely breakfast sausage resists rewrapping in plastic and becomes such an ugly mess of folds, creases, and tears, I give up and toss it in a bin.

My phone rings.

"Hoi," I say, just to piss her off. "Who is this?"

"You know damn well who it is," Cathy snarls, her already tinny voice accentuated by the phone's tiny speaker.

Our daughter eloped a week ago. Didn't need to be psychic to know she wanted to blame me for it.

I say, "Hello, Catherine."

"Don't you 'Hello Catherine' me. How dare you do that to my daughter?"

She doesn't know I'm psychic. I told her, of course. You do stupid stuff when you're in love. But she never believed me because—well, you do stupid stuff when you're in love.

"What did I do this time?"

"You helped her!"

"I did?"

"Of course you did, you wanker. Edie just texted me from Hawaii. Said she won some all-expense-paid trip. She denies it, but I know it was you!"

My neck shivers and spine runs cold. I'm not surprised I didn't see it. I don't know everything—especially if it doesn't involve me—but this sorta does.

Bastard knew I wouldn't go for his little game, so he invented a reason. He lured in my daughter for leverage. Maybe even kidnapped her. It's a good ruse, I reckon. And he didn't even need to be psychic, just smart. Too smart.

I let Cathy scream at me for a few more seconds while I think. Is Edie in danger? No. At least, not if I go. There's no reason to hurt her in advance. And a kidnapping would draw attention to his little experiment. But if I'm the only one who won't go, she and her husband could die in an accident as a warning to others refusing a future invitation.

I tell my ex that I'll handle it and hang up.

It'd be an odd thing, six psychics sitting in one place for a game of poker. What's the worst that could happen?

I imagine I should go.

Brisbane to Honolulu takes twenty-six hours, two transfers, and half of a fifth.

Blue sky. Yellow beach. Ugly shirts. Not much different from where I left.

A little robot at the airport waves a sign reading *T. Young* and leads me to a driverless cab. I'm surprised by both, but go along with them. It makes sense. I don't predict events. I predict people. Computers and drones and acts of God are beyond my ability. Which explains my third wife, but that's another story.

My beard itches something terrible from sweat. I'd shave, but I'd look beet red and stupid. I scratch my chin and squint, to appear unfriendly and tunnel my vision. Don't want to inadvertently spy trouble, especially round tourists. Their penchant for drama could sweep me away.

The car drops me off at a resort. It's tall and wide and glittering white. I pass under some Loulu palms to reach the front desk. They wave a bit. I don't wave back.

The receptionist, a young gentleman I don't dare curse in front of, takes my name and my phone number. As he hands me a key, his smile ripples. *Oh no.* I brace. Time and space fold over between us. Ever so briefly, he looks like a cubist portrait or something surreal, wearing bits of his past and future and true heart's desire on his sleeve. Luckily, he's a kind bloke and I get nothing untoward. His shift ends in an hour and he's got a hot date with his boyfriend named Keith. Tame stuff, really. What a relief.

The room is empty, so I go in. It's one simple bedroom. No

suite. Mr. Anonymous has suddenly got cheap. I laugh and check the fridge. Oddly, no booze.

I plop on the bed and decide I'm not going to go. I made it this far. I could fake sleeping in. Or order up cocktails and get so hammered, I can't. Maybe I'll wander the streets and get lost. Let my phone die of charge to be sure. Can't hurt my kiddo if I'm just stupid lazy. I hope.

They're all pretty good plans—but his is better. The door won't unlock.

I call down, but the staff won't pick up. I get cycled through menu after menu to select from, but can't seem to find the button that will get me out of the room. I go to the balcony to climb down. Twelve stories of vertigo says I don't.

I dial Cathy, but hang up. I dial Edie, but hang up. I know they won't answer, each for their own reasons. I dial triple zero. Three naughts appear on my phone before I realize I'm not home. I dial nine, nine, nine, but get nothing. What's the emergency number in this hell? I curse at the top of my lungs. I don't know it. I should know it. But I've never needed emergency before. I've never let myself get into trouble.

Charles Darwin is laughing.

I flop on the bed and tell him off.

The sun sets and the telly drones on about different kinds of fish. It skips from a hideous lamprey to a cute local boy. I practice its name 'cause I'm bored.

"Hoomoo...hoomoo...nookoo...nookoo...ahpoo...aha."

I'm surprised at how easy it is, but know I'll forget.

I get hungry and gnaw on a pouch of Nobby's Beer Nuts from my flight. My lips parch from the salt, so I suck down a five-dollar water.

The phone rings and I spit.

It's gotta be Anonymous.

I have to answer it.

"Hoi," I say, just to piss him off. "Who is this?"

But the voice is recorded. "Your seat is ready in the King's Ballroom."

There's no inflection or character to discern anything. It's another robot to keep me in the dark. Then it hits me. It's an experiment. I'm not a genius. I just remembered the letter. But to keep it scientifically valid, the researcher keeps distant.

My fear slightly wanes. I don't want to go. I refuse to be prodded and pricked. Whoever wins this will be a target for sure. And if they're not dissected, they'd be pressed into service for someone for some*thing*. I shudder at both.

The door *schlicks* unlocked. I feel like a lion whose cage door just opened to fake grassland. I want to run through it, free. But I know what's beyond is not right. There could be hunters or doctors with shears ready to snip, or worse . . . tourists.

I've decided not to play. Not well, at least. Certainly not to win. No psychic abilities in this bloke, they'll say. Must have been a mistake. Our research was wrong. Let his girl go if we got her. I'll lose quickly and scram. Grab some tucker and a beer and my daughter and fly back to—

The hallway's not empty.

I see five other souls wandering round, all confused. Well, except one man whose nose looks like it got tattooed by a bus. He looks determined.

None of us say hi. We don't have to. It's like we know each other by scents cast off the trembling of each other's plastic reality.

Imani's the oldest. A grandmother from the southern US. She's black as the night, but carries a smile that would blind you. She doesn't show it. Not today.

Gregg with two g's is a young guy. His blue eyes and black tats have seen time, and I mean hard. Murdered someone to stop something worse. We understand the temptation and nod.

Omar's a sheik, but not really. He plays up the part for free food. The resort terrifies him, afraid his lies might just find him. I chuckle. He glowers, embarrassed. He knows that I know.

Ingvar's a fisherman. He doesn't belong here. He knows

454

where to drop nets and when. His long silver hair is caked with salt, as if someone dragged him through surf.

Nate Nguyen is the gambler. His broken pug nose wrinkles in fear. He thinks he alone has been set up by our captor, until he sees me. I look less like a pigeon than some.

Then there's me, Tyson Young, a bludger by trade who somehow invests in enough stocks to stay solvent.

We shuffle to the ballroom. It's towering and wide, with gold carpet and crystals vomiting from the ceiling and sconces. One table sits lonely in the center, with six chairs and a robot dealer. To our relief, there's a buffet fit for a king. We all dive in, almost smiling. The only chitchat between us consists of pleased grunts at the spread. No beer, unfortunately. Or wine. Not even coffee. Just water and juice.

This guy's a cruel one.

The doors lock.

The robot calls us to quarter. It looks like a person of sorts—copper skin, red vest, and a hat. Probably expensive, but no money was spent on its looks.

We go to the black-felt table, dragging our feet and our fare.

There's a mark at each place with our name. I sit across from the robot. Gregg holds Imani's chair as she sits to my left. I wish I'd thought of that. Then he sits to my right. Omar and Ingvar take their time. Omar is twitching, too paranoid. Ingvar's plate is too full. Nate sits down with resolve.

The robot speaks like an American.

"Welcome to the first international Psychic Poker game," it drones. "I will explain how to play and help you adhere to the rules. The game is seven-card no-limit Texas Hold'em. The best five-card hand wins the round. You must buy into each hand, paying a minimum of 10,000 yuan. You each get two cards to use privately. Afterward, I will deal three community cards faceup for all to use. Then the first round of betting begins...."

None of us care. Half already know the rules. Half want to punch the thing.

It drones on and doles out chips in towering stacks that

sparkle from LEDs in their sides. Each face is a screen displaying a value. The smallest I read is ¥*10,000*.

Gregg whistles. Nate grabs a chip worth one hundred grand and bites it for good luck. The rest of us stare at him. He's welcome to win, we all think. But he sneers, just as unhappy as us.

The robot orders us to ante in, but none of us move. It thinks we're confused, so it plucks chips from us all and starts dealing.

Two cards fall at our fingertips. We don't turn them over. I pull the world gently, stretching enough to see my four and a red king. A little more tug and I know Imani has twin nines. Gregg has a ten and a smiling jack. Ingvar has a two and a five, and I'm jealous. Omar and Nate share a pair of red aces between them. But Nate has a seven while Omar a queen.

The robot flops cards in the center, a mismatched set of three, six, and nine.

Gregg chuckles.

We wait.

And wait.

Each of us touches an edge of clingy time-space, not daring to move. We just look.

Ten sympathetic eyes slide to Imani as she purses her lips at her three nines. Poor woman. I'm no expert at poker, but I know simple odds. She will win this, if it's just about cards. But she'll fold before that happens.

That leaves advantage to Omar with his ace high and queen. He swallows.

Nate's got a bigger problem. He's automatically bet, so if everyone folds, he will win by default. He won't show any psychic abilities—good for him—but that's not sustainable for a whole game. Worse, he can't control what we do.

Ingvar is first to bet, but isn't sure of the game. If he bets anything, the game goes longer for him. Unless he can lose quite a bit. But he could win from everyone folding. But we won't. He doesn't know how to bluff. We all know his hand sucks. Letting him win is too obvious. At least his hand is so bad he can fold without anyone suspecting this time. So, he will. But next hand he will squirm like Nate.

Gregg won't risk a new prison, no matter the money. He'd lose more from winning than most. He could call next—matching the bet—and still have a good chance of losing. But this is not normal. Unless an ace turns up next, both Omar and Nate will fold, claiming they can't read a crook, and leaving him in the lead. So, Gregg'll play to a type and fold his cards face up. His bluff will be blustering, obtuse, to look unpredictable. Just another criminal who doesn't follow the rules.

Then it's my turn. The king is the problem. If the aces jump ship, I'm lost. But the four gives me reason to hope. I'll fold. I'll snack. I'll feel good about my dumb luck and hope every hand is as bad.

Imani will fold, as we all know. No glamour or glory. No pouting or pontificating. She'll just end it.

Omar is sweating. He must fold—but as a grifter with vices, the money's a tease. He could win the whole thing if we let him. But how long before his creditors find out? Twelve mil is a lot to a sane man. But a spender like Omar won't last. And then there's the chance this is all just a trap. No. He will fold and regret it.

So, Nate wins that hand. The next cards will be dealt and Ingvar's the target. We see how it works and all fold once again. Nate loses a bit. Ingvar makes up for his loss from before. The next hand is Gregg's—who loses the same way. Then me and Imani and Omar, in turn.

And we're back where we started, with the same stack as before, playing poker in a room with a robot and our lives on the line.

Hours pass. Not a single card flipped. No chip changing hands. We all need to piss.

Gregg stretches and paces a bit, like he's still in prison. "Don't let me see your cards," he jokes.

TENZIN RANGDOL

We laugh but don't feel better for it. We're too taut.

We think about playing for real. Not using our powers, just luck. Maybe jaw a little in between to act casual. But nothing now is friendly. Nate is too good and Ingvar's too bad. Gregg is too emotional. Imani would have fun until she starts to lose. The conflict would color her smile worse than tea. Omar's so desperate, he'd accuse me of cheating. Or almost. He'd realize the only way to cheat would be to be psychic, and he won't admit that is real.

No. A friendly game is out of the question.

But they're stiff competition. Even in chess, the greats like Kasparov and Carlsen only had to deal with one opponent at a time. They might imagine ten or twenty moves ahead but only consider a few alternate paths into the future. We're six psychics warping to see six possible futures for each of the others. Six to the power of six—I use my calculator and whistle—that's 46,656 sights... *if* we stay on task. Add another six and we'd be knockin' on someone's door.

Nate's ego thinks he should win. He plots a new plan. Poker is about probability. Twenty-five percent of the deck is any suit—minus the suits revealed so far. Each card is $\frac{1}{52}$ of the whole and doubling the decks doesn't change that. But any card you need is one out of the total remaining cards unknown to you, which is less than fifty-two. But that's only if you care about the suit. Otherwise your chance of hitting the correct face or pip of any suit is $\frac{1}{13}$ of the remaining cards, plus or minus—blah, blah, blah. None of that matters. Nate sucks at math. He never needed it before.

But maybe, he thinks, just maybe he's picked up enough from his opponents through osmosis to give him the advantage over the rest. Maybe he could throw us a curve to distract our predictions and he could use our confusion to win the whole thing.

The money would be incredible. Better yet, the boost to his reputation would be... devastating. He'd never be allowed in another game, ever. Unless he kept silent. But bragging is better than money. It's the whole point of playing. He'd prefer death to that loss.

He sneers at Ingvar.

Ingvar doesn't care. He wants to be here less than any of us. He's not even got his land legs back. Win or lose, he just wants to go home. Besides, with a five and a two, why bother planning at all? He'll only lose money, so he'll call and be done with it.

He grunts toward Gregg.

Gregg feels forced. His life is a disaster and money would solve most of his problems. And Ingvar's hand is so terrible, playing on is almost a sure win. The question isn't whether to play or fold. It's to call or raise.

They tug and look through me.

The two have me in straights. I've got one of the worst hands. Four and king are so far apart to be useless. Everybody knows that. Imani plays after me. With the best hand by far, she's sure to question folding now. I probably won't win, but how much could I lose in one hand? If Gregg calls, I'd have to raise. I could raise by a bit and whittle myself over an hour. Or I could raise large, using the king as my excuse. If Gregg raises small instead, then I'd have the same options. If he raised large, I could call and ride it out or raise again. Raising again, small or large, would seriously anger Imani, but that's not my problem.

Imani glowers, displeased.

Gambling is a sin. The Devil uses it to elevate his disciples and ruin the faithful. So, she absolutely won't play. Unless…maybe Jesus sent her to counter the Devil. Three cards of the same number should be real good. The rest of us seem afraid of it. And with God's will on her side, she doesn't need to rely on the Devil's luck. So, she'll match the bet. Or raise it. Depending on what I do. But only a little. And only if I raise a little. If I raise a lot, she won't raise at all. Well, maybe a little. Or a lot. In any case, she'd be committing no sin because she's not coveting, simply letting God work His will through her. Her reward then would be added to our punishment for our hubris. Or is it her own hubris she should fear? *Lord, lead me not into temptation.*

What if this is a test? Should she resist like old Job or show faith in His will and teach these sinners a lesson?

She's so cross-eyed, she can't bring herself to look at poor Omar.

Omar is obsessed with himself. What would he buy if he wins? Who would he pay off—both in debts and bribes? Imani is his first hurdle to financial freedom, no matter how brief. He has the best hand after hers. If he got lucky, he could crush her on the first hand and never let her get back up. But he usually leaves nothing to chance, preferring to lie, cheat, and steal. He could play her own ego, instead. Let her raise round after round, thinking him a fool, and then go all-in at the end, drowning her in chips and confidence. He could prick her with doubt. She doesn't know the order of hands. She doesn't know odds.

But what if she's unshakable? What if her belief in her god is so set, she can't fail? And what if Nate follows suit? Or even me? The wrong card at the wrong time can end it all.

Then how would he escape? What ID should he use? Who would he dupe out of funds? For how long? Which air or cruise line? Which city would have him?

Every prediction he makes in this room wrinkles his future outside.

Nate glitches.

We all felt it coming. His soul creases and clings to itself. Realities overlap, a conundrum of possibilities entangle and threaten to tear. He backs off to smooth it.

It's too late.

We see it all now.

Nate doesn't care what happens to Omar, except how it affects what he does. Nate could afford a new wife. Or win back an old one. Which could lead to kids. Unless he lost now. Then he'd have to survive alone. Or find a new wife. Or win back an old one. But he'd likely fail both. Unless he'd learn something. Maybe change for the better. But that was as likely as winning this game against five psychics, a set of nines, and dumb luck. His fingers fade slightly, glowing chips falling through them.

Ingvar stamps his feet down. He must not give in. Just lose and get out. But what if the others don't let him. Our collective push on reality is straining it. Probabilities gather, warp, and stretch. He might even win. His soles sink into the carpet.

Gregg won't even hear it. He's desperate for good luck after all he's been through, like a mess of bad turns owes dividends he's earned. We see all his realities. Grooms at his weddings and children they adopt. He shoots up alone in abandoned warehouses, no friend in the world but his fix. He accepts an award. He's thrown back in prison. He's elected to office. He lies, ancient, addicted, and dying faceup in a sun-burnt desert lot, leaving no trace he existed. Tattoos slide from his skin to the arms of his chair.

What the hell?

I toss over a plate of cheese, in case it's drugged—but I know it's not. I can feel the warp tug my skin like wet rubber. Ain't got a plan. All bets are off, but they're not.

The game's worse than cling-wrap pulled by a toddler who's all thumbs. It's a whole schoolyard of kiddos dragging clear plastic like kites, tangling them as they run this way and that, stretching them beyond sanity to the brink.

Nate grabs all the blinking chips left and dissolves into nothing.

Omar's flesh glistens. His lips spread, slippery and taut, showing barbs and a rasp 'stead of teeth. His neck swells and splits into gills. He squirts as he screams. Then coils in on himself and sucks his own gut 'til he's gone.

The past is best forgotten. The present is twisting and torn. The future folds into a funnel, dragging us through it. We can't stop predicting. That too-long-to-name fish will vanish. The Hawaiian volcano will erupt in reverse. Edie and hubbo and Cathy and the rest won't escape.

The table pinches and whines then shrinks with a pop. The robot implodes. Time-space collapses and drags us in, through, and down. Our bodies stretch out like palms flailing. Resort, city, jungle, sky, moon, planets, and galaxies lash around us in a collide-o-scope of fractal shards lunging at us. Math screams an unbearable sound as it shatters.

My ears burst. My heart bleats. Lungs strain. I hold tight to what I think is left of reality, but fate pulls me in, spinning, and wraps me. I think I might suffocate but it's twisted like twine into laser-sharp webbing. My blood sprays into horrific mandalas.

I scream to Imani for help, but she's white as a ghost, her teeth hollow, words empty. Christ ain't saving her now, as we fall toward whatever hell's at the end.

Ingvar turns into stone, banging and bruising us poor flotsam in the temporal surf.

Gregg weaves plots like a madman, hope driving him headlong into the collapse. I hope he breaks through. But he snaps in twelve pieces and melts.

Imani shrieks as her soul is consumed by clear flames.

I'm all that is left in the vortex.

Or would be, if I went.

So, I imagine I shouldn't go.

I shake loose from my future and blink several times.

Blue sky. Check. Yellow sand. Check. Ugly shirts. Check, check, and check.

The caravan's fridge is just within reach, and I snag a cold tinnie. I crack it and sip it and sit back, staring at that damned ticket.

I'll call the others to be sure they don't go.

Edie and her hubbo's at risk if I skip alone. But when all of us do, Mr. Anonymous will be ruined. Not just 'cause he failed to motivate us. He'll wonder, Why? What did we foresee? Why won't we come? And that lack of knowing will put him in a tailspin, 'stead of us.

No one'll get hurt. No hands will be dealt. No pots will be lost or won. The world will remain a mess, but intact. And that's all right by me.

I'm that kind of legend.

No one is supposed to know what I do.

The Year in the Contests

The Greek philosopher Heraclitus once said, "The only constant in life is change." Here at Writers of the Future, most of our change comes in the form of growth.

CONTEST GROWTH

The number of entries to both the writing and illustration Contests rose to the highest ever, and this volume features winners from ten countries: Australia, China, England, India, Iran, Jamaica, Portugal, Singapore, Spain, and United States.

Entries this year continued to rise in overall quality. In part, this might be because, in 2020, we introduced an online workshop for anyone who would like to become a better writer. The course takes the author through the journey of writing a story: from formulating the idea to a finished draft. Over 6,000 students have enrolled in the course. It is free to enter, and access to the information is unlimited. You can learn more about it at www.WritersoftheFuture.com.

The Writers of the Future Podcast has also exploded in popularity. Hosted by the publishers of this anthology, the podcast features interviews with author and illustrator judges, past winners, editors, and other industry professionals. The podcast became syndicated this year, and many episodes have been listened to more than a million times.

Despite the pandemic, when deemed safe, the publishers of Writers of the Future continue to promote the Contest by traveling around the US or holding online events, inviting judges and past winners as guests. This year we appeared at 20Booksto50K in Las Vegas; Life, the Universe & Everything in Utah; Dragon Con in Atlanta; FanX in Utah; and at other popular venues.

LAST YEAR'S ANTHOLOGY

The anthologies continue to grow in popularity, too. Last year's anthology, volume 37, hit #1 on Amazon's bestseller list in the US in seven categories and even appeared for a time with volume 36—so we had two bestselling anthologies at once. It also topped bestseller lists in Australia and the UK.

Reviews have been excellent for volume 37. The Midwest Book Review hailed it as the latest in a "trend setting series" and noted that the Contest has "contributed more talent than any other source to the genre," while *Tangent* magazine offered a thoughtful analysis of each story and praised several authors.

The anthologies continue to amass awards. Volume 36 was a Foreword Indies 2020 Silver Winner in Science Fiction and a Finalist in Anthologies. The Critters Readers' Poll awarded the Writers of the Future Forum as the Best Writers' Discussion Forum.

FAREWELL TO THREE CONTEST JUDGES

Right before press time, and after this book was finalized, David Farland tragically left us. One of his last acts was to make this book the best it could be, and honor the writers in these pages. He also wrote his last story for this volume to accompany the cover by Bob Eggleton. Dave will be missed in all ways going forward, from his selfless help to young writers in his editing and teaching, to his amazing ability to drive the Contest forward into a bright future. Thank you, Dave.

We were sad to lose two illustrator judges. Gary Meyer passed away in February 2021, a renowned illustrator of such iconic art as the *Jaws* movie poster, *Star Wars*, album covers, and classic aerial art. He'd been a judge since 2012.

Ron Lindahn passed away in May; he'd been a judge since 1989. He succeeded Frank Kelly Freas as the Illustrators' Contest Coordinating Judge. He had an impact on many young artists.

WELCOMING NEW CONTEST JUDGES

We proudly welcome two new illustrator judges: past winner Brittany Jackson, who is best known for her children's book illustrations, and fantasy artist Tom Wood, whose creations of dragons and medieval, death-defying warriors have become iconic images of fantasy culture across the globe.

We also added a fine new writer judge, popular science fiction author S. M. Stirling, who has published over forty novels and is a wonderful addition to our writing workshop instructors.

NOTABLE ACCOMPLISHMENTS FROM ALUMNI AND JUDGES

So many of our authors and illustrators have good news, new books and stories to offer that we can't discuss them all, but here are highlights from the year:

Contest judges Brian Herbert and Kevin J. Anderson celebrated a hugely successful *Dune* movie release. International box-office numbers are well over $390 million (as of December 2021) and still climbing.

Brittany Jackson, grand prize illustrator for volume 24, had her second *New York Times* bestseller with her cover art for the LeBron James's middle-grade novel *We Are Family*.

Aliya Chen, grand prize illustrator for volume 35, is now a concept artist at Netflix.

Jason Fischer (Vol. 26) from Australia released a novel in all formats, *Papa Lucy & the Boneman*.

Dutch winner Floris Kleijne (Vol. 20) released a thriller entitled *KlaverBlad*. It won the Schaduwprijs (Shadow Award) for the best debut thriller of the year, a significant thriller genre award in the Dutch language.

Michael Michera, grand prize illustrator for volume 33, is now working for Paramount Pictures as a concept artist.

The summer 2021 edition of *DreamForge Magazine* featured Wulf Moon (Vol. 35).

Past winner (Vol. 18) and judge Nnedi Okorafor released her new novel *Remote Control*.

Irvin Rodriguez, grand prize illustrator from volume 27, opened a gallery show in Pennsylvania.

At our Awards Ceremony in Hollywood, keynote speaker Toni Weisskopf from Baen Books, one of the largest speculative fiction publishers in the US, mentioned she has now published over fifty Writers and Illustrators of the Future Contest judges and winners.

AWARDS FOR WINNERS

We're very proud of our Contest judges and winners who were honored with prestigious awards in the past year. Here are some highlights:

Analog Analytical Laboratory (AnLab) Readers' Poll
Finalist: Best Fact Article—Coauthors Contest judges Gregory
    Benford and Larry Niven "Big Smart Objects"
Finalist: Best Fact Article—Contest judge Gregory Benford
    "Veiling the Earth"
Finalist: Best Cover Artist—Eldar Zakirov (Vol. 22)

Asimov's Readers' Poll
Finalist: Best Novella—Contest judge Nancy Kress "Semper
    Augustus"
Finalist: Best Novella—Contest judge Kristine Kathryn Rusch
    "Maelstrom"
Finalist: Best Novelette—Contest judge Kevin J. Anderson
    "The Hind"
Finalist: Best Cover Artist—Eldar Zakirov (Vol. 22)

Aurealis Awards
Winner: Best Science Fiction Novella—T. R. Napper (Vol. 31)
    for "The Weight of the Air, The Weight of the World"
Finalist: Best Science Fiction Short Story—T. R. Napper (Vol. 31)
    for "Jack's Fine Dining"
Finalist: Best Horror Novella—Michael Gardner (Vol. 36) for
    "Foundations" appearing in *Writers of the Future Volume 36*!

Finalist: Best Children's Fiction—Contest judge Sean Williams for *Her Perilous Mansion*

Finalist: Best Collection—Cat Sparks (Vol. 21) for *Dark Harvest*

Aurora Awards

Finalist: Best Novel—Contest judge Robert J. Sawyer for *The Oppenheimer Alternative*

Baen Awards

Winner: Fantasy Adventure Award—M. Elizabeth Ticknor (Vol. 38) for "Echoes of Meridian"

Grand Prize: Jim Baen Memorial Short Story Award—G. Scott Huggins (Vol. 15) for "Salvage Judgment"

First Runner-up: Jim Baen Memorial Short Story Award—C. Stuart Hardwick (Vol. 30) for "Reaction Time"

Chesley Awards

Finalist: Best Cover Illustration—Madolyn Locke (Vol. 37) for *Valian Styrke: Knight of Fate*

Finalist: Best Color Work: Unpublished—Bruce Brenneise (Vol. 34) for "Garden of Solitude"

Ditmar Awards

Winner: Best Collected Work—Cat Sparks (Vol. 21) for *Dark Harvest*

Finalist: Best Collected Work—T. R. Napper (Vol. 31) for *Neon Leviathan*

Finalist: Best Novelette—T. R. Napper (Vol. 31) for "The Weight of the Air, The Weight of the World"

Hugo Awards

Finalist: Best Novelette—Aliette de Bodard (Vol. 23) for "The Inaccessibility of Heaven"

Finalist: Best Related Work—Vida Cruz (Vol. 34) for *FIYAHCON*

Locus Awards
Winner: Collection—Ken Liu (Vol. 19) for *The Hidden Girl and Other Stories*
Finalist: Novella—Aliette de Bodard (Vol. 23) for *Of Dragons, Feasts and Murders* and *Seven of Infinities*
Finalist: Best Novelette—Aliette de Bodard (Vol. 23) for "The Inaccessibility of Heaven"
Finalist: Best Novelette—Ken Liu (Vol. 19) for "A Whisper of Blue"
Finalist: Short Story—Aliette de Bodard (Vol. 23) for "In the Lands of the Spills"
Finalist: Short Story—Ken Liu (Vol. 19) for "50 Things Every AI Working with Humans Should Know"
Finalist: Artist—Contest judges Shaun Tan (Vol. 8) and Bob Eggleton
Finalist: Illustrated and Art Book—*Fantastic Paintings of Frazetta* art by Contest judge Frank Frazetta

Mike Resnick Memorial Award
Winner: Best Unpublished Science Fiction Short Story— Z. T. Bright (Vol. 38) for "The Measure of a Mother's Love"

Theodore Sturgeon Memorial Award
Finalist—Ken Liu (Vol. 19) for "50 Things Every AI Working with Humans Should Know"

Of course, with so many winners, we're at a point where we can't list everything here, but dozens of published short stories and novels can be found listed on the Contests' blog.

That's it for this year. Looking forward to next year and a spectacular future!

For Contest year 38, the winners are:

Writers of the Future Contest Winners

FIRST QUARTER

1. *Mike Jack Stoumbos*
   "THE SQUID IS MY BROTHER"

2. *Brittany Rainsdon*
   "THE LAST DYING SEASON"

3. *J. A. Becker*
   "FOR THE FEDERATION"

SECOND QUARTER

1. *M. Elizabeth Ticknor*
   "THE PHANTOM CARNIVAL"

2. *John Coming*
   "THE ISLAND ON THE LAKE"

3. *Azure Arther*
   "AGATHA'S MONSTER"

THIRD QUARTER

1. *Lazarus Black*
   "PSYCHIC POKER"

2. *Em Dupre*
   "THE GREATER GOOD"

3. *N. V. Haskell*
   "THE MYSTICAL FARRAGO"

FOURTH QUARTER

1. *Desmond Astaire*
   "GALLOWS"

2. *Z. T. Bright*
   "THE MAGIC BOOK OF ACCIDENTAL CITY DESTRUCTION: A BOOK WIZARD'S GUIDE"

3. *Michael Panter*
   "LILT OF A LARK"

FINALIST

Rebecca E. Treasure, "TSUU, TSUU, KASVA SUUREMASSE"

THE YEAR IN THE CONTESTS

Illustrators of the Future Contest Winners

FIRST QUARTER

Majid Saberinejad
Natalia Salvador
Jerome Tieh

SECOND QUARTER

Arthur M. Doweyko
Zaine Lodhi
Xiaomeng Zhang

THIRD QUARTER

Nick Jizba
Brett Stump
Annalee Wu

FOURTH QUARTER

Ari Zaritsky
Jim Zaccaria
Tenzin Rangdol

L. Ron Hubbard's
Writers of the Future Contest

The most enduring and influential
contest in the history of SF and Fantasy

Open to new and amateur SF & Fantasy writers

Prizes each quarter: $1,000, $750, $500
Quarterly 1st place winners compete for $5,000
additional annual prize!

ALL JUDGING DONE BY
PROFESSIONAL WRITERS ONLY

No entry fee is required

Entrants retain all publication rights

Don't delay! Send your entry now!

To submit your entry electronically go to:
www.writersofthefuture.com/enter-writer-contest

Email: contests@authorservicesinc.com

To submit your entry via mail send to:
L. Ron Hubbard's Writers of the Future Contest
7051 Hollywood Blvd.
Los Angeles, California 90028

1. No entry fee is required, and all rights in the story remain the property of the author. All types of science fiction, fantasy, and dark fantasy are welcome.

2. By submitting to the Contest, the entrant agrees to abide by all Contest rules.

3. All entries must be original works by the entrant, in English. Plagiarism, which includes the use of third-party poetry, song lyrics, characters, or another person's universe, without written permission, will result in disqualification. Excessive violence or sex, determined by the judges, will result in disqualification. Entries may not have been previously published in professional media.

4. To be eligible, entries must be a short story of fantasy, science fiction, or light speculative horror. Your story has no minimum length requirement, however it may not be longer than 17,000 words.

   We regret we cannot consider novels, poetry, screenplays, or works intended for children.

5. The Contest is open only to those who have not professionally published a novel or short novel, or more than one novelette, or more than three short stories, in any medium. Professional publication is deemed to be payment of at least eight cents per word, and at least 5,000 copies, or 5,000 hits.

6. Entries submitted in hard copy must be typewritten or a computer printout in black ink on white paper, printed only on the front of the paper, double-spaced, with numbered

pages. All other formats will be disqualified. Each entry must have a cover page with the title of the work, the author's legal name, a pen name if applicable, address, telephone number, email address and an approximate word count. Every subsequent page must carry the title and a page number, but the author's name must be deleted to facilitate fair, anonymous judging.

Entries submitted electronically must be double-spaced and must include the title and page number on each page, but not the author's name. Electronic submissions will separately include the author's legal name, pen name if applicable, address, telephone number, email address, and approximate word count.

7. Manuscripts will be returned after judging only if the author has provided return postage on a self-addressed envelope.

8. We accept only entries that do not require a delivery signature for us to receive them.

9. There shall be three cash prizes in each quarter: a First Prize of $1,000, a Second Prize of $750, and a Third Prize of $500, in US dollars. In addition, at the end of the year the First Place winners will have their entries judged by a panel of judges, and a Grand Prize winner shall be determined and receive an additional $5,000. All winners will also receive trophies. The Grand Prize winner shall be announced and awarded, along with the trophies to winners, at the L. Ron Hubbard awards ceremony held in the following year or when it is able to be held due to government regulations.

10. The Contest has four quarters, beginning on October 1, January 1, April 1, and July 1. The year will end on September 30. To be eligible for judging in its quarter, an entry must be postmarked or received electronically no later than

midnight on the last day of the quarter. Late entries will be included in the following quarter and the Contest Administration will so notify the entrant.

11. Each entrant may submit only one manuscript per quarter. Winners are ineligible to make further entries in the Contest.

12. All entries for each quarter are final. No revisions are accepted.

13. Entries will be judged by professional authors. The decisions of the judges are entirely their own, and are final and binding.

14. Winners in each quarter will be individually notified of the results by phone, mail, or email.

15. This Contest is void where prohibited by law.

16. To send your entry electronically, go to:
www.writersofthefuture.com/enter-writer-contest
and follow the instructions.
To send your entry in hard copy, mail it to:
L. Ron Hubbard's Writers of the Future Contest
7051 Hollywood Blvd., Los Angeles, California 90028

17. Visit the website for any Contest rules update at:
www.writersofthefuture.com

1. The Contest is open to entrants from all nations. (However, entrants should provide themselves with some means for written communication in English.) All themes of science fiction and fantasy illustrations are welcome: every entry is judged on its own merits only. No entry fee is required and all rights to the entry remain the property of the artist.

2. By submitting to the Contest, the entrant agrees to abide by all Contest rules.

3. The Contest is open to new and amateur artists who have not been professionally published and paid for more than three black-and-white story illustrations, or more than one process-color painting, in media distributed broadly to the general public. The ultimate eligibility criterion, however, is defined by the word "amateur"—in other words, the artist has not been paid for his artwork. If you are not sure of your eligibility, please write a letter to the Contest Administration with details regarding your publication history. Include a self-addressed and stamped envelope for the reply. You may also send your questions to the Contest Administration via email.

4. Each entrant may submit only one set of illustrations in each Contest quarter. The entry must be original to the entrant and previously unpublished. Plagiarism, infringement of the rights of others, or other violations of the Contest rules will result in disqualification. Winners in previous quarters are not eligible to make further entries.

5. The entry shall consist of three illustrations done by the entrant in a color or black-and-white medium created from the artist's imagination. Use of gray scale in illustrations

and mixed media, computer generated art, and the use of photography in the illustrations are accepted. Each illustration must represent a subject different from the other two.

6. Electronic submissions will separately include the artist's legal name, address, telephone number, email address which will identify each of three pieces of art and the artist's signature on the art should be deleted. Only .jpg, .jpeg, and .png files will be accepted, a maximum file size of 10 MB.

7. HARD COPY ENTRIES SHOULD NOT BE THE ORIGINAL DRAWINGS, but should be color or black-and-white reproductions of the originals of a quality satisfactory to the entrant. Entries must be submitted unfolded and flat, in an envelope no larger than 9 inches by 12 inches. Images submitted electronically must be a minimum of 300 dpi, a minimum of 5 × 7 inches and a maximum of 8.5 × 11 inches.

All hard copy entries must be accompanied by a self-addressed return envelope of the appropriate size, with the correct US postage affixed. (Non-US entrants should enclose international postage reply coupons.) If the entrant does not want the reproductions returned, the entry should be clearly marked DISPOSABLE COPIES: DO NOT RETURN. A business-size self-addressed envelope with correct postage (or valid email address) should be included so that the judging results may be returned to the entrant. We only accept entries that do not require a delivery signature for us to receive them.

To facilitate anonymous judging, each of the three photocopies must be accompanied by a removable cover sheet bearing the artist's name, address, telephone number, email address, and an identifying title for that work. The reproduction of the work should carry the same identifying title on the front of the illustration and the artist's signature should be deleted. The Contest Administration will remove and file the cover sheets, and forward only the anonymous entry to the judges.

8. There will be three cowinners in each quarter. Each winner will receive a cash prize of US $500 and will be awarded a trophy. Winners will also receive eligibility to compete for the annual Grand Prize of $5,000 together with the annual Grand Prize trophy.

9. For the annual Grand Prize Contest, the quarterly winners will be furnished with a specification sheet and a winning story from the Writers of the Future Contest to illustrate. In order to retain eligibility for the Grand Prize, each winner shall send to the Contest address his/her illustration of the assigned story within thirty (30) days of receipt of the story assignment.

The yearly Grand Prize winner shall be determined by a panel of judges on the following basis only: Each Grand Prize judge's personal opinion on the extent to which it makes the judge want to read the story it illustrates.

The Grand Prize winner shall be announced and awarded, along with the trophies to the winners, at the L. Ron Hubbard awards ceremony held in the following year or when it is able to be held due to government regulations.

10. The Contest has four quarters, beginning on October 1, January 1, April 1, and July 1. The year will end on September 30. To be eligible for judging in its quarter, an entry must be postmarked or received electronically no later than midnight on the last day of the quarter. Late entries will

be included in the following quarter and the Contest Administration will so notify the entrant.

11. Entries will be judged by professional artists only. Each quarterly judging and the Grand Prize judging may have different panels of judges. The decisions of the judges are entirely their own and are final and binding.

12. Winners in each quarter will be individually notified of the results by phone, mail, or email.

13. This Contest is void where prohibited by law.

14. To send your entry electronically, go to: www.writersofthefuture.com/enter-the-illustrator-contest and follow the instructions.
To send your entry via mail send it to:
L. Ron Hubbard's Illustrators of the Future Contest
7051 Hollywood Blvd., Los Angeles, California 90028

15. Visit the website for any Contest rules update at: www.illustratorsofthefuture.com